Praise for *M*

"Splendid debut novel . . . Movi.., ..ortlessly beyond mere fictionalized biography, Kelly delivers a richly lyrical and thought-provoking novel with closing twists that feel as impossible, inevitable, and satisfying—as magical, in short—as one of Houdini's own illusions."

—*Publishers Weekly* (starred review)

"A grand story of secrets, codes, and magic befitting one of history's greatest illusionists and the love of his life. . . . Kelly animates the love story of this historic couple with a smooth blending of research and artistry. . . . Dazzling and enchanting, *Mrs. Houdini* will captivate readers in a fashion that would make Harry and Bess proud."

—*Shelf Awareness* (starred review)

"*Mrs. Houdini* is a dazzling blend of adventure, love, betrayal, and redemption."

—Historical Novel Society, Editor's Choice

"Victoria Kelly brings immense imaginative empathy to bear on the fascinating story of the woman who stood beside Harry Houdini, on stage, in life, and after his early death. Resonant, haunting, and deeply felt, this is a stellar debut from a novelist to watch."

—Geraldine Brooks, Pulitzer Prize–winning author

"Kelly confidently peels back layers of Bess, revealing a fiercely intelligent and independent woman trying to heal spiritual, emotional, and metaphysical wounds. Had the man who made an elephant disappear before hundreds of people pulled a similar trick on her and with her heart no less? Or, is love the deepest mystery and biggest illusion of them all?"

—NY1.com

"Victoria Kelly's impressive debut is a magical, poignantly romantic tale of the world's greatest escape artist and the remarkable woman who was his devoted partner, both onstage and off. In *Mrs. Houdini,* love proves to be the most mysterious and powerful of all death-defying acts."

—Jennifer Chiaverini, *New York Times* bestselling author

"A magical trip through a magical time—a fresh and absorbing read."

—Kate Alcott, *New York Times* bestselling author of *The Dressmaker*

"[Kelly] has a deft hand in setting a scene."

—*Library Journal*

"*Mrs. Houdini* is a delightful read, and will resonate with anyone who's ever been struck by the illogical but nonetheless compelling notion that a lost beloved may yet reappear, despite all rational evidence to the contrary. The book answers that great 'What if?' and does so in an eminently pleasurable way."

—*Star Tribune*

"Poignant portrait of a satisfying marriage, the rupture of grief, and the seemingly magical ability of love to survive the grave."

—*Forward*

"This author's debut novel will keep you turning the pages to find out if Harry finally reaches Bess."

—*Missourian*

"By the time the sparkling ending is reached—an ending that couldn't be more perfect—you'll be entranced . . . especially if a bit of gauzy illusion is what you'd love in a romance. . . . *Mrs. Houdini* is great escapism."

"*Mrs. Houdini* is an engaging addition to the tradition of books that seek to put flesh onto historical, but often obscure, women attached to famous men."

"*Mrs. Houdini* is, in its way, a ghost story, and like every good ghost story, it comes with an ending that will make you shiver. But it's not a shiver of fear that Kelly's fine debut provokes, though there's more than a hint of the uncanny in its pages. It's the shiver one gets from an excellent story skillfully told, with characters whose fates are fully and sympathetically realized."

"Bess Houdini was swept into history by an impulsive and passionate love, and then left when her world-renowned husband died too soon. And that is where we find her at the beginning of the novel. Kelly has drawn Bess with such charm and moxie that I felt myself pulled into the pages, racing alongside her to uncover the clues Harry left behind, then stunned and weeping when she discovers the future he imagined for her."

ALSO BY VICTORIA KELLY

When the Men Go Off to War: Poems

Mrs. HOUDINI

a novel

Victoria Kelly

WASHINGTON SQUARE PRESS

NEW YORK   LONDON   TORONTO   SYDNEY   NEW DELHI

WASHINGTON SQUARE PRESS
An Imprint of Simon & Schuster, Inc.
1230 Avenue of the Americas
New York, NY 10020

First Washington Square Press trade paperback edition March 2017

WASHINGTON SQUARE PRESS and colophon are registered trademarks of Simon & Schuster, Inc.

For information about special discounts for bulk purchases, please contact Simon & Schuster Special Sales at 1-866-506-1949 or business@simonandschuster.com.

The Simon & Schuster Speakers Bureau can bring authors to your live event. For more information or to book an event, contact the Simon & Schuster Speakers Bureau at 1-866-248-3049 or visit our website at www.simonspeakers.com.

Interior design by Kyoko Watanabe

Manufactured in the United States of America

10 9 8 7 6 5 4 3 2 1

The Library of Congress has cataloged the Atria Books edition as follows:

Kelly, Victoria.
  Mrs. Houdini : a novel / by Victoria Kelly. — First Atria books hardcover edition.
     pages ; cm
  I. Title.
  PS3611.E4575M77 2016
  813'.6—dc23

                              2015026564

ISBN 978-1-5011-1090-0
ISBN 978-1-5011-1091-7 (pbk)
ISBN 978-1-5011-1092-4 (ebook)

For my dad

The world is full of magic things, patiently waiting for our senses to grow sharper.

—W. B. YEATS

Prologue

GALENA, KANSAS

January 9, 1898

"Where is my brother, John Murphy?" Harry held the card to the light. "I have not heard from him in nineteen years." He returned the note to its envelope and surveyed the audience. Outside the hall, the winter roared over the cracked-earth streets, the horses stamping at their posts.

"It's my question." A woman's small voice rose from the back of the theater.

Bess was seated in a wooden chair in the middle of the stage, a black lace veil draped over her head. She glanced at Harry, then peered into the darkness. This was not routine.

"The cards are meant to remain anonymous," Harry said. "It is what the spirits prefer."

The woman stood up, her face in the shadows. "But how are you supposed to answer without knowing me?"

Bess began to cough. The hall was filthy, the clay floor kicked up by hundreds of feet, and the dust hung like an iron around her neck. The words wouldn't come. For these types of questions the answer was always evasive, *he is on the way to you, he is coming;* for others, the answers apprehended ahead of time—recent deaths, small-town gossip—she could be more specific.

"Mrs. Houdini." Harry rushed to her side. "Are you all right? What is coming to you?"

"It's—John Murphy," she stammered, abandoning her heavy, affected stage voice. "I think you will find him at East Seventy-Second Street in New York."

"New York?" the woman said. "Why would he be there?"

Bess broke protocol again and looked directly at Harry. Another fit of coughing overtook her. The veil slipped to the floor.

Harry stood up. "My wife is ill. The spirits are accosting her. We shall have to conclude here." He ushered Bess backstage and placed his hand against the back of her neck. "My God, are you all right?" He searched her face. "What's the matter?"

Bess shook her head. "It was the dust. I couldn't breathe."

"The dust?" He pulled away, irritated. "You shouldn't have done that. We go by the plan, Bess. You know that."

"I don't know where it came from. I kept thinking of John Murphy who owns the ice cream parlor near your mother's apartment, and the words just came out." She wiped her face. "I'm sorry."

"And what happens when the real Murphy turns out to be dead, or in jail?"

"What does it matter? By then we'll be halfway to Milwaukee."

Harry frowned. "I suppose. If the storm lets up."

She took his hand. "It's all a trick one way or another, whatever we say."

❋

In the frigid gray of morning, the trunks packed and the bill settled, Bess was stopped outside the hotel by a small, agitated woman, wrapped from ears to feet in a heavy wool coat.

"Mrs. Houdini," she said, her breath white as smoke. "It's Mary Murphy."

"Mary Murphy?"

"You told me about my brother."

Bess feigned innocence. "I'm afraid I don't remember."

Harry came up behind them. "If it's about last night, Mrs. Houdini isn't entirely conscious during the readings," he explained. "It's not really her who's speaking. She can't be held accountable."

The woman pressed her hand against Harry's arm, urgently. "Your wife was right. My brother works on Seventy-Second Street in New York."

Bess froze. "Pardon?"

"I wired a friend of mine last night and asked her to investigate. She found him. He's alive and well."

Bess saw Harry's jaw go tight. "I'm so glad," he said coolly, wrapping his arm around her waist and pulling her toward the hotel. "But I'm afraid we're very late."

Mary Murphy stood in the snow, startled, and watched them leave.

In the crowded lobby, Bess pulled free of Harry's grip. "My God," she said, trembling. "What have we done?"

Harry ran his hand through his hair. "Clearly it's a matter of coincidence."

"Harry—have we sold our souls for a little applause?"

"It was an innocent enough answer."

Bess took a ragged breath. "This is what we've been looking for, though, isn't it? This is real magic."

"What does that even mean?" He bent over to pick up their bags, but she could tell he was frightened. "You know I don't put stock in religion."

"It's not religion. It's . . . knowing more than we should. Connecting with the other side. We've been pretending all this time to speak with the dead—what if we really can?" She lowered her voice. "How do we know what—or who—is really over there?"

Harry's eyes glistened. "Isn't that what everyone wants—to know what is beyond?"

"No. Not me." She shivered, remembering her childhood fear of darkness, the shadows that assembled themselves into gruesome shapes on her bedroom ceiling at night, and the hours of prayer it took to dispel them.

"I think," Harry said slowly, "you want to know more than you think you do. And I think 'our magic'—if we can call it that—is something that happens when we're together. It's not evil." The daylight rippled like water across his face. Outside the window, Mary Murphy had disappeared.

It was true. Since she had married Harry, Bess felt as if her senses had been illuminated. Colors were brighter; lights flamed in the dark. But she was afraid. "Let's put a stop to the séances. You won't find it, Harry—whatever it is you're hoping to uncover." She looked out toward the snow-covered plains, the white, blinding landscape where the street met the grass.

Harry looked, too, searching the emptiness as if waiting for a parade of spirits to march into view, dissolving like icicles into the frozen earth.

Chapter 1

CONEY ISLAND

June 1894

Besides the beach, there was no better place to spend a humid Saturday afternoon on Coney Island than inside Vacca's Theater, where it was cool and dark. There were enough seats to make the place seem popular, but few enough that the stage always looked close, as if it were just on the other side of your living room. Bess had performed there three weeks earlier, right after she'd turned eighteen and joined the Floral Sisters, and the audience had been kind, throwing pink roses onto the stage. She and the girls knew better than to give their real names, which were dull, German names, and there would always be a crowd of eager men waiting by the theater doors afterward, wanting to know if they were really sisters, and was their last name really Floral?

This morning one of the girls had persuaded Bess to come with her. Her real name was Nora but everyone called her Doll, because she had tiny, rose-pink fingernails and eyes like moons. It was going to be a real riot, she said; a magician named Dash had saved her two seats and promised her a good show.

"You know, the other magician's his brother," Doll told her as they crossed the street from their boardinghouse onto the fairground. "And he's unattached as well."

"Of course he is," Bess said. "And they're always brothers."

Doll rolled her eyes. "No, his *real* brother."

"That's what he told you, at least." Doll was always giddy with the anticipation of love, always bringing Bess along on dates, and the worst were the dates with other performers. They all made their livings pretending to be something they were not—Bess and Doll included—but it was difficult for the men especially to be both charming and sincere at the same time, when in show business you could really only be one or the other.

Their seats were in the third row, left, and they had a good view of the stage when the two magicians stepped out and announced themselves to the crowd. They spoke loudly, and with authority, but the reception from the audience was merely polite. They were not transported yet; everyone could still hear the bells and laughter of the carnival outside, not quite muffled by the humidity of the afternoon. The women fanned their faces lazily, and no one was quite sure exactly who the Brothers Houdini were, although they billed themselves as "escape artists."

"Which one's Dash?" Bess asked, and Doll pointed to the taller of the two, who was tying the other inside a black cloth sack.

She wasn't sure whether to be disappointed, because the one Doll called Harry wasn't as tall as Dash, or pleased, because Harry was clearly the more athletic of the two, with darker hair and a rounder jaw. She had always liked dark-haired men. In high school, she had come close to losing her way with a waiter who'd kissed her so hard he'd bitten her. Still, she had been charmed by his coal-black hair and the swagger of a hot summer.

Still inside the sack, Harry knelt down in a steamer trunk, which Dash then locked and wrapped with a heavy braided rope. There was no sound or movement from inside the trunk. Dash pulled a curtain around the trunk and himself so that both men were completely obscured from view.

"Ladies and gentlemen," he declared from behind the curtain, raising his voice to drown out the sounds of the music outside. Doll pressed her palms together in anticipation. "Behold"—he clapped three times—"a miracle!"

The curtain was opened by unseen hands, and there, on the other side, stood Harry, completely free, arms raised triumphantly in the air. The audience murmured and then broke into loud applause.

Bess leaned toward Doll. "That was slick."

"Wait," Doll said, grabbing her arm. "I don't think it's over yet."

Harry, his white shirt miraculously undirtied, proceeded to unwind the rope from around the trunk and open the latch. Inside, emerging somehow from the cloth sack, also unrumpled, was Dash.

The audience cheered. "Bravo!" Doll called, getting to her feet. From the stage, Dash noticed them and smiled. Bess was impressed and curious. It had been a matter of only a few minutes since Harry himself had been tied up in that sack. How could he have managed to get himself out, and Dash in, so quickly?

Then, from the back of the theater, a voice broke out. "Youse a bunch of fakers!" someone cried. The crowd parted to reveal a scowling, gray-haired man with his fists in the air. "I know fakers when I sees them, and youse two are some fakers!"

Onstage, Dash and Harry looked at each other. "I beg to differ with you, sir," Harry said, and the audience laughed.

"What you have here is a fake box, and I'm gonna show this thing up," the man cried.

"Do it!" someone else called. "Go up there and do it!"

Bess felt sorry for the Houdinis. She wished she could save them. She saw Dash wince, and she looked at Doll. "Those poor boys. He's ruining their act." But neither brother seemed the least bit flustered.

The man made his way up to the stage, cheered by the audience, and when he arrived he stood face-to-face with Harry and Dash, his cheeks flaming red.

"I can get myself outta that cheap box," he announced. "I been doin' acts for thirty years, and you're dirtyin' the stage with your fake tricks."

"Please," Harry said, motioning toward the trunk still sitting in the middle of the stage. The audience laughed again, nervously this time.

The man climbed inside the sack and pulled it up to his shoulders and then over his head, still muttering to himself. When he was completely enclosed, Harry tied the sack and helped him kneel down inside the trunk. Dash closed the latch and locked it, then pulled the curtain around the trunk, and Harry and Dash sat down on the edge of the stage to wait, their legs dangling just above the floor.

For the first few minutes everyone was quiet; Bess was not quite sure whether they were rooting for the old man or for the Houdinis; it would make for an unexpected show either way. By the start of the third minute, the crowd began to murmur.

Doll looked at Bess and beamed. "Dash promised a riot, didn't he? I'll tell you what, this is wonderful fun. I wonder how long he'll stay in there."

Bess wasn't so sure. By the fifth minute it was becoming apparent that something was wrong. The crowd was restless, and some people were beginning to boo. Harry stood up from his seat at the corner of the stage and held up his hand.

As the voices died down, the muffled cries behind the curtain became louder. Someone on the other side was calling for help. Dash jumped to his feet, and he and Harry yanked the curtain aside to reveal the trunk, still roped shut. Dash sliced the ropes, and together the brothers helped pull the man, still inside the sack, from the confinement of the trunk. He was writhing inside the cloth, and when they untied it and the fabric fell to his feet, he stood for a moment in the middle of the stage, his body damp with perspiration, and then collapsed on the floor.

The crowd cheered.

※

The brothers had promised to meet them at the stage door a half hour after the show. Doll begged Bess to go back to their room so she could change. "I hate this skirt." She tugged at the coarse blue fabric. "I should have worn the red."

"Won't Anna be mad when she sees you brought me instead of her?"

"Nah." Doll shrugged. "She's got a beau of her own tonight anyway."

Bess smiled, but she knew why Doll had asked her instead of Anna. Of the three of them, Bess was the plainest; she had the smallest bust and the cruelest shape. Anna, on the other hand, with her corn-blond hair and pillowed cheeks, was the principal among them, and always took the middle spot when they sang.

They lived, with most of the other performers, in West Brighton, in a neighborhood nicknamed the Gut. The rough half a dozen blocks were crammed with shanties, beer halls, and cabarets. The three of them lived in a cheap hotel alongside chorus girls who danced in the bars and hustled customers by slipping hydrate of chloral into their drinks and stealing their wallets. It was Bess's dream to one day earn enough to stay in the Brighton Beach Hotel, with its white veranda and geranium-lined walkways.

In their room, in the tiny aisle between the bunk and the single bed, each with its own tiny brass lamp, Doll leaned into a hand mirror and examined her eyelashes. "I hate it in here," she said. "It's so crammed, and there's hardly any light."

Bess nodded but couldn't complain. It was the most independence she'd had, having grown up under first her mother's constant religious admonitions, then the protective watchfulness of her older sister. And she did not regret leaving her sister's tiny apartment on Grand Street, where the wealthier townhomes of Bedford were always just within view, their elaborate stonework and silk-draped windows a reminder of what she could never have. When Doll and Anna had asked her to join the singing troupe, she'd had nothing to lose. She had only a year of high school left, and the careers ahead of her were wife, nun, or shopgirl.

Most of the Gut had burned down a decade earlier, but it was still a wicked place to live, and no girl walked alone there at night. They practiced their act instead in the afternoons, in the park adjacent to the Manhattan Beach Hotel. The performance consisted mainly of love ballads for soprano and alto, accompanied by swaying hips and flickering eyelashes. Onstage, they wore feathers in their hair, black ankle boots, and skirts hemmed to their shins. After a half hour of rehearsal, sprawled on the cool hotel grass, they listened to the guests splashing in the saltwater bathhouses next door and plotted how to win a spot in Henderson's Music Hall, with its polished wood stage, red velvet seats, and gilded balconies. Bess had been in Coney Island for only three weeks, but already she was lulled by the routine of their lazy afternoons, their evenings at the clam bars or the racetrack, the easy and unpoliced flirtation between men and women. None of it seemed scandalous to her. It did not seem like Gomorrah but rather like Eden, the carousels and the ivory sand and the hotels with their burning lights and pastel awnings, the thick, syrupy smell of the confectioners in the lobbies. She could almost forget the hot, baked sidewalks of Grand Street, the raging nightly altercations of the couple who lived on the other side of the apartment wall. When she was onstage with the girls, the evening air drifting through open windows and the piano music echoing behind her, she could imagine herself living this life forever, accountable to no one, her dark hair braided with pink feathers and the sound of her voice carrying, *After the ball is over, after the break of morn, after the dancers' leaving, after the stars are gone.*

Dash met them first, swinging his stage jacket over his shoulder and cracking some joke about Harry primping like a girl. He picked Doll up by the waist and spun her in a quick circle, pressing his mouth against hers. "I was hoping you'd come," he said.

"Oh, the act was wonderful," she breathed. "We wouldn't have missed it for anything."

He turned to Bess. "I'm Dash," he said, pumping her hand. "My brother and I saw you in your show last weekend." He nodded at Doll. "I stopped this one on her way out."

Bess felt her cheeks burning. She hadn't noticed them. "I usually don't pay attention to faces," she mumbled. "I'm sorry. I know that seems rude."

Dash shrugged. "Nah."

"Are you two really brothers?" she asked.

"We are."

"You don't look much alike."

"We're Hungarian," he said, as if it were an explanation. Bess didn't press him further, because the one Doll had called Harry had come outside and was striding over to them. His hair was newly brushed and he'd changed his shoes, but while Dash had switched shirts, Harry wore the same clothing she'd seen onstage. She couldn't see any stains of perspiration on his shirt. She wondered if that, too, was a trick, whether he'd simply changed into an identical shirt to make it seem as if it had all been easy. If so, it had worked; she was impressed.

"Well, that was good fun," he said, putting his hand on his brother's shoulder. "Now who are these lovely women here?" He spoke with a slight European accent, enunciating each word carefully, as if he were being especially cautious not to give himself away. Bess wondered what he'd make of learning that her real name was heavily German.

She introduced herself as Bess. When she held out her hand, he turned it over and, boldly, kissed the middle of her palm. She snatched it away, surprised and a little scandalized.

"My mother always told me never to shake a woman's hand," he said. "It's disrespectful."

Doll laughed and reached for Dash's arm. "You magicians are quite cheeky, aren't you?"

Bess considered Harry's bold gesture. She wasn't sure what to make of him. He was taller than she was, which was easy considering she was still the height of a child, but he had an arrogance about him that unnerved her.

"Are we going to the beach?" Doll asked. "Let's, please. It's sweltering out here."

The sun was going down behind them, but guests were still pouring onto the grounds, and the streetlamps blazed like the white eyes of ghosts. Bess recalled her mother's shame when she'd left home, but it was worth it, wasn't it, to be here in the summer lights in this jewel-encrusted palace, a place with more color and life than she'd ever known.

None of the performers spent much of their free time in the fairground, though. The Bowery was always crowded, the food was expensive, and they didn't get any of it for free. But mostly, there was always the possibility that theatergoers might recognize or accost them. Even worse than that, although no one said it out loud, was the possibility that they would actually be mistaken for the theatergoers themselves, ordinary men and women who ate hot dogs or waited in line for a goat-cart ride or the Switchback dime railroad. And the idea of it—such tedious, immaculate ordinariness—was abhorrent. They had all come to Coney Island to forge extraordinary, resplendent lives under the lights. Perhaps her sister would be content to wait in line, but Bess would not be one of the onlookers anymore.

"To the beach," Dash agreed and took Doll's hand, and Harry fell in step behind them. Bess walked beside him, as she had nowhere else to go, but he didn't speak to her again. She was unsettled by his silence, and slightly insulted. It seemed outside the bounds of common decency. He was young—almost as young as she—and she wondered if he had ever even been with a woman before. Doll—who was an expert in such matters—had explained to her that when men made a show of their confidence it was often to disguise some sexual insecurity.

Finally she gave in and spoke first. "Tell me something." She lowered her voice so Dash and Doll wouldn't hear. "You knew that man in the audience was going to challenge you tonight, didn't you? You knew he'd never be able to get out of that trunk."

Harry smiled. "Why would you think that?"

"Or maybe it was all made up, and you paid him to get stuck in there so you could look like a hero." She surprised herself with this. She hadn't meant to be so brash. But she was stewing in the insult of his silence, and it had brought out another, harsher side to her.

His smile faded. "I'll tell you one thing—not a soul in the whole state of New York can get out of that trunk except Dash and me. And I certainly don't need to pay anyone to try."

"You don't have to snap at me." She paused. "I could get out of that trunk."

He looked at her, amused. "Could you?"

Bess nodded. "You're clearly very skilled with ropes—that's the most difficult part. You had your hands untied behind your back before Dash even pulled the sack up over your head. But the rope tying the sack was tricked—I suspect you just had to pull on it from the inside for it to open the bag. Then there's the trick panel on the rear of the trunk."

Harry's smirk vanished. "You're wrong."

"I'm not saying it doesn't take a great deal of skill and practice to do it so quickly. I do think you should bind your ankles as well though. It would make the escape seem even more miraculous." She saw Harry's face darken and realized she had gone too far.

"I'll tell you my own secret," she said, more kindly. "My real name's much worse than Floral. It's Wilhelmina Beatrice Rahner. The Bess comes from Beatrice."

Harry's anger seemed to soften. "*That's* your secret? It's not that bad."

"Of course it is. It sounds like the name of some fat headmistress."

"Beatrice was the name of Dante's muse," he argued. "He wrote her into Paradise."

Bess glanced up at the dim figures of Dash and Doll, ahead of them, growing farther and farther away. "You've read Dante?"

"I've read everything there is to do with magic. Or at least I intend to, anyway."

"But Dante's books are about religion." She recalled her teacher's lecture on the *Inferno* in high school. She wouldn't classify it as a study in magic—fantasy, maybe, if you took it lightly. But to Bess, the nine circles of hell were a Catholic warning against sin, about how carefully everyone treaded in this world, and how quickly fortune could be taken away. The Italian girls flaunted their untranslated copies of the book to show up the German girls, whom they considered bland and unsophisticated.

Of course, on Sundays they all went to the same church, and outside their neighborhood, in the wealthier parts of the city, all of them tried equally hard not to give away any trace of their heritages, using American nicknames to disguise Old World names and American makeup to hide ethnic imperfections.

Harry snorted. "Magic and religion are the same thing."

"You mean miracles?"

"Miracles don't exist. I mean real magic." He frowned. "Growing up, I watched my father pace uselessly around the room when the rent came due, saying, 'The Lord will provide, the Lord will provide.' But it wasn't the Lord who found ways to pay our rent. It was me."

Bess was taken aback. "I have to say I disagree with you. Miracles *do* exist."

"Have you ever seen one?"

"No, but—"

"So how would you know?"

"It depends on how you look at it. A baby being born—that's a miracle, don't you think?" She felt her cheeks flush. It was becoming clear how young she was, how little experience she had outside the few blocks she grew up on. She knew the priests did not have all the answers; in fact, one of the ones she'd encountered in a church near the Gut had tried to run his hand along her leg. But it was difficult to admit that, to some extent, life was one great pool of floundering souls, everyone clutching for something to believe in. Church had always set her at ease—when her father died, when her mother remarried, and the house was full of screaming children—she could sit for an hour among the trembling brightness of the candles, the windows the colors of jewels, and all that breathless beauty, and be still.

"Listen," Harry said. "The only miracle I've seen yet is the one that led me to meeting you tonight."

Bess blinked at him. She wondered if he was making fun of her. She had insulted him, perhaps even humiliated him, and now he was proclaiming some kind of tenderness toward her? He hadn't even touched her hand, but she felt as if he'd run his fingers down her back. She wrapped her arms instinctively around her waist. "You're—you're quite straightforward."

Harry reached toward her. "Are you cold?"

She shook her head and changed the subject. "Are you saying you don't believe in religion then?"

"Of course I do. My father was a Jewish scholar."

"Oh," she stammered, confused. "You're . . . Jewish then?" She wasn't quite sure which was worse—that he was Jewish, or that he seemed to have mocked her own beliefs. Or that neither of these changed the fact that she couldn't quite bring herself to step away from him.

"I suppose."

"Do you still practice it?"

"No." He looked her up and down. "And you're Catholic, then?"

"Why would you suppose that?"

He smiled. "You said *Jewish* with such forced politeness."

She blushed. "I did not. And it's not that. My mother's very strict about her faith."

"So you became a dancer. How very Catholic of you." He frowned. "You seem to put a lot of stock in what you've learned from other people—teachers, parents, priests. But what about what you've learned for yourself?"

She felt, in a way, that, by standing here alone with Harry, she had made a decision without intending to. His breath was so warm she felt as if it might scald her. She realized now that she wouldn't—couldn't—go back. What she had once considered sinful did not seem wrong anymore. The routines of her new life—the wide-eyed stares of the men in the audience; the giggling late-night confessions of Anna and Doll in the bunk across from her—seemed not only harmless but honest and real. She had been looking for something during those hours she spent in the solitude of a church pew, but she had found it here instead, in Harry's smooth, unblemished face, and in the way he seemed to want her not for being smooth or unblemished but for being wonderfully complicated, emerging from the banality of her past life to something enthralling.

They had reached the beach now, and the ocean, black as cloth in the distance, the froth of the waves cascading like plumage, was less than a hundred feet away. There was something spectacular about the sea at night—it was dangerous, unexplored; and if there was such a thing as magic, then it was certainly somewhere out there, in all that humid darkness.

They stood with their feet buried in the sand, looking out at the water. Dash and Doll were nowhere to be seen, but she could hear the unmistakable chirp of Doll's laughter, somewhere down the beach. "You believe in miracles. But don't you believe in magic?" Harry asked her, his dark eyes suddenly serious.

Bess blinked. "I—I don't think so. You mean like flying carpets? No."

"I'm going to tell you a secret, then. And it is essential that you know this." He took both her hands and looked at her. A current of electricity shot through her. "There is no such thing as magic."

Bess felt herself shiver, but she didn't pull away. "Why do you say that?"

"Because if it was real, I'd know it."

"That's a ridiculous answer."

He shrugged. "Perhaps."

She was suddenly nervous to be alone with him. She didn't care much for propriety, but it was odd that the beach was empty, even at this hour. A few hundred feet away was a thick, salty marshland, and swarming the air by their faces, clouds of tiny black bugs found their way into Bess's hair and mouth. She was becoming more and more uncomfortable next to Harry. There was something animal-like about his movements, the strength with which he'd grabbed her. He had seemed to joke with her before, but there was not a trace of play in his black eyes now. He was watching her with intent.

"I wrote you off, back when I watched you perform," he said. "I thought you were just another flirt singing silly songs."

"Oh," she said, alarmed. "Well, I don't know what to say to that."

"But you knew about tonight. You were right that we were onto that lackey who tried to discredit us. And the trunk trick . . . I'm not saying you were right about that. I'm just saying no one's ever come so close to seeing through one of my tricks. You're smarter than I expected. And bolder, too, I guess."

She could feel herself growing dizzy in the heat. The waves seemed to be pressing in on them both.

Something occurred to her. "How many times did you see me perform?"

"Three or four."

"I didn't see you."

"I was in the back. You wouldn't have seen me. But we passed each other in the Bowery a few times."

Bess was startled. "Why didn't you say anything to me? Did you know it was going to be me here with Doll tonight?"

Harry slid his hands into his pockets. "I asked Dash to take Doll out, so you'd come."

"Oh, that's mean. Now she thinks he likes her. You should have just asked me."

"Would you have said yes?"

"Sure."

He smiled. "How much do you like me?" he asked.

"What?"

"Enough to marry me?"

Bess laughed. She couldn't tell if he was serious now, or mocking her. "That's a lark. And I don't see how you'll win me over by making fun of me."

"I'm not making fun. I'm serious. I'm twenty and you're what—eighteen?"

She nodded. "Yes, we're still young. What's the rush?" She was playing along now.

"You're not a child anymore, Bess. You're a woman. Don't you feel that's what you are?" He put his hand on the back of her neck. She felt the churn in her stomach. "You're old enough by now to know what it is you want."

"I suppose I am." The words didn't sound as playful as she intended. He was as confusing a man as she had ever met. No one had ever professed his love to her before. In fact, some of the men Doll had introduced her to had told her frankly that they couldn't take her seriously; she looked too much like a child with her curly hair and small lips. Now this man she had just met—who was, perhaps, as much still a boy as she was a girl—was declaring himself to her, and she wasn't sure whether to be flattered or suspicious.

"Don't you want me?" he asked, with utter seriousness.

She shook her head. "I don't know what you mean by that exactly. I'm not the kind of girl you might be thinking I am."

He removed his hand from her neck and brushed a strand of hair behind her ear. "I mean, don't you want to marry me?"

Rationally, it didn't make sense. Neither of them had any money. She had known him for a night. He could turn out to be the kind of man who drank, who hit her when he was angry. He could miscalculate one of his tricks and die young. And she'd been in Coney Island only three weeks. Three weeks earlier, she'd been a schoolgirl, working at a shop counter in the evenings. She hadn't had enough time to become someone else. What would she do if she became a mother? People who got married had children. Did she even want a child?

The sand hills loomed like mountains beside her, the scattered shells dimly white in the moonlight. She bent down and held one in her hand. The front was smooth, the inside rough with salt. She looked at Harry. He had his hands in his pockets and was staring at her expectantly. She laid her palm against her forehead. Harry knelt down beside her. "What's wrong? Are you sick?"

She thought of what her mother would say if she brought home a Jew. "I can't believe you're actually serious right now. I can't marry you, Harry. You don't know a thing about me, nor I you."

He considered this. "Harry's not my real name. My real name is Ehrich Weiss. And no one here knows that but Dash, and you, now."

"So you see then? I don't even know what to call you."

"You can call me whatever you like."

"Harry—" she began.

He pulled her to her feet. "Come with me."

"No, I can't."

"I'll carry you then." He picked her up like a trinket, laughing, then hooked his arms around her shoulders and knees, like a groom carrying a bride. "You're very light."

"This is preposterous," she cried, but he was already walking in long strides across the sand, toward the marsh. "Where are we going?"

The marsh, they discovered, was really a quick rush of water the ocean had made into a river, through the sand. It had dug itself deep over time, and someone had built a small bridge across it. He put her down in the middle of the bridge. "Can you stand?" he asked.

"I can, you brute. But you're mad. What in the world makes you think we can get married when we've only just met?"

"Damn it, Bess! How can you not see it?" His outburst startled her, and she stepped back. "We're the *same*, you and me." He wrapped his hands around her waist and held her tightly. "We see things. Things other people don't."

"Why do you say that?"

"Because you didn't see *me*. When you were onstage you were looking right at me, and yet you didn't see me. Because you were seeing something else. Am I right?"

Bess nodded. She'd learned that when she sang, the songs enveloped her. She saw sensations in front of her—colors, the heat of the afternoon like smoke rising, brightness like the sun on glass.

He went on, breathlessly, as if the realization had consumed him. "There's something else out there, beyond what the mind can perceive. Maybe it's religion, maybe it's not. It's not magic the way we think of it—that kind of magic is a game. It's something else, something truer than that. Some people believe in it. A few can sense it. But me—I can see it. And then I met you. And I think—I think you can actually reach it."

Bess was stricken. She could feel the pulse of his hands around her waist as if the blood was throbbing through his fingers. "Reach *what*, Harry?"

"What is out there. The other place."

"Like heaven?"

"White gates and all that? No, no. I think there's another plane of living right here where we're standing. People who have been, people who have yet to be, what if they are right here with us? And yet most of us aren't even aware of them." His eyes danced. There was a madness to his passion, but he was not insane. There was something real and familiar about him. She felt he was putting words to something she had always known. And what if he was right? What if she possessed something extraordinary? No one, before Doll and Anna approached her and asked her to sing, had ever believed she was extraordinary.

"Speaking with the dead is sacrilege."

"I don't care if you speak with them or not. I was only trying to explain why I love you." He seemed suddenly nervous, as if, in his arrogance, he had only just now realized that she could reject him. "I was trying to say that you're perceptive. And I think you could make me better."

He stepped back slightly, turning to face the lights of the Bowery in the distance. "I've never been one to take anything slow. I've got these great expectations, you know. I'm going to be famous, and very wealthy, and I'm going to take care of my mother so she never has to worry again, and I simply can't do that living like everyone else. When you caught on to my tricks, I thought, This is it. This is the girl. And if I know you're the girl, why should I wait to tell you?"

Bess blushed. "Surely you can't tell that from one—"

"That song you sing in your act—what was it? O'er me you cast a spell, something-something-something."

"Rosabel."

He grinned. "Yes, that was it. Rosabel. I loved that song. How does it go?"

"Rosabel, sweet Rosabel," she said hurriedly, speaking instead of singing, "I love her more than I can tell, over me she casts a spell, my charming black-eyed Rosabel—" She broke off. "I thought you said it was silly."

"No, I said the *songs* were silly." He shook his head; he had been listening, rapt. "But that one's beautiful. I started to love you then—your face lit up when you sang it. I thought, This is a girl who hopes for things. She probably doesn't know a thing about love yet, but once she has it, she's never giving it up. And then, after you sang the last verse, it was as if you realized you'd revealed too much. So you laughed and did that little jig, kicking your feet up, and the audience was charmed. But I knew. Your face had given it all away."

Bess stared at him. She felt herself being swept up by his certitude. There was a kind of grandeur about him, about the way he seemed to feel emotions so strongly, as if the rest of the world lay glazed with sleep while he danced furiously. "I feel like—you may know my thoughts better than I do." She had always believed herself decisive, self-reliant, but now she felt flustered.

"It's the other way around. Tonight, you saw through me—you saw *me* . . . It was you who cast the spell."

Bess thought about the morning of her thirteenth birthday, when her mother had first proposed the idea of her entering the nunnery. Her mother had taken her to a shabby brownstone in the middle of Manhattan where rows of old ladies in black robes were seated silently on benches, stringing rosaries. Outside, the city roared with life. She couldn't imagine spending the rest of her life as one of those somber women, while just outside the door there was so much incandescence, so many elegant shops and sharply dressed men waiting to love her.

But her mother was a strict, unforgiving German woman, whose body had borne ten children, and whose second husband was in and out of the house, most of the time stinking of beer, a poor replacement for Bess's gentle father, who had died years earlier. That afternoon, Bess had vowed to accept the first opportunity that would take her away from home. The opportunity came four years later, in the form of two nineteen-year-old girls named Nora Koch and Anna Kappel, who had been slightly ahead of her in high school but had left when they were fifteen, with dreams of being in vaudeville. She ran into them on the street outside the grocer's; they had had some minor success as a singing duo, but they were looking for a third, and invited her to go with them to Coney Island, where they had booked an act for the summer, and longer, if they succeeded. But recently the thought had occurred to her that if they reached September without a larger booking, they could not continue, and what would she do then?

The act was barely making them enough money to afford their room in the boardinghouse, and she couldn't imagine going back to Brooklyn, even to Stella's, and having Sunday lunch with her family once again and hearing her stepfather crashing through the door, slurring those terrible old German songs, and seeing all her brothers and sisters crammed into two bedrooms. If she were married, she would have a home of her own. She wasn't quite sure what love felt like, but she liked the way she felt when Harry touched her. And he said he wanted her. No one in her life had seemed to want to love her so much as he did.

"All right," she said softly. "I'll marry you."

"You see? That's part of what I love about you. You always do the unexpected."

Then he resumed his strange seriousness. From the other side of Coney Island came the echo of church bells chiming the hour. They seemed an anomaly against the faint cacophony of voices drifting from the Bowery. "There's something you need to promise me first," he said. "Before we get married."

"What is it?"

Harry took her hands and lifted them straight up, clasping his palms against hers. They were rough as sandpaper. "Beatrice," he said. "Raise your hands to heaven and swear that you will be true to me. Never betray me in any way, so help you God."

There was not an animal in the water beneath them, not a single creature shuffling through the sand. Everything was stillness.

"I will never betray you," Bess murmured. She could not take her eyes off him. His intensity was hypnotic.

"What I do—I have many secrets. When you're my wife, you'll know all of them. You'll know everything about me. You'll know more than Dash, even. And if you agree to marry me, it must be forever. You can never go back home again."

There was something about the lateness of the hour, the bridge in the marshland, and the dramatic vow he'd made her take that gave her pause. She wondered if she was standing face-to-face with a madman. But there was something thrilling about what had just transpired. Harry was promising her a life of possibility, of magic, and it was unlike anything she had ever imagined for herself. And she could not help but envision, now, what it would be like to be his wife, to wake up beside him, to watch him stand in front of her, silhouetted against the window, the muscles in his back sharp as lines of charcoal. She wanted him to kiss her. She thought of that black-haired waiter in Brooklyn and the taste of blood on her lip where he'd bitten her; she had been frightened then, but she wanted Harry to put his mouth on her now. She wanted him to say he would never love anyone but her. She thought of the sheer strength he must have to pull off that escape trick onstage, and she wondered what it would feel like to know that strength.

She thought about what her friends would say when she told them she had fallen in love with him. Doll would be both thrilled and heartbroken. Anna would despise her for leaving the group, certainly.

"Don't be nervous." Harry put his arm around her shoulder. "I will take care of you."

"Harry," she whispered. "When we are old, I want you to think of me as I am on our wedding night." She didn't know where the words came from. "I want to please you. I want you to remember me." It seemed a more binding vow than the one he had asked her to swear.

He pulled her to him then, for the first time, so their bodies were against each other, their arms intertwined. She could feel his stomach harden. He pressed his mouth against hers and kissed her. Gently, he lowered her onto the wood of the bridge so they were kneeling face-to-face.

She heard Dash and Doll coming up the beach toward them, breaking their solitude. They stood up quickly, wiping the mud off their clothes. Doll was waving. "Yoo-hoo!" she called.

"You devil, Harry!" Dash shouted. "We knew you two were up to something!"

"Do you think Dash will be cross when you tell him?" Bess whispered.

"No." Harry shrugged. "And it doesn't matter now. We've made our vows."

"But—we'll have a ceremony?"

"Of course." Harry took her chin in his hand and kissed her again.

They bought her ring in the morning, at a secondhand jewelry store, pooling what little money they had. When it was polished it looked almost new, and Harry had the gold engraved inside with the word *Rosabel,* which would come to symbolize a time in their lives when everything was simplest, when a man could declare his love on a bridge in the middle of a humid night and everything usual or proper could be disregarded. In the afternoon they were married by the local ward boss, with his secretary as witness, and by the evening Bess had packed a suitcase with her few sets of clothes and photographs and moved into Harry's room in the hotel across the street. He told her they would be leaving in a week, because Vacca's was stiffing him and he'd heard of some opportunities in the South. She tried to imagine what her mother was doing at the very moment—some kind of embroidery, probably, or washing the pots, and she wondered what she herself would be doing thirty years later, when she was her mother's age, and whether there would be anything left of the girl Harry fell in love with. She looked out at the roller coaster across the street, and the young girls in their white summer dresses and the boys staring after them, and the memories, beating with life, like tiny birds, before her eyes.

Chapter 2

THE TEAROOM

May 1929

"He's here, Bess. Can't you hear him? He's with us now."

She could hear the voice beside her clearly, but it sounded nothing like Harry's. The man at her bedside, grasping her palm, was not her husband but the reverend and medium Arthur Ford—a handsome, dark-eyed man in his early forties who had proclaimed he could entice Harry to speak to him. Ford had, over the past several months, become a fixture in Bess's social circle. A few nights before, dizzy with champagne, she had taken a fall as she danced and banged her head against a railing, and Ford had taken her home and wrapped her head in white cloth. Now, he put his other hand on her cheek and brushed a strand of hair out of her eyes so she could see his face.

"Mrs. Houdini, he says that when this message comes through there will be a veritable storm, that many will seek to destroy you. You must be prepared for this."

They were not alone. Seated in a semicircle around Bess's chaise were Bess's press agent, two reporters, an editor at *Scientific American* and his wife, and a wealthy friend of Ford's who'd come for the spectacle of the séance. The blinds had been drawn, but the city still burned behind them. On the street, the taxicabs were crowded with kissing couples and red-lipped, white-toothed women who went on laughing under the streetlamps, and how divine it would have been to be young with Harry on a night like this, to be on his arm on the way to a party. But Harry was gone, wasn't he? She had been left behind, and it was the end of a dream.

Ford strengthened his grip on her hand. "He's coming through clearly now," he insisted, closing his eyes and hunching his shoulders, as if with the weight of some invisible force. "A man who says he is Harry Houdini, but whose real name is Ehrich Weiss, is here. He tells me to say, 'Hello, Bess, sweetheart,' and he wants me to convey his message."

"Yes." The words emerged like small breaths in the cold. "Go on," she said. "Tell me what it is."

Arthur Ford fixed his eyes on Bess. "The code, he says, is the one you used to use in one of your secret mind-reading acts, to communicate information to each other." His voice was chillingly quiet.

Bess used her elbow to push herself into a sitting position. Her head was still pounding from her injury. In the three years since Harry's death, she had become unmoored, searching for the sparks of her own identity while continuing to cling to Harry's. She did not want to forget him, and she did not want him to be forgotten. He had made it publicly clear before his death that when he was gone, he was going to try to come back, through the communication of a private code he and Bess had established.

Then, in 1926, he had died suddenly, and young, at fifty-two; and the world had grieved with her. But what had surprised Bess was how desperately the public clung to Harry's vow that he would return to speak to her. In these wild and unanchored years, people needed something to believe in; religious or not, they needed to know if there was some kind of life after death. They believed Bess's retrieval of the code would provide the assurances they were looking for.

And so, while she had spent the recent, grieving years sorting through Harry's estate, and fielding interviews, and attempting two failed businesses of her own, she had also been participating in dozens of unsuccessful séances a month. At first she had believed she could channel Harry herself; every Sunday she set aside two still, private hours waiting for him to reach her. But nothing came of those hours. Whatever powers she, or Harry, had once believed she possessed, failed her. Finally she opened herself up to the idea that he might use someone else to speak to her. Harry had followed this same logic after his mother died, at first reaching out to her spirit himself, in the privacy of their home, then asking Bess to participate, unsuccessfully. Increasingly desperate, he had ventured into the parlors of the spiritualists.

In the three years since Harry's death, the public's fascination with Houdini's legacy hadn't waned; she still received thousands of letters from mediums claiming to know the message Harry had left her before he died—the message that would prove, once and for all, that it was possible for the dead to come back and speak to the living. But all of these claims had been false.

Only Bess knew how desperately Harry himself had wished to be certain of such a possibility. But none of the séances he had attended had ever convinced him. And she could never speak to anyone, not even his siblings, the truth that the great Houdini had died afraid of what was to come.

Then, two months ago, Arthur Ford had come into her tearoom. He was a man of God. She had sensed that there was something different about him. He had kissed her, and promised her honesty, and Bess was convinced that he, of all people, could contact Harry. In the end, it was she who had asked him for a séance.

Ford continued. "This is the code. It is ten words." Bess nodded; that was correct. She pulled her white silk robe closer around her shoulders. "And it is: Rosabel. Answer. Tell. Pray. Answer. Look. Tell. Answer. Answer. Tell." The room was completely silent, the eyes of all the witnesses focused on Bess. "He wants you to tell him whether they are right or not."

Bess was still. "Yes," she said at last. "Yes, they are." There was a murmur of amazement from the witnesses.

Ford opened his eyes. "Harry smiles and says thank you. Now I can go on. He tells you to take off your wedding ring and tell them what Rosabel means."

She had lost so much weight in her widowed years that the ring slid easily off her finger. She traced the letters engraved on the inside. She held it out, trembling, for Ford to inspect, and she heard, from somewhere long ago, the words of the song: *Rosabel, sweet Rosabel, I love her more than I can tell, over me she casts a spell, my charming black-eyed Rosabel . . .*

I'll come back for you, Harry had promised. On his deathbed, he had struggled to convey a message he was unable to finish.

"And now, the words we just established—*answer, tell, pray,* and so on—signify another word in your code, which used common phrases or groups of phrases to indicate certain letters," Ford's voice went on. "And that word after Rosabel is *believe.* The message Harry wants to send back to you is 'Rosabel, believe.' Is that right?"

Bess looked at him, stunned. "Is it possible?" she whispered. "Is he really—is he really here?" The sounds of the city seemed to rush in upon her like a great wind. She could hear rain outside, sheets of it pounding on the sidewalk. "Someone close the windows, please!" she cried.

"But—they are closed," she heard the editor's wife say.

"Mrs. Houdini? Are you all right?" another voice asked. There was commotion in the room; chairs scraped against the floor. Someone leaned over her.

Then she heard Ford's voice, louder than before. "He says, 'Tell the whole world that Harry still lives!'"

Across the room, the door burst open. "What is this intrusion?" she heard Ford cry out. "What is going on?"

Bess's eyes focused again. Her sister Stella was pushing her way through the semicircle of chairs, her hair matted with rain under a black cloche hat. She stood dripping beside Bess's couch.

"Bess, don't believe it!" she cried. "It's all a hoax. This woman"— she pointed to one of the journalists—"has already sent a story to the *Graphic* that accuses you of faking this séance! It's going to be the biggest scandal since the Ponzi scheme."

Ford stood up. "What do you think you are doing?"

"Bess," Stella urged, wringing the bottom of her dress, "Ford's known the code all along. He didn't get it through Harry just now. The message has already been printed in Rea Jaure's story. And the story's going to say that Harry and I were sleeping together, and that he told *me* the message, and I gave it to Ford, and you knew all along, and we're all a bunch of fakes."

Bess shook her head. She swung her body around to look at Ford and then back at Stella. "But—that's impossible. That was our private message. No one knew it but Harry and me."

"No." Stella shook her head. "Someone else knew. One of the nurses heard him say it in the hospital, and she sold the information to Ford." She glared at him from across the room. "*Rosabel, believe.* That's it, isn't it?"

The editor's wife gasped. "How could you know that? We've only all just heard it for the first time."

Bess looked at Ford, her eyes steely with anger. "Is this true,

Arthur? Were you just manipulating me this whole time?" She felt like a fool. How could she have been so naïve?

Ford learned toward her and reached for her elbow. A combed-back strand of hair fell over his forehead. His eyes were wide with disbelief. And yet there was a glimmer in his voice of something she hadn't recognized before—the overenunciated diction of a lie. "Darling, no. It's real, I promise. Harry was here."

"It's all going to come out tomorrow, Bess," Stella said.

"Everyone get out!" Bess cried. She looked at her agent. "Vernon, get them out! Get them out! I want everyone out!" She threw the covers off the couch and stood up, the neckline of her robe slipping down her shoulder. Ford reached toward her to pull the edge back up, but Bess pushed him away.

"Darling—" he protested. "You need to lie down. You're not well."

Bess's voice was frigid. "*Don't* call me darling; I'm not your darling. I never should have believed you—Harry never would have believed you! You're nothing but a fraud!"

The room was in an uproar. Bess's agent pushed everyone toward the door, and in the chaos somebody knocked over a vase, which shattered on the floor, sending shards of clay skittering across the tile mosaic *B* that Harry had had installed. Her agent stooped to pick up the pieces.

Bess waved him away. "Please, just leave me with Stella."

He looked at her. "Will you be all right?"

"Yes, yes, I'll be fine."

When everyone had gone, Stella sat down on the couch beside her. "I never slept with Harry," she said. "That would have been—practically incestuous. And he never told me about the message."

"Of course not. It's preposterous."

"They're going to slander us both in the papers. It's going to be horrible." She picked at a run in her green silk stockings.

"Yes, I know." Bess's whole body ached. It seemed as if everything she had tried to accomplish over the past three years had crumbled. She hated looking like a fool, but she hated even more having Harry's legacy slandered. Would she be able to continue with the séances after this? Or would she and Harry be the laughingstocks of the press? She needed to reach him, notoriety or not. The public wanted Harry's code revealed because it would be proof that one could live beyond death. But to Bess, the code was only a stepping-stone. Before Harry died he had told her that there was some kind of essential message, some private knowledge, that he could communicate to her only after he had gone; now, she needed to hear the code first, so that she knew it was truly Harry coming through.

She hoped they wouldn't go after Harry's sister, Gladys, as well. She must telephone her immediately in the morning.

"Will you be all right?" Stella asked. "It's going to be a madhouse around here for a while."

"I'll be fine. Maybe the scandal will rustle up some more business for the tearoom."

Stella laughed. "Always the silver lining."

Bess stopped herself from saying more. Even in the aftermath of another disastrous evening, she still had one last secret to propel her onward. Not a soul on earth—not Arthur Ford, not even Stella or Gladys—knew that Harry, who had always been one for contingencies, had left her with *two* codes before he died. Yes, there was *Rosabel, believe,* and soon the whole world would know about that. But there was a second code, too, which went back to one of their very first nights together. And when she heard those words—which she surely would, she had to—she would know, with certainty, that Harry had found her. Because it was impossible that anyone could have heard the second code; it had not been spoken out loud in decades.

"I'm sorry about Arthur, though," Stella said, mixing two glasses of ice and gin. "I know how much he meant to you."

Ford *had* meant something to her, briefly. He had a rare combination of confidence and schoolboyish sincerity that reminded her of Harry, and she had met him during a vulnerable evening, when she had discovered another of Harry's old love letters hidden in the bookshelf. He had assuaged her loneliness, for a while. But she would recover.

"It is a shame, isn't it?" Bess sighed. "Of course, he was no Harry. But he was such a handsome man."

She woke in the morning with a splitting headache, curled in the chair in her living room. It appeared to be late morning, and the white city light was bleeding through the curtains. The house was unbearably quiet, except for some voices on the street. The housekeeper didn't usually come until noon, and she wasn't sure what had happened to the butler; she imagined he had taken the dog for a walk. It was such a large house for her to be living in, essentially alone—four stories of heavy brownstone, two balconies, and a dozen rooms, the tall windows framed by intricate woodwork and mirroring marble-slabbed fireplaces. Most of the rooms were unused now. When Harry had been alive there was always noise, always a parade of friends and strangers coming in and out, always Alfred Becks, Harry's librarian, with another delivery of books and John Sargent, his secretary, with a pile of letters. Harry had adored fame; he had liked to be admired, hated to be alone.

Even when it was just the two of them he had taken the rooms on the fourth floor for his study area, and she had taken the rooms on the third, where she would hear his voice call down three or four times before noon: "Mrs. Houdini, is my lunch ready?" While he wrote his books, he would send her letters, too, via the maid, who carried them down from the fourth floor on a silver tray. It was his little game. They were always elegantly packaged, even though the content was sometimes frivolous—lines from a poem, perhaps, or comments about the weather. Even when he was far, he always felt near. How ironic that during the fever of their marriage, the frenzied traveling schedule and public appearances, she had sometimes wished for time to herself. Now, it was she who hated to be alone. For the first time in her life since that one young month in Coney Island, she had independence, and was living off her own merit. And she still felt, and needed, Harry's presence. His death, as had his life, consumed her, and until she reached him she did not feel that she could be in possession of herself entirely.

Perhaps that was why she had trusted Ford. His easy arrogance, the enormity of his charisma, had filled a void. And she had hoped, for the first time after so many failed occasions, that someone had gotten through.

Bess rubbed her face and looked at the clock, then jumped out of the chair. She fumbled for her robe. It wasn't morning at all; it was already midafternoon. Could it possibly be two o'clock already? She couldn't remember having slept so late since her circus days with Harry. She had to get to the tearoom. The vegetable orders were being delivered, and she couldn't rely on anyone else to stand up to the deliveryman; bruised produce meant lost profit.

When Harry died, he had left her greatly in debt. She hadn't known the extent of it until his creditors came calling a few days after his funeral, demanding payment. When she totaled the figures, the amount was staggering—more than she could possibly hope to pay with what remained to her. Harry had made enormous sums of money onstage over the last ten years of his life, but he had spent it just as quickly—rare books worth tens of thousands of dollars, unreasonably large gifts to friends, vast investments lost in the moving picture business. Bess was left with state inheritance taxes, funeral costs, and debts on a variety of their purchases, and a life insurance policy that would barely cover those figures.

She had already sold a great deal of Harry's collection of magic books, articles, and papers, but she hadn't had the heart to sell it all, and despite what she had parted with, the house was still packed with his belongings. He had always liked to brag, in his later years, that he possessed the world's largest magic collection and one of the world's largest dramatic collections. There was not a single wall in the four-story home on which bookshelves had not been built, and filled to capacity. She herself opened very few of these books, and even Harry, once he had cataloged them, read only a few pages of interest, then shelved them. He had had very little time to read either, especially as he got older and more renowned. Before he died he wrote seven books on magic, and what little time he had went to writing and research. He had never been the kind of man to drink or eat to excess, but collecting had been an addiction for him: he was consumed by the thrill of acquisition, which Bess attributed to his poverty as a child. Still, she disapproved of his limitless spending, and after a while she caught on that Becks was having the books delivered through the side door to avoid her seeing them. Even after Harry's death, the books he had ordered kept arriving, by post or courier, to the tune of a twenty-thousand-dollar debt.

Even the house she had lived in with him would be quietly put on the market within the year. She had narrowly avoided bankruptcy, and now she was wrapped up in a sordid affair, thanks to Ford. Outside, the sounds on the street were growing steadily louder. Pulling back one of the curtains, she saw a crowd of reporters gathered on the sidewalk. They were pounding on the walls and waving their notebooks in the air. One of them looked up and noticed her face in the window and gave a shout, and the others followed suit, crying to her to come down. "Mrs. Houdini!" they shouted. "Can you tell us why you did it?" Bess closed the curtains.

So Stella had been right; there would be a backlash against her. How anyone could imagine she would betray Harry's memory in such a way, she did not know. But few people knew how much they had lived through together, how they had spent the first five years of their marriage sleeping on cots and in hallways and stealing potatoes to survive. There hadn't been a day in twenty years that she and Harry had spent apart. After his mother died, especially, he clung to her. He couldn't even choose his own clothes without her. Perhaps it was because he felt that Bess was the only one still living who really knew him; in public, he would always be the showman, but at home he was only Harry.

Stella alone knew the full extent of Bess's financial struggles. After Harry's death Stella had asked her, "How could you not hate him for leaving you poor?" Bess had only shaken her head. How could she explain what no one would understand? Her loyalty to Harry, and her belief in his promises, was absolute.

"Harry wouldn't leave me destitute," she had told Stella.

Stella had looked at her pityingly. "But he did, darling. Look at all the bills."

"No. There's money somewhere. I'm sure of it."

Stella had laughed. "Where? Hidden in the attic? In the soles of his shoes?"

"Perhaps. I don't know."

"Be realistic, Bess."

Now Bess tried to push aside the memories and imagine what Harry would advise. She applied pink lipstick and changed into a new white dress and gloves. She would dress as the innocent, as she had early in her marriage, when she had played at being nothing more than an assistant unaware of the secrets behind the tricks. She would go to work as usual, and serve lunch, and avoid the crowds, and she would get by.

A year after Harry's death, Bess had opened a speakeasy with Stella, which had quickly failed, largely due to bad investments—the same lack of business acumen that had always plagued Harry. But the thought of sitting alone in the house all day was abhorrent. After giving herself up to brandy and cigarettes and late nights on Broadway, she found herself dancing the Charleston on the edge of the Biltmore Hotel rooftop one Saturday night, kicking her feet out twenty-seven stories above Madison Avenue, and decided she ought to pursue a steadier occupation.

Finally, six months ago, she went into business on her own, in a more civilized operation, and opened a tearoom on West Forty-Ninth called Mrs. Harry Houdini's Rendezvous, where struggling magicians could find work, and wealthy women could eat and be entertained. She hired a Negro woman to do the cooking, rented a vacant space, and decorated it simply with candles, some toy rabbits, white-clothed tables, and framed portraits of herself and Harry. At the entrance she posted a red-winged parrot named Oscar, who called, "Welcome, welcome!" when customers came through the door. The back of the restaurant opened onto a garden patio, the tables shaded in the summertime with lace-trimmed red and black umbrellas.

The tearoom brought back her verve. She was capitalizing on Harry's fame, yes, but it was the first thing she could call her own. Her identity had always been so dependent on Harry's, her name so inextricably linked with his; even after his death she could not escape him. Both before and after he died so unexpectedly, she was completely consumed by his notoriety. But in her younger days, when they had started out, performing as a pair, they had been the Great Houdinis; she had considered herself his equal. When they were doing the dime museums, they had resorted to the pretense of clairvoyants in order to make enough money to live on. Harry would put her into a trance and she would deliver messages, which were carefully orchestrated between them, through an elaborate code of seemingly harmless blinks, hand and feet motions, and conversational words. So much of their marriage, it seemed to her now, had been defined by the codes they created.

Sneaking out the back of the house into the alley and hailing a cab two blocks down, she managed to avoid the crowd of reporters on the street. And when she stepped out of the car on Forty-Ninth Street, she felt a renewed sense of strength; she felt, for the first time, like it would be possible to start her life over the way she had started over at eighteen, or at twenty-three, when she and Harry had become famous. If she could get over this new obstacle, and focus again on reaching Harry, she would be all right. She didn't need much; she only needed to make a living, and to have a reason to get up in the morning. And she needed to prove there was something more beyond this life—that Harry, who had once blazed with an indomitable spirit, had not vanished into some eternal darkness.

When she stepped into the tearoom at half past two, she was greeted by the clatter of plates and the muffled calls of the kitchen staff. How beautiful that these sounds belonged to her. Along the far wall, the pastries, iced in pastel, were on display in pristine glass cases; behind them, the soda fountain had just been installed. The green and pink glasses with their tiny curved rims were lined neatly on mahogany shelves behind the bar.

At a table across the room, one of the other magicians was

entertaining a woman and a little girl with a needle-swallowing trick. The girl was enthralled. She pulled on the magician's sleeve. "Tell me how you did it!" she begged in a tiny voice.

When they were younger Bess and Harry used to talk about adopting children. "We'll take in dozens of them, when we settle down," Harry used to say. "We'll have a bigger family than yours even." But the time to settle down never came.

They never did figure out what problems prevented them from having children. She never became pregnant. Harry seemed to think he had been sterilized as a result of X-ray exposure. When he was younger, he had befriended a radiologist and used to X-ray himself out of fascination with his insides.

Years ago, Harry had created an imaginary child named Mayer Samuel, whose life story he told to Bess in notes delivered from the fourth floor of their New York house to the third—his admission to Harvard, his marriage to a Boston heiress named Norma, his terms in the Senate. The story culminated in Mayer Samuel's election as president of the United States, and then the fun seemed to fizzle out, and Mayer Samuel disappeared from their lives. Then, instead of children, they adopted dogs.

Standing in the doorway between the kitchen and the tearoom, watching the woman and her daughter, Bess was overcome by a sense of loss. She was over fifty now, and her childbearing days were far behind her. But she had never thought, in the rush of life while Harry was alive, what she would do without him, if she didn't have children or grandchildren. She'd always assumed they'd grow old together. He was so healthy, so strong and vital, she never imagined he'd die so young. After his death, she realized he had kept every scrap of paper she had ever written to him, dating from their very first week together. Some of the notes were trivial, written on napkins, with addresses or questions about dinner. But he had filed every one of them away, and she had never known. How much more, she wondered, had she not known about him?

Bess saw the girl's mother turn and catch her eye. The woman looked away quickly. Bess hurried into the dining room to check on the orders.

One of the magicians—a tall kid who, in his youngest years, used to follow Houdini around to all his New York performances—rushed to her side, asking, "Mrs. Houdini? What are you doing here?" She tried to wave him away, but he ushered her into the kitchen and seated her in an empty chair in the corner.

"For goodness' sakes, I'm not ill, Billy. Just disgraced."

He stared at her with his mouth open.

"I'm joking."

"Oh." He let out a small, forced laugh and cleared his throat.

At the kitchen door, Dolores, whom she'd hired as a book-keeper, was beckoning to her. Mamie, the cook, was sweating in front of the stove and assembling the cooked-meat sandwiches. Bess saw a glimmer of suspicion in her eyes. So everyone has read the papers, she thought. And they've got to decide now whether I've tried to trick them or not. The truth was that she had a great deal to gain from a successful séance. Not only would it legitimize Harry's lifetime of work but the publicity would help ease her financial difficulties. It would mean the success of her tearoom, requests for interviews, value added to Harry's collectibles . . . It was no wonder people suspected her of fakery.

She ought to be out in the dining room, she knew, going from table to table as she usually did. The functioning of the place depended on her; without her presence, it lost its charm. But today seemed a day to remain behind the scenes.

In the corner, she found Dolores standing over a cardboard box with her hands on her face. "Mrs. Houdini," she said. "These are ruined. We can't serve them."

Bess looked in the box at over a hundred tomatoes, half of them crushed.

"They were delivered to the back. There's half a dozen other boxes out there, too."

"You mean the deliveryman just *left* them there? Without getting a signature?" She was fuming. "I won't pay for these!"

"You shouldn't, ma'am," Mamie cut in. "They're tryin' to put one over on you. They probably thought you wouldn't come in today. Or wouldn't notice if you did."

Bess sat down and tried to think. It was unacceptable. She'd have to find another vendor. But the other vendors charged more. Either way, she'd be losing money.

She could hear the clatter of teacups, in the dining room, and the delighted claps from the customers as Billy went table to table doing his card tricks. He was one of the best in the world at cards, she told everyone. She had discovered him when he was a boy and convinced Harry to mentor him. She hated wasting too much time in the back. She had built this business as a way to get herself out of the house, a way to get back into society after a period of reclusion, and she liked being actively involved in its running. "I wouldn't recommend it as a rest cure," she had once joked to a reporter during an interview. "But it does keep a woman busy."

"What do you say," the man had asked her, "to the claim that you're a regular Rosalind? A symbol of the age?"

Bess was charmed. "I would say," she had replied, "that I wish I were as young as Rosalind."

From the dining room, she heard a rush of commotion. "Oh, Jesus, are those reporters? They can't come in here! Would you call the police, Dolores, please?"

Dolores stuck her head out the door, then closed it quickly. "It's not reporters, Mrs. Houdini. It's Lou Gehrig! He's in the dining room!"

Bess jumped to her feet. "Lou's here?"

"He had a helluva night last night," she said. "He hit three consecutive home runs against the Tigers. The Yankees won eleven to nine. Everyone's talking about it."

Bess hurried into the dining room to find the baseball star dressed inconspicuously in summer-white slacks, signing autographs in the foyer. "Lou!" she called from the back of the crowd. She reached for his arm and led him away from the chaos, toward a corner table. "Is it just you today?"

He nodded. "I'm hungry for a cold sandwich. I was hoping not to attract any attention." He held up a copy of *Dodsworth*. "Just planning to read."

Bess laughed. "I heard you're the talk of the town today. It's going to be hard to read."

"I heard we're *both* the talk of the town." He smiled grimly. "Don't let those saps get you down, Bess."

"I'll try not to."

"You haven't been to any games lately. You know I've got a seat for you whenever you want it."

"Thank you. You know . . . it's not that I don't want to come." Bess lowered her eyes. He was such a good kid. She and Harry had first met Lou when he was just a nineteen-year-old college student with a strong arm, who loved magic. She'd known him for years, but she'd seen him only a handful of times, about town or in the tearoom, since Harry's funeral. The truth was, after Harry died, she couldn't bear going to games alone, and Lou's new fame had put demands on him, a burden she understood too well.

"You and Harry were always kind to me," Lou said, taking a sip of water. "There were times I thought, Well, this man's advice is just as swell as my father's. He always knew what to say about handling the press, good or bad. And I think he would tell you to ignore what's going on now."

Bess nodded. "I know you want some quiet. But it was good of you to come," she said. "Really. I'll send Billy over with a menu." She caught sight of the young magician hovering eagerly in the kitchen doorway. She leaned toward him. "He idolizes you."

Standing, Bess picked up an empty tray from the sideboard. She wrapped her hands around the cool metal and breathed a private sigh of relief. Word of Lou's appearance today would certainly get around town; it would drum up some more business, for a time. She also hoped it would help keep the papers from condemning her.

She turned toward the kitchen to go back to the tomatoes, but not before she was blinded by a momentary flash of light. When the whiteness receded it seemed everything in front of her was magnified, the colors scattering like shards of glass. And behind her, a reflection glimmering in the silver of the serving tray, she could see Harry's ghostly face, as if it had been flung across the room. He appeared like a haunting, his face veiled in shadows, his features misshapen. But then his eyes came into view, and everything else followed, and it was unmistakably him.

She turned around, dropping the tray. The metal clattered as it hit the floor and the colors righted themselves and the light and shadows were gone.

Billy rushed to her side. "Mrs. Houdini?"

"It was Harry!" she cried, incredulous.

He squinted at her. "What was Harry?"

"His face—in the tray." She stopped. In the mirror across the room, she saw it again—the same face she had just seen in the tray. She spun around to see a photograph of Harry, gazing at her, on the wall. It was a photograph she had hung there herself, when the tearoom first opened. His appearance in the tray had been nothing but a reflection of a photograph—something Harry himself would have laughed at her for mistaking. Not a visitation at all.

She had to step outside. She was embarrassing herself. She told Billy that she was going over to Thirty-Fifth Street to sort out the vendor problems. "You look out for Lou and Gladys while I'm gone."

Apparently Billy had heard the commotion in the kitchen. "If you're gonna fire the produce people, you could just call 'em. It'd be easier."

"No, no. I like to do things in person. It's the honorable way." She turned toward the street, still shaken. She had never admitted to anyone her hope that Harry's return would be more than the code revealed, more even than a message that followed—that when he came to her, he would appear physically somehow. She would see him, perhaps be able to touch him. She knew she was expecting more than death allowed; even the idea that he could reach far enough across the divide to communicate the code to her was preposterous. But she hoped. Harry had always managed to achieve the impossible.

It was already after four when she arrived back at the tearoom. The walk had served her well. After Harry's death, she began to love the city. Its daily pandemonium was a relief from the chaos of her own mind. She loved the cathedral bells and the cramped alleys, the gold-tipped tops of the skyscrapers at dawn, the buildings lined up like army troops as far as she could see. And she loved the stone statues in the parks and the beaded dresses in the department store windows and the gnarled faces of the old men who sat on their stoops in the afternoons. She rarely went back to Brooklyn now, and only to visit Stella; she preferred Manhattan, its parade of colored taxicabs and wild energy.

The streets were crowded with gray-suited men and women walking briskly home from their offices. She could not imagine having lived a life that stuck her to a desk for eight or ten hours a day. Stella's husband, Fred, had worked at a bank for many years, and she knew he came home every night stooped by the tedium of the business. Really, it was the business side of running the tearoom that was the most taxing. Her argument with the produce vendors had lasted half an hour. It had ended badly; they claimed the tomatoes had been perfect when they were delivered, and Bess had had no choice but to end their contract.

In the dining room, the remaining staff was clearing the tables and turning out the lamps. Gladys was sitting patiently by the window, her cane propped against the wall. Bess pressed her hand to her sister-in-law's shoulder and sat down across from her, out of breath. "It's me. I'm so sorry I'm late."

Gladys shrugged. "It's very peaceful here when it empties out." She looked, as usual, calm and well; she had worn only black since her mother's death seventeen years prior, but she cut a trim, stylish figure, and black seemed more fashionable than miserable on her. At forty-four, she looked ten years younger, and had a childlike innocence about her. But she carried herself with a Victorian composure that defied the flapper irreverence of the era. She wound her dark hair into a tight bun at the nape of her neck and sat straight, always, two inches from the back of the chair, her ears studded with tiny pearls and her vacant blue eyes staring.

Bess stretched her legs in front of her and reached for Gladys's drink. "Is this gin?" She took a sip. It was water; Gladys, like Harry, almost always drank water.

"It was a terrible thing that they put in the papers this morning."

Bess pressed her hand into Gladys's. "But you know I didn't engineer that séance."

Gladys nodded reasonably. "Of course, you were tricked."

Bess felt her face flush. She didn't want to be the object of anyone else's pity, especially not Gladys's. They had always enjoyed a cool, levelheaded friendship. And for all her life's difficulties, Gladys had never felt sorry for herself, and Bess would be damned if she would let some gossip get to her.

Gladys was the one person, besides Harry's mother, who could do no wrong in his eyes. She had been almost completely blinded as a child in a gas lamp explosion, and when he died Harry had left her with a sum of money large enough for her to purchase her own small apartment and hire a sight companion, full-time. Bess had offered her a room in the town house, but Gladys had wanted to live on her own. The two women weren't close during Harry's lifetime, but in the years following his death their friendship had blossomed. Now they met every afternoon for cake and walked back to Gladys's apartment together after four o'clock closing. It was the twilight hour—the tinkling spoons quieting as the room emptied out, the light settling into evening, the spring air cooling.

As Gladys and Harry's mother had gotten older, Gladys and Mrs. Weiss had cared for each other; they had a symbiotic relationship that worked well, each doing the things the other could not—Mrs. Weiss still had her vision but was lacking strength, and Gladys had plenty of strength but no vision. But when Mrs. Weiss died it was like a light went off in Gladys. Only with their own growing friendship had Bess seen a change in her.

"I had a little shock this afternoon. You'll think I'm mad, but I thought I saw Harry—here in the dining room." She saw Gladys's frown and added quickly, "Of course, it wasn't him. It was a trick of the mind." She looked over at the photograph she had seen reflected in the tray. It was one of her favorites; Harry was facing the camera with his tight, pursed smile. He looked very mysterious, which made it perfect for the tearoom, and she felt silly recalling her earlier panic. "But never mind that. What did you do this morning?"

But something was off, she realized. There was something wrong with the photograph.

"I did manage to get some dictation done earlier," Gladys said—she wrote advertising copy, from home, for women's products.

Bess tried to listen, but she was agitated. She couldn't put her finger on why. "Let me get you another glass of water," she said, standing up. She wanted to examine the photograph more closely. "Keep talking, I can hear you. I'll just run into the kitchen."

"I had a magazine page to do today—about soap. You can't imagine how horribly boring it is to find something to say about *soap*." Gladys had worked for the agency for so long that her blindness was hardly a disability any longer; her longtime employer, a gentleman in his early seventies, had given her the position at first as a favor to Harry. But she had shown such a knack for a quick turn of phrase that he kept her on.

Bess stared at the photograph. Had something *changed*? It didn't appear so. It was still the same Harry, in the same necktie, with the same alluring expression. But something felt different.

It suddenly came to her. It wasn't that the *photograph* had changed; it was the reflection. In the image she had seen in the tray earlier, Harry had been serious; in the photograph, he was smiling. She felt her whole body begin to tingle. It was a sensation she had experienced only a handful of times in her life, the same electricity she had felt when she'd had the vision of John Murphy so many years ago.

In the kitchen she found the serving tray she had been using earlier. Mamie had left everything in its proper place, washed and dried, and the silver was sparkling. Taking it back into the dining room, Bess couldn't keep herself from trembling. She was glad Gladys couldn't see her.

"Bess?" Gladys called. "Are you all right?"

"I'm . . . I was just looking at this photograph." Bess tried to remember where she had been standing when she'd seen the reflection. She had just turned away from Table 8, where Lou had been sitting. She hadn't taken more than a step toward the kitchen when she'd seen the image in the silver. Standing in front of Table 8 again now, exactly as she had been, with her back to Harry's photograph, she held up the tray with shaking hands.

In the silver, she could see only the empty papered wall.

She turned around. Harry's photograph was on the left. It hadn't moved; but from where she'd been standing when she first saw his face, she saw now that it couldn't have been a reflection from the photograph. The picture was simply hung too far over to catch the mirrored surface of the tray.

So what had she seen, exactly?

"Which photograph?"

Gladys's question startled her back to clarity. But Bess could barely find the words to answer her. What could she say that wouldn't sound cracked? "The portrait of Harry—I thought . . . I thought his expression was serious, but I'm looking at it now and he's smiling."

Gladys paused. "If there's one thing I learned from Harry," she said from across the room, "it's that images aren't always what they first appear to be. Neither was he, after all. As we both know."

Chapter 3

THE BEER HALL

June 1894

The night they were married, he came to the window with her as the moon rose, flaming like a phoenix, over the steaming white heat of the afternoon. A few blocks away, they could see a crowd of Italians swarming a carriage that was making its way slowly down the street. Inside was a woman Bess's age, in a white veil, next to a man in a black suit, and he was kissing her passionately. The members of the crowd were throwing flowers into the carriage, and the summer blazed.

"Do you wish that was you?" Harry frowned. "That you had a proper wedding?"

"I don't need all that," she reassured him, although there was a part of her that wondered whether she would ever be as happy as that bride, who had probably known her groom since grade school; that was the way the Italians did it. It was the same with the Germans, and if she had stayed at home she would doubtless have married one of the boys she had played with in the street as a child. But she had entered into a different life now, and she would never relinquish it for afternoons stitching clothes and cutting noodles, the tedium of the Brooklyn winters and the endless counting of rosary beads after dinner.

She turned to Harry, wondering how it was supposed to happen next, now that they were married. "I really don't know what to call you," she said. "And what will we call each other?"

Harry kissed her forehead. "We'll call each other Mr. and Mrs. Houdini."

"But those are just stage names. It seems odd to address you as Harry Houdini."

"When I was twelve," Harry said, "after my brother Herman died, and my father's school failed and he moved us to Milwaukee, I made him a promise that I would take care of my mother, if anything should happen to him. But I couldn't do that there. I ran away from home, to Missouri, and I began studying magic, and I gave up on Ehrich Weiss." A dark cloud passed over his face. "Ehrich Weiss has nothing to offer me anymore."

Bess felt her cheeks flush. She had never known a person to just decide he was going to be someone new, and commit to it so wholeheartedly. She felt she had entered into a world where anything could happen, where magic folded itself around them like a live thing. This was the kind of woman she wanted to be—not a timid, unripe girl, afraid of the dark, but the kind who left home and fell in love and married the man instead of waffling over him in confession for months on end. She wanted to live with Harry's unapologetic certitude.

Harry bent down to retrieve something from the cabinet behind him. When he turned around, he was holding a glistening bottle of champagne. Bess clapped her hands. "Where did you get that?" They'd barely had enough money to buy the rings.

"Don't worry about that," he said, and then, shrugging, "a gift from Dash." He stuck a pocketknife into the cork, and the top popped off and shot across the room.

Bess shrieked. "Is it supposed to do that?" Harry filled a pewter cup with the shimmering liquid and handed it to her. "Aren't you going to have any?" she asked him.

He shook his head. "I never drink alcohol. It slows my reflexes."

Bess considered her own glass. She had never had champagne before, and she'd been drunk only once in her life. "Well, fine," she said and poured the contents down her throat in one gulp.

Harry blinked at her, then burst out laughing. "You'll feel that," he said.

Her throat was already burning. She stepped toward him and, almost imperceptibly, brushed her hand against his. "But that's what I want," she said. "I want to feel everything."

Harry stepped back and looked at her, then reached out a hand and placed it on her back, where the laces of her dress were tied. Even in the dark she could sense his uncertainty, the utter seriousness of the moment. She turned so he could untie her. He fumbled with the knots, but after some effort they came free, and the dress slid to her ankles. She stepped out of it and stood before him, shivering even in the heat. He took her hand. Her corset and drawers had yet to be removed, but she could feel the rise and fall of her chest, the white flesh visible. She lifted his hand to her and stepped against him so she could feel his breath, like a sacred thing.

"We're married now," she said quietly. "You can do what you like."

His hand shook as he held it to her breast. "No one—no one's ever said that to me before."

"You've never been married before."

"Will you sing something?" he asked her. "I like your voice."

She looked at him. Was it possible that he was nervous? The same Harry Houdini who had held her gaze so intensely on the beach, who was so sure she would marry him? The lyrics of an

Irish love song she learned as a girl in school came rushing back to her. She hadn't heard it in a long time, but the words had etched themselves on her and she pulled them out like tiny, glimmering threads. "I'll take you home again, Kathleen," she began, her voice quiet, "across the ocean wild and wide, to where your heart has ever been, since first you were my bonnie bride."

"Keep going," he begged. There was a flicker of recognition in his eyes, perhaps a longing for the old world his parents had told him about when he was a child, before the cold Milwaukee winters and the tragedy of poverty had hardened him.

Bess's voice shook. "To that dear home beyond the sea, my Kathleen shall again return, and when thy old friends welcome thee, thy loving heart will cease to yearn."

Harry closed his eyes, and when he opened them again he said, "It's sad."

"Yes," she said. "It is sad."

He took her to the bed and undressed her completely, then himself, so that they were lying against each other. The humidity pressed down on them, heavy as stone, and Bess pushed the blanket to the side of the bed. "I don't know what I'm doing, Harry," she said softly. She had never seen a man's naked body before, except her stepfather's flaccid form when he was drunk and had fallen asleep, naked, on the kitchen floor. But there had been something pitiful and contemptible about him that was not present here, in Harry. She could see the dim form of every muscle on his chest, spangled with sweat, and he was beautiful, and she could feel him trembling, too. His breath was hot against her face.

"It will hurt," he said.

"I know." But she was brave. What powers she possessed beneath those clothes, she had never imagined. Her mother had never broached the subject with her, but her sister Stella, who was already married, had alluded to it. Tomorrow she would have to bring Harry home and tell them both, she realized, and she would not be a little girl in that house anymore.

"Do you think I look like a child?" she asked him. "Men have said I look like a child."

Harry's eyes widened. "A child? Far from that." He laughed, holding her against him. Her concern seemed to ease his nerves somewhat. She waited for what came next, for the agony of the wait to be over, and the rush of pain, but also the way she knew it would change them both, how they would emerge, not unscathed but happier.

"You are my own," he said.

As a performer, Harry had determined that true power belonged to those who knew how to create not merely illusions but transformations. It was a fact of human nature, he said, that people wished to become something else. They wanted to travel to that mysterious in-between place that lives only in magic, which ordinary men and women cannot reach. Characters in fairy tales were awakened from death as if they had only been asleep—they hovered, suspended, between two worlds—and Harry knew that people wanted this experience for themselves. If they could go to that place, and come back from it, they would somehow be different—they, too, would be anointed and saved.

This was the secret that drove the success of Harry's Metamorphosis trick—when one person was locked inside the trunk, and disappeared, and then reemerged free and unbound; it was as if he had been able to pass through walls, to fade into the ether in which the secret, dreamed-about places lay, and come back from it changed.

It was with great surprise that after their first night together, as the morning breathed itself through the open window of Harry's room, Bess learned that she was expected to take Dash's place in the trick. Dash wanted to strike out on his own, Harry said; he had never quite been comfortable with the uncertainty of the profession, and he wanted to return to the city and try his hand at other things.

"You and I will be the Houdinis now," he said, beaming. "Harry and Bess. We'll be on the billing together."

Bess was aghast. "You can't be serious. A few days isn't enough time for me to practice all those tricks."

"You'll be fine. You're much smaller than Dash—it will actually be better this way."

Of course, she knew that what he was doing was merely deception, and if one knew the secret one could easily step into another's part. Surely, as a Floral Sister she had been playing a part. Still, knowing how tricks were done and doing them were two different things altogether.

"What should I wear? I don't imagine I could wear one of my singing costumes, with all those feathers."

Harry went over to his dresser and pulled out a pair of thin black tights. "You can wear these."

Bess took one look at the tights, hanging limply from his hand like a wrinkled snakeskin, and burst out laughing.

"I couldn't possibly! You'll—you'll have me look like a prostitute, in front of all those people?"

"Oh, don't be embarrassed, Bess. I've been to plenty of shows—circuses, things like that. This is what the women wear. You'll have some kind of a dress on, too. Just—not so much as you're used to."

"I don't think I can step onto a stage in that." Out of costume, her usual nonstage underclothes alone consisted of drawers and an undershirt, a drawstring corset, a petticoat, a long-sleeved chemise, silk stockings and garters. "I've never shown so much of myself."

Harry laughed. "Yes, you have."

"My singing costume wasn't that—"

"With me. Last night."

Bess glared at him. "You're a lousy brute!"

Harry shrugged. He was much more cavalier when he was talking about his act—a different person altogether, not the tender, nervous boy of the night before. Still, his stage arrogance— the confidence, the clear-eyed determination—was alluring.

"Besides, I'll bet you know how to do half of my magic already. I'll test you. The ropes—"

She shook her head. "Now you are trying to fool me. That's the one thing that's not a trick. I'll bet you really do know how to break out of those ropes and all kinds of fasteners. It's your talent."

He laughed. "You're a smart one."

She hesitated. "There's one more thing, and it's something I can't control. Whenever I'm nervous, my hands shake. I've tried, but I can't stop it. What if they shake onstage?"

Harry smoothed her head. "You won't have to do any of the difficult restraints. Just leave those to me."

"Fine. But you have to do something for me first." She hesitated. Voicing her request made her anxious. She wasn't even sure it was what she wanted. "We're married now. I want to introduce you to my mother."

"She's not going to like me, you said so yourself," Harry said, frowning.

Bess thought about it. He was probably right. "We'll see."

"I'm ashamed that I'm poor, but I'm not going to be ashamed that I'm Jewish."

"No one's asking you to be."

He folded the tights and put them back into the drawer among his other costumes, which had been carelessly stuffed inside. "Why does it matter to you that I meet her? You said you had moved in with your sister."

"Because," Bess said, "if you want me to meet your mother—and you said you did—it's only fair that you meet mine. We're not going to start this marriage off unfairly. You said it yourself—you want me on your billing, by your side. Not in the wings."

Harry sighed. "All right. Let's go today then, and we'll meet each other's mothers. And anyway, we're leaving next week for the circus, and we'll have to tell them."

Bess glanced around his room, seeing it clearly now, for the first time in daylight. It was disastrous. His clothes lay in piles in the corners, covered in dust and dirt, and the place smelled strongly of sweat. Empty lemonade bottles were stacked on the bureau. Harry came up behind her and wrapped his arms around her waist. "It's only temporary," he said, as if reading her mind.

Bess grimaced. "That's good."

"There's a Yiddish word my mother used to use: *balaboosta*. It means homemaker. That's what she was. Always very organized. As you can see, I don't have those same skills. Now you'll be my balaboosta." He grinned.

"Oh, I will?" Bess wasn't sure she wanted to be anyone's balaboosta. She had grown up in a house full of children and had never envied her mother the enormous tasks of housekeeping she faced every day.

Harry pulled her down onto the bed and flipped her over so he was lying on top of her. For a moment she wasn't sure whether he was going to smack her or kiss her. Then he ran his fingers under her dress and began to tickle her mercilessly. Bess shrieked.

"Say you will!" He laughed. "Say you'll do it!"

"Okay, okay!" Bess cried, squirming under his grip. "I'll be your balaboosta!"

Harry sat up and smiled at her. "Good. I knew you'd come to your senses."

She tried to push him over, but he was too strong. "You are so infuriating!"

Harry took her chin in his hand and kissed her. "But I'll do my part," he said. "I'm going to take care of you. I promise. You'll have everything you want."

Looking around the room, she wasn't so sure this would be true. But despite his flaws, she already loved this stranger beside her. She had loved his swagger onstage and his dark, impenetrable eyes, and now even his incompetence at housekeeping.

She lay back on the bed and closed her eyes. "Have you ever been inside the Brighton Beach Hotel?"

"Not yet."

"Neither have I. But I've memorized their menu. Littleneck clams, baked bluefish, meringue for dessert."

"One day," Harry said, "we can go there. We'll come with our servants and stay the whole summer. We'll watch the races along Ocean Parkway on Sundays. And we'll have one dinner in the hotel and after the fireworks we'll go over to Tappan's for a second dinner."

Bess laughed. "Yes. Instead of Paddy Shea's. Anna thinks that's the height of elegance. But then again, she also dreams of staying in the Elephant Hotel on her honeymoon." Compared to the Brighton Beach Hotel, with its white curtains and silver chargers in the dining room, the Elephant Hotel was garish; it was built in the shape of an elephant, with rooms that were cramped and dark.

"With the cigar shop in front? You're kidding."

Bess shook her head. "What did you do before you were Harry Houdini?" she asked. "Do you have any skills beside magic?"

"Do you mean how will I support you if I fail at magic? Well, I won't fail," he said. "But, to humor you, I can tell you I was very efficient as an assistant necktie cutter for a little while. At H. Richter's Sons in New York."

Bess sat up. "H. Richter's? Next to Siegel-Cooper? I worked as a waitress in their café during high school! Do you think we've met before?"

Harry thought about it. "I quit five years ago. So you would have just started."

Bess tried to remember the faces of the patrons who used to frequent the restaurant, but they were only shadows. "I do think it's possible. The men from H. Richter's came in for coffee all the time."

"What were you doing working at fourteen anyway?"

The hair rose on Bess's arms. "My stepfather was—is still, I suppose—a terrible drunk. I don't think he'll be there when we go to Brooklyn, thank God. He's never there. But after my mother married him, he used to come into my room at night. At first it was nothing—just friendly kisses on the cheek, to say good night. Then one night, when I was sixteen, he tried to climb into bed with me. I kicked him so hard he was laid up for a week. After that, I moved into my sister's apartment with her and her new husband. So I got a job to help pay my part of the rent."

Harry stroked her head. "You poor thing." His expression was pensive. "I think a part of me remembers meeting you and a part of you remembers me. Even if the memories are not on the surface right now. Maybe that's why I was so drawn to you."

"I thought you didn't believe in things like fate?"

Harry shrugged. "Well, I believe in stories. Sometimes we can make them true even when they're not."

Mrs. Weiss lived in a walk-up tenement apartment on East Sixty-Ninth Street with Harry's younger sister, Gladys, and brother Leo. Leo worked on the docks and was rarely at home, but Gladys led them into the living area. She was a tiny girl, barely twelve years old, and very frail, her wrists thin as rope. Bess saw her standing in the doorway—she was clearly blind and stared right past them into the darkness of the hallway; the right side of her face was marred with faint scars. Harry hadn't told her anything about his siblings, never mind a blind sister who had certainly been the victim of some kind of accident—but it was clear the girl worshiped him. She grasped his arm as he led her toward the faded pink sofa where Mrs. Weiss was waiting in a black lace church dress, hands clasped in her lap, to receive them. Her gray hair was tied neatly behind her head in a low bun.

"Mein geliebter Sohn!" she cried, reaching up to embrace Harry, tears streaming down her face. She kissed both sides of his face three times. Harry had told Bess that Mrs. Weiss didn't know a word of English. German was the language of the household, and Bess had fortunately learned a conversational use of it in her own house, although her parents spoke mainly in English. She had not mentioned this to Harry; she was eager to hear how he would present her if he did not think she could understand him.

"Mother, dearest," Harry said, motioning to Bess, "this is my wife, Beatrice."

Mrs. Weiss looked at her sharply. "You love each other very much?" she asked Harry.

"Yes, we do."

Bess could see Mrs. Weiss's hesitation as she considered her response. Finally she smiled. "Then I have not lost a son," she said. "I have gained a daughter."

"It's a pleasure to meet you," Bess responded in German, dipping into a relieved curtsy. Harry turned to her in surprise, and Bess smiled. She had managed to trick the trickster himself.

She had the sense that Harry expected her to treat his mother as he did, as one would treat a queen. She was suddenly grateful that her new name was Houdini and she would never have to be the second Mrs. Weiss. It would be difficult, if not impossible, to be held in compare by Harry with this woman, with her high, chiseled cheekbones and perfectly rounded nails. She had done more in her lifetime than Bess could dream of doing—moved across the world, survived ferocious Wisconsin winters, been widowed, and dragged her family out of abject poverty. And yet she still carried herself with the kind of softness and grace one saw in the most polished society women. Bess was terrified that Mrs. Weiss would secretly despise her for marrying Harry, but this did not appear to be the case. Instead, she seemed eager to impress her. She took Bess by the hand and led her to a far wall, where a worn prayer rug had been given a place of prominence, hanging beside the family photographs.

"Kaiserin Josephine walked on this many times. It used to belong to an orphan asylum in Budapest. This is a family treasure." Her face lit up. "My husband was quite a well-known scholar in the old country. He was able to obtain artifacts like this. Ehrich is going to be equally famous here, in the new country."

"Yes, I know," Bess said, because she felt this was the proper response, although secretly she wondered what would come of his mother's dreams for him. Bess and Harry both had come from poor upbringings. The circus and vaudeville business was a tricky profession, and one did not easily find fame or fortune in it.

Mrs. Weiss leaned in so Harry could not hear her. "You know my son will be"—she began in English and then had difficulty finding the words, and finished in German—"always a boy at heart?"

Bess laughed, not sure how to respond.

"He has a soft heart but a fiery temper. You will have to learn to manage his moods."

Bess glanced at Harry, and he shrugged.

Mrs. Weiss had made strawberry pie, Harry's favorite, and

they stayed for lunch before leaving for the Rahners' residence in Brooklyn. Gladys chattered away about neighborhood gossip, and when the dishes were cleaned, Bess took Gladys's hand and squeezed it. "We will see you again soon," she said in English, and Gladys beamed.

Before they left Mrs. Weiss went into the bedroom and came out with a paper bag. "Don't be offended," she said, reaching in to pull out a woman's long skirt. "But you should not be traveling with Harry in those clothes. You look much too young. You will be turned away for lodging."

Bess bit her lip. "Thank you," she said, looking at Harry, whose face was frozen in horror. "That is very practical advice." She glanced down at her own skirt, her face hot with humiliation, but knew there was some truth to it. Her small size, small breasts, and curly hair gave the wrong impression of her age. She did not want to have to pretend to be Harry's sister when she had only just become his wife.

When they left, after a long series of kisses and good-byes, Bess turned to Harry. "How did I do? Was I all right?"

"Wonderful," he said. "But you didn't tell me you could speak German."

She smiled. "Are you still glad you married me?"

He laughed and pulled her into an alcove at the end of the hallway. "My dear girl," he said, wrapping his hands around her waist, "my mother might claim me as her son, but you are my wife. The two loves do not conflict."

"But you love her so much."

"Of course. She's my mother, and I have to take care of her. I have to do what my father could not." He lifted the bottom of her skirt and ran his fingers over her knees. "I only have three devotions—you, my mother, and my magic act. I promise you I will be faithful to those my entire life."

Bess pulled down her skirt. "Harry! Someone could come up the stairs."

He grew serious. "What you told me about your stepfather— you should know, no one will ever hurt you again. Not while I'm here."

Bess wrapped her arms around his neck. "What about you? Your mother warned me that you have a temper."

Harry was horrified. "I would never lay a finger on you."

"You can lay a finger on me," she said playfully. "It's all right."

He blinked at her. "But you just said—?"

"Don't you want to?"

"Of course," he stuttered.

"You don't have to be gentle with me, you know. I'm not fragile." She untucked his shirt. There was something exhilarating about hiding in the hallway of his family's building. She had never done anything so daring. "I'm your wife, Harry."

Harry brought her leg up around him. He clasped his hand over her mouth and held on to her thigh so tightly that she could feel the flesh bruising. No one had ever loved her this much. She felt she had lived most of her years numb, and had come out of a white snow burning with life. She wanted to feel every part of her life now; she wanted to feel all the facets of love, all its joys and agonies.

Certainly, she was breathing, but she could hear nothing. Around them, there was only quiet, that beautiful, abundant quiet.

＊

Mrs. Rahner's apartment was halfway down Driggs Avenue, in a decrepit building split into eight units. It was larger than the Weisses', but there had been twelve of them living in it at one point. It was not, however, nearly as clean, and as they climbed to the third floor Bess noticed the rows of dead plants, the carcasses of gifts her stepfather had brought home after his many binges, bought with money they could not afford to spend. Harry would not hold her hand, and she realized when she took it anyway that it was because his palms were wet with sweat. It dawned on her that Harry Houdini—who pretended to be afraid of nothing— was terrified of this meeting. It was a revelation that made him seem suddenly more human.

"We'll only stay an hour," she whispered as they waited for someone to come to the door. "Don't worry." Despite everything that had happened with her stepfather, she still felt an allegiance to her mother. Mrs. Rahner had displayed little affection as Bess was growing up, but there had always been love there.

Inside, they could hear the cries of Bess's younger siblings, and feet running across the wooden floors. Finally, the door opened, and Bess's sister Stella, a full-figured blonde four years older than Bess, stood in the foyer.

"What are you doing here?" Bess threw herself into Stella's arms.

"Mother's got a terrible cold," Stella said. "She's run ragged. I came over to help."

"Well, she's not going to like what I have to say, then."

Stella glanced at Harry, who was frozen in the hallway, his hands pressed against his sides. "You're not . . . planning to move back in with Mother, are you?"

"No, it's the opposite. I'm married. I'm not coming home again."

Stella laughed.

"I am, really. This is Harry, and he and I are married."

Stella gaped at her. "That's ridiculous. How could you be married? You only just left for Coney Island a month ago."

Bess thought back to Harry's own tactics with his family. "I know. But we love each other."

Stella stared at them for a moment longer, and her face softened. "Well, congratulations then. I'm happy for you."

Bess looked past her into the apartment, but she didn't see her mother. She had been inside the rooms only on Sundays since she had moved in with Stella two years earlier. "Darling, you have to tell her for me. I can't bear to do it. You know how she is. Go in and ask her if she'll see us."

Stella wiped her hands on the dish towel she was holding. "Why are you so nervous about it? She wasn't upset when I got married at eighteen. If you've had a proper Catholic wedding, you know she'll be happy."

Bess bit her lip. "Well, I didn't have one, you see." She hesitated. "Harry's Jewish, for one, and—the other thing is, you see, he's a magician, and we're leaving next week for the show circuit in the South."

"Oh, Lord Almighty," Stella said.

"Please," Bess begged. "Tell her for me and see if she'll see us?"

"Wait here a minute." Stella shook her head. "I don't know what she'll say."

Stella retreated to the back bedroom to find Mrs. Rahner. The smaller children, hearing voices, came running to the door, and squealed when they saw Bess. They clung to her arms and legs.

"Why won't you go inside?" Harry asked.

"I've got a frightful headache," Bess said. "And I don't want to get into an argument. I'd rather go back to Coney Island if there's just going to be a row." She paused, recalling Mrs. Weiss's gentleness. "Your mother was so kind to me. You won't understand mine. She won't be as kind to you."

Harry seemed relieved to hear they might be leaving. He hung back awkwardly as Bess greeted the children.

"Do some magic for them," she whispered. "Don't just stand there."

Harry seemed to relax at the suggestion. "Hey, look at this!" He reached behind one of the girl's ears and brought a tiny paper flower into view. "Presto," he said, waving the flower with a flourish. The children released Bess immediately and crowded around him instead.

From the back of the apartment, they heard a loud wail. Mrs. Rahner came out of the bedroom in her nightgown, brandishing a chain of rosary beads, Stella trailing after her. "You get out of my house!" she cried, in her heavy German accent, rushing toward the door. "Beatrice, you have condemned yourself! How could you? You've gotten yourself in league with the devil!"

The children scampered into the kitchen, laughing, but Harry stepped backward into the hallway, clearly startled. Bess just stared. Her mother's green eyes were full of fear and rage, the skin beneath them paper-thin. Her face and body were thin, too, so that even in her assault she seemed frail as a bird.

Stella stepped in front of her mother and tried to calm her. But Mrs. Rahner grabbed a vial of holy water and began splashing it all over the foyer and in the doorway where Bess and Harry stood.

"What in the world is going on?" Harry said, as the water splashed over his feet. She could see his cheeks reddening angrily.

Bess grabbed his arm. "Oh, be rational, Mama. He's not the devil. We just came to say good-bye before we leave."

"If you've married this man, I don't want to see you again. Do you hear me? You've gotten yourself into an unholy marriage, and you've put a curse upon yourself. Your father would be ashamed of you." She broke into a series of vehement Hail Marys and Our Fathers.

"I don't care!" Bess cried, losing her composure. "I love him!" Her heart was breaking. She had spent years both hating her mother for remarrying and vying for her love. After her father died, Bess had done everything she could to make her mother happy again, but nothing ever seemed enough. Now, she was being pushed out of the apartment for a second time. "Please, won't you try to understand?"

"You'd better go." Stella attempted to wrestle the water from her mother's grasp. "Leave me your address and I'll write you. Just give it time."

Bess turned and ran down the stairs and into the white city sunlight, her chest heaving. Harry followed her and pulled her back before she could run into the road.

Bess was shaking. "She's—a nasty woman," she said between choked breaths. She vowed she would not give her mother the satisfaction of making her cry. "She treated you—so rudely."

A shadow crossed over Harry's face. "Don't leave me because of this," he begged, grasping her hand. "Come home with me. None of this will matter tomorrow."

Bess was so surprised to see him overcome with worry that she regained her calm. "That's ridiculous. We've only just gotten married. How could I leave?" The idea hadn't occurred to her, but now she saw that, if she wanted, she could still be free of him; after all, they had not had a proper wedding. She could still return home, to Stella's house and her mother's cooking on Sundays and the rooms smelling of salt and perfume and the red-brick views outside her old bedroom window.

Harry took her by the elbow. Above them, the city sky was colorless, bisected by buildings whose shadows did nothing to cool the sidewalks. "It's too hot out. Let's have some dinner and go meet the train."

Bess shook her head and pulled her arm away. "I'm serious, Harry. I won't ever speak to her again. Your mother can be mother enough for the two of us. She was very kind to me, and she didn't have to be. For all she knew I was nothing but a little hussy."

Harry smiled. "Nonsense. You look far too young to be a hussy."

He took her hand and walked her down Fulton Street, stopping at the shop windows and making promises of what he would buy her one day. Bess kissed him in front of a diamond cross but could not help hearing the voice of her soft-spoken Brooklyn priest, warning that a rich man can never be admitted into heaven. Harry's fixation on money worried her. She wondered if there was some truth to her mother's fears, and whether there were some of his tricks that were in fact not tricks after all.

❄

"The brothers Houdini, who for years have mystified the world with their mysterious box mystery, known as 'Metamorphosis,' are no more, and the team will hereafter be known as the Houdinis. The new partner is Miss Bessie Raymond, the petite soubrette, who was married to Mr. Harry Houdini this month. First and final show in Coney Island tomorrow evening."

Bess held up the page she had torn from *The New York Clipper* and frowned. "They got my name wrong."

Harry took it from her and read it again. "That's all right," he said. "It's a splendid article. Raymond, Rahner, it doesn't matter what you were before. You're a Houdini now. This should draw us a big crowd. It's not often people see a husband and wife performing together."

Bess lay back on the bed, fanning herself with the rest of the newspaper. "How do you think we're going to manage in the South? It's supposed to be sweltering."

"You'll like it," Harry said. "People are dignified there, I hear." He pulled his cardboard suitcase from under the bed and began sorting through the clothes he'd thrown around the room. "When I am rich," he said, "I'll take you anywhere you want to go. We can go to California if you'd like, and buy a swimming pool, and hire a servant who'll spray you with water all day, and you'll never be hot again."

Bess smiled. "Don't pack all your clothes yet," she cautioned him. "Save something nice for tonight." Doll and Dash and some of the other performers were giving a party for them. "And please don't wear something that's wrinkled."

Harry surveyed the room. "Everything I have is wrinkled."

Bess wet a cloth and leaned toward him, sticking the fabric inside his ear.

Harry jumped. "What on earth are you doing?"

"Your ears are filthy. Don't you ever clean them?"

Harry thought about this and then sat down on the bed. He winced as she finished the job. "You're not still upset about your mother, are you? She'll come around."

Bess shook her head. "She won't, but I'm not upset."

Downstairs, they heard the loud thumping of a bed against the wall. Another married couple had moved into the apartment directly below them, and it seemed as if they spent half their day in bed. Bess blushed.

Harry heard the thumping, too, and pulled her down with him onto the pillows. "Kiss me," he said.

She did. He was a confident kisser, and he had the most wonderful, strong hands. But he still seemed unsure of himself at times.

"I want to try something," he murmured, struggling out of his clothes. He pulled her hand down his stomach, between his legs. He gasped when she touched him, and she held him in her hand, her own body throbbing. "I want you to put your mouth . . . down here," he told her. "I want to see what it feels like."

Bess snatched her hand away and sat up. "I will not!" she said. "That's—that's a *whore's* behavior."

Harry sat up beside her, his voice livid. "And what do you think making love in the hallway of my mother's apartment building was? That certainly wasn't a *lady's* behavior."

Bess slapped him hard across the cheek. Harry sat back, startled.

For a moment, she was afraid he was going to hit her back. She threw her arms over her face. Harry yanked them away. "Who do you think I am?" he demanded. "Do you think I'm the kind of man who would strike his wife?"

"I'm not sure what kind of man you are," she said slowly, realizing it only as she sounded out the words. She had fallen in love with his love for her, with the certainty of his devotion. "I don't really know you."

Harry stood up in disgust and pulled on his clothes. "Get dressed," he ordered. "We're going to be late for our own party. I'll wait for you outside." He paused in the doorway. "Sometimes, you look at me like I'm not a good man," he said sadly. "And it's not fair."

They were met with cheers in the beer hall, where Doll and Dash waited to greet them with beer and flowers. The other performers, crowding the hall, raised their glasses, calling, "Hooray for the newlyweds!"

It appeared they had been waiting for some time, and almost everyone was already drunk. Bess looked around at the group of them, her friends—Billy the strongman, and Doll and Anna and the other musicians, and Tony the fire-breather, and the comedians. She had known them for only a month, but she would miss them if she and Harry made up and went south after all. Bess took a yellow flower to match her skirt and put it behind her ear. She was wearing one of the outfits Mrs. Weiss had given her, and she felt older and more like the kind of woman who could do such things, even if they were in a beer hall. It was all anyone could afford, but she hated the place—the waiters with their stained white aprons and the smell of stale tobacco and the constant influx of drunken sailors, who spat lewd, drunken comments at the women. She imagined the kinds of places she would frequent if she were wealthier—tearooms papered in pink and white, quiet except for low voices and the tinkle of porcelain cups. Working in the restaurant at Siegel-Cooper had spoiled her; she had seen how it was possible to live. She had carefully observed the dress and mannerisms of the women who came for lunch, admiring their flowered silk gowns and egret plume hats. Of course, she couldn't imitate their polished behaviors with her own friends—they would only laugh at her—but she filed the memories away for later use.

She and Harry parted almost immediately—he toward a group of men in the back and she toward the excited chatter of Doll and Anna. They had found a new performer for their group, who would be joining them the following week, and they had given up their short-lived grudge against Bess for abandoning them.

"What is it like to be married?" Doll asked. "Do you feel like a different person?"

Bess shook her head, tears pooling in her eyes. Doll grabbed her hand. "What's wrong? Did I say something?"

"We had an argument," Bess said. "Harry and me. Just before coming here."

Anna laughed. "Oh, is that all? Darling, married people argue all the time. It's nothing."

Bess covered her face with her handkerchief. "This was different." She wanted to tell them what Harry had asked her to do, but she was too embarrassed.

"That's what everyone says. I know my fair share of married women—I've got six married cousins, you know—and they all say that." She handed her a heavy glass of beer. "Drink this. It will make you feel better."

Bess took the glass and swallowed the contents in four gulps. It was thick and bitter, and she almost retched it back up. "This is the worst beer I've ever had," she said.

Anna shrugged. "Of course it is. We're in the Gut."

"Champagne tastes better." Her mother had forbidden alcohol in the apartment—an order her stepfather never tolerated—but she would not forget the champagne Harry had opened after their wedding, the sensation of the bubbles popping against her tongue.

"*Of course* champagne tastes better," Doll said. "What a silly thing to say."

Bess looked across the room at Harry, who was seated at a far table with his legs stretched out in front of him, laughing. Evatima Tardo, the snake charmer, was seated beside him, her hand on his thigh. She was a strange, black-haired Cuban beauty, who spoke English with a heavy, seductive accent and performed a miraculous act—she enticed rattlesnakes to bite her bare shoulder and was able to sing beautifully as dozens of pins were pushed into her face. She had a mysterious tolerance for pain and poison that Harry envied. She claimed she had been bitten by a poisonous fer-de-lance as a child, which had immunized her, but Harry was certain she was lying and was always trying to entice her to tell him her secret.

Now she was brazenly flirting with him, leaning into him and saying something that was making him laugh. She had the tiniest waist Bess had ever seen, and Bess watched as Harry reached out and placed his hand on her hip.

"Bess." Doll put her arm around Bess's shoulder. "Don't worry about them, love. He's just trying to make you jealous. He's *your* husband."

Behind them, Bess heard a cork popping, and she turned to see one of the sailors holding a bottle of champagne over his head, the white froth pouring down the sides and onto the table.

"Where did you get that?" Bess asked him.

He grinned at her. "Wouldn't you like to know?" When she shrugged he said, "We just got back from a haul, and I've got a stash of money. Want a glass?"

Bess nodded. "I would, please."

"You'll have to do a little something to get it."

Bess blushed. "I don't think so. I'm no chorus girl."

"Nothing as bad as *you're* thinking, you dirty girl," he said coyly, holding up an empty beer glass. "You see, I only have this one glass to drink out of. Just come sit on my lap for a few minutes, and we can share it."

Bess looked over at Harry again; his arm was still around Evatima's waist.

"All right," she said and moved cautiously to the sailor's table. He was actually quite handsome, and clean, too—unlike most of the men she encountered in the beer halls. He looked about Harry's age, and had similar dark features and a rounded chin.

"Are you Catholic?" she asked him as he handed her the glass.

He laughed. "I look it, don't I? *Sono italiano*."

"My mother would like you then." She took a large gulp of the liquid and wiped her mouth.

"Is she that easy to please?"

"That *hard* to please, you mean."

He put one arm around her stomach to keep her from falling off his knee. She could feel his hardness under her dress. "And what about you?" he asked. "Are you easy to please?"

Bess laughed. "Sometimes." The champagne was going to her head, and she felt light with alcohol and flattery. Too late, she wondered what kinds of men she would have been able to attract if she hadn't been so eager to marry Harry.

She leaned back against the sailor and lay her head on his shoulder. He bent over, pushing the hair out of her face, and kissed her hard on the mouth.

Out of the corner of her eye she caught a glimpse of Harry, still seated at his far table, staring at her. Evatima was gone, and he was wearing a look of such incredulous horror that she felt as if she had been struck in the gut.

He stood up, almost mechanically, and made his way to the door. She scrambled off the sailor's lap and followed him outside. She found him sitting on the sidewalk, his face in his hands, crying.

"Harry," she said. "It was nothing. It was a mistake."

"How could you?"

She put her hand on his shoulder. "Darling, please don't be mad. It was just a kiss."

"I need you to leave," he said, lifting his head.

Bess looked at him, startled. "Leave? What do you mean?"

"I want you to go to your sister's. I'll take you to the train station."

"That's ridiculous. *You* were flirting, too, to make *me* jealous. What about your promises?"

"You betrayed me, Bess. You swore you never would, and you did."

She felt as if she were on the edge of hysteria. "If I go to my sister's, will you come find me?"

Harry stood up. "Come on. Let's go."

"We can't leave—all those people inside are there for *us*." She watched him walk away, his gait stiff and unnatural. She was terrified, but also inflamed by the alcohol, and by the memory of his flirtations with Evatima. She ran after him. "Fine," she cried. "If this is what you want, I'll go! You'll regret it!"

They didn't speak on the walk. The last train to Grand Street left at ten. Harry bought her ticket and stood with her on the platform until the train pulled in. "Good-bye, Mr. Houdini," she said when the doors opened, trying to maintain her dignity.

Harry looked at her coldly. "Good-bye. I'll wire your sister to tell her you're coming."

Bess's knees trembled as she climbed the steps onto the train. She half expected Harry to come running after her, but when she looked out the window he was still standing there, his face unforgiving in the blue moonlight. She wondered what she would say to Stella, when just a week before she had so brazenly declared herself willing to give up everything for a man who was now abandoning her.

She sat shaken, as if in a dream, during the thirty-minute ride. How did one go about getting a divorce? she wondered. And how would she arrange one if Harry was leaving in two days for the circus? She felt herself choking back tears, imagining him doing the act without her. Just a short time ago he had proclaimed her extraordinary, and she had believed him. But then he had cast her off just as quickly, and she was a fool. By the time the train pulled into the station she was sobbing quietly, much to the horror of her seatmate, an elderly woman clasping a heavy brocade handbag.

Bess looked around for her own case and realized, alarmed, that she hadn't brought one—all she had was her little purse with powder and a few coins. When she saw her sister's tall figure standing on the platform, waiting for her, she knew it was true—Harry had wired her after all, and he wasn't coming back for her. She took the steps two at a time and threw herself into Stella's arms.

"I'm so sorry, I'm so sorry," she sobbed. "I was wrong about Harry."

Stella stroked her hair. "He's a brute. You've been badly abused, Bess."

"But I loved him—I love him."

"I know. But you can live with me now. And Fred will give him a good thrashing if he ever sees him again."

Stella took her home and made her drink a glass of whiskey. Then she put her to sleep in the big bedroom, with its crisp embroidered sheets, and she and Fred took the little bed. Fred was livid about Harry; Bess could hear him storming around the kitchen.

At two in the morning, she awoke to the sound of someone knocking loudly on the front door. She could hear Fred stumbling out of bed, and then she heard voices in the foyer, and Stella whispering, and she knew Harry had come back for her. Bess flew to the door in her sister's nightgown and threw her arms around his neck. Harry kissed the top of her head over and over.

"See, darling," he said. "I told you I would send you away, but I didn't say I wouldn't fly after you and bring you back."

Chapter 4

THE FRIDAY BOYS

May 1929

Bess stood in the hall outside Gladys's apartment, holding a blue beaded dress wrapped in paper. Gladys answered the door herself; her Irish girl, Colleen, had the night off.

She reached out to touch the fabric of the dress and then felt Bess's own apricot crepe dress. "I don't know about this. It seems very flimsy. Can you see through it?"

"There was always a bit of the harem in that covering up your arms and legs business, don't you think?"

Gladys was only one size larger than Bess, and the dress slipped on her easily, even though she still wore the thick ribbed corset of the old decade. Bess zipped the dress and then lifted her sister-in-law's hair and dropped it back onto her shoulders. "You should cut this, you know. No one wears their hair long anymore." She had bobbed her own hair years ago, bleaching it when it started to gray, to a hue so blond it appeared almost white. "I'm not saying Eton crop or anything dramatic like that. Just a little shorter."

Gladys shook her head. She was beautiful with her dark,

draping hair and soft eyes. "My mother always loved my hair long."

"Well, let's get creative then. We can pin it and make it look short." Bess gathered her sister-in-law's hair together. "You know what I was thinking on my way over here? Do you remember how they used to arrest women on Fifth Avenue for smoking?"

Gladys smiled. "That was years ago, wasn't it? I can't believe they used to do that. But it's not much different from Prohibition, I suppose. Trying to enforce morality."

"At least they arrest both men and women now," Bess said.

"Let's try not to get arrested tonight. At least promise me that."

An hour later they were made up with rouge and lipstick, stepping out of the taxicab onto Forty-Ninth Street. They entered a crowd of strangers who were weaving their way down the sidewalk.

Gladys hung on Bess's elbow. "I can't remember the last time I went to a party," she said. "It's exciting."

Bess pushed open the door to the tearoom. "They're much different now. Very slick. All kinds of debauchery."

There was an illicit sort of caution about public drunkenness. But there was a thrill, too, in going into the back room of a Long Acre pharmacy for "smoke"—water with fuel alcohol—and sneaking from one tawdry speakeasy to another, their walls papered with lithographs of nude women.

She led Gladys into the lounge, where someone was playing the piano raucously at the end of the room.

Gladys tightened her grip on Bess's arm. "Don't leave me."

It wasn't late—only nine o'clock—but it was a cool evening, and that always made people want to get out of their own apartments and go somewhere else. There were at least fifty people inside already—the whole place fit only about a hundred, and tightly. Someone had brought a roulette board, and a crowd was calling out bets.

On Fridays, when the lunches and sodas and teas had been cleared away and the liquor cabinet was unlocked, Bess let Oscar, the parrot, out of his cage to play, which signaled the start of the night. She had acquired him from an exotic birds dealer in Harlem, and he was the star of the place, really. He walked with such muscular control that he was sometimes mistaken for a sophisticated automaton. Now, Oscar was strutting through the middle of the room with enviable precision, showing off his party-red feathers.

"Good day, good day, good day," he called in his shrill voice, craning his neck to see the figures looming over him.

Stella came in, short of breath, sporting a new straight-silhouetted dress of copper crepe de chine. Fred had recently come into money after a favorable oil investment, and she had embraced her newfound wealth and status as eagerly as she had once embraced motherhood. She started when she saw Oscar gazing at her in the entryway, then laughed, dropping her purse on a table. "Do you have any booze? I've just come from dinner with Fred's friends and I'm bored out of my mind." She threw herself onto the sofa in the lounge and began flipping through the thick, glossy pages of a recent edition of *McClure's* that was lying on the console table.

Bess loved Stella's briskness, and she embraced the chaos her sister brought. They were their best selves at parties. She thought about all the lonely Sunday hours she had spent meditating on Harry's photograph, wishing he would appear. Sometimes she thought she heard voices, but they turned out to be only men shouting on the street below. Once, when she was especially exhausted, she thought she had seen her name written in steam on the bathroom mirror. But when she woke up it was no longer there, and she couldn't remember if she had dreamed it or imagined it, and it never appeared again. Something similar had happened to her years before, when she and Harry had been trying to contact Mrs. Weiss's spirit. She had stumbled, blurry-eyed, into the bathroom in the middle of the night to find a bloom of thin white lines feathered across the mirror. She wasn't sure what it meant, and when she'd turned on the light they had gone.

"I have something to confess to you," Stella said, pulling Bess away from Gladys and onto the couch with her. "But you can't be cross with me. Do you promise?"

"What is it?"

Stella hesitated. "Please don't be upset."

"For God's sake, I won't—now tell me!"

She took a breath. "Fred and I—we're having another baby."

Bess looked at her, confused; Stella was four years older than she was. She had three children, already grown. "But—that's impossible."

Stella pressed her hands together in her lap. "Of course *I'm* not pregnant. But Abby—she's gotten herself into a situation, you see. And she was supposed to go off to Europe in the fall. She doesn't want the baby."

Abby was Stella's youngest daughter; she was seventeen, and unmarried. She'd thrown herself into the Broadway scene, recklessly, and gotten lost in the lights.

"Well that's— I'm not sure what to say. It's wonderful, in a way. Isn't it?"

"Is it? I'm rather concerned I'm too old to be raising a baby."

"Nonsense."

"I didn't want to tell you. I was worried it might upset you."

Bess shook her head, reaching to adjust the garnet-studded brooch she had pinned into her hair. She was aware that Stella had always spoken of children cautiously around her. "I'm happy for you. Really. You'll enjoy it."

Stella smiled, relieved.

"How is Fred reacting?"

"He's furious of course; you know Fred. He's been storming all over the house day and night since Abby saw the doctor. But I think he's excited about it, too. He always did love babies. But it's still early yet, of course. And Abby might change her mind and decide she wants it after all. That does tend to happen." Her eye caught one of the other magazines on the table. "Is this *The Delineator*? I haven't read this in years; I thought it'd gone out of print." She picked it up. "Where did you find this?"

Bess shrugged. "Gladys brought it over the other day. She said that girl who helps her—you know, Colleen—bought it uptown. There's apparently an article in there about Harry."

She turned to see a group of loud, smooth-faced men crowding the doorway. The "boys," as she called them—the young, rowdy magician set—had arrived. They always came in for drinks after their Friday shows. At first she'd kept the place open mainly for them, but then word got around and soon there were just as many women, too, each hoping to end the night pie-eyed with a man on her arm. They came in their best rayon dresses, trimmed with velvet, their tiny beaded chain-strapped purses hanging from their elbows. Bess watched them with a kind of removed clarity, their bodies lit by the old familiar glamour of the city—all the beautiful, ordinary people milling about, bearing the heightened sense that they *mattered*, that they were living in an age that mattered.

Niall Robbins was her favorite of the boys. He was a strange character; three years earlier, he'd been a reckless, handsome playboy, the son of a wealthy stockbroker. Then, for a year or so, he'd become pious and, just as suddenly, went back to the parties and declared his ambition to become a magician. He could drink with the best of them, and he got crazy doing it—they'd once spent a half hour going round and round in the Commodore Hotel's revolving door.

Bess greeted Niall in the lounge. "Darling, how are you? I was hoping I'd see you." She stepped back. "This is Harry's sister Gladys."

"You don't say. It's a real pleasure." Niall pumped Gladys's hand. "But I should be asking how *you* are," he called to Bess over the noise. He beckoned a server with a tray of cocktails. There were more than two dozen people crammed into the lobby alone now, and more pouring through the door. Zingoni, one of New York's most popular magicians, had just come from a performance, and his crew was raucous. One of them was pounding out "Bambalina" on the piano.

Bess shrugged. "It'll be out of the news tomorrow."

"Listen," Niall said, "I've told you, it's not going to happen the way you're imagining it. There has never yet been a séance that has produced any actual results."

Bess was beginning to agree with him. Surely all the hours she had sat in those large, smoky rooms with women spewing their disgusting ectoplasm and claiming they were holy had been a grave mistake. The hundreds of mediums she had encountered worked only in the dark and adopted false voices—just as she had done during her circus days, touting falsehoods to small-town folks. Harry would never come back to her in that way. It was degrading. But what if she herself really did possess the clarity of vision, the gift of sight that Harry had always believed in? She had tried to access it after his death, but perhaps she had been going about it all wrong.

She had always prided herself on understanding Harry when no one else could, on being able to solve the mysteries and riddles he presented her with during their marriage—just as she had seen through his Metamorphosis trick when she first saw him onstage.

She needed to channel his spirit—not his ghost, but his being, wherever he was. Her search, she realized, should be guided not by the conventional methods of the time—the endless séances and prayer vigils—but by following Harry's *rejection* of convention. She only had to figure out what that meant.

A friend of Stella's came up behind Bess and grabbed her arm, swaying to the music. "Is it true Lou Gehrig was here the other day? I was hoping he would come in tonight! Do you think he might?"

"He only came for lunch." Bess shrugged. "I don't think he stays out late."

"Stella says you're friends with dozens of celebrities."

Bess smiled. "A lady never tells."

Niall rolled his eyes. "You're a right old pontificator." He turned to the woman. "She knows them all, and they know her— Josephine Baker, Al Jolson, Jack Dempsey. They've all been in here at one time or another."

The woman shrieked and wandered off in search of anyone famous who might be lingering among the crowd.

When she left, Bess shook her head. "I do know them, but it's not true they've all come in here. Josephine Baker and Al Jolson live in California."

"Oops." Niall threw up his hands. "So it'll bring a little more business your way. How else do you think places become popular? Rumors. That's how. I'll tell you, if this was my place, I'd do whatever I had to do to keep it strong. Did you ever consider dating someone else famous? At least for the papers? I heard that's how it's done in Hollywood. One person's fame boosts the fame of the other, and vice versa. You get a few photographs taken together, and you don't even have to go out on a real date. Of course, you can sleep with the good-looking ones."

"I've been on dates. Just not ones I flaunt in the papers." Bess turned to survey the antics in the dining room. A small cigarette fire had started on one of the tables but appeared to have been extinguished.

"Why not? Do you really think Harry would blame you? What was it you said to that reporter last month? 'I'll practice temperance when I'm old'?"

"Oh, come on. That was just publicity for the tearoom. I've got to make this place seem like someplace where anything could happen."

Niall followed Bess's gaze to a young redhead who had stripped down to her pink checkered stockings and wrapped herself in a tablecloth. "Well, it certainly is that."

The woman saw them and stumbled over. Niall held out his hand to help her stand.

"This is Marlene," he told Bess and Gladys. "I brought her with me." She was beautiful, and very young—only twenty or so—with coiffed auburn hair and black eyelashes. "Marlene's husband went away to prison, you see. But he managed to hide away enough of their money to get her a little apartment near the park."

Marlene noted Gladys's surprise and added, "It's all right. Everyone knows about my husband. We used to give fabulous dinners."

Niall nodded. "They did, that's true."

Bess turned to the bar, where bowls of oranges and lemons were set out beside blue glass bottles. It looked like a painting; she had stayed late after the lunch hour to set up for tonight. "Let's have a drink." She poured two gin rickeys and handed one to Gladys, who took a tentative sip.

"We're talking about finding ourselves some men," Bess said. Marlene clapped her hands. "Oh!" she cried. "I have the perfect men for you. They're brothers. I just met them a few moments ago." She looked around. "I think they were brothers." She wandered off, still holding the tablecloth around her shoulders.

Bess raised her eyebrows at Niall. "Why, she's as beautiful as a peacock and stupid as a goose."

"Don't be cruel," he said, throwing up his hands. "She lives in the apartment next to mine, and she caught me on my way out."

Gladys reached for Bess's elbow. "Would you sit with me for a moment?" she asked. "I'm feeling a little light-headed."

"Oh no." Bess led her over to the lounge and settled her onto the couch. "I shouldn't have given you that stuff. It's practically poison."

"I'm just overwhelmed is all."

Bess fumbled around in her purse for a cigarette. "Sometimes, I feel this city is so large that it makes me feel small." She reached for the issue of *The Delineator* buried among the magazines on the coffee table. "I haven't had a chance to read that article you told me about yet."

"Colleen read it to me. It's in the back somewhere, I think. It's very sweet."

Bess flipped through the pages. The artistic renderings of the women were always like her—small and boyish, with thin hips and breasts flattened by side-laced bras. Years ago she had been ridiculed for her shape, and called a child. How ironic that it was only when she was a woman of middle age did she finally possess an enviable form. Still, she knew she was getting older. An advertisement for Palmolive facial cream asked, "The kindly candles of last night, the telltale revealments of noon! Do you fear the contrast they may offer?" And she did, she did fear it.

Toward the back of the issue she found the article, a short piece championing successful Hollywood marriages. It briefly mentioned her and Harry, with an accompanying photograph of them at a medical charity auction five years earlier, along with others like Douglas Fairbanks and Mary Pickford. She recalled Harry's nerves that night, how he had clung to her, how he stood in a room full of great doctors and philanthropists and wondered if he would ever stop feeling like the lesser, less refined man.

Those rare moments of vulnerability had always devastated her. Now, she knew he was out there in some unfamiliar place looking for her, just as she was looking for him. When he died she had seen how afraid he was, how uncertain, and the thought of him alone, lonely, trying to find her, was almost too much to bear. She looked at Gladys and lowered her voice. "Do you think . . . he'll ever come back?"

Gladys reached for her hand and peered at her with empty blue eyes. "He's not coming back," she said gently. "He's not, Bess."

"But he is *somewhere*."

It was the one thing on which the two women fiercely disagreed. If there was anyone who could find a way to cross between the two worlds, it would be Harry. But Gladys, perhaps because of her own tragedy, had never subscribed to any romantic notions. Sometimes Bess wondered what it was Gladys saw in the blackness of the world around her. If she didn't see another, spiritual world, what did she see?

Bess studied the yellow liquid sparkling at the bottom of her glass. "But, you see, he promised he'd come back. In all his life, he never broke a promise to me."

"Maybe he *can't* come back," Gladys said.

Bess shook her head. There was something she'd kept from Gladys. "He promised something else, too. A few years before he died, I came in to find him in the library one night, hunched over some paperwork on his desk. I said, 'Harry, what are you still doing in here? It's late.' And he turned to me, smiling, and said, 'It's all right, Bess. I'm making sure you'll be taken care of if something happens to me.' I said, 'Nothing's going to happen to you,' and he said, 'Don't worry. I'm arranging everything.'"

"What did he mean?" Gladys asked. "Life insurance?"

"No. It wasn't that. He had a policy, of course, but he could never be certain they would pay out if something happened while he was performing. He'd arranged for something else."

"Like what?"

"Money of some sort. Hidden, where no one else could find it. He was always so paranoid, especially after that night we were burgled. Before he died, he tried to tell me something. I think it may have been about that. But he couldn't get the words out." On nights when she couldn't sleep, Bess searched the house. There were enough papers and hidden panels and loose floorboards to last her years. But so far, she had found nothing.

"Have you called the banks? The reasonable thing would have been for him to keep it in a safe-deposit box."

Bess nodded. "I've checked every one in the city. I've even called banks in Wisconsin."

"That would have been smart of him. Not many people would think to look where we grew up."

Bess held up her hands. "But there was nothing. Under the names Houdini or Weiss or Rahner."

Gladys pressed her lips together. "What will happen if you don't find it? Are things really that bad?"

"I'll have to sell what's left, I suppose. Harry's things. People want them. That's why I'm pinning my hopes on this business." She couldn't bring herself to tell Gladys that the house would have to go, too; in another year the mortgage would bleed the remnants of her accounts dry. She had already spoken to a broker, who could not contain his eagerness to list the property. But what would she have left of Harry once the house was gone? And what if the money Harry had left her was hidden somewhere inside?

She could not shake the feeling that the house held secrets she was meant to discover. She needed to hold on to it for as long as possible.

"Bess—" Gladys began.

"Don't say it. That's why I didn't tell you."

"I shouldn't have taken what Harry left for me. That should have been your money."

"Don't be ridiculous. Harry left that to *you*. How else were you supposed to afford an aide? I'm not having this conversation." Bess turned back to the magazine on her lap as the music picked up and the noise of the party, of the sweating, concrete city, swelled louder around them. At the bottom of the page was an article calling for the return of the Miss America pageants, which had been cancelled a year prior. She and Harry had been in attendance for the first official pageant, in 1921, when the "Most Beautiful Bathing Girl in America" had been awarded the title of Golden Mermaid. A hundred thousand people had crowded the boardwalk that day to watch a little dark-haired Norma Shearer look-alike win the hundred-dollar prize. The winner, a pretty teenager named Margaret Gorman, had asked Harry for an autograph after the competition. Harry had been tickled by this. "I'll trade mine for yours," he had told her. "You're famous too now, after all."

The magazine had a photograph of Margaret, an American flag draped around her shoulders and a string of white beads hanging from her neck. She had embodied the youthful energy of the age; a city girl, from Washington, she had later married and entered society as a minor celebrity. Below her was the caption "I am afraid I am going to wake up and find this has all been a dream."

There were photographs of the subsequent competitions, too, as they had gained notoriety, even amid the harsh protestations of women's groups. In one of the photographs, a full-figured blond girl smiled in a black bathing suit, her hands on her hips. "Kathleen O'Neill of Philadelphia," the caption read, "competing in the 1924 pageant." Behind her, a poster advertising the film *Walkin' Home, Again* was plastered on the side of a bathhouse, the word *Walkin'* cut off by the girl's elbow.

Bess sat back, startled, before leaning in to look at the picture more closely. Was she really seeing what she thought she was seeing? There were the words from Harry's second code, in plain sight in front of her eyes. *I'll take you home again, Kathleen*, the song began. Their wedding night was the first and only time she'd sung it to him, but it had stayed with him, until his deathbed. And somehow she had stumbled across the photograph of this girl, Kathleen—who had not even won the pageant—the words "Home Again" clearly visible behind her.

Harry had always protested the idea that photographs could reveal spirits that could not be seen by the naked eye, at the same time conceding that there was something eerie and almost otherworldly about the idea of using light and darkness to capture a moment in time on paper. He had wondered, privately to Bess, whether some part of a person was left behind every time their photograph was taken. But the spiritualists' use of photography to show fake ghosts and spirits angered him; in one public demonstration, he showed how he could manipulate the development of film to portray Abraham Lincoln's "ghost" behind him. He always insisted that his own magic was different from the spiritualists' endeavors. His magic was an illusion—something clearly impossible becoming possible. But it didn't claim to be more than that—not divinely sanctioned or preordained. He and Bess had once flirted with that kind of deception, and they could never shake the feeling that there was a darkness behind their fraud.

Bess thought back to her vision of Harry in the silver tray. She had been fooled, she thought, by his photograph on the wall; but then she was not so certain. Was it possible that there was something about that photograph that tied in to the photograph of Kathleen O'Neill?

She thought back to the afternoon of his death. It was definitely possible that a nurse had overheard the first code; but Harry had only ever referred to the second code as "the song you sang for me on our wedding night." They had never spoken the lyrics out loud. No one knew the details of that night.

She shook her head. She had to get some air and think of something else. "I'm going to get you some water," she told Gladys.

Gladys shook her head. "Please, I'm fine."

"It's no trouble." Bess stood up and bumped into a man she didn't recognize, slightly younger and shorter than herself. The underarms of his shirt were damp with sweat.

"Hey, you're Bess Houdini," he said, grabbing her arm. "I've seen you before. Three times actually. When your husband performed here in New York. He was something else."

She hated when conversations began like that. She never knew whether people were being polite or fishing for information about Harry. She looked around desperately for someone to pull her away. Another of Niall's friends, whose name she had forgotten, was walking past; she grabbed his hand and pulled herself toward him. "Oh, Burt! I've been looking for you."

The man looked at her, surprised for a moment, and then put his arm around her jovially. "Well," he said. "Here I am."

"Come with me into the kitchen." She took him by the hand and led him through the double doors. "Oh, thank you," she breathed, collapsing into a chair. Her mind was still racing over what she'd seen in the magazine.

He laughed, bending to turn on a lamp. "You actually almost got my name right. It's Robert. Bobby."

She looked up at him distractedly. "What's that? Oh. That is funny. I've never been very good with names, especially ones I've made up myself."

"What's yours?"

"My what?"

He smiled. "Your name."

Bess blinked at him. "You mean you don't know?"

"We've never met before, have we?"

"No." She wondered if she should tell him. As soon as they left the kitchen it would become embarrassingly obvious. She stood up.

"Don't go yet," he said. "I was beginning to enjoy myself."

Bess looked at him skeptically. "I'm sure you know you're handsome, but I'm also almost twenty years older than you. If I had to guess."

He shrugged. "I prefer older women."

"Are you married?" she asked him.

"No. Are you?"

Bess hesitated. She touched her hand instinctively, for the wedding ring she'd left at home after the Ford disaster. "Not anymore."

"Well, that's good. We must keep up the pretense of decency, mustn't we? We wouldn't want to do anything to get people talking."

Bess was amused. She liked his humor; it took her out of her head. There had been a period after Harry's death, in the haze of grief and champagne, when she'd lost her way with a number of men, many of them younger than she. There was a certain thrill to an affair with a man who was young, especially one who didn't know who she was. But after a while it had only made her long for some kind of real love.

"I ought to go," she said. "What I really need is to get some air. You are funny though."

"Well, you shouldn't go alone." He followed her out the door that led into the alley beside the building and then onto Forty-Ninth Street. Next to the tearoom, a little jewelry store had opened up a few days earlier, selling hammered gold bespoke pieces. It was dark out and there was a breeze going; she closed her eyes and leaned against the glass storefront.

"That's better," she said. "It's so hot in there."

Robert pulled her against him and pressed his mouth hard against hers. Bess opened her eyes, startled. For a moment she wasn't sure what to do. Finally she did nothing, and let him kiss her. It felt good to feel someone's lips against hers again, even if it didn't mean anything.

He took her tightly by the waist. "Really," he said. "You can't possibly be twenty years older than me. You barely look forty."

"I can assure you I'm not forty."

Someone whistled from the sidewalk. "Yoo-hoo, Bess!" She looked over to see a girlfriend of hers grinning at her from across the street.

Robert's hands fell from her waist. "*You're* Bess Houdini?" He was aghast. "Good God! I didn't recognize you!"

"Yes, I know. It was nice."

"I'm—sorry. I didn't mean—I really should go." He stumbled onto the sidewalk. Bess stared after him. She wasn't surprised he'd run off. The scandal surrounding her was still fresh, after all. Besides, men didn't like women who were famous for being other men's wives. And they certainly didn't like women who famously held séances for their dead husbands. Now she was alone, and the piano music from next door was falling softly into the street.

She rested her face against the cool glass of the jewelry store. She was happy something so innocuous had opened in the space, and not another restaurant to compete with hers. In the window, the female mannequin was dressed in a white silk shirtwaist with a red necktie and a wrist wrapped in gold. She was standing in front of an enlarged black-and-white photograph of a yacht, tied in the harbor at dusk; in the background, a man was leaning over the edge of the boat, waving to someone off camera.

Bess looked longingly at the mannequin's bracelets. No one had bought her jewelry since Harry died. She could buy herself dresses and hats and shoes, but jewelry was something else; it wasn't something one bought for oneself.

There was something familiar about the charm on the mannequin, she realized. It looked like one Harry had bought for her years before, on their first trip to London. She still had it in a wooden box on her dressing table. It was a tiny gold ladybug, the tips of its wings dotted with red paint. Hers was much smaller, of course; they had had very little money at the time, but it was the first piece of gold jewelry she'd ever owned, other than her wedding ring.

Below the man's hand in the photo, the name of the yacht was barely visible. *Home Again*, it said, the words painted in curled black letters.

Bess froze. It couldn't be. She pressed her palms against the glass and searched the image for something else she recognized, but there was nothing familiar at all about the scene.

At the back of the store, she saw a light burning under a closed door. Someone was in there. She pounded on the window glass. After a moment the door opened and a thin old man hobbled toward her, removing a head-strap magnifier.

"What do you want?" he called through the front door. "We're closed."

"I own the tearoom next door!" she yelled back. "I need to talk to you!"

The jeweler unlocked the door and let her in. "Bess Houdini? Why didn't you say so? This damn magnifier does things to my vision." He frowned. "What's the matter?"

Bess hesitated. "I'm sorry about the noise next door."

He shrugged. "I like the noise. Makes it seem less lonely in here. To be honest I came into work so late because I knew it would be chaos in there."

"The picture in your window," she said. "I need to know where you got it."

He blinked at her. "What do you mean?"

"That yacht. Did you take that photograph yourself?"

"No. My son made the display for me. That's him in the picture. But it was taken years ago."

Bess examined it. It didn't look familiar. "Where was it taken?"

"I'm not sure. I just said I needed something for a display, and he pulled it out of his album and had it enlarged."

"Do you have a copy of the photograph?" She wasn't sure what she was going to find, but she felt, if she could study it at home, something would come of it.

He looked confused. "What's this about?"

"I know it's an odd request. You see," she lied, "it looks just like a boat my father used to own when I was a girl."

He shook his head. "My son has the negatives. But he lives in Chicago now."

She must have looked crestfallen, because she saw the glaze of pity in his eyes. He thought about it, then waved his hand. "You know what? You can have it—the one in the window."

"Oh no, I couldn't take that. It's your display." Bess turned around. The cardboard was over two feet tall.

But he was already striding over to the window and undoing the ties. "It's all right. It hasn't been very successful at drawing customers. I was going to replace it with something else. I thought it was elegant, but I think I need something flashier."

Bess kissed him on the cheek. "Oh, you're a doll!" she cried. "And don't worry about your business. I'll make sure all my friends come in and buy something expensive from you."

She hauled the cardboard through the alley and left it against the outside wall of the tearoom. Then she went back inside in search of Gladys. Niall was blotto, leaning against the doorway, a dreamy look in his eyes. "I love this place, Bess," he murmured. "It feels like home."

"You looking for your friend?" She turned to see the man with the sweaty underarms, holding a cigarette in each hand. "The blind one?"

"Yes. Where did she go?"

"She left with some fella. Said to tell you he would get her home."

"She did?" Bess was alarmed for a moment, then laughed to herself. "Well, that's something."

She brought the picture of the yacht inside and leaned it against the wall in front of her. There were other white boats in the background, their names obscured, and in the distance, a striped lighthouse, a thin beam of light stretched across the water. It must have been some kind of yachting club.

But she noticed something new. The photographer's name, Charles Radley—scrawled in black ink in the corner—had been obscured in the window by the mannequin. Bess had never heard of him. Beneath his name, the photograph was dated April 2, 1925.

The issue of *The Delineator* was still on the coffee table. She sat down on the sofa and turned the pages with trembling hands. There she was, that girl Kathleen still staring out at her, the look in her eyes penetrating—as if, all those years ago, she'd known—and the words "Home Again" blurred behind her.

Bess tore out the photograph of Kathleen. On the bottom edge of the magazine page, there was also a photographer's name, printed in italic letters so small she had to squint to decipher it, the words barely visible as they ran against the corner of the bathhouse.

"Charles Radley," it read.

Chapter 5

THE CIRCUS

July 1894

They joined the Welsh Brothers circus in the green, sleepy town of Lancaster, Pennsylvania, arriving at the train station in the thrashing nighttime rain. No one was waiting to greet them, and as the platform cleared they managed to find the stationmaster and asked him where the circus tents were. He directed them to a field three miles away, toward the center of town, but they had no money to spare and walked the distance in the mud and darkness. Each of them hauled a heavy trunk, one almost half filled with playing cards. Bess had come up with the idea to make up special packs of cards and sell them between their acts, along with the secret to a sleight-of-hand trick.

They arrived at the field drenched and exhausted. They had eaten the last of their food—bread and cheese—on the train, and hadn't had a meal for hours. Around them half a dozen tattered tents had been erected, and a dozen trucks parked, but there were no people. Everyone, it appeared, was inside taking shelter from the rain. They stopped in a little alley between two of the tents, panting.

"Hey, you!" a voice called to them in the darkness. Bess looked around and saw a light burning in the distance. A figure was standing in a doorway that had been cut into the back of one of the trucks. "You the Houdinis?"

"Oh, thank God," she said to Harry. "We've been found."

The figure waved them toward the truck, and they discovered that the inside had been cleared out and done over as makeshift living quarters, with a few cots and a table and chair. A gas lamp was burning on the table, and Bess could make out the rounded, sweating face of the figure who had called them over, a heavyset man in greased black pants and loose suspenders.

"I'm Welsh," he said. "You're the Houdinis, right?"

Harry nodded. "Harry and Bess." His uneasiness was noticeable immediately to Bess. She had known him only a short time, but she already felt she could read his slightest expressions. Welsh was intimidating, and much larger than Harry.

Welsh sat down at the table and thumbed through a notebook. He didn't motion for them to sit, but even if he had, there were no other seats besides the bed, and Bess certainly did not feel comfortable sitting on another man's cot. "What do you do?" he asked, pulling out a pen.

Harry shrugged. "Anything."

Welsh nodded. "You two do Punch and Judy. And mind reading. Houdini, you do the magic, the wife singing and dancing, and of course your trunk trick, and the handcuff act. Twenty-five a week and cakes."

Bess glanced at Harry to see if he knew what cakes were, but she couldn't catch his eye. Harry didn't seem concerned. He pushed his hand forward and grasped Welsh's. "That's fine."

Welsh led them to another car, where their own living space had been partitioned off from another, larger space, which appeared to house a group of men. The men were playing cards and nodded to them as they passed through but didn't look up. There was nothing in the room they had been assigned but a narrow cot—no space even for a table. The division between their space and the men's was nothing but a thin piece of wood. She could hear every word they were saying. They seemed to be the rougher ones that Harry had called canvas men.

Harry was horrified. "This is worse than Coney Island," he said. "I thought we were here for something better."

Bess took his hand and led him over to the bed. "This is fine," she said, pulling off his soaking shirt and handing him a dry one. "This is all we need." She smoothed his hair and kissed him. "We're living simply, remember? We're on the road life." She tried to disguise her own nervousness—especially about the men living right on the other side of the thin wall—but she couldn't bear to see Harry so hopeless, sitting beside her with his head in his hands.

"It *will* get better," she added, although she couldn't stop shivering in her wet dress. "Once we do the act and people start noticing us, there'll be more and more money coming our way."

"Do you really believe that?"

Bess wasn't sure she did. But she nodded anyway.

"I'm afraid—" He lowered his voice. "I'm afraid I may have failed you already. And we haven't even begun."

"We have to start somewhere." She nodded toward the wall. "And you better start by making friends with some of those men. They'll tell you how things are run around here."

Harry bit his lip. "How do I do that?"

Bess stared at him. "Haven't you made a friend before?"

He shrugged. "Dash was always the social one, not me."

Back in Coney Island, she had seen how his stage charm wore to awkwardness offstage. But she hadn't realized the extent of Harry's shyness until now. "When I met you, you were so confident. You have to be like that."

"I'm always like that after a show. It's the act—it stays with me for a little while."

"Pretend you just got offstage," she said.

But Harry only shook his head. "It's not like that."

"Well, I can't make friends for you—" she began, then stopped herself. Or could she? She poked her head around the partition. The men were deeply engaged in their game. "Hello, gentlemen," she called over the pounding of the rain outside. "Does anyone know where I could find an oven around here? I was going to make an almond cake in the morning if anybody wants some."

The men put down their cards and looked up. One of them eyed her suspiciously. "Who are you?"

"I'm Bess." She pulled Harry out behind her. She realized she must look a mess with her hair matted to her head and her dress dripping, but she forged ahead. "This is my husband, Harry. We're the Houdinis."

The heavy, bearded man at the head of the table pushed back his chair. "You're the Houdinis?" He stood up and went to shake Harry's hand. "I'm Eddie Saint. I heard you do some damn fine performing."

Harry seemed to find his footing. "Well, it's my wife, really, who's the star."

"He's being modest," Bess said. "He's head billing."

Harry shook his head. "Oh, no. You see, we have to tell everyone it's me because Bess looks so young, Welsh would try to pay her as a child, and we couldn't live off that."

The men laughed and clapped him on the back. "I'll take some of that cake," one of them said.

Saint looked at Bess. "Don't you have a towel?" He turned to one of the younger players. "Lenny, get 'em a towel, would you? Don't you have any manners?"

Bess looked over at Harry and smiled.

✳

Bess didn't notice until the morning that there was a tiny window cut into the side of the truck. When she woke up Harry was gone, and the day was bright and warm; there was no trace in the sky of the storm of the night before. She hurried to get dressed, then wandered around the grounds until she found the breakfast area. Half a dozen long pine tables had been set up under one of the open tents, and there was a sour-faced woman cooking eggs and toast on the far side of the dining area, in the shade. Another woman, wearing a warm, crooked smile, came up to her as she stood hesitantly at the entrance to the tent.

"Come on, you'll sit with me, dear," the woman said. "You don't want nothin' to do with those men over there. Are you a Houdini?"

Bess nodded.

"I'm Mrs. McCarthy. I'm a juggler. We've been waiting for you. Heard you got a good show going on. And you see we ain't got nearly enough women here."

"Yes . . . I see that." Bess looked around at the men who were shoveling food into their mouths, spilling much of it onto the tables.

"Did Welsh really put you in the trailer with the canvas men? Does he want you to up and quit before you even start?" Mrs. McCarthy led her into a smaller tent adjacent to the breakfast tent. "Come on. The performers eat in here. Breakfast is almost over."

"They're not so bad," Bess said.

Mrs. McCarthy appeared to be in her late thirties, and she was dressed decently enough, in a cream-and-purple-patterned day dress. The performers' tent was much quieter than the other. The men and women—there was only Mrs. McCarthy and one other woman—sat together, and the younger one flirted with a blond-haired man in low whispers. There was a sense of familiarity to it, almost like home. Here, in this Pennsylvania field, the grass dusted with the dew of last night's storm and the veil of light coming through the canvas, everything seemed still; Bess wanted to hold this gleaming moment before it slid away.

She spotted Harry at one of the tables and took a seat next to him. He raised her hand to his lips and kissed it. "Good morning. I didn't want to wake you. You're not mad I left you, are you?"

Bess shook her head. "Of course not." She was stunned he had ventured off on his own.

A waiter put a cup of black coffee in front of her. "Ham or—?" He stopped. Bess looked at Harry, confused.

"One ham, one or, please," Harry said, and everyone laughed.

"*Or* means eggs," Mrs. McCarthy told Bess from across the table. "You can only pick one." But she was amused. Harry looked at Bess, pleased with himself.

They both ordered eggs, and Bess turned back to Mrs. McCarthy. "Last night, Welsh said something about cakes. What are cakes?"

Mrs. McCarthy laughed again; it came from deep in her stomach, a kind of bellow. "*Cakes* means meals. He means you get your meals included when you work here."

Bess nodded, relieved. At least they wouldn't have to worry about food for the time being. She wondered what they would do with their salary if they didn't have to pay for meals or lodging. She supposed Harry would want them to save it.

"Does anyone ever take a room in town, away from the trucks?" she asked, out of curiosity. She worried how Harry would fare in their close quarters over time.

Mrs. McCarthy shook her head. "I wouldn't do that, hon. It'll look bad for you. Everyone here does everything together. That's the way it's always been. There ain't no privacy, but that's the life."

Bess looked over at Harry, who was talking to two of the men animatedly about their acts. She turned back to Mrs. McCarthy. "I almost forgot. Do you know where I can find an oven?"

"Bribed some of the men with food, did ya?" She nodded toward the back of the tent. "There's no oven, but there's a stove back there. I did the same thing when I first got here. It's about the only way to get 'em to like ya if you can't sleep with 'em."

"What a sweet creature—what a beautiful face my wife has!"

Harry knelt beside Bess behind the curtained puppet theater, voicing the role of the male puppet, Punch. Beyond the stage, ten circus goers had gathered to watch their performance. Most seemed only minimally interested; the men were chewing tobacco and the children were looking around the tent. In the back corner, Welsh leaned against the pole, his face cool as stone.

Bess slapped Harry's puppet with hers and looked down at the script. "Keep quiet, dummy! You're a terrible husband."

"Don't be cross, my dear. Give me a kiss."

"Oh, all right." Bess kissed his puppet with hers and leaned toward his lips behind the stage. Harry grinned and cupped her brassiere.

"Stop!" Bess slapped his hand away. She whispered, "Do you want to get fired?"

"I didn't come all the way down here to do some dumb puppet show. Who wrote this script anyway?"

"I don't know. Welsh said do Punch and Judy before our magic. When we start getting known for our real act we can stop." In front of the curtain, she maneuvered her puppet's arms around Punch. "You have sweet lips," she said in Judy's high, shrewish voice. "Will you dance with me?"

Punch hit Judy on the nose. "Get out of the way! You don't dance well enough for me! Go and fetch the baby."

Bess raised her voice. "You get the baby, you lazy idiot. I'm making the dumplings."

Bess shoved the puppet baby toward Harry. For the next part of the act, Punch was supposed to get annoyed at its wailing and hit its head against the wall.

"I can't do it," Harry whispered.

The audience began to boo. "Git the hook!" one of them cried. "Git 'em outta here!"

Harry stood up from behind the curtain. "Oh, all right!" he cried, throwing down his puppet. "I don't like this damn doll show any more than you do. Let's get on with the magic!"

The audience hooted. Bess dropped her puppet, relieved, and stood up beside Harry.

"Ladies and gentlemen," Harry began with a flourish. "I am Harry Houdini, and this is my assistant, Madame Houdini. We are the Master Monarchs of Modern Mystery, and today, you will be the first to witness the greatest novelty mystery act in the world!"

The audience cheered.

Bess retrieved a pair of handcuffs from inside a black bag. "Now you can see," Harry went on, "that I have nothing—no keys—up my sleeve. Any escapes will be completely unaided and authentic." He held up his arm. "Now Madame Houdini is going to handcuff my hands behind my back."

Bess secured the handcuffs tightly. It was a new innovation to the Metamorphosis trick that Harry had devised on one of their afternoon walks through town, when they had passed a man with his hands behind his back being led into the local police station. "Now," Harry said, "you may have seen ordinary escape tricks before. But I can assure you this is no ordinary escape. We are not using ropes. There has never before been an escape done while handcuffed."

Bess felt surprisingly at ease. Her new role in Harry's magic was much more thrilling than her short-lived singing career. She hadn't been able to draw men's eyes the way Anna had, but her childlike size was perfectly suited to the manipulations Harry's tricks required. What was more, Harry was more confident when she was beside him onstage. He seemed to her the best version of himself.

Bess pulled the large cloth bag over Harry's head and secured it at the top, so he was completely unseen. Then she guided him into the trunk, which she locked and strapped with a long belt. She looked out into the faces of the crowd; their chewing had stopped. She had their attention now. She stood on top of the trunk and drew a curtain in front of herself so that only her head was visible, then announced, "When I clap my hands three times, I will have disappeared. You will all be witness to a marvelous mystery, performed with the greatest speed and dexterity." Then she drew the curtain completely above her head and clapped three times. With the third clap, the curtain dropped, and Harry was standing on the trunk in Bess's place.

His hands were uncuffed and resting on his hips. The crowd murmured.

"Where's your pretty assistant?" one of the men called.

"She probably just ran offstage," someone else said.

"Offstage?" Harry feigned confusion. "Oh, no." He stepped off the trunk and began to undo the belts. "You see, she's inside this trunk."

The crowd burst into applause.

Backstage, on the lawn behind the tent, Bess wiped the sweat from her forehead. "How many of these do we have to do today?"

"Ten," Harry said. "Give or take."

"I'm exhausted already. I don't know how you do it."

Harry tapped his foot in the grass. He was as spirited as a caged animal. He beamed at her. "Didn't you see? They loved us."

Welsh came striding toward them from inside the tent, frowning.

"Uh-oh," Bess said. "We made a mess of his Punch and Judy."

Welsh stuck out his hand. "Helluva magic act, Houdini," he said. "But you ain't no comedian. Scratch the Punch and Judy from now on. Have Bess start with a song instead."

"I can do that," she said, relieved.

"You two got a good thing going. Needs some polish though. Don't rush through it as much. You need to drag it out more."

Harry nodded. "That's a good suggestion."

"Of course it is," Welsh snapped. "And another thing. Have someone in the audience inspect the cuffs. People will think they're trick cuffs if you don't." He cleared his throat. "They aren't trick cuffs, are they?"

"No, sir."

"Good. Now, we need you in Tent Five. They're demanding a Wild Man, but we ain't got one. So you're it."

Bess looked at Harry in his slacks and shirt. "How are we going to do that?"

"Rumple his hair a bit, tear up some sacks for clothes, and make him wild with some raw meat. He's supposed to be a native of the jungle, but who really cares?"

When Welsh left Harry said, "What do you think he meant when he said we should drag the act out? I thought we already were."

Bess thought about it. "Maybe we should give them a hint of danger. Make them think your life is really at stake. People want drama."

Harry kissed her. "My little ingenue."

*

Harry embraced the challenges. The Wild Man drew a crowd of fifty to his first show. The ringmaster claimed Harry was living on a diet of meat and tobacco, so at the end of the show the men threw cigarettes and cigars at the cage. Between this act and the Metamorphosis, Harry gave away a stash of loot to the canvas men.

Of their twenty-five dollars a week, he insisted on saving half and sending the other half to his mother in New York. In return, Bess would receive the loveliest letters from Mrs. Weiss. The letters never mentioned Bess's mother (although Bess was certain Harry had told her about being thrown out of the house) but Bess understood that Mrs. Weiss was offering herself up as a mothering figure, advising her on how to do laundry on the road, and how to evade the drunk circus goers.

Most of the performers, Bess learned, were related to each other. Mrs. McCarthy was married to the ringmaster, and her brother was the fire-eater, and her husband's cousin was one of the canvas men. The other woman, Moira, did the costumes, and made Bess a new dress she could wear in the show. In return, whenever they could find poultry, Bess cooked up platters of fried chicken on Friday nights.

She didn't mind the lack of spending money as much as she minded the lack of privacy. She couldn't think about doing anything intimate in their living space, which was nearly the same as doing it in public as far as she was concerned. But she began to be haunted by the faces of the babies she saw in the audience.

Harry was against the idea. "We can't support a child right now," he told her. "And you wouldn't be able to perform for a year. Who would take your place?" She knew his ambitions were elsewhere. He was spending an hour every day on his exercises, doing push-ups and intricate stretches, and another hour with his cards, practicing his finger work. Sometimes he would revert to the old standby he had learned in his youth—hanging upside down from a suspended bar and picking up needles with his eyelids. A more complicated task was swallowing the needles, then regurgitating them.

Bess undid his collar. "Please, darling. Think how much fun we'll have in trying. Just meet me here on Fridays during lunch so we're alone. You can be tired. I'll take care of you." And he relented.

He made the most extraordinary discovery in the quaint, sweltering town of Birmingham, Alabama, which charmed Bess with its shop-lined streets and immaculately dressed southern women. After the show one night Harry met a doctor who mentioned that he worked at a nearby insane asylum, and asked him if he would like to visit. Bess was curious and insisted on accompanying him. Mrs. McCarthy thought she was out of her mind. "You don't want to see what goes on in places like that," she told her. "The rest of us are going swimming in the river. Come with us."

But Harry's excitement was infectious. Dr. Steeves had told him that he had a possible new idea for an escape trick, only he wouldn't tell him what it was.

The institution was set back from the road, near a lake, on freshly manicured grounds. It seemed to Bess, from the outside, to be more of a hotel than a hospital, except for the bars on the windows. The sun was shining on the red bricks, and she slid her hand into Harry's as they waited at the front entrance.

They were greeted by Dr. Steeves, who was flushed with eagerness. He ushered them past the nurses' station and the recreation room, and through a long corridor of patient rooms. Some of the doors were partially ajar, and Bess could see the shadows of the patients moving about inside the rooms. Finally, she caught a glimpse of one of the patients in the flesh; it was a woman about her age, her dark hair pulled loosely from her face, sitting still by the window, staring out at the lawn. A vision of the woman as a child, playing with a doll in a railway car, flashed before her eyes. She wasn't sure whether it was based in any truth, but it made Bess alarmingly sad. She was not quite sure what separated a woman like that from one like her; did one see madness coming, she wondered, or did it come quietly, like a thief at night? She shivered. She would rather die than lose her mind.

At the end of the corridor was one final door, which looked to Bess just like all the others. But when Dr. Steeves unlocked it, he stepped in front of them and held up his hand. "Stay back," he warned. "This patient is quite dangerous."

Inside, the room was completely padded in cream-colored canvas. There were no windows, and it was stiflingly quiet, except for the panting of a man rolling about on the floor.

"My God!" Harry cried, horrified. "What is that?"

The man was wearing what appeared to be a normal jacket, except the sleeves were exceptionally long, and they were wrapped once around the man's torso and tied behind his back. Bess had never seen anything like it. She grabbed Harry's arm. He had used restraint muffs in his act before, but never anything like this. The man on the ground was straining every muscle in his body, but he could not get loose. His legs were jerking wildly, desperately, underneath him, and his forehead was dripping with sweat.

"It's called a straitjacket," Dr. Steeves remarked proudly. "It's impossible to get free of it."

Bess could see the flicker of eagerness in Harry's eyes at the word *impossible*.

"Can I borrow one?" he asked the doctor.

By the end of the week he had perfected the new trick, and the cigarettes were pouring onto the stage. Harry played up his experience in the asylum, making the patients out to be criminally inclined, dangerous men, and the feat he was accomplishing onstage seemed all the more daring because of it. But Bess could not forget how that young girl sat stick-still in her chair by the window, looking out onto the Alabama fields and thinking of God knows what life she'd had, or who had loved her once.

❋

"We have just recently become aware of a tragic situation in this good town of De Land, Illinois," Harry began. Bess, in a dress of cream-colored lace, sat blindfolded in a chair beside him. "A man who walked in these very streets beside you has only recently been found murdered."

After a few months on the circuit, Harry had tired of the Metamorphosis. Bess, longing for a break from the physical exertion, came up with a new angle. She began to notice how many people lingered after the show, wondering if Harry was somehow working actual magic. They were longing, she saw, for something real. Possessing true knowledge made them more than players on the stage; it made them powerful. She asked Welsh to begin billing them as "Celebrated Clairvoyants" and saying they could communicate freely with the dead.

They worked on the trick together. Whenever they stopped in a new town, Harry paid a visit to the local cemetery, asking about recent deaths, while Bess disguised herself and gossiped with women at church teas. In the small towns where the circus pitched its tents, it was easy to learn the local rumors. Everyone knew everyone's business, a phenomenon that astounded Bess and Harry, having come from a place as large as New York City.

By now, the Houdinis' audiences had swelled to the hundreds. Word of their coming seemed to reach the small towns before the circus wagons arrived. "My wife, beside me, has the ability to speak with those we have lost," Harry declared. Bess suddenly slumped over in her chair. "She is in a trance state," Harry said. He rubbed his chin and feigned nervous energy. "My darling, what messages have you to give us today?"

Bess spoke in a high, unfamiliar voice. "I am looking for the killers of Benny Carter."

"Killers?" Harry asked, alarmed. "Were there more than one?"

"Yes."

"Were these killers known to Mr. Carter?"

"Yes."

Harry began to pace back and forth. "Could you tell us, my dear, how this murder was accomplished?"

"With a razor."

The audience was enthralled. Bess could hear their heavy silence, waiting for what she might say next.

"I see the blood," she said, her voice trembling. "Oh, God!" Harry ran to her side and gripped her shoulders. Bess began throwing her body back and forth. "I can't hold on!" she cried. "God help me, I can't hold on!"

"Tell us their names!" Harry said. Bess didn't answer. "What are their names?"

Bess's movements grew increasingly violent. She began to bang her head against the back of the chair.

"Their names!" Harry demanded.

"Bill Doakes and Jim Saunders!" she said. "Benny is here. He won't—he won't let me go. Harry, tell him to let me go! He warns them, 'You boys better put those razors away, or yous goin' to be where I is now.'"

Then she collapsed onto the ground and lay still. From behind her blindfold she heard the commotion and the sound of a chair scraping the makeshift wooden floorboards. She knew one of the men she had just accused had been present and fled the room. She fought a smile. Harry had learned about the murder in a De Land barroom. It was not a sad one. Carter, Doakes, and Saunders were three local criminals who had gone about town together. Consensus was that Carter had stolen from the others and paid the price.

"My God!" someone shouted. "You know things that only the Almighty knows!"

Bess knew she had been right; give them a taste of danger, and talk about death, and they would be hooked.

For more in-depth communications, they used an elaborate code system Harry had devised. It involved signals that relied on the positions of the hands and feet, as well as facial expressions and spoken words. Each word corresponded with a number, so that *pray,* for example, meant 1 and *tell* meant 5. During the act, Harry, ever the showman, blindfolded Bess as she pretended to go into a trance. Harry was passed a coin by a member of the audience, and through their system of communication, he would speak to the spirits inside Bess, asking them "pray tell" when the coin was minted. The words he used in his question gave Bess the answer she was supposed to supply. Other questions and answers they would discuss ahead of time; Bess had the idea to disguise themselves and go door to door selling Bibles, which would give them access to the homes of the townspeople, allowing them to reveal information about those people during the séance.

It was a game she enjoyed, fooling such large groups. No one suspected them of fakery, especially not with Bess's childlike appearance. But one night after a show in southern Missouri, after a particularly thorny revelation about one woman's dead son, she removed her blindfold to see tears streaming down the face of a frail, bonneted old lady. She swelled with regret; the thrill of the deceit was gone. What had she been doing? She had betrayed every moral code she believed in; she had spit in the face of the God she'd been taught to worship. She wondered if the girl she'd been a year ago would ever have imagined she would stoop so low.

Her mother clung to her Catholic faith because she had to; she'd lost a husband, only to gain a derelict one, and she struggled to care for an enormous family. Bess thought Harry's situation had been similar. His father—an immigrant and floundering rabbi—clutched at his own Jewish faith because without it, he was just a failed man preaching about fairies. He had forced his faith on the family with what Harry saw as simpleminded naïveté. Harry didn't see his father's God saving his family; instead, he saw the slow deaths of a brother and his father, the silent desperation of his mother, her defeated shoulders. And so he turned to magic—tricks that played on people's credulity—and it was magic that saved them, the money he earned from traveling the show circuit on his own as a boy. He made no apologies for his agnosticism, but Bess knew there was a part of him that was always wondering whether there was a being out there whose magic was greater than his own.

Bess still believed in God. She believed in the serenity of a quiet church, in the rituals of beads and prayer. In the tumult of her childhood she had seen compassion from neighbors who brought meals, from strangers who led her home when she was lost, and there was something godlike in that. But she also loved Harry, and she loved his practical magic.

She glanced at Harry. He was still immersed in the trick, pacing the stage. She saw the other performers, her friends, huddled in the back of the room, awed. Afterward, Moira came up to her privately.

"I know you've got a trick up your sleeve. How are you knowing those things about people?"

Bess shook her head. "I can't say."

"But it's not real, is it?" Moira asked, a lilt of hope in her voice.

Bess's heart sank. She reached for Moira's arm. "It's not real." It was bad enough fooling strangers, but the thought of fooling these people who had become her friends made her ill. She groped for an explanation and ended up quoting Harry's mechanical voice: "We are only acting by physical, not psychical, means."

Harry found her in their bedroom after. She had ripped off her dress and was clawing at her corset. "I can't breathe," she said. "God help me, I can't breathe." Harry put his arms around her and tried to calm her, but she couldn't stop shaking. It had come upon her so suddenly, the sickening feeling of foreboding, the voice saying they would go straight to hell, and the quick footprints of the rain on the roof.

The room felt unbearably hot. She pushed her way out of the car and into the thrashing rain. Thank goodness, the grass was cold. "Bess!" Harry followed her outside. She could barely see him through the downpour. The doors of the car were flapping wildly, and everywhere around them in the darkening night the circus goers were running to take shelter.

"You're half naked!" Harry shouted. "Get back inside, would you?"

Bess shook her head.

"I don't know how to help you!" he said. "I don't know what you want!"

"I know why I'm not getting pregnant," she called back. "It's a punishment. We've pulled each other into something sinister, Harry."

Harry looked at her in awe, then burst out laughing. "Is that what you think?"

"Then why can't I have children?"

"Come inside out of the rain," he said. "This isn't like you. It makes me feel—uncentered."

He looked so helpless. She imagined what she must look like, her hair matted with rain and all the pins falling out, and she thought about those "delicate" girls she hated, the ones who needed smelling salts and daytime rest. Harry could never love a girl like that. Offstage, he needed her to be the engaging one, the sensible one. She followed him back to the cot.

He wrapped her in a blanket. "There," he said. "That's better now."

"You don't have to coddle me." She wrung out her hair. "I'm better now. It was a momentary loss of sense."

"Over what?"

"That we've done something unforgivable." It seemed to her now, in the flickering candlelight, that this world they had created around themselves could collapse at any moment. Harry was afraid, too, she knew, but of different things—that they wouldn't be able to make it last after all, this career of magicianship, and that he wouldn't be able to support her and he would let her down, by forcing her to go to work in some factory sewing socks, or some boardinghouse kitchen. Harry's fears were physical, Bess's metaphysical. On this account they differed.

"I don't know about the children," he said, "but let me show you something." He took a scrap of paper out of his pocket and held it beside the candle so it would dry enough for him to be able to write on it. "You never told me the first name of your father, did you?"

She thought about it. "I don't think so."

"Write it now on this paper, and then burn it. Don't show it to me."

Bess did, then crumpled the paper in her hand and held it over the flame.

Harry dropped it into a bowl and let it burn. When it had been reduced to ashes, he pulled up his shirtsleeve, revealing his muscled forearm. With his other hand he rubbed the black remnants onto his bare skin, and almost immediately Bess's father's name, Gebhardt, appeared on his arm in red lettering.

Bess's hand flew to her mouth. "You *are* the devil," she said.

"Silly kid." Harry laughed. "Don't you know me by now? It was only a trick!"

"How? How was it a trick?"

"You guess."

She frowned at him. "Give me a pen." Harry grinned and handed her one, and she wrote on her arm with the sharp end and, with her fingertip, rubbed the skin where the inkless nib had touched. She watched as the letters of her father's name appeared.

"It's a trick of the body," Harry explained. "Do you remember what I told you the night we met? There is no such thing as magic." He laughed. "Still, my greatest dream is to slip one by you at some point. You figure them all out too fast."

"But how did you know my father's name?"

"Stella mentioned it in one of her letters."

Bess let out a short laugh. She felt ridiculous. "You scared me for a minute."

Harry peeled the top of the corset off her and climbed into the bed beside her. "There's an explanation for everything."

Bess closed her eyes. "I'm sorry I doubted you," she said. Outside, the wind had calmed to a whisper.

"Do you want to go back to the Metamorphosis?"

She shook her head.

"We can't cut the séances just yet—we'll be poor without them." He traced her eyelids with his fingertips.

Their existence seemed suddenly cozy, not terrible at all. They were together; they knew things about each other no one else knew. The thrill and the fear were gone, and out there on the other side of the storm, the scattered gaslights of the little town flamed and fell, flamed and fell.

Chapter 6

ATLANTIC CITY

June 1929

Mid-June in Atlantic City was crowded, and the heat was scalding. Even in the early evening, the beaches were a patchwork of colored blankets, on top of which parents had placed picnic baskets and sleeping babies in white Moses baskets. Young women lounged in kelly green bathing costumes and stockings rolled down to the knees. The crash of the surf reached all the way to the boardwalk, where Bess stood scanning the row of hotels that stretched for miles.

Locating the photographer Charles Radley had not been difficult. Harry's old secretary had found him easily enough, in under two weeks, through a few letters of inquiry to friends in Atlantic City. Bess felt certain this man was safeguarding some secret of Harry's; perhaps Harry had even left with him the message he intended for Bess. But Charles Radley, it turned out, was no more than a newspaperman, a photographer for *The Atlantic City Daily Press* who also did some freelance work on his own time. She had never heard of him. She herself had only been to Atlantic City a handful of times with Harry, when he had performed his bridge-jumping stunts during the busy summer months.

She had written to Mr. Radley under a pseudonym, asking him to meet her at the United States Hotel. She had heard he did free-lance photography, she said, and she wanted to hire him for a job.

When Stella heard Bess was traveling to Atlantic City for the weekend, she jumped at the chance to accompany her. The baby was due in the fall, and she wanted to be home with Abby when she got bigger. And Fred was so busy at work. She desperately needed a vacation, she said.

Bess couldn't tell her that the trip was really about following the trail of the second code—she knew Stella would think she was imagining things—but still, she hated to travel alone. She told Stella she was going for some business meetings related to Harry's estate, but she would mostly be free. Niall had offered to look after the café while she was gone, and they traveled by train into New Jersey and arrived only an hour before Bess was scheduled to meet with Mr. Radley. She left Stella in the hotel room and made her way downstairs to the lobby.

She was uneasy about the meeting. So much of her marriage with Harry had been about the written word, the notes they left for each other in one room or another; and so much of Harry's career had involved using images to mislead, that it did seem plausible that he could be communicating his second code to her through the words inside photographs. But what if she was wrong? She wasn't sure she would be able to believe in much if she could not believe in this.

The United States Hotel was massive and garish; it spanned fourteen acres between Atlantic, Pacific, Delaware, and Maryland Avenues. It was the largest hotel in the nation, and a marvel of architecture. She and Harry had stayed there after it had first been built; the hotel was hosting Harry's performances for two weeks, and a suite of rooms was included in the contract, for the Houdinis as well as their employees. Bess had been delighted by the ghastly size of the property; she had found the place to be a playground. From the outside, the building was an identical series of brick stories with long white balconies; on the inside, the corridors were carpeted in the same red carpet throughout. While Harry buried himself in work, she went swimming and came back holding pink boxes of saltwater taffy and newspapers with his picture on the front page. Even after fame had found him, he never ceased being thrilled by his face on newsprint.

She didn't really have the money to be staying here now, but she thought it prudent to keep up pretenses, in case it proved necessary. Bess recalled the first time she and Harry had stayed in a real palace, during a trip to Russia. The Grand Duke Sergius, bored and hearing of Harry's escapes, had invited them to St. Petersburg, to give a special exhibition in his ballroom. The duke told them he had spent a month building a steel chest that could not be unlocked. Harry, slightly concerned but knowing how much Bess was longing to see the palace, accepted the challenge. Bess was invited to have tea with the duchess while Harry was performing. Afterward, he recounted to her how he was stripped to his underwear and searched, but managed to open the box nonetheless. She knew how it had been done, the picklock clasped underneath his left toes; he had tested it with her the night before. That night they slept in gray silk sheets in a room decorated with candlelight and heavy tapestries. Breakfast was brought in on a tray and eaten on the balcony, which overlooked the gardens.

She had asked Charles Radley to meet her in the lobby at six. Wanting to make sure he was there before her, she arrived at a quarter past six and scanned the cream-colored sofas for a man sitting alone. She had no idea what he looked like or how old he was, but she estimated that he would be wearing a less expensive suit than most of the men there, and would probably wait about a half hour before he gave up on her.

It was a hot evening, but the lobby was cool. The wall was lined with tall, open glass windows bordered by sheer white curtains. Stiff-collared waiters were bringing around drinks of lemonade, and a piano player was playing a soft rendition of "Rhapsody in Blue." Although the room was crowded, most of the men and women were already in evening dress, the women leaning against armchairs in their jewel-colored chiffon. But there was only one man alone, sweating in a gray wool suit, tapping his foot in an armchair next to the soft carpeted staircase. She was disappointed; she felt certain she would recognize him when she saw him, that it would be instantly clear why Harry had directed her to him. But she had never seen him before; he didn't seem like the bearer of any kind of message. She sat down quietly in a chair by the door and pulled a novel from her purse so she could study him a moment longer. She had given him a man's name for the meeting, and she didn't think he would recognize her at first.

He was much younger than she had imagined. He was clean-shaven and attractive, in his early thirties, his dark eyes hidden behind a thin pair of spectacles. Something about him made her uneasy, though she could not identify what. He seemed harmless enough. He crossed two thin hands over a leather briefcase, which Bess imagined contained a selection of his work. He did not have the body or the demeanor of a dangerous man, although Stella liked to talk about the debauchery of Atlantic City—where the Prohibition laws were essentially unenforced—being even worse than Manhattan's.

After a few minutes he glanced at his watch, looked around the room once more, and stood up. Bess stood up as well and went after him. She followed him across the lobby, toward the dining room, and through a tall mahogany door next to the kitchen. She found herself standing in what appeared to have once been a library. It was completely windowless, lit only by tall brass lamps and shaded sconces. Red leather couches were scattered around the room, and the walls held floor-to-ceiling bookshelves. It reminded her of Harry's library at home. The thick, woody odor of cigar smoke wafted through the doorway. In front of one of the bookshelves, a makeshift wooden bar had been set up and was manned by a bartender, who was retrieving drinks from a fully stocked liquor cabinet behind the bar.

Charles took a seat on one of the barstools and asked for a glass of soda water, pulling a folded newspaper from his briefcase and laying it out in front of him. To his right was a young woman, a Mary Hay look-alike, in a blue embroidered evening dress. He leaned over to speak to her and laid his hand on her arm. Bess sat down on the seat to his left and ordered herself a gin on ice.

It became clear to her immediately that Charles and the woman on his right had just become acquainted. But he had told her his name was Wallace, and she was asking him about his work in the bank. For a moment Bess was alarmed; she wondered if the real Charles Radley was still waiting for her in the lobby somewhere, until it occurred to her that he was very likely making up stories about himself to impress the girl.

After a few minutes the woman in the blue dress stood up. "My friends have arrived," she said. "Perhaps we can chat more later."

Charles's shoulders fell. "Oh. Of course." Bess felt a wave of affection for him. He was not skilled with women.

"Your name isn't really Wallace, is it?" she asked Charles when the woman had left.

He turned to her, alarmed. "Pardon?" She saw a look of recognition cross his face. "Why—you're Bess Houdini, aren't you?"

"I am. But you're not a banker. I know when a man is lying to impress a woman."

He blinked at her, startled. She looked at his glass. "Why bother coming to a place like this if you're only going to drink water?" She called over the bartender and ordered him a whiskey.

He stared at her. "Do you always order whiskey for men you've just met?" He pushed the glass away. "I don't drink whiskey."

His candor surprised her. "I'm—I'm sorry." She was mortified; she had tried too hard to charm him and had ended up coming off as domineering. She may just have ruined the one chance she had to gain his confidence.

Around them, the room was filling up with people. The conversations grew louder, and the smoke thicker.

"My name is actually Charles, not Wallace," he said, pulling his water glass back toward himself.

She looked down. "I know."

He sat up straighter. "How do you know?"

"I'm John Thomas Wilson."

Charles stared at her, confused. "*You're* the one who wrote to me?"

"I'm sorry for the deception. I didn't want there to be any expectations, you see. But I needed to speak with you." Bess took a long sip of her drink, trying to keep her nerves at bay. "My husband and I used to come here. Many years ago, before he died."

"But—how do you know who I am? We've never met—have we?"

She shook her head. "I don't think so. But that's what I came here to find out."

He laughed. "Are you really Bess Houdini? Is this some kind of a joke?"

"It's not, I promise you. I have something very important to discuss with you. I'm here because . . . I believe you may have some kind of information for me. About my husband."

"About *Harry Houdini*?" Charles looked at her with disbelief. "I don't know what kind of information I could have. The closest I ever got to him was seeing his jump at Young's Pier, when I was a kid."

Her heart sunk. "So—you don't have anything for me? You never knew him?"

He shook his head. "Sorry, no." He looked at her pityingly. "I read about what happened to you," he said gently. "For what it's worth, I believe you were duped."

"Thank you." The speed of the music was picking up. She felt she had to find out more about him; surely, there was something of importance there. "Is there somewhere else we could talk that's quieter?"

He shrugged. "We could go over to Doc's Oyster House. They have a good seafood menu."

"What about your woman in blue?"

Charles looked around the room, locating her on one of the leather sofas between two men, flirtatiously fingering the tiny white buttons at her neckline. His face turned red. "Oh, that was nothing. And it's not every day I get to have dinner with Bess Houdini."

"It's probably just as well."

"Oh?" He raised his eyebrows.

"She's too pretty to be respectable. That's advice coming from a woman who was never very pretty."

Charles laughed. "Pretty? What do you need pretty for? You're Mrs. Harry Houdini!" He caught himself. "What I mean is, you've got glamour."

Bess shook her head. "Everyone with money is glamorous to those who don't have it."

He frowned. "I was the one who photographed Evelyn Nesbit in a nightclub the night before her husband murdered her lover. It brought me quite a bit of glamour of my own, for a few weeks."

"You see, being a photographer is far more interesting than being a banker. You should use the truth to impress the ladies instead."

Charles laughed. "This coming from a woman who met me under false pretenses?"

She turned to see Stella coming through the door. "Oh no." She stood up. "I have to go. Could you meet me tomorrow? It's imperative that I speak with you about this." She put on her gloves. "I'll pay for the drinks. I'm sorry I was presumptuous."

Charles shook his head. He took a paper bill out of his wallet and placed it on the bar, then handed her his card. "You can meet me at the press offices tomorrow, if you'd like. I'm there all day on Saturdays."

Stella saw her and waved, making her way over to the bar. Bess intercepted her before she could reach Charles. "Hello! I was just on my way out."

"Is that the estate man? He's very handsome."

"Yes, yes, he is." Bess took her elbow. "Shall we go to dinner?"

Outside, the sun had gone down, but the boardwalk blazed with light. It reminded Bess so much of Coney Island, only livelier. She had to keep herself from searching for Harry in the crowd. The boardwalk had changed quite a bit since the first time she had been there with him. Back then, women rarely walked alone; now, there seemed to be more single women out than single men. And the names on the billboards had changed entirely; instead of Old Dutch Cleanser and Bixby's Shu-Wite, Coca-Cola and Lucky Strike advertised on every block.

Stella said, "I heard from a lady in the hotel that we shouldn't expect to see any celebrities while we're here. They never come when it's this hot. They mostly travel to Europe in the summer. All the well-dressed women are the gamblers' mistresses, apparently, and the prostitutes."

Bess laughed. "I don't care very much for celebrities."

"Funny, given you are one."

"You know what?" She turned to Stella. "Let's take dinner in our room tonight."

"*This,* from Bess Houdini? You've never been home on a Friday night before midnight!" Stella teased. "Is there something the matter? You haven't been yourself lately. Since the Arthur Ford episode." She hesitated. "You weren't really in love with him, were you?"

"God, no."

"Then what is it?"

Bess couldn't take her mind off Charles. There *had* to be something she was missing.

She wondered if his father had been someone they had known, or someone Harry had corresponded with—someone in the bookselling or magic field? "I've just had a bad reaction to what I was drinking earlier," she said. "I think I'll go to bed early."

Stella took Bess's arm. "Off to the room then, darling. I'm going to take a bath. Would you order me dinner?"

Their suite was on the second floor, on the ocean side; it had two bedrooms and a sitting room in between. The maid had left the windows open so the breeze would cool the room. Bess felt lost; her meeting with Charles had accomplished nothing. She had always been small, but over the years she felt herself growing smaller, shrinking with age, as if Harry's death had been eating away at her, physically, every day. Draping her wrap over the sofa, she listened to the people on the pier and wished she were in Russia again, the gardens blanketed with snow, and men and women roaming about in furs and capes. Harry was there, and in the warmth of the fire they were talking about his performance that evening, during which he had asked all of the guests assembled in the ballroom to write down something impossible they would like to see performed.

"It is my job," he explained, "to make the impossible possible again."

The duke selected one of the papers and unfolded it. "You are being asked to ring the bells of the Kremlin," he said and shook his head sadly. "But those bells haven't rung in a hundred years. They are too old."

The question, of course, was a plant; Harry went to the window that overlooked Palace Square. He removed his handkerchief from his pocket and waved it out the open window. As he did so, the bells began to ring. The duke could not speak for several minutes; one of the women fainted onto the couch. For his success, Harry had been handsomely rewarded with a purse full of money. They were certain he was some sort of mystic, or the devil himself. Bess, as his wife, received a white Pomeranian whom she named Carla.

The truth was that Harry's assistant, waiting outside, had fired a pistol at the bells. Even though the ropes holding them had rotted away, the sound was accomplished.

Many people had known some of his secrets. Franz, who fired the pistol, knew most of his tricks. Harry's secretary knew of his correspondence. Alfred knew the extent of his expenditures. But only Bess knew everything. Only Bess knew how his mouth twitched when he slept, and how he looked in the middle of the night when he was not Harry Houdini but Ehrich Weiss. Only she knew. There were no children, no children's children, to know his preference for strawberry jam in the mornings; it was always just her.

Now, she felt something pulling her back to the bar where

she had left Charles. The only way she would find out whether the photographs were a coincidence or a message was to come clean with him, and tell him everything. If he had any knowledge that would help her, she needed to find it out. She didn't care if he called her a madwoman. She grabbed her purse and went into the sitting room. She could hear Stella running the bath, and she left quietly.

In the bar, everything was as it had been fifteen minutes earlier. The man pouring drinks was whistling; the piano music was going; the woman in blue was sitting on the lap of another man, smoking a cigarette. Bess looked around, but she didn't see Charles. He had gone.

She leaned over the wooden bar and waved to the bartender. "Excuse me," she called, slightly out of breath. "The man who was sitting here—when did he leave?"

The bartender shrugged. "I don't know. Ten minutes ago, maybe?"

If Charles had been gone that long, it was too late to catch him. She wondered if she should try that restaurant he had mentioned, but she didn't want Stella to come out and find her missing. On top of the varnished wooden bar, the newspaper he had been reading was still there, folded in half. Bess sat down, spent. She had little interest in the news, but she wondered if the story about her séance was still lingering in the press.

Opening the paper, she breathed a sigh of relief. It appeared to be only local news, innocuous at that. The front page carried a dull story about the Atlantic City lighthouse being repaired in time for the regatta. Another photographer—not Charles—had taken the accompanying photograph. The caption beneath it read, "The Absecon Light has only been out once before in its seventy-two-year history, for eighty-five hours from April 1 to April 4, 1925."

Bess recognized the black-and-white-striped structure. It was the same lighthouse that was in the background of the yacht photograph she had found in the jeweler's window. So it was as she had suspected; that image had been taken by Charles in the Atlantic City Harbor.

But the date was familiar, too—April 1925. Bess reread the newspaper caption. "The Absecon Light has only been out once before . . ." She folded the paper quickly and put it on her lap. It was impossible. The article must be incorrect. In the photograph Charles had taken of the yacht—at dusk on April 2, 1925, according to the scribble underneath his signature—the light from the lighthouse had clearly been working. But the newspaper said the light had been out all day; so how had it been shining in the photograph?

Chapter 7

EUROPE

June 1900

The crowd blew kisses at the departing boat, and many of them cried. Some of the passengers, certainly, would not be back again—illness would strike them, or poverty, or love. Bess and Harry stood at the railing and waved their handkerchiefs to Mrs. Weiss and Gladys, who had come to New York Harbor to see them off to Europe. Tears were pouring down Mrs. Weiss's face; Gladys, pretty at eighteen years old, clung to her mother's arm. The passengers on the boat released colored paper streamers into the water, and somewhere close to the bow, outside the first-class dining room, an orchestra was playing "Believe Me, If All Those Endearing Young Charms."

In a low moment, Bess and Harry had moved back into the cramped Weiss apartment in Manhattan. It was certainly better accommodations than their makeshift circus rooms had been, but still, it was difficult to be a wife without a home of their own to care for, and Harry carried the burden of that humiliation around with him daily. He could barely drag himself out of bed knowing that he had been unable to live up to his promises. Their time with the Welsh troupe hadn't been a failure, exactly; but attendance at the shows had dwindled gradually, until there was barely enough to support the troupe's travel, and eventually the circus had closed. There were larger acts springing up all over the country, mostly with animals—an elephant kneeling before a man was a sight to behold—but Mr. Welsh couldn't afford to purchase any animals, and he couldn't afford to continue without them. After their last night in Louisville, Bess found herself standing on the railway platform beside Harry, with their old black trunk between them, saying good-bye to the friends they had made. Many of them, like the Houdinis, were trying to continue on the vaudeville circuit; they boarded separate trains to places like New York, Chicago, or Atlanta. Others had purchased tickets to California, where they had heard there were industrial and farming jobs. Mrs. McCarthy handed her a pink shawl she had knitted herself.

"For that baby girl you're gonna have someday," she said. She herself was headed to Idaho, where her daughter and her daughter's husband owned a small potato farm. "From the potato fields of Ireland to the potato fields of America," she remarked sadly. "It's not what I'd dreamed of." Bess noticed, for the first time, the thin brown lines that marked her forehead.

Mr. Welsh hooked one hand in his suspenders and shook Harry's hand with his other. "Good luck in Chicago, son. You'll do fine there." He couldn't look Harry in the eye; Bess knew he'd bankrupted himself, and she wasn't sure what he was going to do next. He wasn't a young man anymore; thank God, she thought, she and Harry had their youth to fall back on. Harry had already been gaining notoriety in small towns by escaping from various jail cells, a trick that began when the whole troupe was arrested one afternoon in Georgia for performing on a Sunday. Charlotte, the Fat Woman and a new addition to the troupe, had bawled half the night, squeezed with the rest of the group into a concrete twelve-by-twelve cell. When the jailer fell asleep, Harry had picked the lock and let everyone out, and they had sneaked away to a new town before daylight. Now he had plans to bust out of a Chicago cell in front of a group of reporters, where it would be big news, and, he hoped, get himself known before they continued on with another poorly paid act.

Bess had grown to love life on the Welsh circuit. Harry was shy, often keeping to himself and practicing when he wasn't performing, and in those lonely hours Bess had sought the company of the others in the local beer and pool halls. She never again flirted with any of the men she met there but usually cradled a ginger beer and chatted with the women. Harry spent a great deal of time training with an old Japanese man who could swallow oranges and then bring them up again, a practice that thoroughly horrified Bess. But Harry was as fascinated with swallowers as he was with snake charmers, and he spent hours stretching the muscles of his throat to the point of accommodating small potatoes.

But it was in Chicago where Harry found his headlines. He had walked brazenly into the detective headquarters on the afternoon of their arrival and said to the sergeant on duty, "I would like to be locked up, please." The sergeant had laughed out loud and had Harry escorted from the premises. He'd had to return on three consecutive days before anyone would take him seriously, but when they did, and he was handcuffed and locked inside a cell, he'd escaped easily enough. Then he had performed the feat in the city's larger prison, and the following morning his picture was in the paper, next to the headline KING OF HANDCUFFS. He'd woken Bess up waving a stack of newspapers in his hand.

"I'm famous! My picture's in the papers!" He had purchased over a hundred of them, along with envelopes and stamps, and they'd spent all afternoon mailing the clippings to anyone they could think of who might help them get a job.

It had worked. The clippings got the attention of a manager by the name of Martin Beck, the booker for the Orpheum Circuit. He installed Harry and Bess in his popular theater chain, where they gained a temporary notoriety. In *The Omaha Daily News*, Harry was described as "a young lion, with muscles like steel, roaming about the theater like a restless tiger." Bess had never read anything more exquisite. Sometimes, when they were alone at night together, it seemed he thrust his whole being into his dreams. He would wake up heaving, dripping with sweat as if he had just exited some great performance.

They had celebrated that night, but they couldn't maintain their publicity. As the months progressed they booked fewer and fewer acts, and were offered smaller and smaller salaries, until they were forced to move back to New York, where Bess got a sales position in a hat shop. She spent the hours when the shop was empty sewing ribbons onto felt in a cramped back room; Harry went to the offices of the city papers and offered to sell his magic secrets to them for ten dollars. There were no bidders.

Still, through the dark moments, he loved her. He left her notes every morning in the kitchen before going out to search for a booking: *Sunshine of my life, I have had my coffee, have washed out my glass, and am on my way to business.* Sometimes the notes included frivolous poetry: *What is there in the vale of life / half as delightful as a wife?*

After two months, Beck had called with a last-chance offer. If Harry wanted to go to London, he said, he had a contact for him at Scotland Yard. If he could break out of a prison like that, Beck told him, *then* he would be made.

Bess had never traveled abroad. She was desperate to see the elaborate palaces of Europe, the shining taffeta dresses of the

British ladies. The boat was grand, with mahogany banisters and porcelain china. They were staying in the second-class cabin, which had none of those luxuries, but at night she sat on the stairs and listened to the music of the violins from the dining room. She missed her friends from the circus, but not enough to despair; the circus had been one adventure, but Europe was something else entirely. She thought back on her musings that first night on the bridge, that their lives could be glazed with greatness, that intimacy would somehow cascade into remarkable love. The night they married, she had removed her hairpins and her hair had fallen onto her shoulders and she had stood before Harry in the burning lamplight like a spectator of her own performance.

Harry, for his part, was green with seasickness and couldn't keep anything down but ice and lemon juice. By the third evening he was delirious with fever. The pressure of the sorely needed success in Europe, combined with illness, almost broke him. He began talking in his sleep. "They think I break my knuckles to get the cuffs off," he murmured one night, to no one. "They think they know how I does it."

Bess leaned over him and stroked his burning forehead. His eyes were still closed. "It's okay, Harry. You're just dreaming." She looked around. They shared a large dormitory lined with identical cots, but it didn't appear he had woken anyone else.

"But it's not talent," he said. "It's just practicing with every lock till I know how they all work."

Was he conducting an imaginary interview in his sleep? Bess laughed. "I know, Harry."

"I love you, Beth," he muttered, slurring her name. "What would I do without you?"

"I don't know," she said. "I suppose you'd be lost."

When he finally woke up, early the next morning, she was

still awake, watching him. He looked at her intensely, with an expression of such tenderness it made her shiver. He had never looked at her like that before, not even on their wedding night. It was more than infatuation or desire. It was a look that came from years of real love, tested by hardship—the kind of bursting, painful emotion she herself sometimes felt when she cried over tiny babies she'd seen in prams, and he took her in his arms and held her without saying a word.

He tried to stand but ended up knocking over their open vanity cases in the process.

"I've got to get you some more ice," she told him. "You be a good boy while I'm gone." She tied his wrist to the bed, for fear he would somehow stumble out of the room and fall overboard.

"I'll get loose," he said, falling back on the bed. "I've broken outta prisons, you know."

"Not in this condition you won't."

They arrived in Southampton battered and bruised, Harry from his disastrous short trips around the deck for fresh air, and Bess from her many late-night struggles to get him to stay in bed. The port itself was far from glamorous—even more crowded than New York had been, and dirtier. They had to navigate their trunks through a maze of horse droppings to find the railway station. Beck had given them the address of a boardinghouse in London, and they had not even settled in before Harry had swallowed a half gallon of water, washed his face, and sat down at the table with a map of the city to plot out a route to Scotland Yard.

Bess sat down beside him and wrapped her arms around his shoulders. "How do you know they're expecting you?"

"Beck said so."

"What'll you do if they've never heard of you?"

Harry shrugged.

She turned his head toward hers and kissed him. "Don't go just yet. We've only just gotten here. You've only just recovered."

"We're out of money." Harry pulled away. "I've got to go to work."

She knew he was right. "I want to go with you," she said.

Harry looked at her sadly. "My sweet, sweet girl. You know you can't."

"I am your assistant, you know."

Harry thought about it. "I think I have to go in on my own here. Or else they'll think you're helping me somehow. That you sneaked in some kind of lock pick."

Bess surveyed his appearance. "At least change your clothes. You've been wearing those same pants for three days."

Harry looked down. "Have I? I can't remember when I put them on."

After he had gone, in a clean shirt and pressed pants, she fell into a deep sleep. She dreamed of a man who'd grabbed her hand outside her school when she was twelve, a vagabond with swift eyes and tiny crystals of perspiration on his face, and the nun who'd come out of the school lobby and saved her, and the cool glass of water she'd given Bess in her office afterward, and her soft voice saying, "No one will ever hurt you." Except when she looked up the nun wasn't there anymore, and it was Harry standing over her, with his hand on her shoulder.

She had forgotten where she was. She looked out the window and saw clothes flapping from lines in the alley, and two children kicking dust clouds out of the dirt, the shafts of light between the buildings like two wide-open eyes.

"Here's how we fasten the Yankee criminals who come over here and get into trouble," Superintendent William Melville told Harry at the police headquarters. He wrapped Harry's arms around a pillar in the middle of the station and handcuffed him. "Stage handcuffs, they're one thing, but these are real." Melville smiled. "Beck said you'd give me a real laugh. I might just leave you here to teach you a lesson."

Harry smiled back at him, and Melville checked his watch and turned to the door. It was lunchtime.

"Wait," Harry said. "I'll go with you."

When Melville turned around, he saw that Harry had freed himself and was leaning against the pillar, the cuffs dangling from his pinkie finger.

"Here's the way Yankees open handcuffs," he said. Melville looked at him in astonishment, then burst into laughter.

Harry recounted the story to Bess afterward, pacing the room with excitement. "And I convinced him," he went on, "that I'm the real thing, and he put me in touch with an agent here, who booked me for two weeks at fifty dollars a week. He wants me to do the handcuff trick and the Metamorphosis trick."

"Us," Bess corrected. "He wants us to do the tricks."

Harry nodded. "That's what I meant." He took her elbows in his hands. "You and me."

"I think you did it, Harry," she said. "I think we're gonna be something."

"This act isn't going to separate us," Harry said. "It's going to bring us together."

Bess grinned. "Let's go have some tea. Isn't that what people do when they're in London?"

Harry's two-week engagement at the Hippodrome turned into two months. He had thoroughly entertained Superintendent Melville with both his brazenness and his skill, and even though

Victoria Kelly

he would not reveal how his tricks were done, Melville had done him a favor and brought in the papers. A London *Times* reporter was present when Harry broke out of a concrete cell in Scotland Yard in under fifteen minutes, and the paper published the story as an advertisement for his nightly acts. People flooded the theater, bringing with them a dozen handcuffs and restraints, all of which Harry was able to extract himself from. Bess wore her usual white dress and black tights and retrieved the cuffs from the audience members, then brought them to Harry onstage. In the afternoons, while Harry was readying his new tricks to show her, she walked through the London streets, looking in shop windows. She purchased a fancy crimson-covered sketchbook in a department store, and then spent the hours on park benches, drawing. She wanted to remember these days, the small moments you see only when sitting still for a long time—the women in gossamer dresses floating like spirits over the grass, and the lonely carriage drivers who brushed their horses' manes with the tenderness of parents. When she came home, Harry would be fast asleep on the bed. Only half awakening at the sound of the door opening, he would reach out his arms and pull her down with him, and they would nap together until it was time to get up and dress.

A week before they were scheduled to perform in Budapest, Bess convinced Harry to walk with her after lunch. He was too pale, she said. It wasn't healthy. It was cool out, and the sky was glass blue, and she simply had to leave the dark little room in the actors' boardinghouse they had been sharing for weeks. They walked across the park and onto Regent Street, which had some of the most fashionable shopping. The windows were dressed with rope portieres and displayed everything from silver hatpins and porcelain jars of cold cream to glass table lamps.

"The buildings are all so much older than in New York," Bess said. But Harry didn't answer. He was looking up at them with a furrowed brow, and she knew he was thinking of some kind of new trick. "Harry, no—"

"What about bridge jumping?" he mused. "Do you think I could escape the cuffs underwater?"

Bess looked at him, aghast. "Don't you dare."

He shrugged. "I'll think it over."

"Harry, don't. I'm serious." She tried to change the subject. "Look at that." She pointed to a beaded black ball gown with an enormously ballooned bottom, dressing a mannequin in a store window. It was lined with white lace at the cuffs, and exposed the shoulders. "It's exquisite."

Harry looked at her with a twinkle in his eye. "You should try it on."

"That's ridiculous. We can't afford to buy something like that. It wouldn't be decent to go in there and pretend we can afford it."

But Harry was already striding ahead of her, into the shop. "We're Americans," he was saying. "I heard there are so many American heiresses here, looking to marry into titles, that everyone assumes all Americans are rich."

Inside, they learned that the dress was not available for sale. It had been designed for Queen Victoria, the shop owner explained, but her son had recently become ill, and she had cancelled the purchase.

"I'd like to buy it, then," Harry said.

The shop owner raised his eyebrows. "One does not sell Her Majesty's relics, sir."

"How much would it cost if it did not belong to the Queen?"

He thought about it. "Probably fifty pounds. But it's not for sale."

Bess pulled Harry aside. "You most certainly cannot buy me that dress," she whispered. "You're getting carried away. We're not royalty, and we don't have the money."

Harry pressed his hands into hers. "Bess, look at it. It's just my mother's size, don't you think? I'm going to buy it for her."

Bess stepped backward. "Oh," she stammered.

"It's too large for you," he said. "You're such a tiny thing."

She nodded mutely. Harry pulled away and turned to the shopkeeper.

"I'd like to purchase this for my mother," he explained. "She grew up very poor, and I'd like her to have a dress made for a queen. I'll pay you fifty pounds for it."

The shopkeeper shook his head. "I told you, the dress is not for sale."

Harry pulled a bill out of his wallet and waved it at the man. "You're telling me I am standing here as a paying customer and you are refusing to take my money?"

"I am sorry, sir."

Bess put her hand on Harry's arm. "Darling—"

Harry began to shout. "Well why the hell did you put it in your window then?"

The man remained calm. "You Americans are all the same. You come here and think you deserve the world because you have money. But we Britons have something better than money. We have tradition."

"You're a damn fool."

Bess stepped in front of Harry. "Excuse me," she said, assuming as gentle and feminine an air as she could muster, "but I have a proposal for you. What if we promise that this dress will never be worn in Great Britain? We're only passing through. And this would mean the world to my mother-in-law. This way you can earn money on this dress, and you don't have to feel you are betraying your queen."

The shopkeeper's face softened. "It's a matter of respect, you see," he grumbled.

"Of course it is," Bess said. "I would do the same in your shoes."

He considered it. "All right," he agreed. "Provided the dress is never worn here."

They left the store with the dress packaged in pink tissue and tied inside an enormous white box. Harry was pleased but still fuming.

"You'll catch more flies with honey," Bess told him. "You need to work on your temper. You're going to be a public figure."

This brightened his mood. "I am, aren't I?" He smiled. "But that's what I have you for. To be nice for me."

When they got back to the boardinghouse she closed her eyes on the bed to rest and, when she woke, realized it was already the middle of the night. Harry was asleep beside her. He looked so vulnerable in his sleep. She got out of bed for a drink of water, and on the table next to the bed she noticed a box sticking out from underneath the clothes Harry had piled on the surface. Inside was a tiny gold ladybug charm, nestled in velvet.

"Harry." She nudged him awake. "Where did you get this?"

Harry smiled sleepily. "It's for you," he said and closed his eyes again. "He said it's a symbol of love."

"Who said?"

"The jeweler."

She examined the charm. It was intricately made. "When did you do this? I've been with you all day!"

"After my first performance," he murmured. "I wanted the first paycheck to go to you."

Harry wrote to Mrs. Weiss immediately, urging her to meet them in Budapest, where her old home was, and where many of her family members still lived. He had a surprise, he told her, although he would not tell her anything more than that.

Arriving in Budapest was not without its difficulties. As had happened passing through Germany, the police trailed Bess and Harry at all hours of the day and night; they had heard about his feats in Scotland Yard and were convinced he was some kind of undercover agent, spying for Britain. He spent much of the day walking about the cities, thinking about his magic, leaving her to do her stitching, or sketching, or small errands. She knew his work thrived on loneliness. But when he was required to attend any kind of dinner or formal function, he clung to Bess. She pinned up her hair and sat by his side the entire evening, prodding him to speak when she thought he might need to impress someone.

His performance in Hamburg had been a smashing hit, and thirty marks had been charged for admission. This was more than Harry had ever commanded for his act. In America only the poor and the middle class had come to see him perform, but in Hamburg, for the first time, wealthy patrons filled the seats. Men and women wearing furs and polished shoes and carrying crystal spectacles filed into the theater, the room buzzing with anticipation. Martin Beck had been right—the doors were opening for him after all. Bess, concerned that her stage attire was too tawdry for their new audiences, purchased a long dress made of purple taffeta, as they had ceased doing many of the tricks that involved her being bent and locked away, and Harry had taken on the active physical work instead. Her position now was mainly to add an air of femininity to the stage. Harry explained to her that Europeans were much less accepting of women onstage, but Bess understood he was being kind. The audiences responded to him, not to her, and both of them knew it.

Mrs. Weiss traveled across the Atlantic alone, leaving Gladys with Dash, who was selling insurance in Harrison, New Jersey, now and performing small acts of magic at parties on the weekends. She met them at the port in Hamburg, fragile and feverish from the long ocean journey, and they traveled together by train to Budapest, in a second-class coach. Harry had spent most of their savings on the dress, and he was disappointed, Bess knew, to have to take his mother across Europe in such deplorable conditions. He did not tell her what he had in store for her, only kept repeating, to Mrs. Weiss's dismay, that her trip would be unlike anything she had ever experienced. Bess spent much of the train ride with her embroidery on her lap, trying not to interrupt the conversation that flowed back and forth in German between mother and son.

Mrs. Weiss occupied a position in Harry's heart that no one, not even she as his wife, could supplant. She could not help but think of her own mother, and the lack of tenderness they had shared, and how Mrs. Rahner had kept her word and refused to speak to her since her marriage to Harry. The fact was that Harry had both her and Mrs. Weiss, but she had only Harry, and unless she found herself with child soon, this would likely always be so.

If she had thought London dazzling, then Budapest at the turn of the century was even more so. It was the era of the great Hungarian poets—Endre Ady and Mihály Babits, writers she had heard of—and the streets were lined with small coffeehouses with wood-paneled walls and firelit rooms where both men and women bent over books and porcelain cups of hot beverages. Bess wondered why Rabbi and Mrs. Weiss had ever left such a place. There had been some kind of celebration recently, and the buildings were still hung with colored banners.

They entered the city in the pink twilight, the streets echoing with hoofbeats on the hardwood blocks of the great avenues, which were lined with enormous green topiaries. In the carriage on the way to the boardinghouse, Bess looked over at Mrs. Weiss and saw that her eyes were filled with tears. She was gripping her son's hand, but the other hand, the one holding her handkerchief, was white as bone. Bess imagined she was remembering the last time she had been here, with Rabbi Weiss, so many years before, and how young they must have been then, their unlined faces shining on these very streets.

"Has it changed a great deal?" she asked Mrs. Weiss.

The old woman looked toward her, starry-eyed. "Oh, very much. It seems so much . . . more colorful than I remember. All my memories of it are black and gray."

"I imagine my life would be very different if you had not chosen to leave. So I'm grateful that you did," Bess told her.

They stopped at the entrance to a cramped alley, and Harry got out to check on the rooms. Across the street was a covered market, shuttered now with canvas for the evening. Mrs. Weiss shook her head. "Sometimes I wonder—if we had stayed in Pest, would things have been better than they ended up being in America? My husband might not have died so young, and Gladys wouldn't have been injured. And maybe Ehrich wouldn't have left home."

Bess looked around at the paint peeling from the sides of the buildings. Surely this hadn't been what Harry had had in mind? He had planned this trip with such care. "No," she said. "He would have left no matter where you lived. It's just the way he is."

"Yes." Mrs. Weiss nodded. "He is always looking for what is out there."

*

The boardinghouse occupied a narrow space between a grocery and a butcher's shop; inside, the rooms were hardly six feet wide, each fitting only a small bed and a chair. The bathroom was cramped and dirty, at the end of a long hall, and the whole building smelled of cow meat.

The accommodations didn't startle Mrs. Weiss. "*És ist schon,* Harry," she said, studying the view from the window. "It's lovely."

But, as Bess had anticipated, Harry was crestfallen by all the dust. He and Bess usually stayed in lodgings like these, but he had spent more money than they usually did on his mother's room, which was still small and dirty.

Mrs. Weiss waved her hand. "You must leave me now," she said. "I'm tired." Bess imagined it must be difficult for her to have returned to the home she had left so many years ago; when she said good-bye, she must have assumed it would be forever. People who left during those years rarely made it home again. Now she was reunited with the old city, except it was larger and more glamorous than it had been thirty years earlier. There were green parks, and fountains, and stone music halls that had not been there before. Certainly, she could not help being saddened that the place she had loved had become better without her; that she had left for a better life that had disappointed her, and stood now in a past that had blossomed alone.

Through his mother's uncle Heller, whom Harry had contacted upon their arrival, Bess and Harry had planned the surprise party. Uncle Heller gathered everyone who still lived in the old neighborhood and had known the Weisses and took them across Liberty Square toward the Royal Hotel, which Harry had learned was the most luxurious hotel in the city. He and Bess escorted Mrs. Weiss privately into the courtyard of the massive building, where Harry presented her with the voluminous black gown he had purchased in London.

"This," he said, smoothing the fabric, "was made for Queen Victoria." He looked shyly at the ground. "Now it is yours."

Mrs. Weiss cradled the dress in her arms like a fragile child. "What do you mean?" She looked up, confused, at the building with its wide windows and enormous gray cupolas. "This place is like a church," she said. "It is like I am getting married. What are we doing here?"

Harry beamed. "Father never would have imagined I would one day bring you back here like this." He had planned a reception in the palm garden salon, which had been a feat unto itself, as the salon was never used for hosting private parties. Bess, however, had stepped in and won over the management with Harry's story. She had explained how he wanted to crown his mother as a queen, for a few hours. The sentimentality of the plot appealed to the manager. "For so worthy a cause," he told them, "you may have the room for nothing."

When Mrs. Weiss had changed into the dress, Harry led her into the salon, where everyone she had known once who was able to come waited to surprise her. She had not seen any of them in decades; to only a few had she written letters. Uncle Heller, her mother's brother and the family patriarch, had disapproved of her marriage to Rabbi Weiss, and he had disapproved of her move to America. He had told her it would end in disaster. Now, here she was, an old woman standing in the finest hotel in Budapest, in Queen Victoria's gown, and her son was famous, and the walls were papered in gold leaf and she did not have that old life in the squalor of New York any longer, she had only this life, here.

The salon was decorated with black-and-white floor tiles, tapestries, palms, and gilded furniture. In the center of the room was a bubbling blue fountain, the water arcing over the head of a tiny cherub. Mrs. Weiss rested her hands on the edge of the fountain and bent her head.

Bess was alarmed. "Are you all right, Mother?"

"I was just thinking how two weeks ago I was looking at the Sears catalog, thinking that twenty cents for a bread toaster seemed so much. And now here I am standing on the other side of the world in Queen Victoria's dress."

"Ehrich does love you very much. I can only hope I have a son one day who loves me just as much."

The manager entered the room wearing an expensive suit of clothes, the kind that was reserved for royalty. He kissed Mrs. Weiss's hand and knelt before her on one knee. One by one, the other guests, including Harry, knelt as well. The moment had been orchestrated to the last detail.

"Welcome to our establishment," the manager said. "My mother passed away last year, but she would have been proud to see me open this room to you today."

"You are like a fairy queen," Bess whispered, placing a hand on her shoulder. "You are resplendent."

Mrs. Weiss nodded mutely, staring around her in amazement. A line of waiters entered, bearing cups of black coffee and trays of small iced cakes.

Bess stepped aside to allow them to wait on Mrs. Weiss first. "You are happy, though?"

"Oh, yes," she said, taking a cake off the tray. "I keep thinking I'm going to do something wrong. Everyone's looking at me. And I don't know how to be wealthy."

"No one really knows how to be wealthy," Bess said. "Except maybe the king and queen."

"No." Mrs. Weiss shook her head. "You'll be a very good wealthy woman one day. You have vigor."

Bess laughed.

"Did Harry ever tell you that I was a widow when I married the rabbi?"

"You were? I didn't know that."

"Yes. I married my first husband when I was just seventeen. But we were only married for six months. He got involved with some bad men, and lost a great deal of money, and there was an argument over it. He died in a duel."

Bess grabbed her sleeve. "That's terrible!"

She looked around the room. "It was a great scandal. Even my family was ashamed. These people I knew once, they came to this party, but that's still what they all see now, when they look at me." She paused. "I met the rabbi a few years later, and he was much older than I was, but he loved me, and he didn't care that I was a widow. So I married him."

"But did you love him?" Bess asked.

"In time, I did. But you see, when Harry brought you home, I could tell how much you already loved him back. That's why I liked you. Because I knew you'd give him what I never gave my husband." She reached for Bess's hand. "Don't worry," she said. "You'll have a child. God wouldn't make you only to leave you alone."

Bess looked at the floor. "I'm not alone, though. I have Harry."

"He's a good boy," Mrs. Weiss said, patting Bess's hand. "But I can tell he still leaves you lonely sometimes."

Bess glanced at Harry; he was standing in the corner of the room, quietly observing the proceedings. Bess felt a pang of despair. She did feel alone, the only stranger in this salon, among a roomful of people who had once shared a life together. She wondered if Harry felt toward her the same fierce love and sense of duty he felt toward his mother. His black eyes took in the room, proudly. He didn't stand with her, or look out for her. He seemed, in fact, to have forgotten her entirely.

Still, Mrs. Weiss was right. She loved him with a wonder that crushed the flesh against her chest.

"I will never betray you," she had sworn to him, years ago on the golden beach of Coney Island. She had taken a vow, and meant it. And she could be angry with him, or hurt. But she could never un-love him.

Chapter 8

THE PRESS

June 1929

In the crisp white sheets of her hotel room, Bess woke in a cold sweat. "Harry?" She reached for the pillow beside her. "Darling, I thought I heard something."

He was not there. The room was dark except for the sliver of yellow light from the hallway under the door. The space beside her was cool, the sheets unwrinkled. With slow awareness, she put her hands to her face and felt the creped, tender skin under her eyes. She was not in her twenties anymore; she was much older, and Harry was gone. The sea air coming through the window covered her like a fine mist.

Charles had invited her to his offices, not far from her hotel. But there was still the problem of Stella. Bess longed to tell her what she was really doing here in New Jersey. Stella had never understood why Bess had continued to devote herself to Harry wholeheartedly after his death. It should have been a new beginning, she said; but to Bess, Harry's death had never been an end. Besides her financial burdens, she could not rid herself of the knowledge that Harry was desperate to reach her, and that the message he intended for her carried enormous weight. Yet she had, from the minute he closed his eyes for the last time, clung to the hope that it would not be just his words that would reach her but his voice, his whole form. Surely, such a course existed. She liked to think that the dead were separated from the living by a matter almost like cement—fluid, liquid for the first years after death, until it hardened and became impassable. She had to reach him while she still could.

Stella was sitting at the breakfast table in the sitting room, reading the morning papers in a white lace nightgown. She looked up when she saw Bess.

"Good morning," she said, gesturing toward the window. "It's an absolutely divine day. We must get dressed and go to the beach."

Bess leaned down and kissed her on the cheek. "Of course. I have to run out for an hour or so first to sign some paperwork."

Stella sighed. "You work too hard, you know." Bess raised her eyebrows, and Stella laughed. "I just wish you'd sell the tearoom and let Fred and me help you out with money, now that we finally have some. You always helped us and the kids out. Now it's our turn."

Bess shook her head. "I *like* running the tearoom. You just want me to sell it because it has Harry's name on the door."

"Even if it isn't making any profit?"

"It is making a profit!"

"You can't fool me." Stella sighed. "Fred knows business. And he says you don't know a thing about running one. You shouldn't be giving away as much food and drink as you do."

Bess winced. Fred was right; she didn't know anything about keeping books or calculating margins of profit. She knew how to throw a party, and she knew how to fit her body into a wooden trunk; that was all she knew, and little good either of them did her now.

"If you feel the need to criticize," she said coldly, "you're welcome to stay at home the next time I have an event."

Stella set down her teacup. "Oh, come on. I'm sorry. I didn't mean to make you angry. I just meant—at least let Fred give you some advice."

"I'll think about it." Bess had told Stella the extent of her debts, but she hadn't shared her belief that Harry had left her with a way to extricate herself from them. She hid her desperate, late-night searches of the house from her sister. Stella would call her a fool.

"We can lend you money—we don't have to give it to you."

Bess shook her head. "Absolutely not. You need that money. You're going to have a new baby in the house."

Bess recalled how much she'd adored Fred when he started coming to the house in Brooklyn on Friday nights, courting Stella. Bess was in high school at the time, and Fred had seemed so much older, so much more mature than the boys she went to school with. He was tall and handsome, and he used to put his arm around her shoulders, always protective of her. When he married Stella in the courthouse, Bess wore a blue dress and carried a bouquet of lilies and stood behind Stella. All these years later, he still loved Stella, and he still loved Bess as he would a sister.

Harry had often treated Fred poorly, however. It wasn't intentional; Harry had never had any close male friends, and he wasn't successful at making them. Perhaps out of a feeling of insecurity, he'd assumed a superior air around the tall, genial Fred. Harry kept making more and more money, and Fred kept making the same, plodding politely through his days at the bank all those years. But despite his success, Harry had always been envious of Fred. He never said so out loud, but Bess thought she knew why. It was because Fred was a happy man at heart. He never wished for more than he had. The oil investment, which had happened after Harry died, had come about quite by accident. Harry, on the other hand, was never satisfied. The money, the fame, Bess—none of it had brought him peace.

Bess looked at her watch. "You go on down to the beach, and I'll meet you by the bathing house at noon."

Downstairs in the lobby, she asked if she had received any messages. The clerk checked her box and came back empty-handed. She took a sip of tea in the salon for energy but couldn't bear to delay any longer.

The news offices were adjacent to City Hall, set back a few streets from the boardwalk. It was midmorning, and throngs of men rushed back and forth across the green lawns with briefcases in their hands. Apparently, Saturdays were as busy as weekdays for newspapermen.

She entered the office lobby and was greeted by the clatter of two dozen typewriters. It was everything she had imagined—a room full of men in slim-cut suits and knit ties, calling over cubicle walls to each other, the air gray with smoke, the secretaries with their pretty bobbed hair and straight tailored suits. There was no reception desk, and Bess turned to one of the men rushing past her through the double doors. "Pardon me. Can you tell me if there is a Mr. Charles Radley in today?"

The man looked at her blankly for a minute, then waved his hand vaguely in the direction of the back of the room. She scanned the rows of desks but could not identify the top of his head among the dozens crammed into the corners. She removed her gloves; her hands were clammy from the heat. She did not remember there being so much news to write about when she had first come here with Harry. Back then, it had been a city that was still establishing itself. Now, she imagined, given its growing reputation as a symbol of the current age—all the excesses of luxury, crime, and sexuality—there was quite a bit of scandal to fill the pages of newsprint.

She felt a hand on her shoulder. It was Charles, standing just inside the doorway, his glasses slightly askew, a leather satchel slung over his shoulder.

"Oh! You startled me!"

His face reddened. "Did I? I'm sorry."

"No, no, it's all right. I was distracted. I was just . . . remembering." She patted the sweat off her forehead with the edge of her glove. She noticed that a few of the secretaries closest to the door were glancing at them discreetly. He seemed like a lonely man; she was glad to make them think he had some famous friends.

"It's loud in here," he said. "Would you like to go down to the water?"

She nodded, relieved.

"I have to tell you," he said when they stepped onto the lawn, "I didn't expect to see you here today. But it's been on my mind all night. I can't imagine what it is you have to talk to me about."

It was a white morning, and hot; she watched couples in rolling chairs being pushed down the boardwalk, the women inside fanning themselves languidly. The colors were magnificent, the whole city like a confection—the pinks of the taffy, the pale cream of the sand, the yellows of the billboards . . . The piers, too, were crowded with dancers in red taffeta costumes and brightly dressed showmen, trying to lure in tourists. Charles helped her down the ramp onto the beach, where long planks of wood led to the ocean.

"The thing is," Bess said, "I don't think you'll believe a word I have to say."

Charles looked at her strangely. "Why is that?"

"Because you never met my husband. If you had, it might be different."

"But I did," he said. "I met him once."

Bess reached for his arm. Her heart was beating rapidly. "You did? You said last night that you'd never met him."

"I said I never *knew* him. But I shook his hand when he came out to do the jump on Young's Pier, when I was eleven."

Bess's heart sank.

"I was fascinated by your husband."

Bess sighed. She appreciated Harry's fans, but they frustrated her at the same time. "Let me ask you something," she said carefully. "Do you believe in magic?"

"I believed in your husband's magic when I was little. But do I believe in it now?" He laughed. "No."

"Do you believe that after we die . . . we can come back somehow?" She and Harry had had elaborate conversations about what lay beyond death. He had rejected her Catholic notions of white mansions and eternal rest, the whole idea of "rising" to something else. He believed in a murkier afterlife, that the dead still walked beside the living, perhaps only on a different plane. Sometimes, these people were even visible, like gray strands in the midst of color. If you lifted the veil, he said, then you could see them. But how to accomplish that—he did not know.

Charles pressed his lips together. "I'm not sure." He squinted at her. "Why are you asking me all this?"

They had made it to the end of the wooden walkway, and the white-crusted ocean stretched out in front of them, the shoreline crowded with splashing bathers. It was difficult to disguise her nervousness. She felt as if she were courting someone. "You know, as everyone does, that I've been trying to reach Harry. And I think he might be trying to contact me—through you." She looked at him. "Is that . . . strange?"

Charles gazed at her sharply, as if assessing her sincerity. When she didn't crack a smile, his expression turned to one of bewilderment. "Why do you think that he would be using me?"

Her voice was shaking. "Can I trust you?" she asked. "I don't even know you."

"You can trust me."

He seemed so sincere, so genuine. She knew she had no choice but to tell him the truth, crazy as she knew it would sound. "You see," she began, "in the past several weeks, I've come across two photographs which seemed to have a message embedded in them. The strange thing was, when I found out who took them . . . they were both yours." She turned away from him, toward the ocean. "And I'm not sure why that would be, if he didn't have a connection to you. But I'm also afraid . . . I may have been searching for something that wasn't there."

"I believe you," he said softly.

"You do?"

"Yes."

Charles removed his glasses and began polishing them with his shirtsleeve. "You know I'm a photographer at the *Press*. What I didn't tell you is that I've—" He hesitated, as if he were afraid she would laugh at him. "I've applied to the seminary."

Bess blinked at him. "You're going to be a *priest*?"

"I'm not sure yet."

"But—I saw you flirting with that woman last night!"

Charles stuck his hands in his pockets and squinted at the horizon, where the sea receded into the curve of the earth. "I'm shy. I've never even had a real relationship with a woman." The words came out painfully. "I'd like to try to see . . . if it's possible. Before I make any decisions."

"And the lie? About being a banker named Wallace?"

He blushed. "Sometimes it's easier for me to speak to people I don't know if I pretend to be someone else."

Bess felt a twinge of sympathy for him. How many times had she, too, pretended? How many times had she wished no one would recognize her?

"Do you think I'm foolish?"

Bess shook her head. "People treat me differently," she said, "when they know who I am. To the world, I am Harry Houdini's widow. It is nice sometimes to be judged for myself, as my own person."

"Do you think that, possibly, Harry led you to me because of my spiritual leanings? Because he knew I would believe you?"

She considered it. "I've never tried communicating through a priest before. Harry was Jewish, you know. And he wasn't a good Jew. I certainly am not a good Catholic."

"Perhaps it's because I'm *not* a priest yet. I think people who are in between the secular world and the religious world have the most open minds of anyone. Perhaps he thought I could be a link between the two."

Even in her white straw hat she could feel the sun burning on her cheeks. It was the kind of brilliant, steaming day when she wished that she was anywhere else—somewhere like California, in a bungalow by the studios, with a little greenhouse on the property, waiting for lunch to be served in the garden, and for Harry to step out of his office to join her.

"What I think," Charles ventured, "is that you are afraid because you don't know what happened to your husband after he died. You are afraid he had nowhere to go." He looked down, at the sand. "I know because for a very long time I felt that way, after my mother died, when I was still a boy. And I couldn't bear the thought of her becoming . . . nothing."

Late in Harry's career they had found themselves staying in the same hotel as Sarah Bernhardt, in downtown Boston. The great actress had had her right leg amputated a few months before and had sunk into a deep depression, and she came to watch Harry perform. Afterward, they'd shared an automobile back to the hotel. Bess recalled Sarah's heavy black coat, long to her ankles to hide her wooden leg, and her bursting confection of a hat, red and feathered.

"Mr. Houdini," she had said to Harry. "You must possess some extraordinary powers to perform such marvels."

Harry had laughed. But Sarah had gripped his hand in hers. "Won't you use it to restore my limb for me?"

Bess had realized, at the same time as Harry, that the question was not in jest. Sarah was looking at him eagerly, her eyes filling with tears.

"Good heavens," Harry had said, aghast. "You are asking me to do the impossible."

"But you *do* the impossible."

"I'm afraid you exaggerate my abilities," he'd said, and Sarah had studied him for a long moment, as if she were hoping he was testing her, before releasing her grip on his hand.

Bess recognized a glimpse of this desperation in herself now. She remembered Harry's own tears as he got out of the car at the hotel, leaving Sarah inside. He had never meant to deceive anyone. But what if he was deceiving her now, without even realizing it?

Still, a chill ran through her. "There's something about you . . ." she said to Charles. "Something very powerful. I'm not sure what it is." She thought of her initial attraction to Ford, her certainty in his goodness. But those feelings, she realized now, had been tinged with lust, while what she felt toward Charles was more like a friendship.

Charles put his hand on her arm. "You know, nothing may come of your search."

"I know."

"So why did you still want to meet me today? When you found out last night that I didn't know Harry after all?"

"Well," Bess said. "I suppose I was hoping I could see some more of your pictures. That maybe I would find something else."

"You're welcome to see what I have. But"—he held his palms to the air—"I've been a photographer professionally since I was eighteen years old. There are thousands. I'm not sure I even have copies or negatives of all of them."

"My sister is here with me. She thinks we're here for a vacation. But she's going back to New York tomorrow. I could tell her I want to stay on. Do you think we could meet then?"

"Of course." Charles looked out at the ocean.

Bess bent down and slid a handful of sand through her fingers. Despite the heat, it was cool to the touch. "When I was younger, I dreamed of growing old in California, in a house with palm trees and lemon trees in the yard. But now there is too much holding me to New York."

"People probably ask you this all the time. But do you really think your husband had a spiritual connection to something when he did his magic? That, while he was alive, he had some kind of foothold in the other world?"

Bess pursed her lips together. She thought of the eerie incidents that had befallen them over the course of their marriage, the indications that they may have had some kind of reciprocity with the other side that had never quite materialized. "If those kinds of powers could be accessed so easily," she said sadly, "I wouldn't have spent all these years looking for him."

At one she went to find Stella at the bathing house, but she wasn't there. Bess only then realized how long she'd talked with Charles. She was an hour late, and Stella had likely gotten hungry and gone off in search of lunch.

It was so hot that her dress stuck to her. She trudged up the sand back to the hotel and went to the room to change into her swimming costume. Even before she went inside she knew something was wrong. The door was ajar. When she pushed it open she saw clothes everywhere.

"Stella? Stella?"

Stella came out of the bedroom, her hair wet and pulled back into a bun. Her suitcase was in her hand.

"I thought something happened! I thought someone had broken in!" Only then did Bess realize Stella was crying. She stepped back. "What is it? What's wrong?"

"It's Abby," Stella sobbed. "She's in the hospital. Something's wrong with the baby."

"Oh, God."

"I have to go back tonight. But I can't find my train ticket. I've been looking everywhere."

"Don't worry about that. Buy a new one."

"You can stay. I don't want you to cut your weekend short."

Bess thought of Charles. She would have to wire him immediately. She pulled Stella into a hug. "Of course I'll go back with you."

Chapter 9

YOUNG'S PIER

October 1906

Inside the federal prison in the district of Washington, Bess awaited the outcome of Harry's latest stunt. The warden's tiny office was crammed with a dozen deputies, police officials, and reporters.

Warden Harris had been skeptical of Bess's presence. "This prison is no place for a lady," he had explained to Harry, and it had taken some convincing to allow her inside.

It amused Bess that in the course of only a year she had become "a lady." It had not been very long ago that they had happily slept in hotel rooms crawling with bedbugs and washed in basins stained red with rust. But Harry's notoriety in Europe and Russia had found its way back to America, and after fifteen months overseas, far longer than they had anticipated, he was invited to open in New York's Colonial Theatre. Bess assisted him during his act, which began with a new stunt he had perfected, in which he swallowed a packet of needles followed by a few yards of string, then proceeded to remove the items from his mouth, with the needles threaded onto the string. It was a trick he had come across, like many, in an old book of magic in a Paris antiques store.

She dressed like a lady now, too. She shopped the fur and fine dress floors at Macy's and had the boxes delivered directly to their new home on West 113th Street. She purchased haute couture from Paris and wore it to the racetrack in Saratoga, where American designers often hired models to show off their latest designs. In their new home, Harry installed a massive eight-foot mirror in his bathroom, where he practiced his sleight-of-hand tricks, and an even larger tub to practice his underwater breathing techniques.

The United States Jail in Washington was an enormous stone fortress. Getting inside the gates alone had taken twenty minutes. Now Bess, Harry, and ten reporters filed down the hallway and stood with the warden before Cell No. 2 on Murderers' Row. There were seventeen cells in the wing, all of them occupied, and the cheers and shouts of the inmates were deafening.

"This is the cell that held Charles Guiteau after he assassinated President Garfield," the warden explained. He gestured toward a heavily reinforced square room with brick walls and a thick combination lock securing the iron door. "The door has been dug three feet into the earth to fortify it."

"But—it's occupied!" Bess said. Shaking in the corner of the cell was a large black man with his knees drawn to his chest. He looked terrified.

"Mr. Houdini will be safe, won't he?" Harry's press agent, Whitman Osgood, asked the warden. Per the agreement, Harry would be left alone, except for the prisoners, to attempt his escape. Harry laughed. "Whit, I'm the one who asked to do this trick."

"In an *empty* cell," his agent argued.

"We never specified that."

"Harry, it was *assumed*."

Every prisoner housed in this wing was surely a murderer, but Bess felt a wave of compassion for the man in the cell. Everyone was staring at him. "It's all right," she told him. "It's just Harry Houdini. You've heard of him, haven't you?"

"Houdini!" a man called from down the row. "Let us out!"

"We'll have to search you, of course," the warden told Harry. "If you choose to go forward, that is?"

"I would expect no less," Harry replied. He began taking off his shoes and socks. "And yes, I'm going to go on as planned."

The warden cleared his throat and looked at Harry's press agent. "Mr. Osgood. I believe it would be prudent for Mrs. Houdini to retreat to the office at this time?"

Bess burst out laughing. "Trust me, Mr. Harris. I've seen my husband naked many times before."

Harry smiled, embarrassed. "Of course you have, dear, but it's probably best to wait for me there. Or should they handcuff you and lead you off?"

"It's all right, I'll go willingly," she said. She felt the color rush to her cheeks. She was proud of Harry, certainly, but since their trip to Europe it had become clear that he would have more success performing on his own, for exactly such a reason. Many of his escapes required him to expose himself completely to assert the authenticity of the trick. A fully dressed lady beside him, concealing whatever tools a dress might hide, would only discredit her husband.

Bess was escorted to the office and took a seat by the window, where she sipped her tea and listened to the skeptical chatter of the prison guards.

"Do you really think he'll pull it off today?" one of them asked her.

"Of course."

The guard shook his head. He was a heavyset man with a thick head of hair. "I've been working here for fifteen years. It's impossible. I'm telling you—"

"But he did escape from Scotland Yard," one of them interrupted.

"Those good-for-nothin' Brits." The heavy guard shook his head. "They don't know what they're doing."

"Guiteau was hanged here, wasn't he?" Bess asked. "Do things like that ever make you think the place is haunted?"

"I've seen all kinds of strange things here," the guard said. "Things you wouldn't believe."

"You'd be surprised how much I would believe."

The warden and the reporters came into the office. Warden Harris checked his watch. "He's on the clock now. We'll see how he does."

The reporters pulled their chairs around Bess. "Do you know how he does his escapes?" one of them asked her.

Bess always avoided this question; she knew everything, of course, but she liked to keep some mystery around Harry's acts.

"She's not gonna tell us that," the heavy guard said. "Then no one would quit asking her how it's done."

The reporter changed angles. "What would you do if Harry fails to escape today?"

Bess smiled. "Do? Why, I would do what I always do around this time of the afternoon. I would go back to the hotel and wash for dinner."

They were not amused. "But wouldn't you be upset?"

Bess took a long sip of tea before responding. "My husband, you see, has escaped from far more terrible places than this. I imagine he could even find his way into and out of your homes at night without your ever knowing."

The men sat back, startled. Before they could muster any response, there was a knock on the door. The warden opened it to find Harry, standing in the corridor with his clothes back on. Bess looked at her watch. It had been exactly twenty-one minutes.

"I let all of your prisoners out," Harry said, wiping his brow. The guards jumped to their feet. "But then I locked them all in again."

"What the devil are you talking about?" the warden demanded. The group rushed outside to find the eight other prisoners in the cellblock, including the black man from Guiteau's cell, locked in entirely different cells than they'd been in before.

Bess lingered in the back of the group with Harry. "You mustn't do things like that, Harry," she whispered. "People don't understand your humor."

Afterward they took the first train to New York, where Harry had scheduled a series of rehearsals that weekend for an upcoming act. The idleness of waiting for him was difficult. That evening Bess wandered around Macy's department store, looking for something to occupy her time. The building had opened only a few years before, and the floors and walls still glistened. When she had first become wealthy enough for shopping to be a pastime, the department store had enthralled her. It advertised itself as "a place where almost anything may be bought," and she was a woman who could buy almost anything. And people had begun to recognize her; the store clerks whispered when she approached, and stepped up to help her before she had even approached the counters. They called her famous.

And she loved the crowds; she loved the soft smells of the perfumes and the long carpeted avenues between displays. But tonight they had been invited to Sherry's for a party given by the insurance magnate James Hazen Hyde, and she had convinced Harry to give up his work for a few hours. She heard the restaurant had been transformed into a royal French garden for the occasion, with real grass on the floor. And she wanted to surprise

Harry with a new dress, one with the scandalously low Gibson girl neckline coming into style.

She found Harry at his desk at home after she had dressed for dinner; he was scribbling furiously in a notebook.

When he saw her in her diamond earrings, a glass of wine in her hand, he stopped writing. "Dear, I don't think I'm up for dinner tonight. I'm exhausted."

Bess's heart sank; he didn't even mention the dress, how beautiful she looked in it. "That just means you want time to work on your tricks. Instead of spending time with me." A wave of despair came over her. Didn't he see how integral she was to his success? She fielded the questions from reporters so he didn't have to. She sewed his clothes when he ripped them and ran him a bath when his muscles ached from so many rehearsals. His accomplishments in the prison were hers as well as his; she deserved to celebrate with him. And to cancel at the last minute when the hosts had gone to such lengths for the party would be insulting.

He snatched the wineglass from her. "I don't want you drinking this stuff anymore. You never know what you're saying when you drink."

Bess grabbed the glass back, splashing some of the wine onto the carpet. "I know perfectly well what I'm saying. I've had one sip. You didn't even want to come back to New York today until I made you. You hardly even see your mother anymore."

Harry's eyes narrowed. He stood up quickly, and Bess winced. She knew better than to imply any kind of disrespect toward his mother. But he only took a napkin from the table and knelt down on his knees to mop up the spill.

"I'm sorry," she said softly. "I didn't mean that. I only meant that I'm lonely."

"How can you be lonely?" Harry demanded, still blotting the

stain. "You have everything you could have dreamed of. You're a society woman now. You can go anywhere you like."

Bess was quiet. "You know why I'm lonely," she said finally.

Harry stopped cleaning but did not look up. "I can't help you with that, Bess. We're just not meant to have children."

"We could adopt a child."

"You have a dog."

Bess scoffed. "A dog's no substitute for a child." Besides, even Carla, their Russian Pomeranian, was always left behind in New York under the care of the housekeeper when they traveled.

"Well, right now we can't adopt. In a few years, when I'm more secure in my career, then we can talk about it. But you can't drag a child around the world like this. It's not fair." He stood up. "I'm just very, very tired. And we have to pack our cases again tonight. We have to leave earlier than we planned for Atlantic City."

Bess watched him turn away. "Is it because you're afraid there's something wrong with you?" she said. "That maybe you aren't capable of making a child?" Harry stopped but didn't turn around. Bess's voice broke. "Or what if it's me? Did you ever think about that? Did you ever think about what it would feel like to be a woman who can't give her husband a baby? What use am I then? You have your work, but what do I have?"

Harry turned around. The hardness in his face had disappeared. He looked sad, and old for the first time in his life. "Bess," he said. He took her in his arms and ran his fingers through the back of her hair. "You have me."

"But I don't have you. We've been invited to the most beautiful evening of the season, and you won't go with me."

Harry sighed. "You know how I feel about those parties. My head's just too full of work right now to carry on a conversation about business or politics."

Bess set her jaw to keep her lip from trembling. She would not let Harry ruin her night. "It's all right," she said. "I'll go alone."

She expected him to protest, but he only looked at her surprised. "Are you sure?"

"Yes." She picked up her handbag. She thought of the candlelit tables and the chairs garlanded with roses, waiting for her arrival. "I'm very sociable, you know. *I* can talk about politics all night."

✳

Young's Million Dollar Pier had been open for only a few months, but it had become a sensation among tourists. Built as an arcade and amusement hall, it was not yet as famous as Steel Pier, but Harry had chosen it as the location for his jump because the closest jetty was over a hundred yards away. The millionaire John Young, who had built the pier, met them on their arrival and took them to survey the site. He had booked Harry to give a performance to attract attention to his new project. Harry would jump, handcuffed, into the ocean, free himself, and come ashore. The publicity from the jump would help sell tickets to his theater show, which would take place the following three nights in the pier's theater.

Bess took a liking to Young immediately; he was a natural showman, like Harry. Everything about him was grand, down to his colorful neckties and his perfectly coiffed hair. Part of his charm was his careful attentiveness. He complimented Bess on her filigreed brooch, resting at the base of her neck. "The pier is almost two thousand feet long," he explained. "But you don't have to worry. It's very sturdy; it was built with concrete. There's a concert hall, a theater, and a telegraph station inside. We are finishing the aquarium right now. There will be sea creatures on display I guarantee you've never seen."

Harry followed them inside, but Bess could tell he was barely listening. His eyes were darting across the room, examining the structure from every angle. It was early springtime, but the ocean was cold and rough, and the sea spray came up to the windows, the salt caking the glass. She wondered if he was concerned. He rarely told her about any hesitations. "My chief task," he liked to say, "is to conquer my own fear. If I can do that, I can do anything."

The inside of the pier was like a glamorous hotel. There was music playing softly from a piano across the room, and shining white floors. Young led them toward the center of the building, which opened onto a vast lawn, cluttered with sculptures and small potted trees. "This is my home," he boasted. "When the post office delivers my mail, they deliver it to Number One Atlantic Ocean."

Bess was awed. She and Harry had seen a great many spectacles in Europe, but a house in the ocean was not one of them. Across the lawn, the gray stone of Young's residence glistened like glass.

"I had no idea this was here," she said. "From the outside, you can't even tell." A cold burst of air rushed over the lawn. Bess wrapped her mink stole more tightly around herself. "It is cold, isn't it, Harry? Perhaps we'd better go inside so you can warm up before you perform." She could tell he was distracted. He did not like being in the company of others, besides her, for very long.

Harry nodded. "Yes, that's a good idea."

Young led them inside the house, and Bess let out of a cry of amazement. The foyer walls were made entirely of colored seashells.

"It's marvelous."

"My wife designed the inside," he explained. "She apologizes that she cannot be here. She has an engagement in New York and won't be back until tomorrow."

Young had invited them to stay with him. He showed them to

their room so that they could rest before Harry's stunt, which had been billed for four o'clock that afternoon. Over three thousand people were expected to attend.

The room was more traditionally decorated than the foyer, with silk wallpaper and thick Persian carpets. Bess unlaced her shoes and lay down on the bed.

"The water's cold today," Harry said, looking out the window. The room, on the fourth floor of the house, was two stories higher than the pier and looked out over the writhing ocean. "If this were a river, it would be frozen."

Bess tried to sit up but was suddenly overcome by wooziness. She lay down again and put her hand to her forehead. "Maybe you should postpone the stunt if it's too cold."

Harry pressed his hands against the glass. "No. I can survive in cold water."

"Come here and feel my head. I think it's very warm."

Harry sat down next to her and put his palm against her cheeks and forehead. "You are warm. Maybe you shouldn't be outside today."

Bess looked at him. "I have to be there!"

"But you really don't look well," he assured her. "And you know how you can be with these jumps."

He was right about that. Of all his tricks, the bridge and pier jumps were the ones she feared the most. He trained for them, submerging himself in ice baths, gradually lowering the temperature to under thirty degrees to ensure that he could still hold his breath in temperatures so low. "Complete mental serenity" he called his experience in the baths. But Bess had her doubts. She suspected the baths were extremely painful, even for him. She tried to disguise her concern, but the danger in bridge and pier jumping was very real. What the audience never knew was that Harry always had with him a rope man, who was instructed to go down and retrieve him if he did not appear after two minutes. This had not happened yet, but certainly one's luck could not last forever. Harry was often careless with his life. For his Detroit bridge jump, the river had frozen over the night before, and he had had to cut a hole into the ice so he could continue with the performance.

She was feeling poorly, it was true, but she was still saddened by their argument the night before. She hated the coldness that came over Harry whenever he was immersed in his work. While her ability to see through his new tricks had once enthralled him, recently it seemed to frustrate, and even insult, him. When he was attentive to her, he was the most loving man. But now he seemed to be more attentive to his work than to her, on an endless quest to earn larger audiences, greater fame. She suspected it was a result of his having achieved a little fame, but not enough to secure their future. She knew he worried over how to keep himself relevant in an increasingly competitive field. Whenever word reached him that another magician had stolen one of his tricks or claimed he could outdo him, Harry would rush off to the magician's next performance to challenge the man and reclaim his title. She felt so much less a part of his world than she had when they had shared the stage. The more success he achieved on his own, the more Bess's value seemed to lie in assuring his emotional well-being, boosting the confidence that waxed and waned according to his publicity.

Finally she agreed to stay inside and rest for the afternoon. Harry kissed her forehead distractedly and went out to meet his rope man and the rest of the crew, who had just arrived on the train, and to examine the site of the jump more closely. Bess changed into a silk robe, lay on her side, and tried to sleep. Outside she could hear the wind rattling the windows. The sky was growing gray, and the clouds were coming in.

Ten minutes after Harry left, there was a knock on the door.

Relieved, she climbed woozily out of bed and padded her way, barefoot, across the carpet. Of course he had come back to ask her to go with him to the jump. He needed her.

But it wasn't Harry in the hall; it was Young, bearing an armful of white towels.

"My wife told me to put these in your room, but I forgot," he confessed.

Bess blinked. "Thank you. I didn't notice they were missing." Surely someone as rich as he had staff to do such things? "Harry's just left."

Young looked at his watch. "Of course. I should be going out there soon as well. It's already past three o'clock. When are you going down?"

"Actually, I'm staying here to rest. I'm not feeling well." She wondered if he could read from her expression that they had had an argument.

"I'm so sorry to hear that." Young looked past her into the room. "Do you mind if I set these down?"

Bess took a step backward. "Of course, I'm sorry. It is your house after all. Please come in."

Young closed the door behind him and set the towels on a table by the window. Looking at the sky, he said, "It's a good thing we're doing this within the hour. There's bad weather coming in."

Bess went over to his side and followed his gaze out the window. "I'm sure Harry will be fine. He's done this kind of thing before, in much worse weather."

Young turned to her. "I must admit, I was surprised by how young you both are. I had thought you older."

Bess laughed. "Is that a compliment?"

"Of course. Actually, you are much more beautiful than your photographs in the papers."

"That's quite kind, I think." She blushed as his hand brushed against hers. She had never stood so close to any man who was not Harry. She felt that familiar rush of blood run through her. Young was not as handsome as Harry, and he was at least ten years older, but he had a confidence that reminded her of the Harry Houdini she had first seen onstage.

Suddenly, turning from the window, he seized her hand. She looked at him, astonished. "What are you doing?"

He pulled her against him and kissed her, hard, on the mouth.

But she didn't pull back. It felt nice. Not for the first time, she wondered if she had rushed into marriage too soon. If she hadn't married Harry, would her life have been more fulfilled? Could she have had children?

John Young led her toward the bed. She followed him blindly. "You don't have to be afraid," he said. "You do find me attractive, don't you? I find you very attractive."

She tried to picture Harry's face, to inspire her to act quickly, to move away from him before things got out of hand. But strangely, the Harry of her imagination was muted, his features dulled to gray, and the woman who had married him was slipping away, too.

"I'm not afraid," she said.

She stood, trembling, as he reached behind her to untie her robe. She tried to envision that it was not John Young standing in front of her but Harry, and that he desired her the way he had desired her ten years before, when she was an eighteen-year-old girl, and he had gripped her arms and kissed her fiercely on the beach.

Young pulled the robe off her shoulders. She stood naked before him, shivering. He reached out and placed his hand on her back, then pulled her roughly toward him. She arched her back so that her hips were against his. "Beatrice," he moaned.

Bess stepped back, alarmed. No man had ever called her that except Harry. Suddenly, she felt exposed. Outside, there was a loud swell of voices. People had begun cheering. Harry must have arrived on the pier. He was fifty feet below her, right outside the window. She grabbed her robe and covered herself, then reached behind her head and repinned some of the hair that had fallen out. "Go." She tried to steady her voice. "It's already three-thirty."

Young's face reddened. "*You* wanted this," he said angrily. "You're nothing but a goddamn tease." He stalked out the door, slamming it behind him.

When he had gone she fell onto the bed and felt numb. The wind was growing stronger outside. She thought about her mother's warnings, that Harry would make her into a bad woman. She certainly was a bad woman now, but she didn't blame Harry for it, or even Young. She had been willing—frozen, but willing. How could she even have contemplated being with someone else? She felt the emptiness coming over her again, realizing how close she had come to betraying Harry. Was she really so weak that she would break her vows over a few harsh words? She wondered if it was possible that she had imagined it all, that her fever had brought on hallucinations. But when she looked at the table she saw the white towels piled neatly by the window and she knew it had been very real.

There would be three thousand people, Young had said. Usually Harry prefaced the stunt by talking for ten minutes or so, then made a great show of putting on the handcuffs and leaning over the railing to examine the water. When he jumped in, it usually took him only a minute to release himself, although sometimes he took longer to increase the suspense.

She looked at her watch. It was a quarter to four. She pictured Harry at the end of the pier, stripping to bathing trunks in the icy cold, holding out his wrists to a policeman to be handcuffed. He liked to chat with the policemen and some of the reporters before the stunt; it put him at ease. John Young, certainly, would partake in the banter. But he would not say, "I just came from your room." He would not say, "I have seen your wife naked and she is beautiful." He would shake Harry's hand with the same hand that had touched her, and Harry would climb over the railing and one of his assistants would hold him in place until he gave the cue, the rush of wind stronger now than before, and the gray ocean churning underneath; then he would be pushed into a free fall, and he would drop, and no one would see him until he emerged again.

She had to go to him. She could not leave him alone down there. She had been to the brink of a betrayal she could not come back from, but she had stopped herself, and if it took that to convince her that she wanted no one but Harry, then she had to think of it as a blessing. He was the love of her life.

She searched through her trunk and found a long gray skirt and blouse she could dress herself in quickly, and without any help to lace. She checked her hair in the mirror. Her watch now read four o'clock. Perhaps he would still be standing on the pier; ever the showman, he enjoyed watching the crowd's anticipation build. She raced down the corridor and over to the veranda at the end of the hall, which overlooked the edge of the pier. Flinging the doors open, she heard the loud cries of the crowd below. Then, like a fog rushing toward her, came the shrill voice of a newsboy: "Extree! Houdini dead! Extree! Houdini drowned in ocean!"

Bess fell to her knees. She could not breathe. It could not be possible. From the position of the balcony she could not see the spot of Harry's jump, only the crowd milling about in alarm and, in the distance, the ocean, angry and white with froth. She stumbled, as if drugged, down the stairwell onto the first floor, which led outside.

She could not look anyone in the eye as she pushed her way toward the front of the massive throng. She caught sight of John

Young in the distance, leaning searchingly over the railing, and then vomited onto the concrete. Less than an hour ago, she had almost given everything to that man, and now she had lost Harry. How could she not have seen this? She had always thought of the bond between them as something fated, otherworldly—that if something happened to Harry, she would know it. But she felt nothing now but fear.

"Bess." Someone spoke behind her, touching the back of her shoulder. When she turned, dizzily, she could almost make out Harry's form, blue and ghostlike, his hair and body dripping.

"Harry?" she choked in disbelief.

Before he could say anything further, the crowd rushed in on him, separating them, pushed apart only by the policemen and two doctors in white coats, with stethoscopes around their necks. Harry was draped in towels and ushered into the building, and then she couldn't see him anymore.

Harry's assistant, Jim Collins, put his hand on her shoulder. Jim was the first man Harry had hired, and the only person other than Bess he trusted with the workings of his tricks. "He didn't come up after two minutes," Jim explained, his blue eyes soft with relief. "The rope man had to lower himself into the water and go down in search of him. After four minutes the physicians were of the mind that he could not have survived."

"But the newsboys. I heard them—"

"They were dispatched with bulletins. You know how these things work. Call out the news now, write it up later. But after six minutes we saw the top of his head emerge from the water, then his arms, pulling himself in by the rope."

"Six minutes." Bess looked down at the water, stunned. "He's never held his breath that long."

"It's miraculous." She could see Jim still trembling slightly from nerves. He adored Harry, and she adored Jim in return.

She put her hand on his arm. "I have to see him."

"Of course."

Bess looked at John Young, standing by the railing, and caught his eye. Neither of them gave any acknowledgment of what had occurred between them less than an hour earlier. They both were married. Bess had almost lost her husband. John Young had brought in the towels. Nothing more.

Bess found Harry upstairs in their bedroom, immersed in a hot bath, one of the physicians sitting in a chair beside the tub, checking his pulse. She rushed over and seized Harry's hand. His grip was weak. The doctor excused himself politely.

"I thought I'd lost you," she murmured.

"I got caught," he said. "There was an old fishing net down there, and I got the cuffs off easily enough, but I couldn't get my legs free, and then I started losing air, and I couldn't tell top from bottom. I started to pray, and Bess, I swear I could hear my father's voice calling to me from somewhere down there. Then I saw the rope, and I managed to free myself and grab hold of it."

Bess looked at him, surprised. Harry almost never talked about his father, and he certainly didn't consider himself a practicing Jew any longer. She leaned toward him and ran her fingers through his hair. "You think your father saved you?"

"I don't know. But I do know he was *there*." His voice trailed off. "Somehow, he was there . . . It's the first time I've ever been alone but felt . . . not alone." He closed his eyes and laid his head against the edge of the tub. "I'm sorry, Bess."

Bess blinked. "Sorry? What for?"

"I scared you. I didn't do the trick right. I failed."

Bess ran her hand over the top of his head. "Oh, no. It's all right, darling. You didn't fail me at all."

Chapter 10

LONG ISLAND

June 1929

Bess spent the next two days at Mount Sinai Hospital, at Stella's side, leaving only to check on the tearoom for an hour at a time. Abby had woken up that Saturday morning in a pool of blood, such a significant amount that the doctors immediately diagnosed a likely miscarriage. Abby was delirious with medication and grief; but by Saturday night, when Stella and Bess arrived, she claimed she could feel slight stirrings of movement in her belly. Stella worried she was imagining them, but by Sunday morning they were stronger, and there was no more bleeding; the doctors diagnosed her with placenta previa, in which, they explained, the placenta grows over the cervix; this was the cause of the bleeding. They ordered bed rest for the five remaining months of the pregnancy.

Bess felt a sense of culpability that Stella had not been there right away; nothing good seemed to come out of Atlantic City. Fortunately, she had never spoken to John Young again. After the pier jump she had begged Harry to go back to New York, to Gladys and to Mrs. Weiss, whom Harry had moved into the house. She longed to see their tiny dog, Carla, who yelped when she spotted them, ran in circles and then jumped onto the bed.

But that night—their first night home in several months—as they had lain side by side under the thick feather duvet Bess had purchased during their travels in Europe, Bess was certain she heard someone whispering in the hall outside their bedroom. *Lazarus,* the voice said, *come forth.*

She'd sat up immediately and found she could not breathe. It was as if someone was holding her by the throat. She had grown up believing in demons that never appeared, and now, it seemed, they had come for her at last. In the corner of the room, the shadow of a man appeared.

She had touched Harry on the arm, and he'd woken immediately. "Harry," she had said, her throat thick. "They've come for me."

Harry had looked across the room and shouted. He'd jumped from the bed, throwing himself at the shadow. "Darling, no!" Bess had said. "He's here for *me!*" She'd watched the two forms, Harry and the dark man, wrestling in the dark. Then she'd heard Harry yell again, and when she lit the lamp she saw that the shadow was not a ghost, it was a man, and he was wielding a razor blade, and he had attacked Harry, slicing through the skin of his neck.

Harry had managed to wrestle the man out the door and into the parlor, where Mrs. Weiss, woken by the noise, had already called the police. Harry gained control of the weapon, but the man had escaped before the police arrived. Bess had found Harry kneeling in the foyer in a pool of blood, breathing heavily. He had been taken to the hospital, where his wounds were found to be superficial. They'd never learned the identity of the intruder. Bess had been unable to shake the feeling that their lives were in danger now, physically as well as spiritually, that she had brought evil into their life, and like a black tar it covered everything.

Harry, despite having come precariously close to dying, had looked back on that weekend in Atlantic City with fondness. He had been entranced by the thick ocean air, the smell of chocolate fudge being mixed in huge stainless steel vats, the endless parade of lovers walking along the boardwalk, the women with their white parasols. He steadfastly swore he had heard his father speak to him when he was underwater. Years later, on the back of a photograph he had taken of her by the beach, she came across a note Harry had jotted across the bottom: *Many a time I have looked at the silent remembrances of the past, and never have I forgotten the fact that life is but an empty dream.* The experience had drawn his magic toward investigation of the paranormal rather than manipulation of the normal.

Even in the early days of his magic he could make mango trees bloom onstage, the roots bursting upward beneath a black cloth, the fruit flamed with orange, the black cloth floating to the floor and the crowd trembling with excitement. Once Bess had asked him if he felt like he was playing God. But even though his father had been a rabbi, Harry didn't know where to find God. All he knew was that God wasn't in his father's books, and he wasn't under the milky lights of the stage, and he wasn't under the black cloth either. God was somewhere else.

On Tuesday afternoon, when Bess went back to her town house for the first time since leaving for Atlantic City, she was greeted by the sound of the dog sliding across the wooden floors toward her, and by George, white-gloved and nervous, in the foyer.

"Mrs. Houdini," he began hesitantly. "There's a gentleman in the library waiting for you."

"A gentleman?" She rarely had guests at the house, short of

Gladys and Stella, and preferred to do her entertaining at the tearoom.

"I wouldn't have let him in, but he showed me a telegram you sent him."

Bess's pulse quickened. "Charles!" She rushed through the library doors. She had only telegrammed him that there had been an emergency, and she would get back in touch with him, but somehow he had found her.

He was standing by the staircase with his back to her, his luggage at his feet. He turned when she entered. "This is— I've never seen anything like this." He craned his head to see the spiral stairs, which wound through all four floors. "It's so grand."

"You found me."

His face turned red. "I found your address through the paper. Was it presumptuous of me to come? I didn't know what had happened and I thought maybe I could offer some help."

"No, no, it wasn't presumptuous. It was my niece. She's in the hospital, but she's all right now."

"Oh, that's a relief."

Bess nodded.

"I brought the photographs." He gestured toward his luggage. "I brought as many as I could, but I simply couldn't fit them all."

Bess looked down at the leather case and felt herself become dizzy. She had hardly eaten a thing since Saturday, and hardly slept either. Her stay in the hospital at Abby's bedside had stirred up feelings of loneliness she had buried for a long time, and it had called into question the importance of her fixation. Here was a *real* situation, right in front of her—Abby's baby in danger, Stella's family in crisis—and it made her hunt for Harry seem all the more imaginary, and silly. She simply didn't have the energy or the willpower to sort through hundreds of photographs right then. She wasn't even sure she believed in the message anymore.

"Charles," she said, "what would you say if I invited you to a party tonight?" The bespectacled man Gladys had been conversing with at Niall's party had become a full-blown romance, apparently. The man, Lloyd, a stockbroker, was having people out to his country estate.

"Tonight?" Charles blinked, surprised.

"You don't have to go back right away, do you?"

"No, no. I can stay. I just thought—you were so eager to see these photographs."

"I am." Bess's voice caught in her throat. "I am just so tired. And it sounds counterintuitive, I know, but nothing seems more relaxing to me right now than a fun party, full of strangers." She usually spent so many hours in her tearoom, playing hostess and entertaining other guests, that the idea of simply being part of a crowd seemed liberating.

"I'm just not sure—"

Bess gripped his hands. "Please join me. I could use the company."

Charles sighed. "Where are we going? I'm not much for parties."

"I actually don't know the fellow. I've only met him once, but he's got a house out on Long Island. Harry's sister, Gladys, is in love with him I think."

Three hours later they were standing on the lawn of Lloyd's estate, staring out at Long Island Sound. Across the expanse of green grass, Bess could see Gladys, wafting over the grounds on Lloyd's arm, in a yellow dress, as if she had never been reclusive at all. Bess could hardly believe the change in her.

"What do we do now?" Charles asked, fidgeting. The place was swarming with people. A group played croquet, drunkenly, near the water. "Do we approach anyone?"

Bess thought about it. She looked around her at the white

candles floating on the pool, the waiters serving lobster croquettes in the sunken garden. "I don't suppose I usually do that. Usually people approach me." She paused. "That sounded very narcissistic, didn't it?"

"Yes, a bit."

She turned to see Gladys and Lloyd making their way toward them. Lloyd greeted them but then was dragged away by a group of male friends. "Will you be all right here?" he asked Gladys as he left.

Bess found the question insulting. "Of course she'll be all right. I'm here."

Lloyd held up his hands. "Sorry."

Bess leaned toward her sister-in-law when he had gone. "Are you sure he's trustworthy?"

Gladys laughed. It was a sound Bess had not heard in some time. "What could he possibly be taking advantage of? My money? We both know he has loads more than I do." She frowned. "You're the one who encouraged me to get out of the apartment more."

Bess took her hand. "I'm just looking out for you."

"Well, you don't need to." Gladys reached for the concrete edges of a sundial to support herself. "What about you? I can tell you've got a man there. Is that a date?"

"No!" Bess sputtered. "This is Charles Radley. He's—" She thought quickly. "He's a photographer. He's photographing my house."

Charles held out his hand. "Pleasure to meet you."

Gladys looked at him quizzically. "Charles Radley? Your voice sounds familiar. Do you live here?"

"No. I came up from New Jersey."

"That's odd. I'm certain I've met you before. You've never lived in New York?"

"No. I spent a few years in Iowa, but that didn't last."

"Iowa?"

"My mother died when I was eleven. I was sent on an orphan train to live out there."

Bess turned to him, surprised. "I didn't know that. Why did you come back east?"

Charles shrugged. "That's a story for another day."

Gladys held up her hands. "Do you mind if I feel your face?"

Charles blinked and glanced at Bess. "All right, I suppose."

Gladys pushed a strand of dark hair behind her ear and reached for his forehead. She ran her fingers gently over his eyebrows and down the sides of his cheeks. Bess had rarely seen her do this, but she seemed unusually intent tonight. Charles closed his eyes. There seemed to be something between them, she thought, some kind of attraction. At last Gladys said, "You're right. We've never met."

Charles stepped back. Jack Dempsey had arrived—Gladys had said he might—along with his manager and a crowd of other men, and the exclamations of the women were growing noticeably louder.

"Why are you having your house photographed?" Gladys asked. "You're not planning on selling it, are you?"

"No, nothing like that." Bess searched hurriedly for a response. "I feel I owe it to Harry," she said, taking another sip of champagne. "He put a lot of thought into the place, and it ought to be commemorated." She looked at Gladys. Bess could tell she didn't believe her. Gladys had a knack for sorting out truths from falsehoods.

Now that the sun was almost down, the white brick walls of the house took on the pinks and egg blues of the sky. Bess could hear the water splashing faintly against the rocks, past the clatter of the party, and she imagined it could be very peaceful when it was quiet, but also very lonely. All the big houses out here were probably filled with children, and nannies, and tutors, and the children's friends. She wasn't quite sure what one would do, however, without children, or work. Her own days were only partially full taking care of Harry's affairs, and running the tearoom; but she still had empty hours, mostly at night, when a kind of darkness sometimes descended upon her. When Harry was alive, she had felt this emptiness less often, only when he was immersed in his work and excluded her from his thoughts. But looking back, she realized that they were always traveling, and when they were at home, there was Mrs. Weiss puttering about, and Gladys, and all of Harry's business acquaintances passing through the house with some urgent matter or another. She had had no idea how hollow the nights could feel, the bruised blue of the darkness seeming to last forever. She wondered what she would do with herself if her tearoom failed.

"How is Abby?" Gladys asked.

"She's doing much better, as of this morning. Stella is relieved, obviously, but she's also a bit sad. Abby decided she wants to keep the baby for herself. The scare changed her mind, I'm sure."

Gladys nodded. "That is sad for Stella. She thought she was going to have a chance to be young again."

"I remember saying once, in California, 'Life is meant to be enjoyed; I'll behave when I'm old.' And now, of course, I am old, and so is Stella." She looked at Gladys. "Will I see you tomorrow at the tearoom, our usual time?"

"I'm not sure. It depends what time I get back to the city."

"Oh." Bess frowned.

"I'll try," she said.

They stayed another hour, but Bess could tell Charles was uncomfortable in the extravagant gardens. She said good-bye, but as the car was being brought around, Gladys took her aside privately. "Who is that man you brought, really?"

"I met him in Atlantic City. He's a photographer."

"I know. You said that." Gladys seemed agitated.

Bess laughed. "It's not romantic between us, but I don't think *you* should fall in love with him either. He's thinking of becoming a priest."

Charles was waving them over. "The car's here," he called. "Are you coming?"

Bess kissed Glady's cheek. "We'll talk tomorrow."

Bess woke in the middle of the night, struggling for breath. She fumbled for the lamp and sat up in the yellow glow. She couldn't remember what she had been dreaming about, although she felt much more clearheaded than she had when she'd fallen asleep. And she was hungry. Her stomach groaned.

She wrapped herself in a robe and padded downstairs, barefoot, to the kitchen. As she passed the library, she realized the fireplace was lit, and there was a lamp on next to Harry's desk. Charles was sitting in Harry's old chair, hunched over, his back to her.

"What are you doing?" she said. "That's Harry's desk."

He spun around. But instead of looking guilty, he looked stricken. His face was white as a ghost's. "Bess," he said. "What is this?"

In his palm was a tiny rectangular photograph. Bess took it and came up beside him so she could hold it to the light. A young boy gazed back at her from the creased cardboard. He was posing in a studio in front of a painted backdrop of cherubs and clouds, his face solemn.

"I don't know," she said. "Why were you looking through

Harry's things?" Was he trying to steal from her? She realized she didn't know Charles well at all. And she rarely had guests in the house. She felt a small shiver run through her; George was not here tonight, and they were alone.

"I couldn't sleep. I was looking for a book to read." Charles retrieved the photograph, pinching it delicately between two fingers. "I found this inside one of the books. A Forster novel—one of my mother's favorites. And this picture—this is me. As a child."

Bess stared at him. "Are you sure?" It barely looked a thing like him.

"This photograph was part of my mother's possessions. Why would you have this in your house?" He seemed eerily calm.

"I don't know. My husband was a collector. He bought all kinds of things."

"But don't you see," Charles insisted. "This is more than a coincidence. There's something to this. Clearly your husband is trying to come through to us here."

Bess felt her pulse quicken. "What are you saying?"

Charles grabbed her hands and pulled them to his chest. "I'm saying he's *chosen* me, Bess. Just like you said. I have to admit I was skeptical when you came to me. But why would my photograph be in your house? It must have been sold with my mother's things and somehow Harry came into possession of it. In some antiques store, maybe. Some auction."

In her exhaustion she couldn't quite muster up the same enthusiasm. She wasn't sure he was being rational. Instead, she felt a wash of sympathy for him. He seemed suddenly very young, boyish almost, behind his glasses.

"What was it like on the orphan train?" she asked gently. "Was it dreadful?"

"They were very poor conditions." Charles looked away, toward the window. "There was not enough room for all of us. We were not told where we were going. Some of us, who were older, thought we were being taken into the wilderness to be left."

Bess gasped. "But was your new family loving to you, when you arrived?"

"They were kind enough. But they never loved me. They loved their dead son, who had died of fever. I stayed until I was seventeen, but then I left with another boy who hated it out there, too, and came back east."

"What about the rest of your family? There were no brothers or sisters? No aunts or uncles? What about your father?"

Charles shook his head. "I never knew my father. He was a criminal, and died in prison."

Bess wanted to reach out and wrap her arms around him. He was so vulnerable, standing there before her.

"What was your mother like?"

"She was beautiful."

"How did she die?"

"She kept company with all the wrong people. She was shot by a man she loved. He worked with her, in the circus, and one night after a performance they all got drunk and he accused her of being with another man, and he went crazy, and he shot her."

Bess's shoulders stiffened. "Your mother was in the circus?"

"Yes. She performed with snakes. I remember that. She used to keep all kinds of snakes in cages. Most of them were poisonous, too."

Bess's breath caught in her throat. "What was her name?"

"Eva." He looked at her strangely. "Why?"

"Evatima?"

"Yes, but no one ever called her that." His voice turned sharp. "How would you know that?"

"I—knew her. When Harry and I first started out, in Coney Island."

Charles stared. "I think I'm getting the chills. This is all becoming too strange."

Bess had not known Evatima well, but still, she was brought back to those early days, when she and Harry were young, when they lived by the beach. She pictured the woman, alone, cast off by the circus, a single mother with a baby, and Charles, a tiny, tortured boy, sent west on one of those filthy trains she had read about in the papers, brought to a house of strangers to be their son. She was overcome with sadness for all of them, because Evatima was dead, and Harry was dead, and she herself was alone, and Charles was alone. Perhaps, she thought, she and this thin, thoughtful man were more alike than she had first imagined.

Charles cleared his throat. "I think I'm getting too sentimental now. I must be absolutely jagged." He went back to sit at Harry's desk and lay his head in his arms.

Slowly, and then quickly, like a wave, it crashed upon her. The porter coming to inform her that the train was arriving in New York, a tall young man standing in the narrow corridor, his black cap rimmed with red. She was alone, and in tears; and Harry had sent her away, proclaiming their marriage over. She remembered flirting with a man at the beer hall, and across the room, Harry's hand on Evatima's thigh. It was just after they had married, in June, and the train was crowded with sleepy couples with their heads on each other's shoulders, returning from a weekend at the beach. She did not have enough room to think, but rather a narrow seat in second class and a heavyset woman in and out of sleep next to her. And all the way to her sister's she could not get the image of that smoke-filled room out of her head, the flash of glasses on the tables, and Harry's hand stroking the top of Evatima's dark-stockinged thigh.

She had arrived, sobbing, at her sister's door, and Stella had given her a glass of whiskey, and put her to bed. Bess had crept past the babies' room on the way to her own, and seen through the cracks in the doors the tiny forms sleeping under embroidered white sheets, their closed eyes protecting dreams deep as oceans. She had cried herself to sleep because she would never have children with Harry, now that he had left her. And then he had appeared at Stella's door in the middle of the night, full of remorse, and taken her back to Coney Island, to the marriage she thought he had given up on.

She could barely speak. Her hands were shaking uncontrollably. "When—when were you born?" she choked.

Charles looked up at her. "In 1895. Why?"

"It's not possible." When she looked at him all she saw was Harry's son. How she could have overlooked it, before, she did not know. Maybe the glasses had masked Charles's most prominent features. But he had a round chin, she saw, and pronounced cheeks, and these were the chin and cheeks of Ehrich Weiss.

She realized that in the hours after Harry had taken her to the train station, he had gone back to the beer hall, back to the beautiful, exotic Evatima Tardo, and he had made love to her. He had laid his naked body across hers, and put his mouth against hers, and he had given her himself. And a child. The child he could never give to Bess.

She could not think clearly. She stood up and went over to the fireplace. Charles followed her. He put his hand on her shoulder. "What's wrong?" he asked. "Are you all right?"

"This can't be," she whispered.

"What can't be?" Charles frowned.

Harry had sent her to Atlantic City, of course. He had sent her those messages, through the photographs, and led her to Charles. But why would he do such a thing? To hurt her? She had expected his message from the grave to be a profession of love, of reassurance, and instead he had brought her to the doorstep of this man—this boy, really—to confess to her that their marriage had been nothing but a lie.

Perhaps, if she had been able to have children of her own, the blow would not have been so fierce. She had never forgiven herself for those moments with John Young. But—she hadn't gone through with it, in the end. She had been faithful to Harry. And for what? For her whole life to culminate in his indiscretion?

She wondered how long he would have known. Evatima must have sent him that photograph of Charles as a boy. So why had Harry never acknowledged him? Why had he never told Bess, especially after Evatima died, when he knew how desperately she wanted a child? It was cruel, and so unlike the Harry she knew. But then again, it was possible she hadn't really known him at all.

She looked at Charles. She could not help seeing the betrayal in him, Harry's hypocrisy when he had demanded her own loyalty with such forcefulness. She thought back on all the moments of tenderness they had shared and wondered if he had ever really loved her. Or had he simply been trying to assuage his own guilt with gestures of affection? And why had he made her promise to keep looking for him after he died? She had given up three years waiting for him to reach her, only to have dredged up a secret she wished had remained buried.

He should have let her go. He should have let her remarry, become a mother to some other man's children, or a grandmother, and live out her days in some two-bedroom house by the ocean, where she could have spent her afternoons watching the ripples of waves, like tiny dunes, rolling across the water. All the men who had pursued her, whom she had turned away, the kind ones, the widowers, with soft eyes and hands, men who had loved fishing and listening to the radio on weekday nights—what had become of them? And what would have become of her, if she had chosen that kind of life instead?

Charles looked frightened. He was staring at her, mute. She realized she must seem crazed.

"Do you really have no idea?" she demanded. She wondered if Harry had been hiding Charles's photograph all along in the house they shared together, as man and wife, and gazing upon it when she had gone to bed. It was unbearable, to imagine this kind of deception.

Charles shook his head. "No idea about what?"

No; it wasn't possible. Harry would not have betrayed her in such a way. Her mind was racing; there had to be another explanation.

What if Charles was *not* Harry's son? What if Harry had not orchestrated their meeting at all? What if her "discoveries" were merely coincidences that had led her to Charles, and he had taken advantage of this by leading her to believe he was Harry's son? It would not have been impossible for him, working for a newspaper, to do a little digging after they'd met, and manage to contact some of their old Coney Island friends. Someone else besides her surely remembered that night, their sudden departure from their own party and Harry's flirtations with Evatima.

"You want me to think you are his son."

Charles stared at her. "Whose son?"

"Harry's."

Charles took a step backward, alarmed, and then laughed. "You've got to be joking. Are you telling me this photograph is in your house because . . . I'm Harry Houdini's son?"

"Please leave," she said quietly. "I'm sorry I invited you here."

Charles stood there, frozen. "I didn't deceive you. I don't know why you would think that. But I'm not going to stay where I'm not welcome."

He seemed—was it possible?—hurt. His eyes were wide, and he looked suddenly much like the boy in the photograph, young and open—the boy who might have been hers. He put the photograph in his pocket and turned to the door. And then he had gone, and the dog had run upstairs to hide, and the streetlights glowed in the empty dark, and Bess had never felt so utterly, completely alone.

Chapter 11

THE ATLANTIC OCEAN

October 1912

"It is my duty to inform you that by continuing your present regimen you would be committing suicide." Dr. Stone tapped Harry's test results with his forefinger. "You must reconcile yourself, Harry, to the fact that your strenuous days are over."

Bess's jaw dropped, but Harry put his arm around her shoulders and laughed loudly. "How long do you give me?"

Dr. Stone did not look amused. "If you continue as at present, you will be dead within a year."

"Harry!" Bess said.

Harry shook his head and smiled wryly. "Impossible."

"I assure you, it is quite possible. I see patients die every day from lesser conditions. But yours—this ruptured blood vessel in your kidney—it is quite dangerous." Dr. Stone sighed. "Don't be a fool, Harry. Take some time off. No more of these straitjacket escapes. No more stunts. You have other tricks to rely on."

The audience never knows whether the stunt is easy or hard, Harry had once confided to Bess. *Sometimes a stunt that looks easy is in fact exceedingly difficult.* The wet sheet escape he had been performing in Pittsburgh for the past week was a perfect example. For the escape, he had recruited hospital attendants to bind him with sheets and bandages—mummify him, he said—and then pour buckets of water over the bindings. Escaping from these soaking cloths was one of the most physically taxing feats he had ever accomplished, although no one knew this but Bess. The stunt had not been nearly as well received as the time he transported a handkerchief to the top of the Statue of Liberty, or the time he escaped, hanging upside down, from a giant milk jug filled with water.

He was not yet forty, but his body was revealing signs of strain; Bess had started plucking white hairs from his head with tweezers. He could not bear to show any weakness at all. He began spending more time meditating at the cemetery but refused to buy a plot for himself or for Bess. He behaved erratically sometimes, playing silly tricks on Bess at home and concocting various entertaining schemes. Before the Pittsburgh engagement, he had taken Bess, Gladys, and Mrs. Weiss on a vacation to a resort in the Catskills and, in the middle of the first night, had woken his mother by pouring a chest full of gold coins—his salary from a previous engagement—around her sleeping form.

Mrs. Weiss had sat up in bed, terrified, thinking she was drowning. Harry had been giddy as a schoolboy. "Look, Mother! It's all yours!" He'd run his fingers through the gold. "Look what I brought you!"

Mrs. Weiss had looked around her in amazement. She had never possessed so much wealth in her life and had never—especially not during those early, harsh Wisconsin winters—imagined so much existed.

Gladys, who was sleeping in the other bed, had woken next. Harry had pressed a piece of the heavy gold into his sister's hand. "See what I've done," he'd told her. "This is yours."

"What is this?" Gladys had rubbed the coin with her thumb.

"It's gold. And it's real."

Bess had watched the festivities from the doorway, smiling a small, tight smile. She had tried to reconcile with her own mother, only to find the old neighborhood changed, Mrs. Rahner's mind nearly gone. "How can I forgive you?" the withered woman had asked, staring up at her, confused. "I don't even know you."

But it was her sister Ada whose aging haunted Bess. The toothless baby was now a girl of eighteen; she looked startlingly like Bess had at that age. For years Stella had passed along news of the family, as their siblings moved out of New York one by one, leaving only Ada at home—but the others had wanted nothing to do with Bess, and she was almost always traveling.

"I read about you in the papers," Ada had said shyly. "You're very rich."

"Not very. Only a little rich. Have you gotten the money I've sent?"

She'd nodded. "Mother said it was the devil's money, but she kept it anyway." Ada had stepped toward her. "Are you staying tonight?" Her voice rose a little in desperation.

"I can't stay," Bess had said softly. "I'm married now. I live with my husband."

"Harry Houdini."

"Yes."

"You're lucky," Ada had said. "You got out." The wistfulness in her voice had shattered Bess.

Now she could see Harry becoming more and more enamored with this wealth—even if only to give it away—and this worried her. The irony of his situation was not lost on her; he flaunted his gold while obsessing over death—that vast, black arena where one's treasures could not go. Then, in the pink hours of the Catskills morning, as if in response to her fears, Harry had woken her with a small shake.

Victoria Kelly

"Bess," he'd whispered, terrified. "I've just been to the toilet. I've passed some blood."

Bess had called Dr. Stone to Pittsburgh as soon as they arrived. Harry had refused to cancel his show and go back to New York, and so the medical tests were performed in the early hours of the morning, before the day's work began. Dr. Stone slept in the room adjacent to theirs in the hotel; more than once Bess hurried him into their bedroom in the middle of the night, where Harry was writhing in pain, grasping a pillow and shimmering with sweat.

She wished Harry would reconcile himself to the fact that he would never be—as he hoped—invincible. A few months earlier, during a bridge jump into the dark, churning waters of New York Harbor, a corpse had floated to the surface as he sank to the bottom. Bess, along with a thousand spectators, had initially thought the corpse was Harry's, until he appeared a few moments later, his head coming to the surface within a foot of the dead man's arm. Looking over to find the grayed mass bobbing beside him, Harry could not breathe. Flailing in the water, tangled in a cluster of weeds, he'd had to be rescued and dragged to land. For days, neither Bess nor Harry could rid themselves of the image of the man's dark open eyes.

But instead of succumbing to Dr. Stone's diagnosis, Harry resisted it. He declared his new ambition to be buried alive. He had mastered the art of managing his breath, and dirt, he reasoned, would be little different from water. He had Jim Collins bury him, manacled, under one foot of earth, and then two, while he practiced his escapes. Each time it took only a few minutes for him to break free, pushing out of the dirt like a mole. But when Jim put him in a hole at six feet—the depth at which he was intending to perform—he did not emerge. Bess felt a crazed and paralyzing chill come over her, but Jim's eyes were fixed on his watch. He had been instructed to go in after Harry at exactly four and a half minutes. After four excruciating minutes Harry burst into the daylight, choking for air, his face and eyelids black with dirt.

That night when they got home, Harry was very quiet. He lay on the bed with his eyes closed for a long time. Bess lay next to him, afraid to disturb him. When she thought he was asleep, she crept out of the bed and went over to the closet to change into her dressing gown.

She had removed her shirtwaist and drawers when she heard a noise behind her. She turned to see Harry standing there in the dark, watching her. "I thought you were asleep," she said, startled. "Did I wake you?"

He didn't answer. He pushed her against the bedroom wall and pulled her stockings off. "What are you doing, Harry?" she asked. "Are you all right?"

"Are you afraid?" His voice was very quiet.

"No," she said, honestly.

When she was undressed, he turned her around, so that her back was against the blue flowered wallpaper.

She didn't make a sound. Instead she found herself moving as if she were detached from herself, as if she were watching another woman from above. He wrapped his arms around her waist. It felt like she was being filled when she had been empty. She and Harry had not made love this way since they were first married, not with this kind of passion. She turned, lifted her legs, and wrapped them around his waist, and when it was over, she did not feel lonely anymore.

"You can't do the burial stunt again," she said.

"I know." Harry avoided her eyes. "I feel like a failure."

"One failed trick doesn't make you a failure."

"Everyone wonders where people go when they leave this place. I want to perform a trick that makes it seem as if I have gone there, too. To wherever it is people go when they are invisible. But then I will come back again."

Bess wondered if he was purposely avoiding speaking explicitly of death. Instead she said, "I don't want you to go," and he laughed.

"Of course I'm not really *going* anywhere."

"But if you could, hypothetically—if you could really see the other side, I mean—you would."

Harry thought about it. "Yes," he said. "I would go there. If I could come back."

She thought she had a sense of what he was intending to do. He had focused his whole career on pretending to escape death, and now he set his sights on walking into it.

Harry rented workshop space in Midtown, and began working with Jim Collins on constructing a new trick. He had hired other assistants as well, including Jim Vickery, a tall, muscled cabinet-maker who rarely spoke but was, from the beginning, fiercely loyal to Harry. For the first time, Harry refused to tell Bess what the trick entailed. He unveiled it at Hammerstein's Theatre on a damp Friday night in October, the sidewalks silvered with puddles. The stage on which the new trick was performed was covered in deep red carpet. While Harry performed other tricks, a team of bricklayers quickly constructed a brick wall, over ten feet tall, on the stage. After the wall had been built, two black screens were brought out and positioned on either side of it.

Harry stood at the front of the stage now in the suit Bess had ironed for him that morning. It was her small contribution. Harry had a dozen men in his employ now, working as bookers or secretaries or scouts or on construction. He had the young and eager Jim Collins, of course, and Jim Vickery, and his loyal, dignified secretary, John Sargent, with his crop of white hair.

His hair, as usual, was uncombed. "Ladies and gentlemen," he announced, in the booming stage voice that always gave her chills. "I have been preparing myself for years for a performance of this caliber. I have set out to prove to you that while you may think it impossible that one might stand in this very room and yet be somewhere else at the same time, it is quite possible. Indeed, there are realms we do not see, all around us. I have been there. Yet I cannot tell you, in good conscience, what I have witnessed. But when I walk through this wall in front of your eyes, you will know that I have been there, and come back, as the spirits do."

Three audience members were selected to stand behind the brick wall to ensure that he could not sneak around it to the other side. Harry stood behind one of the black screens and waved his hands over the top. "I am here!" he shouted. "Now, ladies and gentlemen, I am going." Only moments later, his hands appeared above the screen on the other side of the wall. "And now, by unknown means, I have crossed over to the other side!" his voice boomed. A stage assistant drew away the second screen, and there stood Harry, clothes and hair disheveled, panting, having crossed through solid brick.

The crowd sat in silence, dumbfounded. Harry bowed proudly.

"They're going to say I am able to dematerialize," he had hinted that morning before he went to prepare for the show. "And I won't protest it. It is not enough to perform magic anymore. One must *be* magic as well." He kissed her, but she turned her mouth away.

"Harry," she murmured, "we said we were never going to do that again." She did not want him exploiting people's beliefs.

He had responded to Dr. Stone's warnings in some unconventional ways. He had purchased the original Martin Luther Bible, with Luther's own notes in the margins, and placed it upon Edgar

Allan Poe's mahogany writing desk, in his study, as if to make some kind of point about dark and light. He had also had his father reburied in the family plot he had purchased in Machpelah Cemetery, insisting on viewing what was left of the body. "There was nothing but skull and bones," he told Bess, rushing eagerly into the house after the process was complete. "Father's teeth were in surprisingly excellent condition."

Now he frowned at her accusations. "This isn't the same as making up stories about people's dead cousins, Bess. This is different. It is the Great Mystery."

"What is the Great Mystery?" she asked him.

He smiled his serene, magician's smile. "Where I go when I am gone."

✳

On April 14 the RMS *Titanic* collided with an iceberg during her maiden voyage. The *Carpathia*, which had rescued some of the survivors from the water, came into port in New York a few days later. Forty thousand people waited on the docks for their arrival, Bess and Harry among them. The mood was frenzied. Some of those waiting recognized Harry and asked if he could communicate with those lost. Harry looked stricken by the suggestion; on flyers thin as tissue paper, representatives of the Metropolitan Opera distributed advertisements for a benefit concert in which the opera star Mary Garden would perform "Nearer My God to Thee."

The solemnity of the tragedy bled into the summer, and even the fall. One could not travel without fear anymore. Bess and Harry said good-bye to Mrs. Weiss in New York the week following Harry's diagnosis. He had been invited to Copenhagen to perform for the Danish royal family. It was a pearl-gray morning in October, and a large crowd had gathered at the dock. There were to be two celebrities on board the ship—Harry Houdini, famous magician, and Theodore Roosevelt, former president of the United States. Neither Bess nor Harry had ever met the president, but Harry was determined to make his acquaintance, and Bess had dressed herself carefully that morning in preparation. She looked about the dock for Mr. Roosevelt but did not see him.

Mrs. Weiss looked awfully small, Bess thought, against the massiveness of the ship floating at the pier. She was dressed in black silk, as she always was when seeing Harry off, as a way of mourning his departure. She clung to Harry's arm and shuffled beside him toward the gangplank.

Harry clasped his mother's hand. "It's only for a month," he said. "John Sargent is going to look after you, and he can arrange for anything you need."

"You know, I'm old," she replied with a small smile. "Perhaps when you come back, I shall not be here."

Harry laughed. "Nonsense. You only like to say those things so I will tell you I love you."

Bess kissed Mrs. Weiss's cheek. "Good-bye, Mother." She picked up her bag quickly, before Harry could do it. Neither of them had told his mother of his kidney, and Bess didn't want him to wince and give it away; it would only worry Mrs. Weiss. They had argued through the night after Dr. Stone left, and Harry had promised her they would take a three-week vacation after Copenhagen, and he would rest in Provence, on the condition that she keep the secret from his mother while he recovered.

Mrs. Weiss shook her hand free of Harry's. "Go."

Harry turned to the crowd that was watching them. "Look, my mother drives me away from her!" They broke out in laughter. Bess flushed; Harry was always the performer, even at the most inconvenient moments.

Bess envied Mrs. Weiss that she had a son like Harry; but

at the same time she felt sorry for the woman. Mrs. Weiss was seventy-one already and increasingly fragile each day, and she had spent the majority of her life saying good-bye to those she loved—her husband, her oldest son, and even Harry, for months at a time, when he traveled around the world doing his magic. Bess, at least, could say that she'd been by his side every night since they met.

"Just go quickly," Mrs. Weiss said, patting his hand, "and come back safely."

Harry pulled Bess up the stairs onto the ship's deck. The passengers were waving their hats and cream-colored gloves, shouting and crying. On the pier, the crowd of Harry's admirers cheered and called his name. The passengers on the boat threw out lines of red paper streamers toward those on the dock. Mrs. Weiss caught Harry's, and as the ship glided slowly away from the dock, Harry leaned farther and farther over the rail, the long wisp of paper dangling between him and his mother, until it snapped and the ends wafted into the murky water.

When the dock was out of sight he turned to Bess, his face already green with seasickness. "Strange how I am a grown man, and still it always feels the same to say good-bye to my mother." He blushed.

"Let's go to the dining hall before you become too ill to eat," she replied.

Harry bowed to her ceremoniously. "What would I do without you to keep track of my meals?"

Bess laughed. "You may be weak on ships, but you're quite strong in character."

Harry smirked. "Now, we both know stubbornness is not the same as strength of character. It's true, though. I'm helpless as a child without you."

She wrapped her arms around his waist and helped him across

the deck. The other passengers watched them, some of the men stopping to clap Harry on the shoulder or shake his hand. Some were amazed that a man like him could be made ill so easily by the ocean. What they didn't understand was that, in all his feats, he was in control; but even his immense abilities were powerless compared to the mighty ocean, writhing like an animal beneath them. Yet this would be a different voyage from their first, years earlier; this time they had a spacious room with a large window, and a butler, and a bed layered in cream silk sheets. Never in her life had Bess imagined she would be quarantined on a ship with a former president of the United States. She imagined dining next to him at tables set with heavy silver.

"It's going to be a helluva trip," Harry said.

But Bess didn't answer. She was staring into the water at the wake.

"Bess? Darling, are you all right? Don't tell me you're ill now, too."

She turned to him with a look of horror on her face. "Look there," she said, pointing. "Do you see it?"

He clutched his stomach and leaned over the railing, staring at the white crests of the waves. "Look at what?"

She leaned over again, this time her eyes scanning the water frantically. "It's gone."

"What's gone?"

"I don't—I don't understand. I saw—"

He gripped her arm. "What is it? What did you see? Tell me."

"It was strange. It was a vision of your mother, in the water. Like a reflection in a pool." Bess craned her head so she could still see the dock full of waving onlookers, like toy soldiers saluting. "It's probably nothing," she said, seeing Harry's terrified face. "Just my mind playing tricks on me." She wondered if she was coming down with whatever malady Harry had and was hallucinating.

Still, she couldn't help thinking that the souls of the *Titanic* passengers were trapped somewhere beneath the trembling waters. One could not travel now without imagining what it must have been like to cling to the rails of the ship in that black night.

"Let's go inside for lunch," she said. "It's terribly chilly out here."

On the second day of the voyage Harry reported to Bess that he had met the president on the deck, doing his morning exercises. The two had walked to breakfast together, and in the dining hall the ship's captain had approached and asked Harry if he would perform as a medium for the passengers.

"What did you say?" Bess asked. "Did you agree?" Recently Harry had begun introducing medium tricks into his act, although he was careful never to claim, as he had long ago, that he was possessed of supernatural powers.

Harry pursed his lips together. "I looked at Mr. Roosevelt, and he said, 'Go on, Mr. Houdini. Give us a little séance.' So I had to agree. But it's all in fun."

Bess frowned. "Be careful. This is the president you're performing for, after all. You don't want to frighten him."

Harry smiled his small, confident smile. "Don't you worry, Mrs. Houdini. I've got a trick or two up my sleeve."

"You mean you're not going to tell me what you're planning?"

"I think I'll make it a surprise."

"You'll have to avoid eating beforehand, remember, so you don't get sick and vomit all over Mr. Roosevelt." Bess kissed him. "What is he like? What kind of man is he?" A few years earlier, Roosevelt had refused to shoot a bear cub he'd been gifted by a group of hunters in Mississippi, and Bess had admired him since.

"He's quite a lively fellow." Harry drew a deck of cards out of his pocket and began shuffling. "I rather like the man. You'll like him, too, I'm certain."

The "reading" took place in the ship's first-class library that evening. It seemed to Bess that the entire roster of first-class passengers was in attendance; the room was filled to capacity, the crew having to bring chairs from the dining hall to accommodate them all.

Bess's seat was on a sofa in the front, next to Mr. Roosevelt. He rose to greet her when she entered, remarking on her dress—a long blue gown, carefully chosen for the occasion. The man was not handsome in the slightest, but he was imposing. What struck Bess immediately about him, besides the thick walrus's mustache that drooped over his mouth, was the softness of his eyes, not nearly as serious as in the photographs she had seen. They reminded her of her late father's eyes—shrewd but kind.

When Harry entered the room, he was greeted with loud applause. He looked around at the filled chairs, pretending bewilderment. "I was told this was to be an informal reading. I suppose I was wrong." Everyone laughed.

Harry began with some card tricks, and then, per his request, the room was dimmed to near dark. The audience was quiet, leaning forward in the shadowy light.

"I would like to ask you, President Roosevelt, to write a question on this slip of paper—a question to which I shall obtain the answer."

Roosevelt chuckled and took the paper, trying to balance it on his knee as he wrote.

"I beg your pardon," Harry said. He reached into the bookcase behind him and handed the former president a book to use as a writing board. Roosevelt thanked him, then turned his back, concealing even the motion of his pencil so Harry couldn't deduce what he was writing. He then sealed the paper in an envelope and inserted the envelope between two blank slates, which were tied together.

"You see," Harry said, "that I will now attempt to make contact with my spirit control, who will answer your question, through me, by writing on these slates."

"Who is your control?" someone called out.

"My control," Harry announced, "is Mr. W. T. Stead. I shall be communicating with him throughout this process." There was a murmur among the crowd. W. T. Stead was a well-known spiritualist writer who had died on the *Titanic*. Bess knew of this control; Harry had practiced using it on her at home. She had warned him it was audacious of him to choose someone who had passed so recently, in such a terrible manner—especially while they were on a ship—but he was committed to the character. Harry closed his eyes and sat in meditative stillness, his palms flat on the knees of his pants.

Roosevelt turned to Bess. "Does this man not terrify you?"

Bess smiled at him. "Sometimes," she replied honestly.

Harry was completely "possessed" now, by his spirit control. The room was hushed. With glazed eyes, he inserted a pencil between the slates and started writing. After a few minutes his body began to quiver violently, and he dropped the slates on the floor at the president's feet, then "emerged" from his unconscious state.

Mr. Roosevelt picked up the slates and examined them. He was quiet for a moment. Then he said, very softly, "Remarkable." He turned to the crowd. "My question was 'Where was I last Christmas?' And he has drawn a map of my entire itinerary in South America! My God, how did you know all this? The papers haven't even published it yet!"

The announcement was met with cheers and great applause. Roosevelt turned back to Harry, who sat calmly in his chair, fully himself now.

"How did you do it, Houdini?" Roosevelt demanded, grinning. "Was that real spiritualism?"

Harry smiled slyly. "Of course not. It was just hocus-pocus."

"Impossible. It must be telepathy."

Harry only laughed.

"Remarkable," Roosevelt said again, standing to shake Harry's hand. The grin had disappeared from his face. Bess could sense the growing unease she had seen time and time again, when one began to doubt all rational certainties about science and magic. If there was one thing Harry's tricks did, it was to make people wonder whether they should be believing in something else.

Later, as they were lying in bed, she rested her head on Harry's chest. "You impressed him, you know."

Harry kissed the top of her head. "And did I impress you, Mrs. Houdini?"

"I have to admit, I'm not sure how you did this one."

Harry sat up on his elbow. "Truly?"

"Truly. Will you tell me?"

He grinned. "You couldn't figure it out because most of it was due to blind chance. The book I handed him to write on had been prepared ahead of time with a hidden carbon sheet inside the front cover. As I replaced the book on the shelf, I snuck a peek at the question, and it was one I had prepared for; when I found out Mr. Roosevelt was going to be on the ship, my man at the London *Telegraph* telegraphed me a copy of the article he was publishing about the South America trip."

"That's incredibly coincidental. What would you have done if he had asked a question you had not prepared for?"

Harry shrugged. "Answered it the best I could, I suppose. Perhaps the spirits really were looking out for me."

"Don't say that. Not if you don't believe it." Bess closed her eyes, taken over by sleep. "Do you believe you'll see me after we die?" she murmured.

Harry ran his fingers through her hair. "Mrs. Houdini, if I die first, I believe you'll see me while you still live. In fact, I promise it."

❋

On their first night in Copenhagen, the sky was overcast, the moon weak through a thick layer of fog. Harry performed at the Cirkus Beketow, the city's premier venue. Young Prince Aage and Prince Axel of the Danish royal family were in attendance, sitting starry-eyed in a box close to stage left. Harry had been rehearsing his Danish and told the audience he was going to attempt to do the entire act in the language.

The Danish people felt an affinity with Harry because of his European origins; he was even more of a sensation in Europe than he was in New York. Moreover, the press had gotten wind of his performance for Roosevelt, and their hotel room floor was papered with messages from press agents requesting interviews, which had been slid under the door by the hotel staff. They had arrived on the continent intact, Harry's seasickness having been much milder than during their last voyage, but he had not been able to shake a feeling of foreboding following Bess's hallucination during their departure. When Bess told him she was going to walk down the Strøget to shop for a dress to wear to his reception, Harry clung to her and begged her not to leave. "I have a feeling something terrible is going to happen to you if you go," he said. They spent the afternoon lying on the bed instead, reading the American papers.

Under the bright lights of the Cirkus Beketow, Harry performed his transference trick splendidly, disappearing on one side of the makeshift wall and reappearing on the other. After the performance the princes welcomed them at a reception in the

Mrs. Houdini

circus foyer. No expense had been spared; tables were laid with cream cloths and plates of poached cod, roast pork, and candied fruit. Through the massive windows, Bess saw that the fog had lifted and the stars were white as pearls. She watched with a glass of champagne in hand as Harry stood on the lobby's velvet carpet in a circle of reporters, stiltedly trying to communicate in the little Danish he knew, until he defaulted to German. He was quivering with excitement, still immersed in the thrill of the performance. She watched as Jim Vickery pushed his way through the crowd and discreetly handed him a telegram. Harry asked the men for their pardon and looked down at the paper.

Bess watched as Harry fell to the floor. She tried to push her way toward him, but the crowd had surged forward, everyone trying to help. She could hear him through the barrier of men, crying out, "Mama, Mama!" but she could not reach him, she could not reach him.

Chapter 12

HARLEM

June 1929

Bess had led Harry by the hand to the door of the circus building and into the taxicab, as if he were a blind man. At the hotel he had sat on the bed, still, as Bess packed their luggage. The telegram, from Dash, who had come to New York from Boston while Harry was gone, had said the situation was dire and urged him to come home and forgo the rest of his performances. In Denmark, at the time, it was a crime to break a contract for any reason—even for family emergencies—and as a result Jim Collins was arrested for a period of days while Harry and Bess were on a train to Berlin.

In New York, they had found Mrs. Weiss lying peacefully in her bed, her form white and unmoving. Dash was there, and Gladys, and John Sargent, and Alfred, but no one had spoken a word. Harry had knelt by her side and taken his mother's hand. "It's cold," he had said, as if he still could not believe she was not merely sleeping. No one had dared touch him then, not even Bess.

"Mother always said, *'Gibt's nicht, nur Mann und Frau,'*" Gladys had murmured softly. "Nothing matters but man and wife. And now she is with the one who loved her most."

At this, Harry had burst into tears. "I loved her most!" he'd shouted. "I loved her most!" Bess had known what he was feeling—that he had failed his mother. He had promised always to take care of her, but he wasn't there at the end, when she needed him most. It had been his duty. The pain from his kidney, which he had dismissed as negligible before, began, suddenly, to cripple him, and he had clutched his side.

This was what Bess had felt when Harry died—a horrid, debilitating pain. And, standing in the library after Charles left, she felt a similar phantom pain sear her insides. She had to believe Charles was a cheat, but still, she could not shake a nagging feeling that perhaps she had been wrong. There was something about him that reminded her of Harry—that same wounded expression, the furrowed eyebrows . . .

The sky was ripe with the first hushed light of morning, and there was a soft knock at the door. Of course Charles had come back; where else would he go? She felt strangely relieved. But it was not Charles standing at her doorstep. It was Gladys.

"What are you doing here at this hour?" Bess asked. "Is everything all right?"

"I came to check on you."

"To check on me? How did you even know I'd be up?"

"I returned to the city last night, actually. I needed to talk to you."

George, who had come off his leave an hour earlier, entered the room, his uniform freshly pressed. "Is everything all right, Mrs. Houdini?"

Bess pulled Gladys into the house and sat her down on the sofa, then turned to the butler. "Would you get us some tea?"

When George had retreated into the kitchen, Gladys said, "You know he's Harry's son, don't you?"

Bess grabbed her hand. "Why do you say that?"

"I knew the moment I touched his face. He has the same bone structure as Harry did. Almost exactly the same. And his voice—I wasn't sure I should say anything, but I couldn't stay at the party. I had Lloyd call me a car soon after you left." She lowered her voice. "Where is he? Is he asleep?"

Bess shook her head. "I sent him away, actually. We had an argument. I accused him . . . of trying to steal from me." She put her head in her hands. "Did you know all these years that Harry had a son? Tell me the truth."

Gladys shook her head fiercely. "I swear I didn't."

"Are you completely certain he is Harry's son? I thought he was trying to deceive me."

Gladys pushed a strand of loose hair behind her ear. "I'm sorry, Bess."

Bess was shaken. Had she made a mistake in sending Charles away? Was she wrong that he had planted the photograph in the library? She couldn't bear the alternative—that Harry had kept the photograph a secret from her, had known for years that he had a son. That their inability to have children had, all along, been her fault and not his. Instead of searching the house for something Harry may have left her for her future, apparently she should have been searching for evidence of his deception.

She could not understand why Harry would have made his transgressions clear *now*, when he was not here to console her or explain to her. Why now, when he had kept the secret from her his entire life? Even on his deathbed, he had mentioned no affair, no lost son, no photograph hidden in the library. It was unbearable to recall the afternoon of Harry's death, the way he'd gripped her hand and looked at her with such unspeakable adoration. To think that even then—in that final moment of brutal honesty—he was concealing something from her . . .

She looked at the clock; it was six in the morning now. She

opened the last of the curtains, and yellow light poured in. In the center of the room, by the fire, was the leather sofa, and Harry's armchair, where he'd liked to close his eyes and rehearse his tricks before he fell asleep. Stuffed in the crevices between Harry's books were papers of all kinds—documents, letters, photographs. She had spent hours over the years opening volume after volume, searching for something that would alleviate her financial burden; but she had found nothing of value. After Harry's passing, George had offered to help her clear the room. At the time, she had contemplated selling the house and moving to California, but when she couldn't bring herself to touch Harry's things, she realized she could not go anywhere; she was a prisoner of her old life, forever.

Even with the room bathed in light, she had the eerie sensation that they were being watched. She rushed to the windows and flung the curtains closed. She stood there feeling as if she was in not her own home but a stranger's, waiting for the owners to return.

"It was that woman from the circus that night, wasn't it?" Gladys murmured.

"How did you know about that?"

"Stella told me, a long time ago."

Bess sighed. "Yes. It was her."

Gladys pressed her hand onto Bess's. "This doesn't change anything," she said. "He still loved you with all his heart."

Bess laughed cruelly. "Of course he didn't."

"He did, Bess. He loved you more than anything."

Bess felt the tears streaming down her face. She had tried so hard, her whole life, to keep her emotions to herself. But now she couldn't help it. "If he loved me so much," she demanded, "why would he want to hurt me so badly?"

"What do you mean? That's why he kept it from you all these years, probably. So he didn't hurt you."

"No." Bess stood up and began pacing the room. "You don't understand. It wasn't a coincidence that I happened to meet Charles when I was in Atlantic City. I went down there specifically to see him. Harry told me to go."

Gladys looked at her, shocked. "What are you talking about? You mean you—you got through to him after all?"

"Think about it. Do you really think, of all the millions of people in this world, that I would have just *happened* upon Harry's lost son? It was Harry's doing." She had been wanting to speak those words for so long that they seemed sacred, profound. She took a deep breath. "I've never told anyone this, but Harry left me a second code—in case the first one made its way into the wrong hands. No one could have possibly known the code but me—we never said it out loud, not once. And a few weeks ago, I came across pieces of this very code in some photographs—both of which were taken by Charles Radley."

Gladys shook her head in disbelief. "It can't be . . ."

"I told you all along." Bess stopped pacing. "I knew Harry was trying to come through to me. What I can't figure out is why the one message he would want to send would be the one that would hurt me the most."

"Maybe he was trying to be honest with you at last," Gladys ventured.

"I would have preferred dishonesty, I think."

"Would you, though? Maybe there is a reason Harry wanted you two to meet. Maybe you just haven't figured it out yet."

In a chest next to Harry's desk—the Poe desk—were albums of letters Bess had compiled when she was still a relatively young wife and had tried to bring some organization to their home. Eventually, she gave up the task, but not before she had filled over four dozen books with all the correspondence she and Harry had written to each other, and some of the photographs they'd collected together. Now, in a moment of clarity, she lifted the heavy lid of the trunk. She'd flipped through them before, many times, but she hadn't known what she was looking for then. Inside, the books were just as she'd left them, stacked neatly in three piles, the covers now black with mold.

Gladys heard the shuffling of papers. "What are you doing?"

"I'm looking for something Harry may have left behind. There must be something in here that mentions Charles."

She began pulling out the books in stacks, rifling through the pages and tossing the albums onto the floor in desperation. Surely, if Harry had been aware of a son, there would be some sign of it in these books, something she would have missed when she put them together. Certainly there would be another photograph, which she herself might even have pasted inside unknowingly, assuming, perhaps, it was of one of Harry's distant cousins.

But she had not prepared herself for the sight of Harry's handwriting. She was beaten back by it as if by a wave. There were all the letters he had written her, all the love professed, the ink still dark as if the words had just been written, as if Harry was only upstairs, having sent the letter down with the butler. *My darling, would you run out for a new silk scarf for my act tonight? My other scarf is frayed. But my love for you is not.*

There had been thousands of these notes over the years. But after Mrs. Weiss's death, the playfulness that had once characterized their marriage had disappeared. Harry had stopped writing letters to Bess and had become consumed with writing long, elaborate sermons to no one. Bess remembered how, during their last encounter, Mrs. Weiss had asked Harry to bring her back a pair of slippers from Denmark; at her funeral, Harry had stooped over the casket and placed two new pink slippers into the grave, as tenderly as if they were babies. He had become melancholy; he'd spoken often of what he called "the mortal valley of death."

He would not accept bookings for performances if they meant leaving New York, because for months he visited her grave every afternoon. His relationship with Dash, which had been tenuous over the years, had become fraught with rivalry; Harry never forgave him for being the only son present for their mother's death.

Would he, Bess had often wondered, have grieved for her the same way, if she had passed first? Looking through the early pages of their letters and all their professions toward her, she liked to believe he would have. But the truth was, she wasn't sure now. There was a part of her that feared that he was happier on the other side of death than he had been with her.

The albums brought back a rush of memories, but there was no mention in any of them of Charles, no indication even that there might have been something Harry was hiding. As she flipped through the pages, she became more and more distraught, more confused and angry, and as she sobbed she began tearing the pages out of the books. She was tired of distrust, tired of searching for things that were not there.

Then she saw it—the postcard from Atlantic City. It was a photograph of the beach outside the Royal Hotel, touched up in color with paint, as postcards from those years often were. She and Harry had returned to the city again several times after Harry's disastrous performance, when he had almost drowned. During one of their return trips he had mailed her this card so she would find it when they arrived home. It was postmarked August 1912, two months before they sailed to Europe. *You are trying to look at what I'm writing as I write this,* the back of the card said, *but I'm not going to let you see, because I am the master of surprises.* She remembered the scene vividly—Harry purchasing the card from a kiosk outside the hotel, leaning on the rail of the boardwalk as he wrote it, his back to her, laughing, Bess trying to peer over his shoulder. He had given another performance at Young's Pier, but

Young himself was not present for it, having been in Europe at the time on business. After a while, she had almost forgotten him. When she tried to recall his face now she could not.

After the show, she and Harry had sat together on the sand, watching the boardwalk lights, like tiny moons, turn on one by one.

Come enjoy the beauty of the ocean, wild and wide, the front of the postcard said, in flowery black script across the top.

Bess caught her breath. *Wild and wide . . .* They were words from the code. The tune rang in her ears: *I'll take you home again, Kathleen, across the ocean wild and wide . . .* She held the card flat in her palm, like a relic, and read it again. *The ocean wild and wide.* The words had not changed; they were still there, engraved into the face of the card. She flipped the postcard over and searched the back for some other clue—anything that would give her an indication of what kind of message was being communicated—but there was nothing but the brief, casual note Harry had jotted to her, which really said nothing at all.

The postcard was written in 1912, before their trip to Europe. She had stood with Harry as he wrote it and placed it in the postbox. She had pasted it in the album herself, years later. It was impossible that Charles, or anyone, could have manufactured its presence.

Gladys felt her way over to where Bess was seated. "What did you find?"

Bess pressed the postcard into her hand. "Another piece of the code. But this postcard was mailed fourteen years before Harry died. All the other clues were in photographs I just discovered. But I've had this for over a decade, and it's unchanged." She touched her hair distractedly. "I'm not sure what this means about how Harry is communicating with me . . . how he's managed to use something that's been in my possession for years."

Gladys ran her fingers along the cardboard. "This code you think you've found—are you sure about it?"

"I think I am."

"I never thought . . ." Gladys began, but her voice trailed off. "I never believed you, Bess."

Bess's mind was racing now; it was as if Harry had somehow plunged into her psyche and was pushing her thoughts forward. His desk . . . Why hadn't she thought of it before? It was Edgar Allan Poe's desk . . . Poe, who had written many times in his stories of secret compartments. Of course his own desk must have had one, or more. But she had never bothered to check. How could she have overlooked something so obvious? She ran her hands along the underside of the desk. She felt a ridge where the wood split in two. As she pressed her fingers along it, the wood slid back, revealing a space beneath the bottom drawer.

"Gladys," she breathed. "I just found a hidden compartment in Harry's desk. There are papers in here." The possibility of finding some kind of hidden money seemed unimportant now; she would give it all up if what she found led her to Harry himself instead.

She lifted the papers out gently; some of them felt very old and brittle. "They're letters." Inside the envelopes, the notes were all handwritten, and they were all from John Sargent, Harry's late secretary, and mailed to the various parts of the country or the world where Bess and Harry had happened to be at the time.

"What do they say?" Gladys held her hand out tentatively to touch them.

The first, at the top of the pile, was dated January 1907.

Harry, you said this lost cousin of yours lives in Atlantic City. I can imagine the shock you must have had to receive the news that a child existed at all. But I searched for his mother and I'm sorry to tell you she has died. No word of the boy's whereabouts. He seems to have disappeared. I'll keep searching. He referred to the boy as Romario Tardo.

Gladys listened with her hand on her mouth. "So Harry knew," she whispered. "He knew he had a son, but he never found out where he was."

"He was clever," Bess said. "He must have told John he was the son of his mother's cousin and enlisted John to help find him."

The next letter was dated a few months later: *Inquired of some neighbors,* Bess read, *and discovered the fate of the boy—he was sent west, it seems, by rail, to be adopted. Have not been able to find him. The records are ill-kept. It seems many of the children are given new names upon arrival.* So Harry had gone as far as to send John, in person, down to Atlantic City, to continue the search. Bess knew the import of this; Harry had relied on his secretary so heavily to manage his correspondence that he rarely liked for him to leave New York, even for business matters.

After that, the letters from John stopped. All future letters were signed by a man named Henry Fletcher, who appeared to be a private investigator of some sort.

"Harry must have worried that John would find out the truth," Bess said. "There was only so far he could take the story of a lost cousin with John."

But with Fletcher, Harry had apparently continued the ruse. Fletcher continued to refer to Romario as Harry's cousin. He had written Harry a letter on January 1 of every year from 1908 to 1926. Each letter detailed the progress, or lack of progress, of the previous year's inquiries.

"Listen to this," Bess said, holding up the letter from 1910. "It's the first time he had a real lead. *Mr. Houdini, I am writing to you with promising news. I have finally managed to trace Romario's journey west, to Des Moines, Iowa.*" But he hadn't been able to locate any more information. The records from that period had been destroyed in a fire.

"So Harry found out about Charles in late 1906 or early

1907," Gladys said thoughtfully. "When he was eleven years old. Clearly Evatima must have decided for some reason to send Harry the photograph and tell him the truth. For what? Money? Fame?"

"Maybe she had a foreboding about her death. She was involved with some dangerous people, it seems."

"Well, she was right. She must have died shortly after she sent the photograph, because by the time Harry began his search, Charles was already on the orphan train."

"And, of course, his new family changed his name. And he decided to keep it, even after he went back to New Jersey."

"These explain part of the mystery, at least. Harry never revealed himself to Charles as his father because it seems he was never been able to find him."

Bess continued reading the letters from Fletcher. By 1915 Harry began including carbon copies of his own replies. It seemed he was growing desperate. Fletcher had gone out to Des Moines to interview everyone he could find. *There is a girl here who remembers Romario,* he wrote to Harry. *She says she was in the same train car. She remembers he went to a childless couple, but she never saw him after that.* The next sentence was scribbled out, and then, it appeared, Fletcher changed his mind and decided to include it after all. *She said he was a nice boy, and he did not seem too afraid.*

Harry's response was anguished. *Damn it, man,* he wrote. *Go back out there if you've got a lead. The expense is no concern.*

In 1918 there was more news to report: Fletcher had located Romario in an archived newspaper photograph taken when the train arrived. He had included a copy of the picture in his letter. Bess held it up to the light. She recognized him from the photograph Charles had shown her; he was standing among a group of children, a cap pulled over his head, looking at something out of view of the camera. Bess stared at the picture for a long time. How might their lives have changed, she thought, if they had found him?

Harry must have kept his discovery a secret, Bess realized, not only because he didn't want to risk damaging their marriage but because he knew how much she had wanted a child. Maybe he couldn't bring himself to tell her that the fault lay in her own body, not his; all those years, he could have left her for someone else, had more children with another woman, but he chose not to. And he couldn't bear to tell her that there was an orphan out there who could be theirs, if she wanted him, only to have her hopes dashed when the boy was never found.

But he had never given up hope; he had looked for Charles for the rest of his life. In the 1926 letter—the last from Fletcher, as Harry had died that year—the trail had grown completely cold. Romario would have been thirty years old by then, and he could have been anywhere. Fletcher suggested dropping the investigation. Harry's response was tortured. *How can I continue my life, surrounded by wealth and fame, knowing somewhere out there this boy is alone? To me, he is not thirty; he will always be a little boy. I will find him, even if it's not in this life.*

His prediction was eerily accurate; it was only in death that Harry had located Charles after all.

Bess clutched the letters to her chest as the clock struck nine. She looked at it, panic setting in. The first trains out of New York began running at five in the morning. Charles could very well be in New Jersey already.

"Gladys," she breathed urgently. "We have to go after him." She scribbled a note for George asking him to call Niall about the tearoom; then she grabbed her fringed wrap from the hall closet and flung open the front door.

"What are you going to tell him?"

"Everything. And we're going to finish piecing together Harry's message."

The one thing Bess couldn't understand, still, as she and Gladys climbed into a taxicab, was why, if Harry was indeed able to communicate with her, as it seemed he was, he would have chosen a method so vague. Why wasn't he simply able to appear to her in a mirror, say, or a dream? Or through a medium? Why all these preposterous clues?

Fifteen minutes later, they emerged from the taxi onto the street corner in front of the terminal. The building was a shining architectural gem, which stood imposingly, its domed windows like the eyes of a giant stone monster. The sunlight gave the rooms inside a dusty, pearl-like glimmer. Bess's hands trembled. She had to find Charles. She felt as if she were on the edge of a precipice.

The massive vestibule was scattered with tired passengers sitting on their luggage, waiting for the trains. Many were sleeping on the benches that ran along the walls. Bess searched the room. Maybe Charles had been bluffing about leaving town. It was possible he was still sleeping at this very moment in some cheap hotel.

But he was there. He stood, his back to her, on the marble staircase, looking at the clock. His coat was hanging over his elbow, and he had one foot on the next step above, looking like a man she had seen before, a man who had waited for her on staircases all over the world. As she approached him, he turned. And for a shimmering moment, he could almost have been young Ehrich Weiss, coming to take her back to Coney Island, to have dinner at the Brighton Beach Hotel.

"Why don't you sing anymore?" Harry had asked her. "I miss your singing." It was a Sunday in Atlantic City; they were waiting for a ride on the carousel, which had been dubbed the Palace of Flying Animals. Hymnals were being passed out for riders to sing along to organ music as they rode.

The funny thing was, she didn't know why she had stopped singing. She could not even remember the words to most of her old songs. She had had a good voice, once.

Harry had handed their tokens to the operator. "You'll go on the Flip-Flap Railroad with me after this, won't you?" His eyes had gleamed.

"Certainly not." The railroad went upside down, in a loop, next to the pier. Many riders had said it had damaged their backs. "You know your body can't handle that kind of stress."

He had laughed and raised his eyebrows suggestively. "My dear, my body can handle anything."

She'd swatted at him. "You shouldn't be vulgar, Harry. You're a public figure now."

"Charles, thank God. I thought you'd be gone." Bess stood at the base of the staircase looking up at the young man, her arm looped through Gladys's elbow. Her lower lip quivered. She reached into her purse and thrust the postcard toward him. "I have to know if you've seen this before."

Charles looked at her with suspicion. "What are you doing here?" He stared at her outstretched hand and seemed to consider it for a moment disdainfully. Finally, he took the card and studied it. His expression changed. "This is my photograph," he said. "It was one of the first photographs I ever sold. I was only seventeen." He looked up at her, his expression still mistrustful. "Why did you come all the way here to show me this?"

Bess lowered her voice. "Harry's brought us together to tell us something, Charles. Please don't leave. I was wrong to accuse you of lying. You *are* his son. Certainly, deep down, you know this. Harry Houdini was your father."

Chapter 13

HOLLYWOOD

June 1923

"Well, Mrs. Houdini." Harry stood in the doorway to the back garden, grinning at her. "We've made it now." He waved a heavy canvas-covered book in the air. "We're in the dictionary!"

Bess closed her novel and blinked at him through the sunlight. "What are you going on about?"

Harry opened the book and began to read. " 'To Houdinize: Verb. To release or extricate oneself, from confinement, bonds, and the like, as by wriggling out.' Ha!" He slammed the book shut again and scooped her off the bench and kissed her.

In a few hours they would be standing outside the Los Angeles premiere of his most recent motion picture, *Haldane of the Secret Service*. The theater was expecting crowds in the thousands.

"Tonight, darling, you should wear the white dress that I love so much."

"But we're still going for a swim with the Londons first? It's so hot."

Harry feigned insult. "You mean you'd rather a double date with those bores than a romantic afternoon with a motion picture star?"

"If it means cooling off a little, yes." Bess stood on her toes and kissed the side of Harry's neck. He smelled different in California. The California air was nothing like New York air. It was cleaner here; they had lemon trees in their yard. And Harry was happier, too, doing his stunts for film as an established movie celebrity, although it had been difficult to get him to agree to leave New York. When he was first offered a leading role in a picture, he had been in a lengthy and dark depression, even though no one who'd seen him perform would have suspected. He had made a five-ton elephant vanish at the New York Hippodrome—the pinnacle of his career—and the papers had had a field day with the trick afterward, quoting Harry's quip, "Fellows, even the elephant does not know how it is done!" But afterward, instead of sleeping, he would retreat to the fireplace in the library and attempt another failed communication with his mother. The house where they had all lived together became a venue for these one-way communications—every mirror a place where she might appear, every Victrola record an opportunity for her voice to come through. But Mrs. Weiss never appeared, and she never spoke to him. Every morning Harry would stare at her photograph and say, "Well, Mama, I have not heard from you. I have not heard." He knew she was his one avenue to prove that the afterlife existed, and he desperately wanted to know what was on the other side.

One evening he came rushing out of the bathroom, his face lathered in shaving cream. "Bess, come quick!" He was nearly delirious with excitement. "I think my mother is trying to reach me!" Bess tossed her needlework aside and ran into the bathroom.

"Listen," he whispered. They stood silently side by side, until Bess began to hear a muted, erratic tapping noise. "It's some kind of code," Harry said.

Bess followed the origin of the noise to the window, and pulled open the shade. Outside, the shutter was hanging loose from its hinges, and the wood was knocking against the house. It almost broke her heart to tell him; for a moment she considered letting him believe, but in the end, she could not.

Harry's face fell. He laughed a little. "How ridiculous of me," he said at last and went back to shaving.

Then the offer from Ben Rolfe at Octagon Films came for Harry to film *The Master Mystery*. Bess begged Harry to do it. California, she knew, could be a new start for them. But it was only after she had convinced John Sargent, Jim Vickery, Jim Collins, and two more men from Harry's crew to come with them that Harry gave in. The men adored Harry, despite his fiery outbursts, the occasions on which he would fire them, then greet them the next morning as if nothing had happened. Periodically, they would raise their own salaries, as Harry always forgot to address such issues. When Bess looked at the books and questioned Harry about the raises, he defended them. "Of course it's okay!" he told her, indignant. "Think of the high cost of living!"

So they were swept into the chaos of Hollywoodland—the poolside parties, the champagne on silver trays, the catered lunches behind painted wooden sets. It was a different world of celebrity from the one they had enjoyed in New York. The enchanted city was, essentially, a desert town, dusty and mountainous, that had been transformed into a kind of fairy tale—a self-made utopia. Everyone was there. They went to places like the El Fay Club and lived large—visiting Rudolph Valentino at Falcon Lair and William Randolph Hearst at San Simeon, his estate enormous with Gothic fireplaces, sundecks, pipe organs, pagodas, and projection rooms.

A month before their departure westward, Harry had surprised Bess with a weekend in Coney Island at the Brighton Beach Hotel. It was as extravagant as she had remembered, gold-gilded and marbled and salt-aired. But it also felt worn-out. Oddly, she had left feeling not nostalgic but indifferent, as if that part of her life had belonged to someone she barely knew, someone she might pass on the street with only a flicker of recognition. California, on the other hand, seemed fraught with glitz and energy, the hotels even more opulent than the Brighton Beach.

The studios were just being built, and Bess marveled at this vast landscape dotted with massive, skylit buildings, the warehouses filled with costumes, the miniature cities built overnight. It all seemed like a grandiose version of the playacting she had done as a child, but these actors performed with more gravity than she had, much the way Harry performed his own art onstage. The streets where the more modest moviemakers lived were lined with orange flowers and white-fenced houses. After supper people sat on their porches until the sun went down, and there was a lazy, dreamy quality to those California evenings that reminded her of the ones she had spent as a little girl in the rowhouse in Brooklyn, when one could still be anything.

Renting the house down the street from them in Laurel Canyon was another well-known couple, Jack and Charmian London. They had come to Hollywood from Sonoma to sort out contracts for screenplays of Jack's work. Some years before, Jack had written a novel titled *The Call of the Wild*, which had garnered him instant fame. He'd led an adventurous life, which he liked to recount during late Friday night dinners. He had lived in Alaska during the Klondike Gold Rush, had spent time in a Japanese prison, and had tended grapes in a vineyard. He and Harry had an eerie number of things in common. Both had massive book collections; Jack's first wife had been named Bess; and his mother had been a spiritualist performer, back when the art had first become popular.

Bess, for her part, was enamored with Charmian, who embodied the freedom of spirit Bess was still trying to achieve. She was dark-haired and voluptuous and seemed, to Bess, to be a more exciting and beautiful version of herself. What distinguished her most of all in Bess's eyes was that Charmian was not simply her husband's companion. She had a career of her own; she was a writer, too, and had published short stories.

"Jack's having a bad day today," Charmian told her, as they set up their sun umbrellas. The seagulls wheeled overhead. Bess looked at the water where the men were wading. Jack London had been sick for years with uremic poisoning, and was on and off morphine.

"Is there anything we can do?" Bess brushed the sand off her arms. "You shouldn't feel obligated to go with us tonight, you know."

Charmian shaded her eyes. "Darling, we wouldn't miss it. We've seen those doorknob tags."

Bess had come up with the idea to distribute thousands of tags promoting Harry's movie; they were printed with the words *This lock is not Houdini-proof.* "Yes," Bess said, "Harry's particularly fond of those."

Charmian laughed. "A picture that will thrill you to the marrows, I've read."

"I certainly hope so. *The Man from Beyond* didn't fare so well. Harry put so much into that one, too." Bess shielded her eyes from the sun. "I feel happy here—happier than I've ever been in New York. And I think Harry's found his first real friend in Jack. What Jack does, his writing, I mean—it's like Harry's art. His account of the San Francisco earthquake in *Collier's*—I'll never forget it. *And for three days and nights this lurid tower swayed in the sky, reddening the sun, darkening the day, and filling the land with smoke.* It was both beautiful and terrifying."

"Yes, but Harry deals in secrets, not in words. That's much

more fascinating. I imagine you know many of them. His secrets, I mean."

For a moment Bess saw herself as she imagined others must see her—glamorous and full of mystery. She wanted to be those things in California. She didn't just want to be, for all her first-class travel and royal introductions, a middle-aged woman who'd loved the right man. As she discovered, people liked her in Hollywood. From the moment they'd arrived, several years before, the invitations had come to their house in her name, too, not just in Harry's. And she felt useful; she enjoyed sweeping about the parties, negotiating Harry's contracts and soliciting others. Since Harry had begun his own production company, putting him in charge of his scripts and casts, there was more than enough work to keep her in the office all afternoon.

And Harry had been infinitely more romantic since they had come to Los Angeles. On occasion he seemed so full of energy that she could see a glimmer of the old Harry. He liked to play little tricks on her. Once she had come home from a luncheon to find a note in her bathroom. *Mrs. Houdini*, it began, *you are a modern woman of liberal ideas. You will not be angry if I keep a date this evening. I expect to meet the most beautiful lady in the world at the corner of Hollywood and Sunset Boulevards at 6:30. I shall be home very late.* She had dressed herself in a blue dress and found Harry waiting where he said he'd be, with a car ready to take them to a jazz club. That night he planned their anniversary party at the Hotel Alexandria, and the long, crystal-bedecked tables they would have, filled with food and orange blossoms and hundreds of people.

"Yes," Bess told Charmian. "I am privy to many of his secrets. But many of them are frightfully mundane."

"Oh, I doubt that."

Bess felt a drop of water on her cheek and looked up to see

Harry standing over her, soaking wet. She squealed and threw him a towel. "You devil, don't get me wet!"

Jack had taken a seat behind Charmian and was cradling her head in his lap, massaging her scalp. It was clear he adored her.

"Come on, Bess." Harry held out his hand. "We should get home and dress."

In 1919, at the premiere of *The Master Mystery*, Bess had stepped out of the car in front of Harry to a dizzying lineup of flashbulbs. The theater had fit only three hundred but there were five times as many as that in the crowd, pushing their way toward the red ropes in front of the entrance. Harry was used to attention, but he wasn't used to the blinding Hollywood fame. Hands had reached out to grab him. He'd turned and looked uncomfortably at Bess.

"It's just like your magic shows," she'd told him, grasping his elbow. "Just hold up your head and smile."

Harry's producer, Rolfe, had swept them through the doors and ushered them into the lobby, where reporters peppered Harry with questions about the logistics of his escape scenes. The movie was a smash. In one scene Harry, hanging by his thumbs, managed to get the antagonist into a chokehold using only his legs. Reaching into the man's pocket with his toes, he extracted a key that freed him from his restraints. The audience had gone wild for it.

Now they stepped out of their car, Bess swathed in white silk, to see a paltry crowd of a hundred or so waiting for autographs. Bess glanced over at Harry, who looked stricken. "There's—there's no one here," he muttered.

"*Don't* let on that you're disappointed," Bess said.

Harry set his jaw and tried to smile. Inside, their friends were waiting to celebrate—Gloria Swanson and the Londons and Sargent and Vickery drinking champagne in the carpeted lobby.

"It's too late," Harry said, his face darkening. "It's failed. I can tell."

"You can't tell a damn thing."

"Well, it's not the *weather* that's keeping them home."

Harry spent the screening slouched in his seat, glancing surreptitiously at the audience for their reactions as they watched him rescue Gladys Leslie from a vile gang of counterfeiters. He'd put his best work into this picture, his most daring escapes, even going so far as to stage an elaborate heist on a Hollywood street to promote the movie, leading to the unveiling of an enormous movie banner.

The screening received polite applause. Afterward, anticipating Harry's dark mood, Bess stood up in his place and invited everyone to join them at Sunset Inn in Santa Monica.

Managed by the famous restaurateur Eddie Brandstatter, Sunset Inn was the place where many of the movie actors spent their evenings, because it was elegant but cheap, and there really wasn't as much money in movies as everyone thought. The restaurant featured a hot and cold buffet and a dizzying rotation of cocktails on illicit menus; California was far from the grips of Prohibition, and everyone knew it. Actors and singers of all levels of fame were encouraged to give impromptu performances. By the time they arrived, Al Jolson was lounging at the bar, and Charles Harrison was on the stage crooning "I'm Always Chasing Rainbows." Bess was quietly awed by these guests. Sometimes it seemed she had invented them, and the whole life she'd stepped into here—the perfume of the women's corsages, the lights glittering at the bottoms of the hills—was just smoke.

Clara Bow hadn't been at the screening, but she was at the restaurant, nursing a glass of red wine. She had Hollywood in a tailspin, claiming engagements with everyone from Gary Cooper to Victor Fleming. Now she came sauntering up to Harry, batting her little-girl eyelashes, and set her glass of wine down on the table beside him. "Well if it isn't the great Harry Houdini," she said in her tiny voice. "I'll tell you. I've been dying to see you do your needle trick."

She blinked at Bess with a small smile. Bess laughed and picked up her own glass. "Go on, Harry," she said, refusing to be baited. "Do a few tricks."

The night before the filming of his first love scene with Marguerite Marsh for *The Master Mystery*, Bess had woken up to find Harry pacing the hallway, unable to sleep. Bess had led him back to bed. "Oh, go ahead and love her, for God's sake," she'd told him. "Customers don't pay to see their leading men be faithful to their off-screen wives." And she had kept her word; she wasn't angry. Flirtations by other women only served to make Harry more appealing as a star.

Now she saw Harry brighten at Clara's invitation to perform. Live magic was his forte; he carried a deck of cards and little tokens of magic in his pocket at all times. "If I can rustle together some needles, I'll swallow them for you," he told the actress.

A crowd had gathered around them. Bess went into the kitchen and came back with an orange. "Forget needles," she told Harry, tossing him the orange. "You know he can swallow this?" she asked the onlookers.

"Oh, do tell me you're kidding," Clara said.

Jack London clapped Harry on the back. "Oh, I've seen it," he said. "I'm not sure whether it's illusion or some kind of grotesque reality."

Bess retreated toward the bar in search of Gloria Swanson; she wanted to talk to the actress about convincing Paramount to allow her a role in Harry's next picture. When she couldn't find her, Bess circled back toward Harry on the other side of the room.

As she approached, Harry stepped out of the crowd. "Mrs.

Houdini," he said, holding out his hand. "Would you care to have dinner with me?"

"Harry, no," she said. "We can't go off by ourselves at your party."

"I've already reserved us a table." He gestured toward one of the many open tables at the back of the room. He led her to her seat and pulled in a nearby server. Bess ordered an Aviation cocktail.

"I do wish you wouldn't have liquor tonight," he said, frowning. "I wanted to talk to you."

Bess pressed her lips together. "Don't lecture me, Harry. It's supposed to be a celebratory night."

His face softened. He reached across the table and took her hand. "You know, when I first came in here, I didn't recognize you. You looked just like a young girl."

"You charmer." Bess smiled. "You know you received another bag of mail today. The old ladies love you."

Between films Harry would occasionally perform in venues around Los Angeles. Since his mother's death, he would bring bouquets of roses with him and incorporate the flowers into his act, tossing them into the lap of any gray-haired lady in the audience. One of his most cherished letters had arrived shortly after the release of his first picture. Among the letters from enthralled moviegoers was one from a frail old woman who had attended one of his shows. *How did you know I needed a rose?* she asked in delicate script. *I am very lonely. I came to your performance to see the crowds, to know there were others on earth. A lonely, lonely woman, and you threw me a rose.* Harry had clutched the letter to his chest, his eyes tearing, as if it were his own mother who had written him.

The waiter came to their table with two menus pasted onto white cardboard. When he left, Harry put down the menu and said, "We can't stay."

Bess looked up. "Why? We have nothing to do tomorrow."

"No. I mean we can't stay here. In California."

Bess laughed. "Of course we can."

Harry cleared his throat. "The picture's a flop."

"How could you know that? It's only just premiered."

"Oh, come on, Bess. You saw the crowd tonight. I may get fan letters, but people have tired of my movies." He rubbed his hand across his face. "I'm not an actor. I'm a magician. I've put everything into the film company when I should have been working on my magic. And the money's nearly gone."

Bess shook her head. "Don't talk to me like a child, Harry. I've seen the books. I know exactly how much money we've spent. There may not be enough to live lavishly, but we're not done—" She stopped as she saw his face darken. Her whole world seemed to be collapsing around her—all the easy simplicity of their new life out West, the dreams she had of their retiring there, adopting children . . . He was taking it all away from her.

Harry slammed his fist on the table. "We are done if I say we're done."

"No, Harry." Bess stiffened. "You don't get to take this away from me. We have a *home* here. You can go crawling back to New York if you'd like. But I'm staying."

"And do what? Everything you have to do here is because of me."

"Oh, you're cruel," she said.

Harry didn't answer. Across the room, Al Jolson had taken the stage and was singing, *There's a lump of sugar down in Dixie and it's all my own, she's the sweetest little bunch of sweetness I have ever known.*

"Mr. Harry Houdini!" A red-cheeked young waiter rushed over to their table and pumped Harry's hand. "Congratulations on your new picture." He hunched toward Bess in an awkward bow. "I didn't get to meet you last night, Mrs. Houdini. But it's a pleasure."

Bess smiled. "You must be mistaken. Harry and I weren't here last night."

The boy looked confused. "But you were sitting at this same table. I nearly spoke to you then, but I couldn't get up the courage."

Harry scribbled an autograph on a napkin and gave it to the boy. "Wonderful to meet you," he said.

The waiter's face turned red. "I'm—I'm sorry for the interruption." He rushed away, clutching the napkin in his hand.

Bess looked at Harry, confused. "You weren't here last night, were you? You said you had a meeting at the studio."

Harry's face grew dark. "It was nothing to mention."

"What was nothing?"

"I had dinner with Charmian."

His voice sounded very far away to her.

"Charmian?" she repeated.

"Please don't be dramatic. I wish you hadn't drunk so much tonight."

"Don't you dare try to turn this back on me!" She couldn't believe what he was telling her. "Are you—are you having an affair with her?"

Harry waved his hand. "No! Nothing like that."

"How could you do this?" Her voice broke. She stood up, knocking the silverware to the floor. "And with Jack being sick—"

"I know Jack's sick, damn it!" Harry banged his fist on the table. He lowered his voice. "Would you sit the hell down? You're making a scene."

"Oh, God forbid I make a scene at *your* party." The room seemed to spin around her. Bess sat down and folded her trembling hands in her lap. "Tell me it's not true, Ehrich."

Harry winced.

"I'm the only one who knew you when you were him. Did you forget that?"

Victoria Kelly

"Damn it, Bess," Harry said. "I'm not sleeping with her. It's not about Charmian anyway. It's about Jack."

"What about Jack?"

"The man's dying, for Christ's sake."

Bess drew in a breath. "What?"

"Charmian's in love with her husband, not with me. She asked me to dinner to talk about Jack. Apparently you got loose-lipped with her about my own kidney injuries. She wanted to know if I could help her find him a doctor."

"And . . . could you?"

Harry shook his head. "He's been to everyone I would have seen."

"Oh, God," Bess said. "Is he really—?"

Harry nodded.

My little lump of sugar down in Dixie, mine all mine, Jolson sang. The room seemed to still around her. The doors to the patio were open and the room was cool with the breeze and the women's long dresses rustled as they danced.

Suddenly none of it seemed to matter any longer—the celebrity, the ocean, the lemon trees in the yard—and the sense that she had her own work, her own value, in Hollywood. She would, Bess realized, leave it all behind for Harry. For perhaps the first time in his career, it wasn't about the money for him. He was asking her to leave California because the place had broken him. People didn't understand that the tricks he did on screen were authentic, that they nearly cost him his life every time. Another actor could replicate them any day with a few well-placed camera angles. His talent was in live performance, where audiences could believe that his magic was real. In Hollywood everything—romances, magic—was manufactured. Harry could never be the Great Houdini in Hollywood. And he couldn't live without being the Great Houdini.

"I bet we're the only people in here who've actually been to Dixie," Bess said quietly. "Remember the tiny trailer we used to live in?"

Harry smiled. "I had to cut holes in the walls of our bedroom, just to try to get some relief from the hot nights."

"Those were some crazy years."

Harry's face crumpled. "Don't you see, Bess? I'm yours till the end. In this life, and after."

Chapter 14

CENTRAL PIER

June 1929

The house was not at all what she expected. It stood, a monument of gray stone, four blocks from the ocean, the porch white as washed linen. The grass was cut to an inch in height, and, inside, the rooms were shining. There were no dishes in the sink, and no shoes in the hall. A single black hat hung on a rack by the door. She would never have guessed that a single man lived there.

"Do you own this?" she asked, running her hands along the wooden banister. She turned to Gladys to describe it. "It's nearly perfect."

Charles shrugged. "I purchased it a few years ago. Thinking, perhaps, I would have a family one day."

"You still can," she said. "You don't have to be a priest, you know. It's not too late to choose a different path."

He continued to surprise her. She had not expected him to forgive her so quickly at the train station, nor had she expected that he would have agreed to let her go back to New Jersey with him. But she was certain now that Harry had brought them together, for some greater purpose.

It made sense, now, why Harry had refused to adopt a child all those years. All along, he had been looking for his own son. Adopting someone else's son while his own was out in the world without him must have seemed unbearable.

Bess looked through the window onto the green, square yard. The house, on the eastern side of Ventnor, was far from the chaos of the Atlantic City tourist area. The lawns of the neighboring houses were cluttered with children's bicycles.

"It's a very pretty neighborhood."

"Yes, I feel sometimes I don't quite fit in here."

The walls, she noticed, were peculiarly bare. In the hallway he had framed three photographs of the boardwalk, which, she assumed, he had taken for the newspaper. Besides these, there was no other artwork in the house. There were no photographs of family or friends, no stacks of books lying about, no indication of what kind of man lived there at all. It was a beautiful, empty house, and he seemed to her suddenly a very lonely boy who was pretending to be grown up. She saw now that he hadn't really come to a decision about his future at all.

She wandered into the parlor, where a tiny upholstered sofa stood, alone, in the center of the room. Charles leaned against the doorway, his hands in his pockets, enjoying the look of surprise on her face as she explored the house.

"You know, Charles, I was wrong about you. I accused you of deception and selfishness—all the bad sides of Harry, perhaps. But the truth is you have many of his good qualities. I don't think you've let the boy grow out of you yet. That was one thing about Harry. He was always young. Even as I got older, he was always young."

Charles's smirk disappeared. "I know you're certain he was trying to find me all those years. But what if you're wrong? What if he knew where I was all along? I'm not sure I want to be his son."

On the train, Bess and Gladys had shown him the letters they'd found in Harry's desk. Charles had confirmed that his name had indeed once been Romario Tardo.

"He didn't know," Gladys said. "Truly he didn't." She lowered herself onto the sofa, and Bess sat next to her.

"What I am certain of," Bess said, "is that there is some sort of message he's trying to send, and you're the only one who can help decipher it." She reached up and clasped his hand. "You're the key to all of this." Her fingers trembled as she took the postcard from her purse. "You read the newspapers when Arthur Ford revealed the code Harry left for me. I suppose . . . I could have loved Arthur, given enough time. But more than that, he almost shattered my hope of ever seeing Harry again." She removed her gloves. She had looked at these hands every day of her life; Harry had touched these hands. But now they were worn. "I told you I thought there was a message from Harry embedded in your photographs. But what I didn't have a chance to tell you before—before our argument—was what that message was. It was a second code."

Charles was stunned. "A second code? Do you know what this means, how many people would be dying to get their hands on that information?"

Bess nodded. "It was to be, Harry said, a safeguard of sorts. No one knew of its existence but us." She handed him the postcard. "In the past week alone, I have found parts of this code in three photographs. All of which were taken by you."

Charles looked at the card and nodded. "So where is the code in this one?"

Bess hesitated. Once she said it out loud, there would be no going back. There was no third code. If Charles broke her trust and sold her secret, Harry might never be able to come back to her. She would never know what had happened to him.

"There was a song I sang," she said, running her hands over

her wedding ring, "when I first met him. Not 'Rosabel'—another song. He was barely Harry Houdini then. His name was Ehrich Weiss." She hummed the tune for Charles.

I'll take you home again, Kathleen
across the ocean wild and wide
to where your heart has ever been
since first you were my bonnie bride.

She gestured toward the door. "In the front pocket of my case, there, are the other two photographs."

Charles rummaged through the case and retrieved the photographs. Bess motioned for him to sit beside her. "This one—this was the first I found." She unfolded the magazine article about the Miss America pageant. "See here, how the billboard and the caption together read 'Home Again Kathleen'? And this one. Your photograph of the yacht—I only had the billboard, so I had a smaller copy photographed to take with me—'Home Again.' And the postcard." She pointed to the flowery script at the top of the card. *"The ocean, wild and wide."*

Charles studied the pictures carefully. "I see the phrases from the song, yes. But—"

Gladys finished his question. "But don't you think there's still a chance this could be a coincidence? That you wanted to find evidence of the code so badly that you found a connection where there was none?"

Bess laughed. "A coincidence? That all these photographs were taken by a son I never knew existed?"

"True," Gladys said. "But what do you hope to gain from this, in the end? Let's say Harry is trying to communicate with you—"

"Which he is."

"Yes. What do these photographs tell us, other than that he

made it to the other side? Maybe the purpose was simply to bring you and Charles together. Maybe there's nothing more to it than what you've already discovered—each other."

"No. There's more to it than we've seen so far. There's a message hidden here." Bess looked at Charles. "When he died, I think Harry intended to come back for me. Physically, I mean. If he could find a way."

Charles ran his hands over the photographs. "So you're saying that . . . what you hope to gain from all this—is that you think you will actually *see* him?"

Bess nodded. "Yes. Somehow, I will."

"As in, he is reborn somehow?"

"No, no, nothing like that. But his whole body of work was so *visual*, you know? He built his life on the seen and unseen. And if he promised he would come back to me—well, I just don't think he would be satisfied with ambiguity."

"But then why hasn't he just appeared to you, say, as a ghost?" Gladys persisted. "Or through a medium? Why all these clues?"

"Because Harry loved tricks. His whole life was an illusion. He *lived* his magic. Nothing was ever what it seemed." Even their marriage, she couldn't help thinking, was an illusion. He had kept secrets even from her.

Charles sat down beside her. "What's next?"

"We have to look at your other photographs."

He ran his fingers through his hair and sighed. "It's a big task," he said, standing up. "Come into the study."

Even though he said he hadn't, Charles, it seemed, had saved a copy of every photograph he'd ever taken, from the time he was seven years old. There were thousands of pictures, haphazardly tossed in boxes stacked end to end across the study floor. The room was overwhelming. Gladys could not contribute; she sat, agitated, on the desk chair and asked one question after another about the progress they were making. Two hours later, they had come up with nothing. The daylight was dimming, and Charles stood to turn on the electric lights. Bess remained on the floor in the pool of photographs, forlorn.

In the fading sunlight she felt suddenly sentimental. She looked at the disorder around her, Charles eagerly sorting through every picture he had ever taken, because, as she did, he believed in the reality, or the myth, of Harry Houdini's spirit.

"I treated you poorly, Charles," she said, looking up at him. He stood above her and pushed his shirtsleeves up his forearms, as Harry used to do. It occurred to her for the first time that she could love this boy—not just in theory, but really, truly, love him. "I'm sorry I lost my temper with you before."

Charles said, "If I ask you something, will you answer me honestly?"

"Of course."

"If your husband had told you about me, would you have taken me in? Another woman's child?"

"You would have been—" Bess stopped. Her voice broke. "You would have been my son. I would have loved you all along."

Charles's hands were white. "I needed a mother and you needed a son. But we didn't find each other until it was too late."

"It's not too late."

"Isn't it? I'm not a little boy anymore."

"Harry loved his mother till the day he died. I used to wonder why we never did adopt any children. We kept saying, later, later. And later never came. And of course, now I realize why he kept putting off the decision; he was hoping he would find you. But I think now, looking back, that Harry was also very much like a boy himself, a kind of Peter Pan, if you will, who never grew up." She paused. "You would have loved him." She cleared her throat and swept her hands through the piles of photographs covering the floor. "We can't possibly have looked at everything, can we? I feel like we are missing something."

Charles ran his hands through his hair again. "I don't know, but I'm exhausted."

Bess tried not to panic. She did not want him to dismiss them to their hotel without finding anything, because she might never get another chance.

Gladys crept over to her side and knelt down beside her. "Perhaps there is another way."

"No, no. There can't be." Bess looked about the room, but there were only those three newspaper photographs on the wall. She'd looked at them a hundred times in desperation, and none of them had any words on them she could decipher from the code.

Then something occurred to her. "What's the biggest bank around here?"

Charles thought about it. "The Boardwalk National Bank, I suppose. Why?"

Gladys's eyes widened. "Of course. It would have to be one he knew would still be around, years later."

"What do you mean?" Charles asked.

"Years before he died," Bess explained, "Harry told me he had arranged some kind of financial security, in case anything ever happened to him. He didn't mean an insurance policy—he never trusted those. I always believed he had hidden money somewhere else. We were never exactly rich; I was always hounding him about spending more than we took in. And he knew there was a debt on the house. So he knew I would have difficulty if he died."

"And you think this money is in a bank here?" Charles asked.

"It makes sense," Gladys said. "Bess inquired at banks in New York. But Harry knew you had lived here at one point. It would have been a safer place to hide it." And Atlantic City had held special meaning for Bess and Harry, too; it had been the place where she had almost lost him once, but had not, in more ways than one.

"But how would he have known you would find it?"

Bess traced Harry's image on one of the photographs. "I found the letters he left, looking for you. I think he knew I would find everything eventually."

She stood up. "And I'm wondering if there's a photograph there, too, that will give us the last piece of the code."

The Boardwalk National Bank was an impressive, columned building with marble floors and crystal chandeliers. A large American flag was draped across one white wall of the lobby, and an enormous wooden clock hung on the other. There were a dozen tellers counting bills and signing forms behind tall glass windows, and every one of their stations was occupied.

"What do we do?" Gladys asked.

"I suppose we just stand in line."

When they reached an open teller, Bess asked for a manager. Fortunately, she was recognized, and ushered into a large office off the lobby, where a trim, mustached man in a pin-striped suit greeted them.

"Mrs. Houdini," the man said, taking her hand. "What a pleasure to meet you. I'm Richard Warren. What can I help you with?" He gestured toward the open seats across from his desk.

Charles helped Gladys into one of them, and then he and Bess sat down. "I believe my husband may have opened an account here," Bess said. "But I'm afraid I'm not sure what kind of account it was, or what name it was under." She slid a piece of paper toward him. "It could have been any of these names."

"Houdini, Weiss, Rahner, Tardo," Warren read. "Well, I can tell you with certainty there is nothing here under the name Houdini. I would have known about it if there was."

"Of course. I didn't think so."

"But if you give me a few minutes, I can check on these other ones for you." He took the paper and went through a door that led to a suite of offices, where an army of pert, manicured secretaries clicked loudly on their typewriters.

"What if it's not here?" Gladys whispered.

"There has to be something," Bess said.

Fifteen minutes later, Warren returned. He was holding a blue card instead of the paper Bess had given him. Bess stood up. "What did you find?"

He handed her the card. "There was no bank account under any of these names. But there is a safe-deposit box. It appears it was paid for in full for a period of twenty-five years. Under the names Beatrice Rahner and Romario Tardo."

Gladys let out of a sigh of relief. "So either name could access it?"

Warren nodded and looked at Gladys and Charles. "But are either of you Rahner or Tardo?"

Bess stepped forward. "I'm Beatrice Rahner."

The manager looked at her. "Mrs. Houdini, really, I can't just—"

"It's my legal name," she explained. "My maiden name."

"It is? I didn't realize." He examined the paper and handed it back to her. "I'll escort you." He opened the door to the offices again and led them down a long corridor to an elevator. Bess squeezed Gladys's hand.

"There has to be something," Gladys assured her.

Warren led them into an enormous vault on the third floor, where thousands of tiny drawers lined the walls from floor to ceiling. Charles stared at them in amazement. "I've never been in a place like this."

Warren walked along the far wall until he found the box

he was looking for and pulled it out of its slot. He set it on the wooden table in the center of the room. "I'm afraid I have to ask. But did your husband leave you a key?"

Bess blinked at him. "A key?"

"Each of these boxes requires two keys to open it—mine and the box owner's." He gestured toward the thin metal box. There were indeed two small brass key slots.

"But—what do you do if the owner's key is lost?" Bess asked.

"Well, in that case, I would have to issue a new key," the manager said. "I'm so sorry. I hate to tell you this. But it takes a week to process the paperwork through the proper channels."

"Oh dear," Bess said. "I'm afraid I'm only in town for today. Couldn't you bypass the paperwork and open it for me now? I can fill out the forms afterward."

Warren shook his head remorsefully. "I'm so sorry, Mrs. Houdini, but I have to follow procedure." He held out his hands. "If the bank owner ever found out, I could lose my job."

Gladys was studying the box with her hands. "Bess," she said slowly. "Are you quite sure you don't have the key after all? Harry did leave you a number of them."

Bess looked at the box and understood what Gladys was getting at. She felt like a dunce for not thinking of it sooner. She pulled her ring of keys out of her purse and thumbed through them. "Well, I'm a fool." She laughed. "He did, didn't he? It must be one of these."

The manager understood. "That solves the problem," he said, nodding. "Surely it must be one of those." He used his own key to open the top lock and then slid the box toward Bess. "I'll leave you in private now." He gestured toward a bell on the wall. "You can use that to call when you are finished. It rings in my office."

When he had gone, Charles looked at Bess. "So how are you going to open this without the key?"

Victoria Kelly

Bess smiled. "I spent thirty years with the world's best lock-smith." She removed one of her hairpins and inserted it into the lock. "It's not too tricky." She closed her eyes and tried to feel around the inside of the lock as Harry had taught her. After a few moments, it clicked open. Gladys heard the noise and clapped.

"What's inside?" she asked.

Bess slid open the lid. Inside, wrapped in velvet, were two dozen heavy gold coins. "Oh, Harry," she said.

"It's gold," Charles said to Gladys. "A lot of it. I've never seen anything like it."

Bess held one in her palm and studied it in amazement. "They're just like the ones he gave your mother on our trip to the Catskills. Do you remember? He must have set some aside." She handed one to Gladys.

"Are they enough to cover your debts?" Gladys asked.

"Yes, and more." She looked at Charles. "But you know, half of these are yours."

Charles stared at her. "Mine? No, I don't think so."

"The box was in both our names. He intended these for us both."

"But you need them."

Bess pressed one of the coins into his hand. "There are more than enough here. Did you think I was really going to bring you into my life and then cast you aside when I got what I wanted?"

Charles looked inside the box again. "But, Bess—there's no photograph."

Bess had almost forgotten about the photograph. She turned the box upside down and examined it, but could find nothing else, even hidden inside. "That can't be . . ."

"There's nothing else?" Gladys asked. "Not even a letter? Nothing?"

Bess's voice cracked. "No."

"Maybe there is no other photograph. Maybe the whole point was to lead you to find this."

"No, no." Bess shook her head. "Money wasn't the point at all. Of course, there was always the debt issue, but I still haven't found *him*. He promised."

Gladys touched her shoulder. "Why do you want to find him so badly? Isn't it enough to know that he loved you?"

Bess's hands began to shake. "It's not enough. I need to know that this isn't the end for us. That I'm going to see him again."

Gladys's voice was soft. "But perhaps it's time to say good-bye and move on."

Bess looked at the cold steel boxes, stacked around them like bricks. "I suppose I'm no different than everyone else. I'm afraid, too, of what there is after all this"—she waved her hand—"is gone."

"I believe you will see him again, in another life," Charles said. "But maybe he just can't find a way to tell you that. You'll just have to believe it will be."

"My whole life, I have *believed*. Believe in the sacraments, my mother said, and I did. I believed. Believe we'll be famous, Harry told me, and I did. Believe people will come see the shows. Believe Hollywood will embrace us. Believe I will come back." Her whole body ached; she could feel herself growing older, the slight papering of her skin, the slow laboring of her heart. "But I'm tired of believing. I just want to *know*."

By the time they arrived back at Charles's house, she felt deflated.

Charles cleared his throat. "Of course you both must stay the night here. There's some food in the kitchen. If you help yourselves, I'll make up the guest rooms for you."

She wasn't hungry. When she was finally alone in her room,

Bess closed the door and stood looking at her case. She barely had the energy to open it. It was still early, but she wanted nothing more than to take a bath and put on her robe. In one sense, her search had been successful, but in another, she felt a long journey had come to an end. She had finally, and definitively it seemed, lost Harry.

Charles had made the bed and placed three folded towels on top of the quilt. On the bedside table, he had leaned the cardboard photograph he had found in Harry's library against the lamp. She lay on her side on the bed and stared at the image. His boyhood face stared out at her, a reminder that perhaps she hadn't lost everything.

Suddenly, she sat up. She went to the door and flung it open. "Charles! Gladys!" she called into the hallway. "Come quickly!"

Charles rushed into her room, Gladys following with her hand on his shoulder. "What is it?" he breathed.

Bess waved the card in front of him. "This is it! This is the last photograph! It was here all along."

Charles looked at her skeptically. "But I didn't take that photograph. And there are no words in it anyway. How can that be the one we were looking for?"

"But you're *in* it. It's practically the same thing. Look!" She pointed to the painted studio backdrop. "Here." Behind Charles's left arm, in the faded black-and-white clouds, was a fat-cheeked baby angel in white sleeves. On the cuff of one of the sleeves was a small embroidered heart. The little symbol seemed, somehow, out of place, as if it had been pasted on.

"It's the expression—wear your heart on your sleeve. *Where your heart has ever been* . . . They're the words from the song." She waved the photograph at him. "Don't look at me like that. I know you think I'm reaching. But this is exactly the kind of game Harry loved. He loved wordplay like this." Riddles had thrilled him. He'd hid them in the notes he passed her from floor to floor of their house, always trying to stump her: palindromes, double entendres, puns, and rebus puzzles, messages hidden in pictures. He would write out the letters of the alphabet, for example, leaving out the letter *u*, to mean *missing you*. Or he would hide their dinner plans in an acrostic disguised as a love poem.

Charles examined the photograph closely. "I suppose . . ."

Bess shivered with excitement. "There's something to this, I'm telling you."

Gladys turned to the light coming through the window. "Let's say you are right—what does it all mean?"

"It means there's a message here."

"But how do you know there are only four pictures you're supposed to be using, and not more?"

"I don't. Can you fetch the other three?" Bess asked Charles. "I need to look at them all."

When he came back, she spread the four photographs on the floor in front of them, in chronological order, starting with the most recent, and squinted at them. She felt a curious energy surging through her. "Charles, help me. My eyes are failing. Do you see anything else on these? Any other words?"

Charles opened a drawer in his desk and rummaged through its contents. After a moment he pulled out a magnifying glass and knelt down beside the picture of the yacht. In the far corner was the back half of another boat, mostly obscured.

"I remember this . . ." he mused. "This was the only boat I've ever come across named after a male. *The William*, it was called."

"But the only letters visible in the photograph are the last three," Bess said. "*I-A-M*."

"Do you think there's something to it?"

"I'm not sure."

In the pageant article, there were a number of other words. A scripted sign on the boardwalk advertised the Velvet Soap Company in tall white letters. Another spelled out "Wrigley's Juicy Fruit chewing gum," and "Frostilla fragrant lotion." And then there was the caption: "Kathleen O'Neill of Philadelphia, waiting for the pageant results." And Charles's own name in the corner.

Bess rubbed her eyes. "What do you see?" she demanded. "Damn it, it's all a blur to me."

Gladys leaned in. "What is it?"

Charles shook his head. "I'm not sure. Let me see the others." He peered down at the postcard. *Come enjoy the beauty of the ocean, wild and wide,* the card read. "I have to admit, it's such a singular phrase, it does seem like more than a coincidence." He flipped the card over. "The caption on the back says, 'Young's Pier, Atlantic City.'" He ran his finger over the card. "It's not possible," he said quietly.

Bess took the postcard, startled. "What is it? What did you find?" She pored over it again, uselessly. She couldn't imagine what she had missed.

"Look—look here. The *ng* of *Young's* has been smudged. Some kind of error in the printing I suppose."

"Yes?"

"If you look at the photographs from latest to earliest"—he handed her the magnifying glass and pointed to the yacht, *The William*, and the visible letters—"*IAM*. I am." He unfolded the magazine article again. "Kathleen O'Neill, waiting for pageant results." He studied the words as if he couldn't quite believe it. "Waiting for . . ."

Bess leaned toward him. "Yes . . ."

"And this one." Charles pointed to the back of the postcard, where the *ng* was rubbed out. "The letters that are left spell *you.*"

"I am waiting for you . . ." Bess couldn't believe it either. Surely it wasn't a coincidence?

"Where?" she demanded. "Waiting for me where?" Was it possible, if she deciphered it, she could reach Harry this very night? She grabbed Charles's cardboard portrait. There were no words at all in the photograph. "Where was this taken, Charles? Please. You must remember."

Charles turned the card over. It was stamped with the studio name and the location: Young's Pier. "I remember, there was an exhibition of dancing horses. I asked my mother if we could see them, but by the time we left the studio, there were no more tickets. I was so angry at her."

"Young's Pier again." It seemed they kept coming back to that place. Bess could feel her heart pulsing wildly. For a moment, she could not move. It did not seem real. Had he really done it, she wondered. Had Harry managed to come back after all? She could not bring herself to stand up and go to him. Because what would she find if she went now, to Young's Pier? Would it be Harry himself, back from the dead? She shuddered, remembering what she had done there with Young himself. How could he want to meet her in the one place where she had nearly betrayed him?

One thing was certain; somehow, from wherever he was at the moment, he was playing with time to reach her. But she didn't know whether his present time coordinated with hers. If it didn't, would they be endlessly chasing each other?

"I have to go there," she said.

She looked at Gladys, whose eyes were wide, her dark hair cascading down her shoulders, then at Charles. "May I borrow your car?"

"Do you think he will be there?" Gladys whispered, incredulous. There were tears on her eyelashes.

"I don't know."

Charles pressed his lips together. "If he is . . . do you think it means . . . he will take you back with him?"

Bess understood what he was asking. What if going to Harry now meant leaving this world to join another? Would it happen suddenly, she wondered, like a heart attack? Would she feel anything? Or would it be simply like stepping through a fog, from one light into another?

Strangely, she was not afraid. But she looked at Charles, sitting cross-legged beside her, his expression grief-stricken, and she realized she could not leave him. She wanted to stay for him. Her life was valuable to someone else. And she had fallen into a kind of love with this lanky, beautiful, vulnerable man.

Bess took his hand. "I'll come back," she promised. And the look of relief on his face broke over her like glass.

Chapter 15

THE SÉANCE

March 1924

Sir Arthur Conan Doyle pulled down the shades, casting the room in shadow. "I always like to begin with a prayer," he said solemnly, "to help us find our way into the Great Beyond."

Bess and Harry sat side by side in the Doyles' parlor in Crowborough, at the edge of Ashdown Forest in England. The Great War in Europe had blazed and dimmed and was over now, and England had already begun to pretend it had moved on, despite the staggering number of crippled soldiers in every town. Harry himself had taken on the preservation of Allied soldiers' lives as his mission, raising millions of dollars in war bonds through his performances and teaching young men how to escape from German handcuffs. But the young and dead who haunted him seemed only to strengthen his desire to contact his mother, whom he believed was somewhere out there, trying to reach him, to reassure him that she still existed, that someone was waiting for him.

Doyle reached for Bess's hand and closed his eyes. Across the circle from Bess, his wife—a pale, pretty thing who had been trained as a mezzo soprano in her younger days—seemed already to be in a meditative state.

"Almighty, we are grateful to you for this breaking down of the walls between two worlds." Sir Arthur's long mustache muffled the words but also, somehow, gave them more weight. "We thirst for another undeniable message from beyond, another call of hope and guidance to the human race at this, the time of its greatest affliction. Can we receive another sign from our friends from beyond?"

Harry, holding Bess's other hand, squeezed her fingers with his; she could sense his nerves. She tried to stifle her own judgments of the process. She wasn't quite sure yet whether to think of it as hocus-pocus or true communication with the other side. Harry himself was fascinated by Doyle's beliefs, and during their time in England he took Bess to the moving pictures but went alone to the graveyards. He said he found peace there, but Bess wasn't entirely sure. He seemed to come home from them paler and grimmer than before. She didn't understand the comfort he claimed he received in such places; she did not think the dead resided there. She had the sense that they preferred to be present among the living.

"I lost my mother, too, you know," Bess had told him. Why couldn't Harry see, she wondered, that she could grieve as well as he could? She simply managed to hide it better. Moreover, she felt she had, in many ways, lost her God by marrying Harry. She had once gone to church weekly, but now she rarely attended. Over the years she had turned to Harry for comfort, when she had once turned to religion. God had become secondary to her marriage. She wasn't sure whether she could ever be forgiven for giving false séances—false hope to grieving widows and parents—during their earlier stage days. Sometimes, memories of her betrayals still rose up to greet her in the middle of the night, like gray ghosts.

When they gave up their California house they traveled to Europe, looking for a change in scenery. In the Suicides' Graveyard in Monte Carlo—where those who had lost their fortunes and killed themselves were buried—Harry wept, and told Bess he loved her, and she forgave him. It didn't seem worth it to be at odds any longer, in the face of all the devastation around them. An obsession with the dead had swept Europe and America, especially among those families mourning sons lost in the war. It seemed every household had purchased a Ouija board and everyone was conducting their own spiritualist experiments. People, it seemed, were possessed by the paranormal.

Harry had begun a correspondence with the noted writer Sir Arthur Conan Doyle, who, like Harry, had started dabbling in spirit photography and embarked upon a quest to contact the dead. "Where are they?" he asked Harry in a letter. "What has become of all those splendid young lives? Are they anywhere?" He told Harry he had been able to reach his son Kingsley—lost to influenza—through a medium. "I am a true believer now," he wrote to Harry, "and I also believe that you are harboring occult powers which you may not even realize."

This, Harry laughed at, but he was impressed by Doyle's steadfast belief that the other side existed. But Harry told Bess he himself was struggling between two opposing forces, that he was both a "skeptic" and "a seeker of the truth." He detested fraud but desperately wanted to find an authentic medium who could prove him wrong.

Bess was frightened by Harry's obsession. Along their European route she searched for Catholic churches on narrow side streets and attended masses in languages she didn't understand. She wasn't sure that the spirits he was attempting to contact were entirely good. Had he forgotten all the trickery they had performed during their early years onstage together, and the eerie power they had seemed to possess despite their fakery—their predictions that had come true? There seemed to be forces at work that they could not control, and Bess was hesitant to rouse them. She bent her head and prayed into the candle smoke and tried to find the faith she'd had as a little girl, but she felt like an impostor, like someone who did not quite belong anymore. She tried to pray, but the words sounded empty.

But Doyle promised he could contact the late Mrs. Weiss. His wife, he claimed, had "a gift."

And so Bess and Harry sat in a small circle across from Sir Arthur and Lady Jean Doyle, who had begun to tap the table with her pencil. She did not look the part of the medium; she was wrapped in a cascade of white fur and filigreed jewelry. "This is the most energetic the forces have ever been," she announced. She drew a cross at the top of the paper laid out in front of her, to ward off evil spirits.

"Who is it?" Doyle asked her eagerly. "Is it Houdini's mother?"

Lady Doyle was furiously scribbling. Doyle jumped to his feet and stood over her shoulder, reading what she was writing. "Oh, my darling, thank God, at last I'm through!" he read. "My beloved boy, tell him not to grieve. Soon he'll get all the evidence he's looking for."

Bess looked over at Harry. His eyes were squeezed tightly shut, and he was sweating profusely.

Doyle continued reading his wife's scribbles. His voice was shrill with excitement. "Tell him I've been with him all the while, all the while. And I have prepared a home for him. It is so different over here, so much larger and bigger and more beautiful. I am so happy in this life." Lady Doyle was convulsing, as if with the weight of the pencil. Even the air around them seemed heavy.

"Why don't you ask her a question?" Bess urged Harry softly.

"I don't know if the spirit will answer direct questions," Doyle said. Lady Doyle shuddered, and her hand began scribbling again.

Sir Arthur read, "If only the world knew the great truth, how different life would be . . . Bless my son, bless him, tell him the gulf will be bridged and his eyes will soon be opened—"

Lady Doyle dropped her pencil and fell back against her chair, weeping.

"I'm sorry, Harry," she said. "She's gone. I'm so sorry." She turned to Sir Arthur. "Dear, raise the shades. I need the light."

Harry was still gripping Bess's hand. His face was white. "Darling, you must let go," she murmured. "You're hurting my hand."

He seemed to rouse himself as if from a deep trance. "What's that, Bess? Oh." He released her hand from his grip.

Later that night, in the privacy of the Doyles' guest room, the frigid English breeze blew through the cracks around the window, and Bess buried her head in Harry's shoulder. "Do you think it was truly your mother coming through?" she asked him. It was difficult even for her to believe that the Doyles—the sincerest Catholics she knew—would resort to manipulation. But Harry had produced all kinds of spooky effects through his own "magic." She had always relied upon him to decipher the real from the fraudulent, and it seemed now, for the first time, he could not. During his own "séances," to prove that such things could be done, he had produced luminous figures that moved through the air. But this was different; this was a séance with a well-known public figure and his wife who insisted they had spoken with his own mother. It was hard for her to call them frauds outright.

Harry wrapped his arm around her and pulled the blanket up to his chin. "I am afraid that I cannot say. Her eyes—they looked at me, but they were not focused on me. It was . . . strange."

It seemed to Bess that her husband was a magician who wanted, desperately, to believe that magic was real.

✳

By that spring, Doyle had become almost as famous for his lectures on spiritualism as he was for his writing. He had crossed the Atlantic for his speaking circuit and traveled the Northeast, giving one lecture in Atlantic City and another in Carnegie Hall in New York. Afterward Harry and Bess invited Doyle and his wife to see a showing of Raymond Hitchcock's *Pinwheel Revue,* then back to their home for dinner. Bess had invited Gladys as well; she had recently moved out of the Houdinis' home and was attempting to live on her own, with the help of an aide, but Bess worried she was often lonely. She had noticed that Gladys still wore only black, and still seemed to grieve her mother's passing even more than Harry did. When they had returned from California, Gladys seemed different to Bess—quieter, more subdued. The energetic girlishness she had once possessed seemed gone.

Harry was eager to show Sir Arthur his collections. He felt he had a kindred spirit in the writer, who appreciated libraries as much as he did. At the same time, having had some time to reflect on the séance he had done with Lady Doyle, Harry had decided that there had been nothing significant in the message that had come through from his mother. He told Bess he would like to test the lady again, if the opportunity arose.

Bess sat beside Gladys and Lady Doyle sat on the large sofa with cups of tea, listening to the men prattle on about London. Bess leaned over to Lady Doyle, trying to entice conversation out of her. The woman was still an enigma to Bess. "Lady Jean, I heard you have a remarkable voice," she said.

Lady Doyle stirred her tea, her large rings flashing. "I did have an admired career once." She had a very British hauteur and seemed to compose her dialogue carefully. "Of course, as you know, being the wife of a recognized figure is work enough now. People say I'm quite a recognized figure as well."

Bess was not impressed by her boasting. She was Doyle's

second wife and had married him at the height of his wealth and fame. Bess had heard rumors that she had convinced him to change his will to leave the daughter of his first wife out of his inheritance.

"Tell me about your mother, Gladys," Lady Doyle continued, as the men talked. "Am I correct that she lived here with you?"

Gladys's jaw tightened. "Yes. She was very happy here."

"She was a lovely woman," Bess added. "She always treated me like a daughter."

"It is a shame about her passing."

"Yes. It certainly was." Bess knew what she was up to. She and Harry had done just such fishing for information in their medium days. She had an idea. "Harry loved her very much. When we were home in New York he used to wear only the clothes she had given him because he thought it would please her."

"How lovely," Lady Doyle said.

By the fireplace, Doyle was surprised to see how many books on spiritualism Harry had amassed. "Good man," he said. "I took you for a skeptic."

Harry laughed. "Oh, no, I still am. That's why I read so much."

Doyle frowned. Bess thought she understood why the man clung to his beliefs with such tenacity, why no one could contradict him, and why he was so eager to convince Harry of his side of things. If he let go of his certainties about life after death, what then? What became of his soul? He was like a buoy tethered in a storm, dancing in black seas; if he were unmoored from his convictions and his beliefs, he would be lost. It was the same way she had felt when she first married Harry, when making her vows meant giving up the life, home, and family she had always thought she could go back to if she wanted. It had left her unmoored as well.

"If you'd only let yourself recognize the powers you possess," Doyle said, "you could be the most powerful man in the world."

He turned to Bess. "Mrs. Houdini, you must convince him to open himself to the remarkable forces he is keeping at bay."

Bess smiled but said nothing. George knocked on the door to inform them that dinner was ready.

Harry held up his hand. "Before we go." He opened his briefcase and removed a small slate, four small cork balls, white ink, and a tablespoon.

Sir Arthur frowned. "What are you up to, Houdini?" Bess looked at Harry as well. She knew he had been preparing something, but he hadn't told her he was going to bring it out that evening.

Lady Jean leaned forward eagerly. "Yes, Mr. Houdini, what are you playing at? Are we to be the unwitting audience for one of your new tricks?"

Harry handed Doyle the cork balls with a small smile. "You are welcome to cut through one of these to see that they are solid cork." Sir Arthur, still frowning, took his pocketknife and sliced one of the balls in half. He nodded. "Yes, yes, I see. What of it?"

Harry took the second ball and, using the spoon, dropped it into the inkwell to soak up the ink. He explained what he was doing out loud, for Gladys's sake. "While I am doing this," he told Sir Arthur, "I would like you to leave the room and write a question or a sentence on a piece of paper. And don't show it to me."

Doyle complied. When he came back in the room, the paper was securely in his pocket. He sat and watched as Harry placed the ink-covered ball on the slate, and Bess, along with the Doyles, watched as the ball began to roll around the surface, on its own, the white ink spelling out a phrase on the black surface. Lady Doyle let out a small cry.

Gradually the words became clear: *Mene, mene, tekel, upharsin*, the slate read, in white letters. "Why, that's what I wrote down," Sir Arthur murmured, aghast. He was visibly shaken. Bess recognized the quotation from the Old Testament. They were the words written on Belshazzar's palace wall by a mysterious hand, which predicted imminent doom for his reign.

Doyle grasped Harry's hands. "Houdini, what powers are you working with?"

Harry shook his head. "I have devoted a lot of time and thought to this illusion. I have been working on it, on and off, for the course of a year. I won't tell you how it was done, but I can assure you it was pure trickery."

Doyle's face was white. "I don't believe you."

"I devised it to show you that such things are possible. I beg of you, Sir Arthur, do not jump to the conclusion that certain things you see are necessarily supernatural, or the work of spirits, just because you cannot explain them. You must be careful in the future of endorsing phenomena just because you cannot explain them."

Doyle smiled. Bess could tell he still did not believe Harry. He thought Harry was obscuring his powers by trying to play them off as tricks. But Bess knew better. She had seen Harry levitate a table, and knew how he did it.

"Come," Bess said, standing up and smoothing out her dress. "Enough of these games. Let's go in to dinner." She did not want to see Doyle's beliefs shattered in front of her; older than Harry by fifteen years, he seemed very fragile under his flinty exterior. As it was, the American press was lambasting him. During an interview he had said he thought men were given whiskey and cigars when they got to heaven, and the papers were already mocking him. And back in England, he had endorsed a young girl's photograph of a fairy as authentic, only to learn that the picture had been doctored, and he had been the object of great ridicule as a result of his naïveté.

As they walked into the dining room, Bess grabbed Harry's arm discreetly. Using the system they had devised during their early stage years, she cautioned him that Lady Doyle had been asking about his mother. She warned him in whispered code—each word, or pairs of words, indicating a different letter—spelling out the word *DECEIVE*: "Now-tell-pray, answer-tell-look-answer-answer-tell." Harry looked alarmed, and disturbed.

They dined on chicken and asparagus and kept up polite conversation about Doyle's lectures. As they finished their dessert of cream cake, Doyle cleared his throat. "Houdini, I must say I was somewhat angered by that article you wrote for *The New York Sun*. You said that after the hundreds of séances you attended, you have never seen anything that could convince you there is a possibility of communication with the beyond."

Harry took a long drink of water. "I am perfectly willing to believe," he said, "but I need significant proof to back any claims I put in print."

Gladys came to her brother's defense. "Certainly you cannot expect Harry to support your claims simply because you are friends. He has a reputation of respectability that he has to uphold." Gladys was more of a skeptic even than Harry and had tried for years to convince him that their mother was not going to come through to them, much to Harry's dismay.

Doyle was insulted. "And I do not have a reputation to uphold? I must tell you, I feel sore about it. You have all the right in the world to your own opinion, but I know the purity of my wife's mediumship, and I saw what the effect was upon you when we were in England. You *believed*."

Lady Doyle sat quietly beside Bess, sipping her wine. She looked neither supportive of nor embarrassed by her husband's outburst.

Sir Arthur stood up. "If agreeable, Lady Doyle will give you a special séance, as she has a feeling that she might have a message coming through. At any rate, she is willing to try." He continued,

"I'd like for her to give you some kind of consolation, and change your mind."

Harry glanced at Bess. "Yes, certainly," he said. "But I assure you I did not mean my article as an affront to you or your wife."

What Bess and Gladys had not told Lady Doyle was that it happened to be Mrs. Weiss's birthday. If this fact came through in the séance, then perhaps Lady Doyle's powers could be proven real. Bess felt a little thrill at being in league with Harry again, as they had been during their stage days. But she also felt sorry for Harry and for Gladys, dredging up all this business with their mother yet again. If Harry had been depressed since her passing, Gladys had been even more so. Mrs. Weiss had been her best friend and confidante, as well as her eyes. Losing Mrs. Weiss had been, surely, like losing a limb. One could never, ever, be the same. Bess only hoped that Gladys wasn't expecting anything to come of this séance, especially having heard Lady Doyle pressing for information earlier.

They proceeded back into the library, and Harry dimmed the lights. They sat in a small circle and placed their hands on the table between them. Once again, Doyle began with a prayer, and Lady Doyle, a pad and pencil in front of her, began by drawing the sign of the cross and asking the spirits, "Do you believe in God? You must say so if you wish us to continue."

Then she began to convulse, and her hand flew across the page, writing furiously.

"It's your mother," Doyle whispered. "It has to be."

I am so happy, my beloved son and daughter, Lady Doyle wrote. *I know that you think of me often, that you often wear the clothes and gifts I've given you because you think it will help you reach me. You must know that you have a guide who is often with you at night. He helps and instructs you over here. He is a very, very high soul, sent especially to work through you on the earth plane. He wants me to say, my dears, that there is much work before you.*

"In this world?" Doyle pressed. His hand was flying, too; he was tearing sheet after sheet from the pad of paper as they filled up.

Yes. It is here in this gray earth that you are needed.

Bess could not bring herself to open her eyes and look at Harry. The whole thing seemed so ridiculous.

Then Lady Doyle's convulsions stilled abruptly. Bess opened her eyes. The woman appeared, suddenly, very composed. It was odd; her dark eyes were open, but there seemed to be a kind of emptiness behind them. Bess shuddered; the room felt very cold and drafty.

Doyle started to read his wife's recent scribbling and paused. He tore off the sheet and handed it to Harry. Bess saw Harry's face grow white. "She writes—" His voice broke. *"My son, you are in danger. My God, my God, save you."*

Bess stood up, knocking the table over. She motioned to Harry and Gladys. "Enough of this! Don't you see what you are doing to them?" She pointed at Lady Doyle, whose forehead was covered in sweat, as if she had exerted great energy. "You are nothing more than a fraud, who has managed to deceive even her own husband! You dare to tell my husband that his life is in danger? Did you know that Cecilia Weiss spoke five languages, but English wasn't one of them? And yet she is somehow writing through your hand in a language she didn't speak."

Sir Arthur took Bess's arm to calm her down. "Of course it's probable that in heaven we can speak all languages, is it not?"

"But if she were trying to convince Harry and Gladys of her authenticity, wouldn't it be even more remarkable if your wife began writing in German, a language she herself doesn't speak?" Bess snatched her arm away. "And today is Mrs. Weiss's birthday—a fact that was never mentioned. You should know that before you try to defend your wife any further. Surely this is proof of her disingenuousness."

Doyle's face reddened. "What are birthdays on the other side? It is the death day which is the real birthday."

Bess shook her head. "How can you say such things?"

"Mrs. Houdini, you are treading on dangerous ground. You invite us into your house and then disrespect my wife's abilities. You are showing the greatest lack of hospitality," Sir Arthur warned.

Harry finally spoke. "That's enough, Bess."

Bess spun to face him. "How can you defend him, Harry? His wife's just tried to threaten you!"

"Because he doesn't know any better."

Doyle grabbed his wife's hand. "Jean, we are leaving." He turned to Harry. "You have ruined a great friendship, you know." He stomped into the hallway and took their coats from the closet. At the doorway, he seemed to hesitate. Without looking back, he murmured, sadly, "Harry, you are to me a perpetual mystery."

Harry watched as they left and did not try to stop them. But Bess could see he was visibly shaken, as was Gladys. When they were gone she regained her composure and realized what she had done. "Darling, I'm sorry I lost my temper," she said.

Gladys shook her head. "The woman was a fraud. There was nothing remotely reminiscent of my mother's voice in her writings. Although I do think Sir Arthur wholeheartedly believes his wife is a medium. I feel sorry for him. Imagine what he has to lose if he decides to confront the truth. His faith, his marriage—it all crumbles before him."

Bess took Harry's hand. "Are you mad at me, my love?"

"No." Harry shook his head, but he wouldn't look at her. He stared through the windows into the darkness as if in a trance. "I was willing to believe," he mused. "Even wanted to believe. My heart was beating so hard. I hoped I might feel my mother's presence . . ."

"But surely you cannot—"

He stopped her. "No. Of course not. My mother was a devoutly Jewish woman. It does not stand to reason that she would have begun her communication with the sign of the cross."

Bess stared at him. "So you were skeptical from the beginning?"

Harry nodded. "I wanted to believe," he said again. "But we can't blind ourselves to the truth." He sighed. "And it doesn't mean I can't be disappointed by it."

Bess thought he had put his hope to the test so often that it was remarkable that any remained.

"The spiritualists—they are going to kill me, you know. Every night they are praying for my death, because I dare to speak out against them."

Bess shuddered. "Don't say those things, Harry." She couldn't bear the idea that he would ever willingly give up on life, when he had spent night after night of his career fighting for it onstage.

Harry shrugged. "But you know it's true. They despise me. Why try to pretend otherwise?"

Chapter 16

THE MESSAGE

June 1929

Bess drove recklessly through the streets of Atlantic City, swerving to avoid the clusters of women in their bathing outfits and straw hats on their way from the beach, laughing down the sidewalks, past the rows of white frame houses with silver chimes. The sky was purpling, and she felt a sense of urgency as she had never felt before. *I am waiting for you at Young's Pier.* This had to be the message Harry had hidden for her in the photographs. She felt, in her heart, that, by some means, he had done it. Harry had called to her, and she would go. She did not know what she would say when she met him. What do you say to someone after such long years apart? Where does one begin?

It was the great irony of Harry's life that he had desired, beyond all measure, to access the realm of the spirits and had been unable to do so, even while the entire public was convinced he had achieved it. By his death Harry had become the nation's foremost expert on spiritualism. He had advertised a money prize to whoever could show him a supernatural act he could not disprove. His book *A Magician Among the Spirits* was published to great fanfare. But after the Doyle séance, he had come close to believing in another's power only one more time, and that was in Margery Crandon, an attractive blue-eyed Canadian woman whom the *American Journal of Psychology* had called "the most brilliant star in physical mediumship." In her presence, golden lights had danced, clocks had stopped, and a white, grotesque substance she called ectoplasm had spewed from her mouth. By the time Harry and Bess met her, the nation and its scientists were already thoroughly under her spell.

Bess recalled the scene of the séance, which had occurred in complete darkness. Harry had begun it with high hopes; men whom he respected greatly had vowed Margery was authentic. It had been a windy autumn evening, the stuff of horror novels, and there were a number of witnesses—scientists and physicians— who'd sat beside her in the Houdinis' parlor in Harlem. Harry had been seated on one side of Mrs. Crandon, and another man was on her right, holding on to her hands and feet to ensure she did not move them to produce any effects. Mrs. Crandon had worn a light kimono with nothing underneath and breathed heavily throughout; she was a woman of overt sexuality, with bulging breasts, and Bess had immediately disliked her, though she imagined the men who were present felt her allure, even from across the room. During the séance, Margery had managed to ring a bell and throw a megaphone without the use of her hands or feet. Bess had been alarmed by the experience; she had felt frigid during the entire evening, even though the room was hot with so many bodies breathing inside.

But afterward, Harry had taken Bess aside and told her he was going to denounce the woman, claiming he could prove that she had rung the bells with her legs, and that the megaphone had been thrown from atop her head. Still, something about her seemed to have unsettled Harry, and afterward he was not the same. He would not set foot in their parlor unless Bess was beside him. He was often fidgety, and he would spend hours at the YMCA, throwing the medicine ball and running the track, as if to invigorate himself out of a deep trance. At the time, she had thought it was a crisis of age, but looking back on it now, Bess thought it was possible Harry had seen some kind of vision of his own death during that séance. Something about it had disturbed him deeply.

Bess's hesitation about Harry's message ran deeper than nervousness. It occurred to her, to her horror, as the car rattled through the Atlantic City streets, that Young's Pier as she and Harry had known it no longer existed. In 1912 a massive fire had destroyed most of the structure. Pictures of the devastation had been in all the New York papers. Young had tried to recoup some of his losses by charging ten cents each to those wanting to see the debris being hauled away. But, ultimately, his efforts had failed. The pier lay in ruins until 1922, when it was finally rebuilt and renamed Central Pier. It would never again eclipse the grandeur of its older competitor, Steel Pier, where earlier in the summer, thousands had watched as swim-capped women on white horses dove into the ocean to the music of John Philip Sousa.

What if Harry couldn't come through after all because the Young's Pier they had known was gone? Charles hadn't tried to stop her, only showed her how to start his automobile and watched from the sidewalk as she drove away. She'd had little experience driving in New York, but Harry had been excited to show her how when he purchased a Model T, and the night felt too urgent to waste any time letting her nerves about the road get to her. But she'd forgotten to ask Charles how to turn on the headlamps, and as the sun descended behind the buildings she raced to the oceanfront so she would not have to get out and walk in the darkness.

The parking attendant at the Royal Hotel recognized her; she left the car at the entrance to the car elevator with him, hastily calling out an invented room number behind her as she ran off. She felt as if she were coming apart at the seams as she ran toward the boardwalk. The lamps were shining already, and the night was almost excruciatingly humid. Bess unpinned her hat and let the breeze cool her head. At the entrance to Central Pier, a carousel was spinning, the painted horses waltzing. Harry would be, she imagined, at the far end of the pier, near the deepest part of the ocean. He would be standing there with his back to her, looking out at the water into which he had jumped so many years before. And then he would turn around and smile at her, and take her hand, and he would tell her what it was like where he had come from, how full of color it was, how many stars there were.

The pier was crowded with people. She could not remember such throngs before. Vaguely, she remembered that the Television exhibit was making its debut. They were calling it the greatest wonder of the electrical world, and there was tremendous bally-hoo over it; everyone was eager to see the new phenomenon. Bess pushed her way through the lines and down the narrow alley of boards on the outside, toward the end of the pier. She could hear the splash of yachts floating in the water. What if Harry wasn't there? What if she didn't recognize him? She chastised herself. Of course he would be there. There was no sense in doubting him; he had never failed to do a single thing he had set his mind to.

It was far different than she remembered. The new pier was smaller than the old one had been, and more modern. The Chamber of Commerce offices occupied most of the interior space. But it hadn't lost any of the vibrant energy it had had that afternoon when Harry performed his escape, and almost died doing it.

This city came alive at night like noplace she had seen, short of New York. The electric lights blazed and the synthetic liquor flowed; women in coral chiffon dresses brushed past her, all the flaming youth of the era congregating in this carnival of color. But something about the scene bothered Bess; she wondered why Harry had lured her here, of all places, especially when he had always loved the quiet more than the crowds. As the Jazz Age swelled around him he had eschewed it, telling Bess he thought New York could sometimes be the loneliest city in the world. After he died, she had cloistered herself inside her huge city home, certain that if Harry were to appear to her it would be there. So why had he chosen this city of sin as their final meeting place?

Rushing down the pier, she could make out a few dim figures by the railing. Most were couples, their hands and arms intertwined, and a few were too young to be Harry, no older than teenagers. But she could see one man, standing alone under the lamppost, hatless, with his elbows on the rail, leaning out over the ocean. Bess caught her breath and froze. She recognized Harry's rumpled hair, the wrinkled black pants he loved. She stopped a few feet from him.

"Ehrich?" she breathed. "Is it really you?" Her hands were trembling violently. She reached to touch his shoulder.

The man turned around and looked at her. He was old—much older than Harry had been when he died—and his eyes were egg blue. There were none of Harry's dark European features in him. "Sorry," he said, shrugging. "I think you meant someone else."

Bess looked past him, as if the real Harry might be hiding on the other side of the rail. It couldn't be . . . She searched the rest of the pier, but she couldn't find him anywhere. The place was loud with laughter and voices and the muffled sounds of orchestra music. She blinked back tears. Certainly, she had interpreted the message correctly . . . hadn't she?

Perhaps Charles had been right. Perhaps Harry's message *was* Charles all along; maybe Harry had merely meant to come back to her through his son, and she was on a fool's errand now, reading silly messages in photographs that were not intended to be messages at all. And she should be happy with this, she knew, with this man who was the closest thing to the family she always wanted. But still, she felt a sadness she could not shake. She sat down on a bench and put her head in her hands.

"Bess!"

She looked up and saw Charles and Gladys standing in front of her. They were both panting, drenched with sweat. They must have taken a taxi after she left and run down the pier.

"I didn't find him," she said, sobbing. "He's not here." Her naïveté became clear to her now; people didn't come back from the dead. How could she have imagined that Harry would have proven himself the exception? And, moreover, that he would return to her at the scene of the most terrible day of her life—when she had kissed another man, and Harry had almost died?

"We know you didn't," Charles said, trying to catch his breath. "He's not here."

Bess frowned. "What do you mean?"

Charles held out a tattered piece of paper. "I found something after you left. It's— Well, look." His eyes were shining. "Well, it's remarkable."

Bess squinted down at the photograph. It was creased with age, and the figures on it were blurred. "There are no words anywhere on this." It was a photograph of Harry's jump, from 1905. In it, she could make out Harry's tiny form hanging over the railing. "You were there," she whispered, incredulous. "I had forgotten you said you were there."

"My mother took me. I begged her to let me go." He wiped the sweat off his brow. "She had bought me a Brownie camera, and I remember I climbed one of the lampposts so I could get a good picture."

Bess could not believe Charles and Harry had come so close to each other. Suddenly it made sense to her why Harry had sent her to Young's Pier; not only was it the day he thought his father had been with him in the water, but it was his singular lost moment, the one time in his life he had walked upon the same ground as his own son. It would have been the greatest regret of his life, looking back on it, that he had not recognized his own son in the crowd.

She peered at the image, looking for a smudge of a young woman holding on to a white hat in the wind, before she remembered that she hadn't come outside until after the jump. Then she sighed, holding out the photograph. "But I don't see what this has to do with my coming here. Look around. Harry's not here."

Charles pressed the paper back into her palm. "You didn't look closely enough." He reached into his pocket and drew out a small magnifying glass. He knelt down beside her and held the glass over the picture. "Look here." He pointed to the crowd. "What do you see?"

Bess followed his finger. The crowd was pressed together, everyone staring intently at Harry hanging over the water, about to jump. It was a moment in time captured by a boy's cheap camera, unaware of what the magician's wife had just done, or what would happen to the magician, or what would happen to the boy himself, only months later, when he would be orphaned. Only the backs of the people's heads were visible to the camera. Except, there was something strange. One man was not looking at the ocean; he was facing the other direction, his face turned upward, staring straight past the heads of the crowd into the camera.

Bess bent over and rubbed her eyes.

"Do you see it?" Charles pressed. "Bess, do you see?"

Through the glass, clear as day, she could make him out. The man looking at the camera—staring right at her, now, as she sat there beside Charles—was, unmistakably, Harry.

Bess let out a small cry. Her eyes went back and forth between the two men in the picture. They were different, but they were the same man. There was a young, dark-haired Harry, dangling perilously from the pier. And there was an older, gray-haired Harry, standing in the crowd.

"Charles," she said softly, "how is it possible?"

Charles pointed to the image. "This is my theory: I think he's living still—in another place, another plane—and he's coming back from the other side, through my photographs."

Gladys sat on the bench beside Bess and took her hands. "Don't you see, Bess? Don't you see what he's done? He's found a way to come back to you!"

Bess started to cry. "I don't understand. How does this keep his promise? What is he playing at here?"

Charles, pacing in front of them, was almost electric with excitement. "You were right about the message!" he pressed. "I think Harry *is* waiting for you—just not in the way you thought." He swept his hand in front of him and gestured toward the crowded pier. "You came out here thinking you would find him here, in the present. But he can't get to you that way. He can only come back through the past. And he's using my photographs to do it."

"So you think . . . he is going back *in time?*"

Charles nodded. "To when these pictures were taken. We didn't think about this, but all of those photographs were taken *before* he died. He's been able to alter the landscape, just slightly, enough for the coded words to come through. You were right about the message—you just didn't interpret it correctly."

Suddenly, it became clear to her what Harry had meant, what Charles had discovered. *I am waiting for you at Young's Pier.* Harry had used the song they'd chosen to relay this message. But the problem was, he couldn't reach her in her own, current, time. Perhaps, in the limbo one entered after death, one could only cross back to the years one had lived, and could go no further. And so Harry was prevented from coming back in all the ways she had been anticipating—through a medium, say, or as a ghost, because he couldn't move beyond 1926. And he wasn't trying to tell her where he would be waiting for her, now, *on this side;* he was trying to tell her where he would be waiting *on the other side.* He was telling her that, when she died, he would be waiting for her here, on Young's Pier, in 1905. And they would go on, together, to what was beckoning.

Bess recalled the agony of that afternoon, the interminable minutes as she'd watched the seething, throbbing blue ocean that had swallowed Harry whole. Afterward she could not get the sound of the crowd out of her head, the small cries of the women as he failed to appear in the water, the shrill voice of the newsboy as he called out the news: "Extree! Houdini dead!"

"I thought I'd lost you," she'd murmured, over and over that night.

"Oh, no," Harry had assured her. "You didn't lose me. I was right there all along."

I was right there all along . . .

It made even more sense now, why Harry had chosen this place to come back to her.

Gladys felt Bess's face. "You're crying," she said softly. "Are you sad because you wish he was here with you now?"

"No." Bess wiped her face. "I'm crying because I don't have to be afraid anymore. Because now I know he's there, and I'll be there with him, too."

Somewhere far away, in a time she'd already lived, the rest of the song was playing:

I'll take you home again, Kathleen
Across the ocean wild and wide
To where your heart has ever been
Since first you were my bonnie bride.

The roses all have left your cheek.
I've watched them fade away and die
Your voice is sad when e'er you speak
And tears bedim your loving eyes.

Oh! I will take you back, Kathleen
To where your heart will feel no pain
And when the fields are fresh and green
I'll take you to your home again!

To that dear home beyond the sea
My Kathleen shall again return.
And when thy old friends welcome thee
Thy loving heart will cease to yearn.

Where laughs the little silver stream
Beside your mother's humble cot
And brightest rays of sunshine gleam
There all your grief will be forgot.

She saw now that the song itself was a love letter from Harry—a promise to take her home again. In his death, he had performed the greatest escape of all. And he had freed her, too, from the glittering loneliness, just as he had freed Charles.

In death he had corrected the two biggest regrets of his life—leaving his son fatherless and leaving his wife childless. He had performed one last remarkable feat, by bringing them together.

"You really love him still, don't you?" Charles marveled. "In spite of finding out about me, and all that."

"No," she said. "Not in spite of."

The motley colors of the summer roared around them, in that iridescent city on the sea, and all the delirious energy of the age was hurtling its way ahead, pulsing with life, into the unknown.

Chapter 17

DETROIT

October 1926

The room in the Château Laurier in Montreal was a fine place for the pair of them to be laid up. The dean of McGill University had arranged for a top-floor suite, with cream curtains, heavy walnut furniture, and a reading library, in English and French, larger than Harry had ever seen in a hotel. Since arriving, however, Bess had been diagnosed with ptomaine poisoning and had been vomiting the contents of her stomach for almost two days. Harry, too, was exhausted, having stayed up all night with her, her fever running so high he was afraid to let her fall asleep. Then, during a lecture and performance at McGill, he had snapped his left ankle and only barely managed to hobble through the rest of the performance. Bess had been able, even through her delirious state, to convince him to see a surgeon, who had set his ankle and declared the rest of him "in the most perfect physical condition."

"You see, Bess?" Harry had boasted. "Other than this ankle, perfect physical condition. I am in the peak of my athleticism." Still, the two of them had spent the afternoon lying on the couch and reading Harry's mail, Harry with his leg propped up on a pillow and Bess with her face still flushed by the remnants of fever. Nevertheless, she took great joy in poking fun at him for the letters he received from young women, then destroying them so he could not respond.

Despite his protestations, she was worried about his health. Lately he had taken on too much; the muscles around his eyes and mouth twitched constantly. He had decided to establish what he was calling a University of Magic and had been designing the curriculum: showmanship, ethics, philosophy. One morning he had come home from the theater to inform Bess that he had enrolled at Columbia University, in an English course. "If I'm going to become the president of my own university," he told her sheepishly, "I need to know how to write better English." Bess knew he had always been ashamed of his lack of education. He had essentially invented a new art form—the art of escape—and he had met a president of the United States and the greatest scholars of the world, but in his mind he had always been second-rate.

Physically, Harry's escapes were becoming more demanding as he aged, not less. He had encased himself in a metal coffin that was then submerged in a hotel swimming pool, and had survived in it for an hour and thirty-one minutes, emerging with close to fatally low blood pressure and high body temperature. And, having accomplished this feat, he was constructing a new stunt in which he would escape from a block of ice.

"Stop thinking that at fifty years you are old," Harry chastised her when she protested. "I'm not old, and I'm older than you. We're not a couple of fiddle-dee-dees. We have our best years before us."

Harry was dictating responses to his letters to a friend of his, Jack Price, who had come up from New York to see the show, when there was a loud knock on the hotel room door. Jack opened it to a large, rather awkward-looking boy of about twenty years, a sketch pad under his arm.

Harry got to his feet. "Sam! Come in, come in." He pumped the boy's hand and gestured toward an armchair. "We were just having a read of some letters."

The boy sat down meekly on the edge of the chair and placed the sketch pad on his knees.

Harry introduced him to Bess. "This young man came to my dressing room after my lecture this afternoon and showed me a sketch he had done of me. It was really rather good. I asked him to come and make another."

Bess smiled weakly, taking a long sip of her water. "How lovely. Are you a student at McGill?"

"Yes, ma'am." He knocked over a vase of roses as he settled himself into the chair. He tried to catch the flowers but failed, letting out a guttural sound of embarrassment. Bess felt her heart go out to the boy, whose body seemed slightly too large for him to manage.

Harry rolled up his shirtsleeves and reclined on the couch, closing his eyes. "Don't worry about it. You'll have to excuse us," he explained. "We're in need of a bit of rest."

The boy stood up again. "I can come back later."

"Nonsense." Harry gestured for him to sit down again.

As Sam sketched, Harry talked languidly about the craft of magic. Sam seemed enthralled by it. He asked Harry if he could explain some of his secrets. Harry smiled and waved his hand. "Aha!" he said. "I'll have to ask my spirits to give me permission."

"He's kidding," Bess interrupted, seeing the boy's eyes widen. "He doesn't have any spirits."

"Would that were true," Harry said solemnly. "Think of the trouble I might have caused if I had used my talents for ill."

"Harry!" she chastised.

As Sam resumed sketching, there was a second knock on the door. Bess sat up. She felt suddenly nauseous. "Harry, don't answer it. You're injured."

Harry waved his hand and stood up. "It's fine. It could be a delivery."

Standing at the door was a muscled, broad-faced man with his hands in his pockets. He was as tall as Sam but heavier, with puckered, sunburned skin and thinning hair. He introduced himself as Gordon Whitehead.

"He's one of my fraternity brothers," Sam explained. "He's all right." Harry ushered him inside.

He was, he said, a theology student, but he looked years older than Sam's twenty, and far too old to be in a fraternity. Bess felt suddenly uneasy, the small sitting room now crowded with people—her nurse, Harry, Jack, Sam, and Gordon. She felt her muscles contract and realized she was clenching her fists. There was something wrong with this new guest, only she couldn't put her finger on it.

Harry gestured for him to take the last open chair. Gordon sat down stiffly. His movements seemed almost manufactured; his eyes darted around the room. Pressing his palms together, he asked Harry to expand on his lecture on spiritualism. Harry told them, laughing, of the many séances to which he had assigned agents— Bess included, working under her maiden name, Wilhelmina Rahner—to sit in the audience and test the mediums' claims. Harry turned to Bess. "Darling, do you remember when John Slater at Carnegie Hall told you, 'You will be taking your first trip to California'—years after we had moved back from Hollywood?" He slapped his knee and turned to the boys. "He also told her, 'My guide says that your sweetheart is not quite as much in love with you as you are with him,' and we all got into an uproar over that. Of course, he didn't have any idea who she really was." He grinned. "The whole world knows I love her more than she loves me."

Sam said, "I think you two may be the most envied couple of the decade, except for maybe Scott and Zelda Fitzgerald."

Bess tried to laugh, to shake off her growing anxiety, but Gordon's face turned serious. "Mr. Houdini, what is your opinion of the miracles mentioned in the Bible?" He leaned forward eagerly.

Sam looked up, startled by the abruptness of the question, but Harry only shrugged. "I prefer not to comment on matters of miracles." Discussions of religion made Harry uneasy. He always felt the ghost of his father, the Jewish scholar, looking over his shoulder. On more than one occasion he had confided to Bess that he thought his father might have disapproved of the career he had chosen. It was one of lonely glamour, and whether in Hollywood or New York, he could not avoid the gaudy, gilded lifestyle celebrity ensured. "I would make one observation, however," Harry added. "What would succeeding generations have said of my feats had I performed them in biblical times? Would they have been referred to as miracles?"

Gordon appeared taken aback. He blinked rapidly and then cleared his throat. "Speaking of miracles," he ventured, "I have heard that you can resist the hardest blows to the abdomen. Is it true?"

Harry, still reclining on the couch, laughed and lifted his shirt. "My forearm and back muscles are like iron! Go on, feel them!"

Bess gripped his wrist nervously. "Don't be a show-off, Harry."

"Would you mind if I delivered a few blows to your abdomen, Mr. Houdini?"

Gordon was staring at Harry intently. It occurred to her that he was serious.

"Why, this is getting out of hand!" she interrupted. Harry would let him, too, she thought; his greatest weakness had always been his pride. But she was the only one who knew of the lingering delicacy of his kidney, and she didn't want to see his health in jeopardy.

But before she could stop him, Harry spoke. "Well, all right," she heard him say, and Gordon, in a flash, bent over him and pounded him with five forceful blows to the stomach. Harry grunted in pain and doubled over on the couch.

Bess screamed. She felt herself falling into a momentary darkness, a kind of white blindness. When she regained her vision, Jack Price was grabbing Gordon by the shoulders and shaking him. "Are you mad?" he yelled.

"He said I could," Gordon protested, pulling away angrily.

Bess rushed to Harry, but he sat up, with some difficulty, and held up his hand to stop her. "That will do," he muttered. He turned to Sam, who was staring at him, stricken. "Would you sign and date your drawing for me before you go?"

Sam did and handed it to him. Harry studied it, keeping one hand on his stomach. "You make me look a little tired in this picture. The truth is, I don't feel so well."

"Get them out of here!" Bess cried. Jack escorted an indignant Gordon and a flabbergasted Sam to the door, then came back to the couch and put his hand on Harry's shoulder. "Are you all right?"

Harry smiled wryly. "Fine, fine. Just wasn't quite prepared for it, that's all. It's only a muscle." He turned back to his pile of mail and began sorting through the letters.

Through the fog of illness, Bess saw Harry's reflection in the mirror over the mantel, and it seemed to her, for the briefest moment, to flicker and disappear. She turned around, in alarm, but her husband was still sitting there, jaw set, slicing an envelope with the hotel's silver letter opener. Still, she could not rid herself of the feeling that the black magic she had been fearing since their wedding day would befall them after all.

A few days earlier, driving past Central Park on their way to the train station, where they were to catch the 6:00 P.M. train to Montreal, Harry had done something unusual. Seven blocks from their home, he had tapped the shoulder of the taxicab driver and asked him to go back.

"Go back where?" the man had asked.

"Go back to the house."

"Why?" Bess had asked, alarmed. "Did you forget something?"

"Please don't ask questions. Just turn around and go back."

Rain was coming down in torrents by the time they reached 113th Street; Bess could barely make out the street signs. When the driver slowed, Harry jumped out of the car and stood under the open sky, looking up at the house, as if it was the last time he would see it.

"Harry, your coat!" Bess cried. "You'll get soaked!"

But he didn't seem to hear. He stood on the sidewalk for a moment and then slowly turned and got back in the car.

"You're sopping wet now!" Bess threw his coat over his shoulders and tried to pat him dry. "Why didn't you go inside?"

Harry shook his head. "I thought I forgot something, but I didn't after all."

After the blow to Harry's stomach, they made their train to Detroit from Montreal, but by the time the curtain went up on Harry's next show, his temperature had soared to 102. During one phase of the first act, he was to pull a thousand yards of silk ribbon from a glass bowl on a table. But he was so weak that he could not finish. He beckoned to Jim Collins to come out and complete the trick. Standing by Jim's side on the open stage, he glanced over at Bess, sitting in the wings. Spread across his face was the saddest expression of humiliation she had ever seen. After the second act she heard him say to the stagehand, "Drop the curtains, I can't go any further." When the curtain descended, he collapsed in her arms.

Harry was admitted into Grace Hospital that evening. Bess

wired Dr. Stone about Harry's condition and asked what to do. He wired back and told her to agree to an operation, and asked if she wanted him to come from New York. She thought about it but declined; she didn't want Harry to think his condition was too serious.

As he was being wheeled into the operating room, Harry tried to stand up and walk. He was almost incoherent, and Bess had to coax him back onto the gurney. As he lay there, staring vacantly at the ceiling, Bess collapsed. Jim Collins, who had not left their side since the theater, rushed to her. "Get someone over here!" he cried. He put his hand on her forehead. "Jesus, she's got a fever of her own."

Harry, in his own state of delirium, did not seem aware that she had fallen. "Say, I could still lick the two of you," she heard him say to the orderlies.

※

When she awoke, Stella was by her bedside. "Are you really awake now?" she asked. "You've been waking up and going back under for days."

"What day is it?" Bess asked groggily. She had a pounding headache. "How did you get here?"

Stella glanced at the clock. "Jim telephoned. He said you and Harry had both been admitted to the hospital, so I rushed out."

Bess heard a sound from the hall. A man appeared in the doorway, his figure obscured by the sun streaming through the windows behind him. "Oh, Harry," Bess said, relieved. "There you are." The man took a step forward into the shadows of the room. It was not Harry; it was Dash Weiss.

"Oh, thank God, she's up," she heard him say.

Stella shook her head. "Only just."

Bess struggled to sit up. "Dash?"

"You have to come to Harry's room. He hasn't got much time."

"Much time for what?" A nurse came in behind him and, seeing that Bess was awake, rushed over to her bedside.

"It's okay, I've got her," Dash told her, helping Bess out of bed and into a wheelchair.

"Come on, we've got to go."

"Time for what?" Bess demanded. No one answered. Stella laid a thin blanket over her lap.

Harry's room was three down from hers. Through the open door, she could see him lying in his hospital bed, unmoving. A tube had been inserted into the side of his mouth. One of the doctors was monitoring his heartbeat with a stethoscope. Nurses were standing along the walls, as if at attention. Bess screamed.

Stella touched her arm gently. "They say he had a gangrenous appendix. He's had two surgeries since he came in. You've been out for days."

Harry's eyes flickered open, and he saw Bess. "Darling," he mumbled. His lips were very dry; the skin was peeling off them. She stumbled out of her wheelchair and onto the edge of the bed. "Remember the code," he whispered, gripping her hand. "Rosabelle, believe."

"No, Harry," Bess sobbed. "Don't say that."

"I have been tired for a long time. Sometime or other we all grow tired."

"Give them a goddamn moment, would you," she heard Dash say, behind her. He ushered everyone out of the room. He himself was the last to go. He put his hand on Harry's shoulder. "I'm sorry, old boy," he murmured. "About our quarreling." They were two men who had lived a century between them, but in that moment they were merely boys again, shuffling cards together in Wisconsin, playing at fame. Bess reached for Dash's hand, the same hand that had shaken hers so many years before, outside Vacca's Theater.

Whatever had become of Doll, she wondered. Pretty, petite Doll, with her ears like perfect shells? And Anna? It seemed like a lifetime ago. She wasn't quite sure what was happening. Just a few moments ago Harry had been going into surgery, and suddenly she was sitting beside him and he looked ten pounds lighter.

In the quiet of the room after everyone left, she could hear Harry's labored breathing. "In almost every respect, I think I am a fake, Bess," he said. He was still lying on his back; he didn't seem to have the strength to turn himself on his side and look at her.

"What are you talking about? You're no fake."

"Remember the song you sang for me on our wedding night. Don't forget."

"How could I forget?"

He looked at something over her shoulder. "I'll come back for you. Promise you'll look for me. Don't give up. I won't be able to rest until I reach you."

Bess's hand trembled against his. "What do you think you'll find when you arrive?"

"There's something I need to tell you . . . but I don't know it all yet myself. I can't know the whole truth of it in this life. But it will change everything."

"How? How will it change everything?"

"We have to look for each other, Bess. Don't give up." His voice broke. "I'm . . . afraid," he whispered. "And I'm afraid to say I'm afraid." Then his eyes seemed to focus on Bess again. "You were such a pretty girl. You said you were too young to marry me. But you were all in white."

He began to cough. He seemed to be struggling to say something else.

"Harry? What is it? Tell me—what are you seeing?" Bess was seized with fear. He could not leave her, he could not go without her.

His eyes fluttered shut. Bess reached for his face, stunned. His cheeks, which had been pink a moment before, seemed to turn blue before her eyes. It occurred to her that she was still holding Harry's hand, but she was alone. She looked frantically around the room. No one was there. Across the room, the clock did not stop. There were voices in the hall, laughter from other rooms. The automobiles coughed outside, four stories below. Smartly dressed women in gray and white stepped onto the sidewalks, carrying sandwiches in brown bags. But somewhere else Harry's afternoon was luminous, luminous with color, and he could not see them.

Chapter 18

THE KNICKERBOCKER HOTEL

Halloween 1936

Bess sat on the roof of the Knickerbocker Hotel in Hollywood in a small semicircle of friends and magicians. Harry's brother Dash was there, and Gladys, with her husband, Lloyd, and other friends of Harry's, including a California judge, several Hollywood actors, and the president of the American Society of Psychical Research. Across from this inner circle, three hundred witnesses waited tensely on a set of wooden bleachers that had been erected for the occasion. Members of the press and various circles of magic had been summoned, by engraved invitation, to observe the tenth anniversary of Harry's death. It was an important night; Bess had made it clear all along that she would discontinue her attempts to contact Harry after a decade had passed. "The whole world is waiting on you tonight," Gladys had told her.

It was unexpectedly cold for October, and the lights of the city glittered, below them, like shards of crystal. On a table in front of Bess was a small altar bearing a picture of Harry Houdini. Above the picture, a tiny red light burned, and beside it, a stand had been set with a locked pair of handcuffs, a pistol, a tambourine, a piece of slate, a bell, and a trumpet.

Hundreds of well-wishers had been waiting for her at Penn Station ten years earlier, when she returned on a train bearing Harry's body; three thousand mourners had gathered outside the Elks Club to witness the funeral procession over the Queensboro Bridge to Machpelah Cemetery. Strangers had wept in each other's arms as Chopin's Funeral March played in the streets, but none of it had brought Harry back.

Bess remembered the weeks that followed as one remembers a storm passing during sleep. Jack Price had cried murder to the press, and demanded to know whether the medium Margery Crandon had orchestrated Gordon Whitehead's violence in retaliation for Harry's humiliating her. But Harry's condition was inconsistent with the blows he had received. Dr. Stone had tried to come up with an explanation as to how Harry could have died of appendicitis when the punches he received had been on the other side of his body; at last he'd concluded that the pain from the blows must have masked the symptoms of Harry's true illness, preventing him from realizing the seriousness of his condition earlier. But Gordon Whitehead had disappeared; no one could locate him again. In her grief, Bess had confronted Mrs. Crandon, who was doing the traveling circuit in New York. Waiting outside her hotel, Bess had taken Margery by the shoulders and shaken her. "If I find out you had anything to do with Harry's death," she'd threatened, her voice quaking, "God help you."

Margery had stared at her vacantly. "Grief does strange things to us, Mrs. Houdini," she'd said. Then she had stepped into a waiting car and turned away from the window.

For so many years Bess had stood on the stage in Harry's shadow; now, it was her performance alone. On the roof of the Knickerbocker, she faced the crowd in a pristine white dress and cape, her lips dabbed with red lipstick, her hair perfectly waved. Promptly at eight o'clock, the orchestra began playing "Pomp and Circumstance." Bess had asked her old carny friend Edward Saint to officiate the séance. When the music was over, he stepped forward to address the gatherers.

"In this cathedral-like atmosphere," he began, placing his hat over his chest, "I wish to remind you that this is a solemn occasion, and that the results of tonight are of a private nature. This is a personal gathering aiding Mrs. Houdini in completing her ten-year vigil. We wish it distinctly understood that in this last and final attempt we are interested in Houdini coming to us, instead of to a stranger."

Bess lifted her head and scanned the crowd. It seemed that everyone she had ever loved, or would again, was there—Stella, a grandmother now, watching with sympathetic eyes; nearby, her sister Ada, alongside three other siblings. Jim Vickery had died, as had Alfred and Dr. Stone and John Sargent, but Jim Collins was there, in the second row next to Harry's old producer, Ben Rolfe, and beside him, Stella's husband, Fred, and the young magicians from her old tearoom. A month after her trip to Atlantic City, she had sold it to Niall for a song; she had discovered that the chaos of the place hadn't held her in its thrall as it once had. It needed someone young and vibrant at the helm—someone who needed something from it, as she had when she first opened it.

Saint continued, "The Houdinis always believed that if you remove the fraud, what is left must be the truth. Before Houdini's death, Mr. Houdini and his wife made a pact that the first to go would contact the survivor. The first year after Houdini's death found Mrs. Houdini every Sunday between the hours of twelve and two o'clock locked up in her own room, waiting for a sign. But at no time has Mrs. Houdini ever received a psychic communication from her husband. We believe that the great Houdini will, in this last authentic séance, come back to Mrs. Houdini, who, for thirty-three years, stood by the side of her beloved Harry, listening to the applause of kings and emperors and the world at large." Saint's voice echoed across the blue night.

On the far end of the bleachers, in the last row, Charles sat quietly with the other members of the press. He wore a badge that identified him as a newspaperman from the *Los Angeles Examiner*. After the stock market crashed, with the East Coast in chaos, he had moved with Bess to California. He had bought a white bungalow, with lemon trees in the yard, across from her own in the Hollywood Hills, where they had pretended to meet as neighbors. He had not gone to seminary. He wanted a child, he told Bess. He wanted to pass along Harry's legacy. Bess, for her part, had begun her marriage to Harry with a trunk of clothes and five dollars to her name; she felt she needed to live once more as if she was only partway through a great adventure.

Gladys had almost gone with them, but then Lloyd had proposed in the garden of his crumbling Long Island estate, and she had accepted. The estate was being sold; he had lost most of his money in stocks but still had some family money remaining. They moved to a three-bedroom house in a quiet town outside the city.

"But will you be all right there?" Bess had asked her. "You won't know anyone."

Gladys had smiled. "Harry never really had any friends."

Bess had laughed. "No, he didn't. He had hundreds of acquaintances. And very loyal employees. But that's not the same as having friends."

"He had you."

"Yes." Bess had thought about it. "I was his best friend."

Now, Saint clasped his hands together. "Let us meditate in prayer," he moaned. "O, mastermind of the universe, please let the spirit of understanding be sent upon us who are gathered in this inner circle tonight. Please bring the light of truth to us tonight. Aid us, guide us, on this most important quest. O, thou disembodied spirits, those of you who have grown old in the mysterious laws of the spirit land, all is in readiness. Please now, the time is at hand. Make yourself known to us. Houdini, are you here?"

He paused; the air around him seemed fragile as lace.

Saint's voice rose to a shout. "Are you here, Houdini? Manifest yourself! Bess is here, your Bess is here, pleading in her heart for a sign. Please manifest yourself by speaking through the trumpet. Lift it, lift it! Levitate the table, move it! Spell out a code, Harry, please! Ring the bell, let it be heard round the world! Come through, Harry!"

In response, there was a deafening silence. The members of the semicircle sat with clasped hands, in meditation, while the crowd craned their heads to see the items laid out on the little black table, which sat, unmoving, where they had been placed at the beginning of the evening.

At last Saint, in a voice that broke, placed his hand over his heart. "Mrs. Houdini," he said. "It seems the zero hour has passed. Have you reached a decision?"

Bess stood to face him on unsteady legs. What she could not tell him was that Harry had, in fact, come through years before. She was done with the humiliating circuses of the spiritualists; she was done with them all. Charles, plagued by the deep-seated fear of public scrutiny, on him and on Bess, had begged her to do the final séance everyone wanted and be done with it all. They had made a pact, together, never to reveal to anyone, with the exception of a future wife, in confidence, that he was Harry's son; Bess had arranged for his inheritance to be passed to him through Gladys, and did not mention him in her will. Nor would they ever reveal the message they had discovered in his photographs.

And so she stood in front of those she had loved dearly, in a recording that would be broadcast around the world, and publicly ended her search for Harry.

"Mrs. Houdini," Saint repeated. "Have you come to a decision?"

Bess looked around her one last time. "Yes," she said. "My husband did not come through. My last hope is gone. I do not believe that Houdini can come back to me, or to anyone. It is now my personal belief that spirit communication is impossible. I do not believe that ghosts or spirits exist."

There was a low murmur from the crowd.

She bent over Harry's photograph on the table and reached for the red lamp. "I now, reverently, turn out the light." She kissed her husband's lips. "Good night, Harry. It is finished."

As she stood there on the rooftop of the hotel, the hush almost sacred in its weight, all the old memories came back: of sitting in church with her mother and her brothers and sisters on either side, and the priest speaking in Latin and waving the incense, and the light burning through the stained glass and if she moved her hand in a certain way it would change color, too. In churches she used to feel as if, perhaps, Harry was just on the other side of the nave, hiding behind some curtain perhaps, waiting to step out to her and say, "Bess, darling, I never really died; it's all been nothing but a trick." Now she knew it was true, only not in the way she had imagined.

She stepped away from the shrine with the sting of tears in her eyes and made her way toward the stairs. A minute after the door closed behind her, the skies opened up with rain. The drops flared around the little table like broken glass. The guests rushed inside, pressing against one another to fit through the small door.

In the lobby of the hotel, the crowd of reporters caught up with her. "Mrs. Houdini! Why do you think your husband didn't come through tonight?" one of them asked.

Bess smoothed her white skirt and looked at the men. "Harry was too grand a magician to come back only to shake little bells or write his name on a piece of slate," she told a reporter named Charles Radley. "He lived in the great moments, and now he is gone."

"Do you think, if he can see us, he's laughing at the attempt?" he asked.

Bess shrugged. "I suppose I'll ask him when I see him."

Epilogue

ANTELOPE VALLEY

February 1944

Charles set down the newspaper and closed his eyes, breathing in the perfume of the house—the comforting smells of toast and clean sheets and shampoo. It was his one afternoon off, and he relished the quiet moments in the middle of the day when the sun was flaring through the windows and he had the house to himself. It was funny how he worked for a newspaper but never had time to actually read one except on his days off.

A year ago, on this day, Bess Houdini had died suddenly of a heart attack at age sixty-seven. Charles had not been there, and he had not been able to argue on her behalf when she was refused burial in her husband's cemetery because she was a Catholic. Instead, he had mourned anonymously, and he had not tried to contact her spirit. She would not have wanted him, he knew, embroiled in the obsessions that had haunted her for so many years.

It was one o'clock now and the children were at school. Margaret was at a Red Cross meeting, folding bandages. The war had been going on for over two years, and the dead kept coming home—they were people he knew, neighbors and the sons of friends—but it was Bess Houdini he was thinking about now.

Every once in a while he took out the photograph of Harry at Young's Pier, as if to reassure himself that it had really happened, that he had not imagined it after all. But Harry was always there, gray-haired and smiling up at the camera in the midst of the crowd. It was the one thing he had kept from Margaret during the seven happy years of their marriage. On their wedding night he had told her his secret—that he was Harry Houdini's son, and that one day, when their children were grown, he and Margaret would tell them together. He had told her the story of meeting Bess and their decision to keep the information private, to avoid slandering Harry's legacy and to keep himself out of the limelight. And when the children were born, he and Bess had created a trust account for them. But he had never told Margaret about the messages in the photographs. By the time he met her, it had seemed almost preposterous that anyone else would believe them. And he couldn't bear the thought of ever speaking the words out loud. He felt it was something private—the one communion that he clung to—that he and his father shared.

He sat at the kitchen table looking again at the photograph. He had seen it so many times that the image was burned into his memory, but it still gave him chills every time he looked at it. Where was Harry now, he wondered. What was he doing?

He thought he heard a car in the driveway, and he hastily slid the photograph back into its envelope. But as he swept his hand across the table, he brushed his cup of coffee, and the black liquid spilled over everything. He let out a small, aching cry; he pulled out the photograph, and it was sopping wet, damaged almost beyond recognition. And the tiny image of Harry was gone, hidden under the black stain.

He almost couldn't believe it. He felt as if his father had died in front of his very eyes. In his despair he glanced over at the window; the car he had heard was in his neighbor's driveway, not his own.

He rushed into his office; he had the negative somewhere, he knew. Bess had made him catalog all his photographs after they moved to California, and they were ordered by date now in neat white boxes. He prayed the negative was inside; he had never looked at it, he realized now, but he knew it must still exist. He threw the boxes on the floor and dumped out the contents, searching like a madman through the strips of miniature images. Finally, he found it, just where it was supposed to be. He held it up to the light and peered at the picture. He could make out some of the scene, even though the image itself was no bigger than a few inches across.

In his darkroom, Charles set up the enlarger head and the easel, turning on the bulb and exposing the image from the negative onto the paper. He worked carefully, dropping the paper into the developing solution, praying that Harry would still be there when he finished. What would he do if the image could never be duplicated again? He wasn't quite sure how the magic worked. What if the tiny, eerie smiling face of his father existed only on the single copy of the photograph he had just ruined?

Underneath the solution, in the red light of the darkroom bulb, he could see the image emerging in front of his eyes. There was young Harry, standing over the water, and there was the woman in the large hat who was always standing behind him. He watched, trembling, as the right edge of the photograph came into focus. He could see the tiny figures in the crowd, and then—he was so grateful he almost cried—he saw him. The gray-haired Harry Houdini, smiling up at a little boy's perch.

"Oh, thank God." Charles moved the paper carefully into the stop bath and the fixing solution, and then into a shallow tray of water. Finally, he turned on the lights and clipped the paper on the line to dry, staring at the image as the water dripped off.

He was so fixated on Harry's face that he almost didn't see it, until he leaned in to adjust the clip. Something else was in the photograph that hadn't been there before.

There, with her arm fastened around Harry's waist, was Bess Houdini, smiling up at him from the center of the crowd.

Author's Note

Years ago, on Halloween—the anniversary of Harry Houdini's death—I came across an article about Bess Houdini's extensive and failed attempts to contact her deceased husband's spirit. The 1920s represented the height of the spiritualist movement, when much of the public believed (with less skepticism than they do today) that the barrier between life and death was permeable. I imagined that Bess's inability to reach Harry, who had been the love of her life, was, for her, the most heartbreaking tragedy. I wanted to create a different ending for her—what if, I wondered, she really had managed to contact Harry? What might have led her to keep such a discovery secret, when she had been so public about her search?

Many of the details in this novel are based on extensive research into the lives of the Houdinis and the period in which they lived. In the years after Harry's death, in an attempt to forge an identity as an entrepreneur in her own right, Bess Houdini opened a tearoom called Mrs. Harry Houdini's Rendezvous on West Forty-Ninth Street in New York City, which was featured in *The Lewiston Daily Sun*. In 1928 she made the unexpected decision to participate in Harold Kellock's biography entitled *Houdini: His Life Story*, granting Kellock extensive interviews about Harry and her relationship with him. Now out of print, this volume was invaluable in helping me construct an honest portrayal of their lives together from Mrs. Houdini's perspective. To achieve as much authenticity as possible, some of the dialogue in the novel has been replicated as she remembered it. I have, however, slightly altered the chronology of certain events and have taken other novelistic liberties throughout.

William Kalush and Larry Sloman's *The Secret Life of Houdini* and Frederick Lewis Allen's *Only Yesterday: An Informal History of the 1920s* also helped in my research, as did many of Houdini's own writings about his magic. Houdini historian John Cox's blog, Wild About Harry, provided a wealth of resources. For my descriptions of Atlantic City, I relied heavily on the recollections of my father, whose family lived and worked there for generations. Still, I was surprised by how little information about Bess's personal life exists. Many accounts of the Houdinis' lives are conflicting, and most sources primarily address Harry's identity as a magician, not as a husband. Given Bess's limited footprint, I was shocked when I purchased a battered secondhand copy of Kellock's book for ten dollars, only to find, opening the book days later, Bess Houdini's signature inside the cover. If there ever was a sign that perhaps her story should be told, I believe that was it.

While I have used research to capture the voices of the characters and the period details in the novel, the intimacies of the Houdinis' relationship are born mainly from my imagination. I can only hope the work lives up to the legacy they left behind.

Acknowledgments

I am tremendously grateful to my agent, Trena Keating, who believed in me long before there was even a book to believe in, and who possesses the uncanny ability to be right about pretty much everything; and to Sarah Cantin, my editor, who is the kind of editor writers talk about, wistfully, as "surely existing somewhere out there." Thank you to Judith Curr and the entire team at Atria, without whom this dream of mine would never have come true.

I am also indebted to these many friends and mentors for their support of my writing and for extraordinary kindnesses done over the years: Dick Allen; Todd Boss and the Motionpoems team; Kevin Brockmeier; Geraldine Brooks and Tony Horwitz; Connie Brothers, Deb West, Jan Zenisek, and the Iowa Writers' Workshop staff; Ethan Canin; Edward Carey; Sam Chang; Leo Damrosch; Gerald Dawe, Deirdre Madden, Lilian Foley, Jonathan Williams, the late E. A. Markham, and the Trinity College Dublin Creative Writing Program; Noah Dorsey; Jennifer duBois; Jehanne Dubrow; Denise Duhamel; Jose Falconi; Jerry Hendrix; Luisa Igloria; Joan Jakobson; Michael Khandelwal, Lisa Hartz, and the Muse Writers Center; David Lehman; Erin McKnight, and Queen's Ferry Press; Jim McPherson; Keija Parssinen; Marilynne Robinson; Tim Seibles; Michael Shinagel; Michael Simms, Guiliana Certo, and Autumn House Press; John Stauffer; Tony Swofford; Gary Thompson and the Naval Institute Press; everyone at Union Literary; Trina Vargo, Mary Lou Hartman, and the U.S.-Ireland Alliance; Katherine Vaz. Thanks also to Gavitt, Kate, Kelly, Laura, Liz, Lizz, Lyndsey, Mallory, Stacey, Eric, Jessica, Lea, Rob, Austin, Josh, Loren, Jason, Alyssa, Dee, Erin, and Isaac, for over a decade of friendship; and to the many cherished friends of the Navy, Virginia Beach, and Galilee I've made over the past several years.

Thank you, especially, to my family—Dad, Mom, Christine, Eric, Laura, Marie, Jim, Chris, Jay, Carolyn, Hank, Josie, Arleen, and Farrell. And to Will, for his love and for our daughters, the greatest gifts of all; if there is magic, surely it's in them.

Mrs. Houdini

Victoria Kelly

A Reader's Club Guide

Topics & Questions for Discussion

1. Harry proposes to Bess the night that he meets her. What about Bess instantly captures his heart? Why do you think she accepts his proposal? How would you react if you were Bess?

2. Harry was a great believer in transformation: "It was a fact of human nature . . . that people wished to become something else. They wanted to travel to that mysterious in-between place that lives only in magic, which ordinary men and women cannot reach." How does Harry use this knowledge in both his escape acts and his personal life?

3. *Mrs. Houdini* contains two hidden codes. Describe their figurative and symbolic significance to Harry and Bess's relationship.

4. According to Bess, Harry's fascination with celebrity "was a result of his having achieved a little fame, but not enough to secure their future." How does this obsession manifest itself on the stage versus in his personal life? Which is more revealing—Harry's desire for fame or Bess's ideas about what drove him?

5. To Bess, Harry was "very much like a boy himself, a kind of Peter Pan, if you will, who never grew up." Why do you think Bess makes this comparison? Do you agree with her?

6. Bess's infertility causes her much grief on a personal and even religious level. In what ways does her inability to conceive—and the knowledge that she is the one at fault—affect Bess as a wife? As a woman? Although the novel is told from Bess's point of view, do you think Harry truly understood his wife's despair? Why or why not?

7. Bess often feels that Harry favors his mother more than her, even wondering "if Harry felt toward her the same fierce love and sense of duty he felt toward his mother." Where do you think Harry's loyalties ultimately lay? Contrast how Bess and Harry are affected by his mother's death.

8. The Houdinis initially perform séances, billing themselves as the "Celebrated Clairvoyants," but Bess eventually fears their act is immoral, realizing she "had spit in the face of the God she'd been taught to worship." How are séances a source of religious conflict? Why is Bess haunted by her participation in them? How does her relationship with religion compare

to her husband's? What role do séances play in the Houdinis' later life?

9. Harry attempts to find Charles throughout his life, even hiring a private investigator. If Harry had found Charles, how would Harry's life have changed? Do you think Bess would be supportive or devastated?

10. Bess feels a deep obligation to communicate with her husband ever since he told her on his deathbed, "I'll come back for you. Promise you'll look for me. Don't give up. I won't be able to rest until I reach you." Do you agree with Bess's decisions to honor her husband's request? In what ways does this devotion harm her life, and it what ways is it necessary for her in order to survive?

11. How would you characterize Bess and Harry's relationship? Although they are very much a team on- and offstage, their marriage is still afflicted with secrets, doubts, and even betrayal. Do you consider it normal for such things to exist in any long-standing relationship? How do you explain Bess and Harry's passion despite their struggles? Does it remind you of any other larger-than-life romances in literature or history?

12. How do you interpret Harry's fascination with death? What is he trying to prove? Is our world permeable?

13. Victoria Kelly did extensive research on the Houdinis and the time in which they lived. How much did you learn about Harry and Bess from reading the book? How has your reading of *Mrs. Houdini* affected your ideas about Harry the man and Harry the magician? How about Bess?

Enhance Your Book Club

1. *Mrs. Houdini* follows Bess and Harry through much of the 1920s. For your next book club meeting, throw a Roaring Twenties–themed party. Consider reading F. Scott Fitzgerald's *The Great Gatsby*, Paula McLain's *The Paris Wife*, or Carl Van Vechten's *Firecrackers* to help set the mood.

2. Choose a historical woman married to a famous man and write a one-page version of his story from her perspective.

3. Read one of Harry Houdini's many published works, such as *The Right Way to Do Wrong: A Unique Selection of Writings by History's Greatest Escape Artist*; *A Magician Among the Spirits*; or *Miracle Mongers and Their Methods: A Complete Exposé*. What did you learn about Harry's life and career? Do you think Victoria Kelly captured the spirit of Harry Houdini in her novel? Discuss your findings with the group.

4. In 2014, the History Channel aired a two-part miniseries *Houdini*, starring Adrien Brody. Watch one or both of these episodes with your book group and compare and contrast the representation of Bess and Harry on-screen and on the page.